Night
Work

First paperback edition August 2021
First hardback edition August 2021
First eBook edition August 2021

www.indiecrime.com

Facebook.com/ChrisCulverBooks

Night Work

A Hana Blackwood Novel

BY

CHRIS CULVER

BOOKS

Other books by Chris Culver

.

Chris Culver

In memory of Roy, my friend.

1

Joseph watched as Lisa Marie Mason knelt in the grass beside the flower bed. Her floppy straw hat may have held the mid-afternoon sun from her eyes, but it did nothing to block his view of her athletic legs and lean torso. Mrs. Mason was thirty-six—eleven years younger than her husband—and had wavy blond hair and big green eyes. Her driver's license claimed she stood five feet ten inches tall and weighed a hundred and thirty pounds, but Joseph doubted she had been truthful with either number. She was a beautiful woman, though, and beautiful women could afford a little vanity.

He hoped he didn't have to kill her.

To avoid traffic cameras, Joseph and Daniel had taken a boat that morning, docked it on a beach roughly a quarter of a mile from the Masons' home, and then walked through the woods and up the hillside. Sweat beaded on Joseph's forehead and down his back. Blisters had already begun forming on his feet.

Phil Mason, Lisa's husband, was a Marine and could shoot a target at three or four hundred yards, but he wouldn't set up an ambush with his wife in the front yard. Joseph and Daniel were fine.

As they approached, Lisa looked over her shoulder and then stood. Joseph looked at Daniel.

"You ready?"

Daniel nodded but said nothing. Though Joseph knew little of Daniel's personal life, they had worked together for six years. Joseph was executive vice president of Lakeside Pools, Inc. Daniel's official title was branch manager.

Contrary to its name, pools were the least of Lakeside's business. Daniel and Joseph solved the company's problems. Sometimes they traveled abroad and delivered cash to suppliers in Southeast Asia, other times they showed up at their employees' homes to remind them of their obligations, and occasionally they met their distribution network to collect payment. Joseph liked the job. It allowed him to use both his mind and the physical skills drilled into him during a fourteen-year career in the Army.

As Lisa walked toward them, the sun lit on her skin, giving her an almost golden glow, while her white shirt stuck to her chest with perspiration. Joseph glanced at his partner.

"The view from the front's nice, too."

Daniel shrugged but said nothing.

"Good talk, friend," said Joseph, shaking his head and starting toward the woman. The dry grass crunched under his feet, and a breeze blew. The air was thick with humidity, and cicadas buzzed from the nearby woods. Joseph smiled. "Morning, Mrs. Mason."

"Good morning," she said, holding her arms rigidly at her sides. She had balled her hands into fists and worked her fingers together nervously. Joseph had called Phil before coming over, so Lisa should have known they were coming. He wondered whether Phil had told her the reason for their visit.

"You own a beautiful home," said Joseph. "It's got room for kids, too. Do you and Phil have any children?"

Joseph knew they didn't, but he hoped he could get her talking all the same. She shook her head.

"No."

"That's a shame. I hear kids are one of life's true joys."

Neither Joseph, Mrs. Mason, nor Daniel spoke for a moment. Then she gestured toward the house.

"Would you like to come in?" she asked. "I can make coffee."

"Is your husband inside?" asked Daniel, his voice soft. Mrs. Mason's eyes traveled up and down him, and she seemed to swallow before shaking her head.

"No. He's out back already."

"Then why would we come in?"

Joseph scowled.

"No need to be rude," he said. "She's offering us coffee. Normal people like coffee."

Daniel raised an eyebrow but said nothing.

"We'll see ourselves to the backyard," said Joseph.

"Phil's on the trail. It goes down to the lake," she said. "He thought you might want some privacy for your…business."

"I appreciate that," said Joseph, forcing a smile to his face once more. "We're all friends here, though. Anything we tell him, we can tell you, too. Would you like to come with us?"

She hesitated and then looked over her shoulder to the flower beds. Azaleas and hostas covered the shaded areas, while rose bushes and annual flowers occupied those spots touched most by the sun. It was a pretty garden, and somehow it fit the log cabin in front of which the couple had planted it.

"I was going to pull some weeds, but I need to pick up sugar and flour at the store," she said. "I've got cookies to bake and decorate for a wedding."

Cookies were a side gig for her. Joseph had never eaten one, but the pictures she posted on Facebook looked great. She had good reviews, too.

"I understand," said Joseph. "Is the trail easy to find?"

"It's the only one behind the house. It leads to

the boathouse and lake. You can't miss it."

"Thank you for your time, Mrs. Mason," said Joseph. He paused until she nodded and turned toward the house again. The view of her backside in those tight shorts was worth the wait. A moment later, he and Daniel walked to the backyard. The home had a walkout basement with big windows that would have made an ordinarily dark space vibrant and bright. A covered hot tub rested on the ground beside the basement door, while a trail led downward at the edge of the yard.

Joseph and Daniel waited in the yard until Mrs. Mason's SUV pulled out of the driveway. Joseph waved. Daniel didn't move. Then, without saying a word, Joseph headed toward the trail and brushed aside the spindly limbs of a pin oak that had encroached upon the walkway.

The path sloped gently downward for a dozen yards, but then the landscape fell away, and the trail shifted from an easy, gentle walk to a hike on hardscrabble terrain. Time, footsteps, and the weather had compacted the dirt until it was as hard as concrete, and the trail cut back on itself as it traversed the hill downward.

About halfway down the embankment, Phil Mason sat on a slab of limestone that jutted from the hillside. His legs dangled over the edge as he looked out over the lake. The water sparkled in the sun, and boaters crisscrossed the surface in jet skis, pontoon boats, and even a few sailboats. It was idyllic.

Sweat dripped down Joseph's brow and beaded between his shoulder blades. He had worn linen pants and a loose-fitting cotton shirt that hung over his belt. His pistol felt heavy at the small of his back. As the wind blew across the lake and up the hill, it rustled his hair and caused his shirt to billow.

"Hey, Phil," said Joseph, stopping on the trail about ten feet from the county sheriff. "When I left my house this morning, I wore loafers. I wish you had told me to expect a hike."

Phil looked from the lake to Joseph and Daniel. He was forty-seven and had won an election to become Bryant County's sheriff nine years ago. He had a master's degree in social work and extensive law enforcement experience. On paper, he looked perfect for the job. In reality, he had secrets and debts that left him vulnerable and unfit for his office.

"Sorry, Mr. Lipscombe," he said, glancing first at Joseph and then to Daniel. "Who's your friend?"

"That's Daniel Nakamura. And stop with this Mr. Lipscombe business. Call me Joseph. No need to stand on formality after all we've done together."

"What do you want?"

Joseph crossed his arms and considered first Phil and then the lake.

"I suspect you know, but we can pretend otherwise."

Phil leaned forward and spit something down

the side of the hill. It plopped a hundred feet below on a rock ledge near the lake.

"I didn't know you chewed tobacco," said Joseph, smiling. "I'll update our files."

Phil glanced at him.

"It's gum. I pop a piece in when I want a cigarette. My doctor says it'll help me quit."

"I hope that works out for you."

Phil considered him for another minute.

"You're here about Oscar Romero."

Joseph crossed his arms.

"I am. A little birdie told us you've been talking to the Romero family about their son."

Phil laced his fingers together and stared at his hands.

"A momma should know what happened to her boy."

Joseph lowered his voice.

"That's not your choice, Phil," he said, reaching into his back pocket and pulling out a thick, unmarked envelope. He tossed it to the ground behind the sheriff. "That's for your trouble. Keep your mouth shut and keep the mouths of those around you shut, and there'll be more in it for you. You know how this works. You have a job. So do we."

Phil hesitated and then nodded before reaching behind him. He opened the envelope and fanned through the wad of hundred-dollar bills before pulling his legs back from the edge and standing.

"You said a little birdie talked to you," said Phil. "Who?"

"You know I won't say," said Joseph. "Don't ask again."

Phil focused on the envelope before shaking his head.

"I can't take your money anymore. It's not worth it."

Joseph forced himself to smile even as he felt the fine hairs on his neck and arms rise.

"Take the money," he said, glancing up the hill toward the log cabin. "Your wife's a beautiful woman, and she's out here alone while you work. I'd hate for something to happen to her."

The sheriff set his jaw and held Joseph's gaze. Then he looked down to the hard-beaten path before shaking his head.

"So that's how this is. I take the money, or you hurt Lisa."

Joseph held up a hand as if he were a police officer directing traffic.

"I'm an honorable man. I swear that I won't touch her," he said. "I can't control everyone, though. And even if I could keep her physically safe, she's got a lot to lose. You both do. You've got your health, this beautiful house, retirement accounts…what more do you want? Tell me. I might be able to help."

"It's hard to sleep at night knowing what I do."

Joseph sighed.

"If you want absolution, talk to a priest. If you talk to the Romero family, though, a lot of people will lose. There's a lot at stake here."

"Maybe that's my penance," said Phil. "Maybe I should lose everything."

Joseph sighed again and looked to Daniel.

"What do you think we should do?"

Daniel brushed past Joseph and walked toward Phil. They squared off, but then Phil's shoulders fell, and he stepped back.

"I can't help you," said Phil, almost pleading. "I hurt the Romero family. That was wrong. I can't keep quiet."

"I understand," said Daniel.

For a moment, no one moved. Then Daniel reached up and pushed Phil. It wasn't hard, but the sheriff stumbled backward. The tip of his foot hit the limestone slab, but his heel hit nothing. His eyes opened wide as he shot his arms forward, twisting and reaching for something that could keep him from falling.

For a split second, the sheriff seemed to hang in midair. Then physics took over, and he plummeted down the hill. Dust kicked up around him, and his arms and legs flailed, making him almost look like a child's doll dropped off the side of the world. He cartwheeled before slamming into a tree.

Joseph sighed.

"I didn't mean for you to do that."

"What'd you expect to happen?" asked Daniel.

Joseph glanced down the hill, trying to see whether the sheriff was moving.

"As talkative as you've been lately, I kind of thought you'd just stare at him," he said. "This was a negotiation. I've got a hundred grand in my car for him. Now we've got to climb down there and make sure he's dead."

Daniel peered down the hill.

"Next time share your plan."

Joseph ignored him and headed down the trail. Phil was about a hundred feet down, but they had to travel a quarter of a mile's worth of switchbacks to reach the sheriff's body. A jagged gash ran across his chin, over his eye, and to his forehead. His femur had broken cleanly and jutted from the meat of his thigh. Blood had already begun pooling on the dry ground beneath him.

The broken femur might have severed Phil's femoral artery—in which case he'd bleed to death—but Daniel and Joseph couldn't take that risk. The sheriff's chest rose and fell, but he was unconscious. Joseph sighed and pointed to a grapefruit-sized rock near Daniel's foot.

"Finish him up," he said. "I'm going to go up and call the boss."

Daniel picked up the rock but didn't hit Phil yet.

"You think we should kill the wife?"

"I hope we don't have to," he said. "Phil kept a lot of people in line for us. Now he can't. Kill him and then come to the car. We'll figure out our next moves. And call your wife. Tell her we're going to be busy the next couple of days. We've got ugly work ahead of us now."

2

My coffee had grown lukewarm, but the sun shone in a nearly cloudless sky. George, my Chesapeake Bay retriever, and I had driven over four hours to reach Pollard, Missouri but now that we were in town, I didn't know what the hell to do. Dr. Kessler, my therapist, had told me to show up and see how I felt, seemingly believing that my mere presence in town would trigger a revelation or epiphany about my life. As I sat there in that public park and drank my lousy coffee, though, and as my dog chased a squirrel up a tree, every suspicion I had about Dr. Kessler's insights into my psyche crystallized into certainty.

She was full of shit.

Three months ago, I had been Detective Hana Jašić Blackwood of the St. Louis County Police Department. I had been a member of the major case squad and a supervisory detective in the family crime unit. From eight in the morning until eight in the evening—and often much later—I had investigated domestic violence and child abuse and sent vile people to prison. My paycheck wouldn't have impressed anyone, but the work had mattered to me. Before that, I had been a combat medic in the United States Army and had spent combat tours in Afghanistan and Iraq. I had helped people.

That was then, though. Now, I was just Hana. I had no job, no responsibilities, and nothing to do. At least the weather was nice.

My coffee wasn't getting any better, so I popped the top and dumped it out on the ground. My adoptive parents had left me a cabin in town, but I hadn't visited since they died years ago. As a kid, I would come to Pollard, wake up with the sunrise, run through the woods, and swim or skip rocks across the lake. Dad and I would have contests to see who could skip a rock the furthest. He always let me win. Mom and I would bake cookies or muffins. It didn't feel right to be here without them.

I began to call my dog to me when I saw movement out of the corner of my eye. An older woman was approaching me from the park's entrance. She wore black slacks and a loose-fitting top that reminded me of a doctor or nurse's scrubs. A plain gold wedding band adorned her right ring finger, and a very pretty brooch in the shape of a hummingbird decorated her light pink cardigan. I wouldn't have thought anything of her except that she wore a mud-caked slipper on one foot and nothing at all on the other.

I gave her a tight smile and called George to me so he wouldn't run up to her and scare her. When I had his leash on, I waved to her. She beamed and walked right toward me.

"Hi," I said. "You out for a walk?"

She nodded and sat beside me on the bench. Neither of us spoke. We just watched the grass sway in the field in front of us and felt the warm afternoon breeze. My new friend was in her late seventies or early eighties, and she smelled like rose oil. By the state of her clothing and jewelry, she had money. Someone should come for her soon. In the meantime, I could keep her company.

"I noticed you lost your shoes," I said. She looked down. Her smile disappeared.

"I guess so," she said. She furrowed her brow and drew in a breath before leaning closer to me. "I think they're trying to kill me again, Emily."

I patted George's shoulder. He panted and seemed to grin. Thankfully, my new friend didn't see that, or she might have been frightened. George was a gentle giant. He had a curly brown coat, bright yellow eyes, and a mind that never stopped working. He was handsome, but he was far oversized for his breed and weighed almost as much as me. When I let him off leash, I kept him in a bright orange vest so people didn't think he was a wild animal.

"I won't let anyone hurt you," I said, still smiling. "Would you like me to call someone for you?"

"There's no one left to call," she said. "It's just you and me now, Emily, and they're trying to kill me, just like they killed Douglas."

I looked at her closer, but I couldn't see any signs of physical injury or malnourishment. She looked well cared for, but her cardigan and blouse could conceal a lot of injuries.

"Has someone hurt you?" I asked.

"They're trying to kill me," she said again. "Robert's gone. You're all I have left. You're not leaving me, too, are you?"

I smiled and shook my head.

"No, I won't leave you," I said. "Sometimes I forget things, though. Do we live together?"

She tilted her face to the side and reached out to touch my hand.

"It's okay, sweetie," she said. "I understand. We haven't lived together since Robert moved us to Pollard."

"I see," I said, nodding. She didn't carry a purse, so I doubted she had an ID hidden on her. "Who's Robert?"

"My husband," she said. "He died a long time ago. It's okay. You spoke at his funeral. He never liked you. He thought you were a trollop. You kind of were, but that's okay."

Her honesty made me smile.

"Do you remember where you live, or do you have it written somewhere?"

"Oh, honey," she said, squeezing my hand again as she tilted her head to the side. "I didn't realize how much you've forgotten."

"It's been rough," I said. "You said somebody's trying to kill you. I'm going to call the police. Maybe they can help."

"No," she said, her voice suddenly fierce. "The police would dig and dig, but they'd never find anything. They wouldn't help with Douglas, and they won't help with me."

"We should call the police, anyway," I said. "We'll talk to them together."

She wrung her hands together but said nothing. I continued smiling as I reached for my purse.

"This will just be—"

Before I could finish my thought, a marked Bryant County Sheriff's Office SUV pulled into the gravel parking lot about two hundred yards away. I nodded to the officer behind the wheel but didn't wave for fear of scaring off my friend. The officer didn't get out. He must have been waiting for my friend's family or a doctor. I looked at her again and slipped my hand out of my purse.

"How long have we lived in Pollard?" I asked, smiling and hoping to make small talk to keep her comfortable and seated until help could arrive. She gave me a soft, kind smile.

"Oh, twenty years, maybe," she said. "We

moved after Robert found out about our nocturnal activities in Miami. I've never seen him so angry, but it wasn't as if his hands were clean, either. He had a girlfriend in every major city on the eastern seaboard, and he never hesitated to visit them on his business trips. With a man like that, you wouldn't think he'd begrudge my sister and I having a little fun with the hoi polloi, but he was unpredictable. We did have fun when we were young, didn't we, sweetie?"

I hadn't anticipated her spilling her marital secrets to me, so I looked away, my face red. Then I drew in a breath.

"My memory isn't what it used to be," I said, smiling. "Let's focus on Robert. How'd you meet him?"

Her eyes grew distant, and she smiled as she relived pleasant memories.

"At a party," she said. "He was the strongest, most handsome man I ever met."

I let her talk for another minute, but I kept my eyes on the sheriff's deputy in the parking lot and wondered what he was waiting for. Then a second SUV pulled into the lot. Three uniformed officers stepped out. The driver, a sergeant with chevrons on her collar, walked to the first SUV and spoke to the officer inside. He pointed to us and then got out of the car.

I looked to my friend on the bench and then wound my hand around George's leash for grip as a tingling sensation began passing over me. No department would send four officers to pick up a lost elderly woman.

"I think we've got a problem," I said, standing and opening my hands, palms toward the officers so they could see I wasn't a threat. They walked toward us. The sergeant smiled but held her right hand on her pistol.

"Afternoon," she called. She flicked a fastener on her holster to release her pistol. She didn't pull it out, but she could very easily. The three officers with her scanned the park around us. One sauntered to my right, while a second hurried to my left. The third stayed a few feet behind his boss. He didn't hide the hand on his weapon.

My heart started beating faster. I kept my hands where they could see them.

"I'm Hana Blackwood," I said, trying to keep my voice calm and even. "Before you come closer, know that my dog is well trained. He's not dangerous. Please don't shoot him. He's big, but he's very gentle."

"Why do you think we'd shoot him?" asked the sergeant.

"Because the deputy to your rear is in a modified Weaver stance, the man to my right is holding his pistol outside his holster with his finger on the trigger guard, and the man to my left looks so jumpy I'd suspect he was on meth had I met him on the street. You look nervous." I paused. "Why are you interested in me?"

"Surveillance cameras spotted your vehicle near the scene of a suspicious death this morning. We've been looking for it ever since," she said. "You have any weapons on you, Ms. Blackwood?"

"Yeah," I said. "I've got a Glock 43 in a holster on my belt and a SIG Sauer P238 in a holster on my right ankle. There's a knife in my left pocket and a razor blade in my wallet that's designed to look like a credit card."

The sergeant whistled.

"You're a well-armed woman," she said. "You know how to use those weapons?"

"Yes."

"Will your dog attack if Deputy Wilson takes his leash?" she asked.

"No."

The deputy took a hesitant step forward but stopped several feet from me when George sat.

"Shouldn't you give him a command or something so he knows I'm friendly?"

"Would that make you feel better?" I asked. He nodded but said nothing, so I looked down to my dog. "George, don't hurt him."

The dog panted. I looked to the deputy again, hoping that was enough. He was in his mid-twenties and had rounded cheeks and thick forearms. His brown hair was buzzed short. He, once more, took a hesitant step forward. George cocked his head to the side, confused but not agitated. As I handed over the leash, George stayed seated and looked at me even as the deputy tried to pull him away.

"He's a big dog," I said. "It's better if you talk to him than try to force him."

The guy cleared his throat and nodded.

"What should I say?"

I shrugged.

"I'd start with hello. That usually works for me."

The guy looked down to George. The deputy to my left tittered.

"Hi," said the deputy. "I'm Bryan."

I patted George's back.

"Go, George."

That was the signal my dog needed. They walked to the parking lot, and I put my hands on top of my head. My elderly friend furrowed her brow at me.

"What's happening, Emily?"

"They're taking me home. We're both safe," I said, smiling at her before looking to the sergeant. "My friend is lost. Can you help her find her way home?"

The sergeant walked to the elderly woman. They talked, and then the older woman stood. The deputies to my left and right walked toward me. One patted me down for weapons, while the other stood nearby with his hand over his firearm. They disarmed me and then had me place my hands behind my back. My heart still beat fast, but I tried to stay calm. I was more likely to avoid getting shot that way.

"You're cooler than I'd expect, Ms. Blackwood," said a deputy, placing a pair of handcuffs around my wrists. "Most murder suspects are twitchy."

I wanted to ask how many he had arrested, but that would only provoke him.

"I didn't kill anybody, but now that I'm in custody, you should read me my rights."

He put a hand on my elbow and began leading me to the parking lot.

"Sounds like you're familiar with the system," he said.

"I am," I said

"Any other pointers?"

I considered and then shrugged.

"Start working on your resume," I said. "If I'm your best suspect in a murder, you should consider another line of work."

3

The Bryant County Sheriff's Office operated out of a single-story, red brick building with mirrored windows. I walked through the station's front door and heard the deep thrum of the air conditioner and the buzz of the lights. The air smelled like old paper and an industrial cleaner likely used on the floor. A throbbing, restless kind of energy suffused the place. At one time, I would have felt at home, but now the hairs on the back of my neck stood and my stomach churned. These cops had no reason to arrest me. I shouldn't have been there.

The front desk was empty on our arrival, but a heavyset woman in her late forties or early fifties hurried toward us, evidently having heard the front door ding. She slowed and appraised me. Like everyone in the station, she wore a khaki uniform and a pistol on her hip. A hair tie pulled her curly brown-and-gray hair from her face. Her name tag read *SUTTON*.

"You the one who killed Phil?" she asked.

I shook my head.

"No."

Ms. Sutton looked to the officer to my left, who shrugged. Then she looked at me with barely disguised disdain.

"Troy wants you in an interrogation room, but I need your information first."

"Sure," I said, nodding. "I'm Hana Jašić Blackwood, and my ID is in my purse. Your officers took it, though, along with my dog. I'll want both back when I leave."

She said nothing, so I gave her my address and other contact information. She looked me up in the license bureau's database and asked a few questions to verify my identity. Then she took my fingerprints and snapped a picture and warned me that she'd be conducting a thorough background investigation that would reveal if I had lied to her. I wished her luck.

Then the uniformed officers led me to a small, windowless interrogation room with a metal table anchored to the floor and two metal folding chairs. Gray paint covered the cinderblock walls, and white linoleum tile designed to look like marble covered the floor, lending the room a harsh, cold feel. The air smelled stale and held just a whiff of bleach. At least it was clean. The officers removed my handcuffs and directed me to sit at the table. I did as they asked, but before they could leave, I cleared my throat.

"Offer me a drink," I said.

"Excuse me?"

"You need to offer me a drink. You should also ask if I need to use the restroom," I said. "If you lock a suspect in a room without meeting her physical needs, your interrogation will look coerced. A defense attorney will argue that her client was thirsty or hungry or had to use the bathroom, but the only way you allowed her to meet her physical needs was by first giving you a statement."

Both officers looked to one another.

"Do you need to use the bathroom, Ms. Blackwood?" asked the one on the left.

"No," I said. "Thanks for offering. Get me a cup of coffee, though. Black, but I'd like two sugars on the side in case it's terrible."

"Anything else?"

"That's it," I said, nodding toward the door. "You can go now."

They left the room, and I slumped into one of the folding chairs and closed my eyes. My body felt heavy. I was equally mad, disgusted, and resigned. Some days, it just felt like I had pissed the universe off, and it was exacting its revenge on me in the most asinine ways possible.

About ten minutes later, the door opened, and a man carrying two cups of coffee stepped inside. He was probably six feet tall and about a hundred and eighty pounds. His slightly uneven sideburns gave his otherwise clean-shaven face a disheveled appearance. In contrast, his khaki uniform looked freshly laundered, his brown hair was coifed, and his smile looked practiced. He had left his firearm elsewhere, so maybe he knew what he was doing. Three stars adorned his collar, marking him as the deputy sheriff. His name tag read *LYONS*.

He set a cup of coffee in front of me and then reached into his pocket for two packets of sugar. I forced my shoulders back and sat straighter.

"I hear you've been ordering my officers around," he said, sitting across from me. I shrugged and reached for the coffee cup. It was hot still, which I appreciated. As I peeled back the lid, I caught a whiff of something like brown sugar and vanilla. It was better than my coffee at home.

"I've been asserting my rights," I said before taking a sip. "Thanks for the coffee. It makes this easier."

"Glad to oblige," he said, picking up his own drink and then leaning back. "We picked you up because we found your car near a murder scene. You want to talk about that?"

I shook my head.

"Not really. If you want to talk, though, go ahead. Who died?"

He looked at me straight in the eye.

"My boss. Sheriff Phil Mason."

The muscles in my back stiffened, and I nodded.

"I'm sorry."

"Me, too," he said, setting his coffee on the table. "Did you know him?"

I shook my head.

"Never heard of him."

"You bought gas at a station half a mile from his house near the time of his death. Half an hour later, you drove past going the other way," he said. "It's a remote station. The owner sells guns, ammunition, and fishing tackle, too. It's how he stays in business. Nobody lives out there except Phil. The road dead-ends just past his cabin at a private marina at the lake. Where were you going?"

I narrowed my eyes and leaned forward.

"Does your boss live in a big log cabin with a pretty garden out front?"

"Sure did."

"He have a pretty wife with blond hair and big boobs?"

Lyons closed his eyes and considered.

"I'm not going to comment on Lisa's anatomy, but she does have blond hair."

"They're my neighbors," I said. "I hadn't been to the cabin since high school, but I went by this morning to check it out. A caretaker used to come by every now and then, but he stopped when Mom and Dad died. I had planned to stay, but the cabin was occupied."

Lyons drew in a slow breath and considered the answer before reaching to his belt for a notepad.

"Who occupied the cabin?"

"A raccoon, I think. Like I said, I haven't been inside in years."

He locked eyes on me and then closed his notepad.

"Are you trying to be funny?" he asked.

I shook my head.

"I'm answering your questions. I didn't kill anybody."

"You're facing a murder charge. If you didn't do it, you should cooperate."

"Thanks for the tip," I said. "I bought gas near your boss's house because I needed gas. That station was near my cabin, which was near your boss's property. Again, I'm sorry he's dead."

Lyons sighed.

"If you didn't kill him, who did? You're the only person to drive by that station all day. Jason—he runs the place— said you looked nervous. Why were you nervous?"

"I wasn't. I had to pee, and his bathroom smelled like a latrine. I didn't want to stay any longer than I had to," I said. "You're wasting your time by focusing on me. You need to talk to your sheriff's wife."

"I already have," said Lyons. "She's heartbroken."

"She's also holding back from you," I said. "She was in the front yard gardening when I drove past."

"She left and drove to Springfield before Phil

died. You were the only person in the area at the time of Phil's death."

I shook my head.

"I didn't kill him, and I don't know what else to tell you," I said. "Now, I'd like an attorney, please. Despite my earlier suggestions to your deputies, no one has read me my rights. You need to retrain your officers before they arrest anyone else. They don't know what they're doing."

Lyons stood. His eyes were cold as they considered me. Then he nodded and left without saying a word. I sipped my coffee and wondered how much worse my day would get.

4

May 20, 1992.
Višegrad, Bosnia and Herzegovina

I lived in the most beautiful town in the world. I
hadn't ever been anywhere else, but Mama had told
me, and she didn't lie. Višegrad had been built on
either side of the Drina River with the mountains
around it forming a V shape that protected it from
wind and severe weather. An old stone bridge with
arches crossed the river. I didn't know why, but
people loved that bridge. The tourists always took
pictures.

The bridge was okay, I guess, but if you closed
your eyes and ran across it fast enough, you
wouldn't even know you were on a bridge.
Somebody wrote a book about it once, but I didn't
understand why that mattered. It wasn't like the
weeping willow in our garden. My weeping willow
grew on a bank of our creek, and its branches just
skimmed the water whenever the wind blew. It

looked like it was dancing in the breeze. That was special. The bridge didn't dance. I guess some people just liked old rocks all piled up.

Mama, Sara, and I were in the living room, but I wished we were outside by my tree. Sara, my sister, was combing my hair. Mama was watching the news. Arman, my little brother, lay on the floor, crashing his trucks. Mama usually told me and Arman to go outside and play when she watched the news, but today she didn't. I didn't know why.

The world had been scary lately. Two months ago, Mama had dragged all our mattresses and blankets down to the basement so we could all sleep there together. We spent a lot of time in the basement now. I used to go to school every day, but then my teacher died when soldiers blew up her house.

A lot of houses in town got blown up lately. Everybody was angry at each other. It was something with the government. Since so many buildings had been blown up, Tata and his employees had been extra busy. They made red tiles and put them on roofs. I was pretty sure that Tata had made every roof in town. He was famous, and lots of people worked for him.

"Why'd the army leave?" asked Sara, pulling my hair back into a ponytail. Mama cleared her throat.

"They just did," she said. "Why doesn't matter."

We lived outside of town, but the Yugoslav army

had surrounded Višegrad about two months ago with their tanks and equipment. Tata said soldiers had surrounded Sarajevo, too. Mama thought we should leave Bosnia, but Tata thought it was safer to stay until the fighting stopped.

"Since the army's gone, will we go back to school?" I asked.

"I don't know," said Mama.

"I miss school and Petra."

"Petra and her family are Serbs," said Mama. "Things are different now. I don't think you should talk to her."

Petra was my best friend, and I had known her my entire life. Mama didn't think that mattered, but I thought it did. Before I could respond, Marko, our dog, barked at something outside. Mama and Sara stiffened and shot their eyes to the door, but then Marko stopped barking.

Things like that happened a lot lately. Mama, Tata, and my older siblings always seemed to be waiting for something, but they never said what. Since we didn't have school, my older brothers, Omar and Hamza, went with Tata to work every morning. One day, they'd take over Tata's company, but for now, they were still learning. Sara, my older sister, didn't put on roofs. She stayed in her room a lot and listened to music. Arman didn't do much, either, because he was four.

"Are we going to leave Bosnia, Mama?" asked Sara.

Mama hesitated before answering. Then she cleared her throat.

"Let's focus on the house for now," she said. "It's a mess. I want it clean when Tata and the boys come home."

The house wasn't a mess, though. We had cleaned it from the basement to the attic two days ago when the army's big trucks drove past. Mama made us clean a lot now. She yelled at us a lot, too. It made my stomach hurt. Tata was worse. He hardly said anything anymore. He just stayed outside with the dog and his gun.

I swept the kitchen floor, while Sara dusted the furniture in the dining room and Mama cleaned the bathroom. Arman stayed in the living room and played with his trucks. I swept for about ten minutes, but I found little dirt. Then Marko started barking again. I leaned the broom against the counter, knowing Mama would tell me to get in the basement soon. Maybe I could bring a puzzle so it wouldn't be so boring.

I started toward my room but then stopped when I realized that Marko was still barking. He usually stopped whenever the car passed on the road. Then I heard the jangle of his collar. The door opened, and Tata called out that he and the boys were home. My chest loosened some, and I smiled. With Tata home, things would be okay. Mama would feel better, Sara would listen to music in her room, and Hamza and I could throw sticks to Marko outside.

I left the kitchen and walked into the living room. Tata was old, but not too old. He had dark brown hair and a neat beard. His hands were so big they could wrap all the way around my fists so I couldn't escape him, and his hugs made me feel as if I were walking on clouds. I smiled at him, but he didn't smile back. Instead, he looked down and sighed.

"Sara, take Arman and Hana downstairs," said Mama. "Please."

My sister didn't move, and Tata didn't make her. Omar stood near the door, and Hamza looked out the window. They had let Marko inside. No one ever let Marko inside.

"What happened?" asked Mama.

"I need some coffee," he said.

Mama nodded and went to make some. Tata sat at the table near the kitchen. Sara and I joined him, but my brothers and the dog stayed in the living room, near the door. When Mama brought Tata his coffee, his hands shook so much he couldn't drink it. I had never seen Tata scared. It made my legs feel weak.

"The police came to the shop this morning. They said Višegrad was a Serb town now and the Muslims had to leave." Tata's eyes looked distant. His hands were balled into fists. "Zaid told them Višegrad was his home and that he'd never leave, so they shot him in the head. Then they shot Sajed. He didn't even say anything. They just shot him."

Mama said nothing. Then I realized she was crying. So was Tata. He licked his lips.

"I thought they were going to kill us, so I gave them the keys to the building and told everybody to leave. By the time I left, a truck had already come to pick up the bodies. It was full."

For a moment, Tata said nothing. I wanted to ask what was going on, but I didn't think they'd answer.

"We'll go to Sarajevo," said Mama. "We'll be safe there."

Mama had wanted to leave weeks ago, but Tata had argued soldiers watched the roads and harassed migrants. Now, he just nodded.

"Get the bags together," he said. "We'll leave as soon as we can."

Mama agreed and started ordering us around. For about an hour, we worked together, getting our house in order. I put three dresses, socks, underwear, and some tights into my backpack along with a drawing of Marko that Sara had made for me. It was my favorite.

Outside, Tata and Omar were already packing the car with bags. I couldn't see Hamza. Tata had told Hamza to stand watch up the road and run back if he saw soldiers. My hands shook so much when I handed Tata my bag that I dropped it. He kissed me and said he loved me before picking it up. He was still trembling. Then he patted my back before going to the house to help Mama. I stayed outside with Omar.

Before we could leave, the truck came.

It was ugly and big, and its engine made the ground rumble. Tata's work trucks were small. This was a hateful thing with a canvas roof, and it made me tremble. Everyone came outside and stood in front of the house.

I walked to Mama and squeezed her hand. She grabbed me by the shoulder and squeezed me behind her. Tata held up his hands and walked forward. Two men jumped out of the vehicle's cab. One wore a camouflage shirt, pants, and a camouflage beret. He looked like a soldier. The other man wore brown slacks, a white shirt, and a brown belt. I had seen him before. He worked for Tata, and his daughter went to my school.

I stepped away from my mother and waved, feelings of relief flooding over me. Mama grabbed me again and forced me behind her. I tried to wiggle away, but her hands were like iron. She had never clutched me so hard in my life.

"But we know him," I said. "Ivana goes to my school. She's his daughter."

As I spoke, Hamza fell out of the back of the truck. He had a gash on his forehead, and blood trailed down his face. Mama flinched and gasped. I tried to run to him, but Mama pulled me back again and then dragged me and Arman into the house. Sara came, too, but Tata and Omar stayed outside.

We crouched in the living room. Every muscle in

my body ached, and I couldn't stop shaking. My stomach hurt. I didn't know what was happening, but I wanted it to stop. Mama clutched Arman and me to her chest and sung us a soft song in her sweet, husky voice. It was the same song she sang to us every night, but it couldn't stop my trembling or my racing heart. Arman cried.

"Mama, what's happening?" he asked, his voice ragged. "Who are they?"

"They're just soldiers," she whispered. "They'll go away."

I knew from the catch in her voice that she had lied to us. My legs begged me to run, but I couldn't move. I had nowhere to go. Then Omar came to the door. Mama held out her arms for him, and he came to her. She held him, and I grabbed onto his leg. He put a hand on my head.

"They want to search the house," he said. "After that, they'll let us go. We have to give them the car, though."

"Fine, fine," said Mama. "Give them the car. How's your brother?"

Omar looked at me and then to Arman before swallowing. I squeezed his leg tighter than I had ever squeezed anyone before.

"He's dizzy, but he'll be okay. We all have to go outside. Come on. They don't want to hurt us. They just want us to leave."

Mama nodded and sucked in a breath. Her jaw was clenched, and her eyes were wet, but she didn't cry.

"Let's go. Omar, carry Hana. I'll carry Arman. Sara, stay behind me. Don't let the soldiers see you."

We shuffled out of the house. Omar was fifteen, so he was almost as big as Tata. I held on to him, and he rubbed my back. Outside, six men in camouflage jumped out of the truck. They weren't actual soldiers—the actual soldiers were young and fit—but they all carried Kalashnikovs. I recognized the weapon because Tata had one hidden beneath his bed. None had their names or any medals or other decorations on their shirts. I recognized two of them from town, but the others were unfamiliar.

We waited while those six men searched our home. At first, my heart had pounded with every bang and thud from inside the home, but nobody hit me or shouted at us. They even let Mama clean the wound on Hamza's forehead.

Then a police car came, and a fat man with big glasses stepped out. Like the soldiers, he wore camouflage. He wore a pistol on his belt. He looked at Tata and motioned for him to come forward.

"I know you," said the police officer. "You put a roof on my house."

"That's what I do," said Tata. "I'm a roofer."

"It leaks," said the officer. "What should I do about that?"

"I'll fix it," said Tata, his voice so quick the words ran together. "Let me get my tools. I'll fix it right now."

"It's too late to fix it. The water's already gotten inside. You ruined my whole house."

"I'll build you a new house. Or take my house. It's beautiful, and the roof is sound and strong."

The officer looked to our house and then to Tata.

"You did it on purpose, didn't you?" he asked, almost smiling. Tata tried to say no, but the officer shook his head. He seemed amused, almost. "It's okay. I understand. This is what you people do. You overcharged us, you provided shoddy work for our houses, and you worked our people like dogs. We're different than you. I understand. You're a Muslim, and I'm a Serb. God made us as we are. Now God is putting it right."

Tata shook his head and furrowed his brow.

"I've never cheated anyone," he said, looking toward the soldiers. "Ask Jovan. He worked for me."

Jovan, my friend Ivana's father, stepped forward. The police officer looked at him.

"Is what he says true?"

Jovan studied my father before sighing and shaking this head.

"He was the worst of them," he said. "He fired me a month ago and refused to pay me because I'm a Serb. That's how they are."

"You were at work yesterday," said Tata. "And I pay you every week. I've never cheated you."

The officer looked at Tata, studying him. Minutes passed in silence. At first, I held my breath, waiting for something to happen, but nothing did.

Then, in a movement so fast I barely saw it, he slapped Tata across the face. Omar put me down, fuming, but Mama grabbed his arm before he could move further.

"Stay," she said, her voice like steel. "You'll only make things worse."

"Good advice," said the fat man. He looked to Sara and motioned her forward, but she didn't move. Then he sighed and reached for the pistol at his side. I clutched onto Omar's leg again. He pushed me back behind him but didn't move, even as the officer pointed the weapon at Tata's head. The tears came to my eyes, then. I couldn't breathe fast enough. The world was spinning. "Send the girl forward."

Mama held a fist to her mouth and cried. Sara did as he asked and stepped forward, tears on her cheeks. She held her arms over her chest as if trying to protect herself.

"She's a child," said Mama, her breath ragged. "Please don't do this."

The officer appraised Sara and then pushed her hands away. He smiled, then, as he reached to her shoulders and tore her dress to her waist. Sara cried and tried to cover herself. Tata held his breath and trembled.

"She's no child," said the police officer. He looked at Jovan. "Your employer owes you back wages. Take his daughter as payment. Put a Serb baby in her belly." Then he looked at Mama. "Take the wife, too. This family owes us all. And boys, take turns this time. No cutting in line. I don't want to break up a fight."

Everybody started moving at once. Omar pushed me back hard and sprinted toward the police officer. The officer raised his pistol and fired. For a split second, my wonderful big brother's body kept moving, but then he fell, dead. Tata grabbed me and Arman before either of us could move.

"We won't fight you," he said, tears streaming down his face. Jovan, my father's worker, dragged Sara toward the house. She screamed and kicked, but he didn't let her go. I wanted to run to her, to save her, but I couldn't. Tata squeezed my arms so tightly I couldn't move. The other soldiers came for Mama next. Her screams pierced something inside me I didn't know was there. Tata didn't stop them. He just held Arman and me. "Don't hurt my children. Please. Let them go."

The officer looked at Arman and then flicked his eyes to me.

"How old is she?"

"Seven," he said, tears choking his voice. "She's a baby. Don't hurt her."

The officer tilted his head left and right, considering. Then he sighed and shook his head.

"She's no good to us," he said. "Take your kids and run. You have ten seconds before we open fire."

Tata hesitated.

"Ten," said the officer. "Nine. Eight."

Tata lifted Arman and me from the ground and sprinted toward the woods as my mother and sister screamed from inside the house. Hamza sprinted after us. Tears streamed down my face, and my ribs ached. I couldn't move. The moment Tata hit the tree line, the soldiers fired at us. It couldn't have been ten seconds. Hamza was ahead of us. He fell first. Then Tata fell beside him. I felt the round that hit him before I heard it.

We hit the ground hard, but Tata didn't let go. Something hot started covering my side. As I reached down, I realized it was blood. Tata pulled us toward Hamza. He put an arm on my brother's back as if to shield him. Hamza covered me with his side, while Tata cradled Arman.

"Don't move," Tata whispered, his voice weak. "No matter what happens. Pretend you're dead. I love you."

I wanted to cry, but I held my breath and didn't move. Arman sobbed beside me, so I held a hand over his mouth as soldiers walked toward us. They shot Hamza and Tata in their backs over and over. Their bodies shuddered with every round. I knew the instant Tata had died because he stopped whispering that he loved us, and I knew the instant Hamza had died because he stopped clutching my hand.

Arman bit my hand, but I held on. Then the shooting stopped, and the soldiers walked back to our house, laughing. I sobbed in my heart but didn't dare make a sound. Arman and I waited there long enough for the blood that caked our clothes to grow cold. Then the sun set. When night finally arrived, a pair of frail hands rolled Tata aside, and I saw my elderly neighbor's lined face. She and Mama were friends, but the moment I saw her, I trembled.

"You're a Serb," I said. "You're one of them."

"I'm not one of them," she said. "Come. We need to go."

"Where's Mama?" I asked, struggling to stand. The night felt cool. Blood and dirt covered my chest and stuck to my hair.

"She's dead."

I might have cried if I had any tears left. Instead, I nodded.

"Where's Sara?"

The older woman drew in a breath.

"God willing, she's dead, too."

I looked to Arman. If the soldiers found us alive, they'd kill us. But first, they'd hurt us. With everyone else dead, it was my job to protect Arman. No one else could.

"Okay," I said. "We'll go."

5

Shortly after Lyons left, Officer Sutton opened the door and leaned against the frame. She crossed her arms. Her lips curled downward into a petulant frown.

"We know you killed Phil," she said, "but we don't know why. Somebody pay you? Was that it?"

I leaned back from the table and crossed my arms but said nothing.

"Maybe you just like killing people," she said, stepping closer to me. "You come down here thinking this little redneck police department wouldn't catch you? That you could do anything you want and lie your way out of trouble?"

She put her hands on the table and leaned forward. Had she been a threat, I would have grabbed her wrists, pulled her arms apart, and slammed her face against the table. Then I would have taken her pistol and shot her. That seemed like overkill for the present situation, but she deserved a response.

"That might be the stupidest thing you've said to me today."

She straightened.

"We're letting you go, but we're going to keep our eyes on you," she said. "One slip up, and you'll be back in our cells. You'll never see daylight again."

"I'll bear that in mind," I said, standing. "Walk me out. I'd hate for your colleagues to see me loose and think I was escaping."

She gestured toward the door and then followed me out. I walked to the lobby, where she handed me a shallow cardboard box that held my purse, phone, and keys. I slipped my phone into my pocket and looked inside my purse to make sure my wallet was where it should be. Then I glanced up.

"Your officers confiscated two firearms and a pair of knives from me, too. Where are they?"

"You have to fill out a form to get those back."

I slung my purse over my shoulder and raised my eyebrows. Sutton blinked but didn't otherwise respond.

"Get me the form," I said.

"Sure," she said, walking around the desk and reaching beneath for a form and clipboard. She handed them both to me. The form had a single page and requested my legal name, home address, phone number, and information about the firearms they had confiscated. It required me to declare that I was in possession of the firearms legally and that I didn't plan to use them in a crime. It also requested that I certify—under penalty of perjury—that the firearms had never been used in a crime.

I looked at Sutton.

"Who created this form?"

Sutton gave me a tight smile and closed her eyes.

"That's none of your concern."

"It's a bullshit form," I said. "You're asking me to swear no one has ever used my firearms in a crime. I can't do that. I can swear that I purchased them from a licensed firearms dealer and that I've never used them to commit a crime, but I have no idea what a previous owner has done."

She shrugged.

"If you can't fill out the forms, you can't get your firearms back. If you've got questions, hire a lawyer. He'll be able to answer them."

I ran my tongue around the inside of my mouth and then clenched my teeth.

"To clarify, you're suggesting I commit a felony to get my pistols back."

She narrowed her eyes.

"How do you figure?"

"You're asking me—and everyone else who fills out these forms—to swear under oath about something I can't possibly know. If you were to go to court and swear you had found a piece of evidence at a crime scene, but you really had no idea where that evidence was found, you'd be lying. Same thing with these forms. They're bullshit."

She shrugged again.

"Like I said, hire a lawyer. Until you fill out these forms, we'll be keeping your firearms in our vault."

I closed my eyes and counted to five in my head.

"Fine. I'll contact a lawyer. Where's my dog?"

"We don't have facilities to house a dog, so Gary took him to the Humane Society."

My mouth popped open, and my eyebrows shot up. I put my hands flat on the front desk.

"Excuse me?"

"You heard me," she said. "You're facing a murder charge. We had to do what we thought was right for the animal."

"So you stole him from me and gave him away."

She rolled her eyes.

"There's a twenty-four-hour hold for all animals taken to the shelter before they're put up for adoption. Just drive over and get him."

I gripped the edge of the desk tight enough that my knuckles started to turn white.

"Did you give my car away, too?"

"Of course not," she said. "Deputy Sheriff Lyons is in his office right now applying for a warrant to search it. It's still at the park under guard."

"This is absurd. You've arrested me without cause, and now you're harassing me."

"My boss and friend is dead," she said. "You'd be wise to remember that before opening your mouth."

She had brought her hand to something under the desk, probably an emergency button. If she pushed that, half a dozen or more officers would come out the back to subdue me. Best-case scenario, I'd get tackled, tased, and shackled. Worst case, my dog would make an adopted family very happy, and I'd be dead.

I held my breath, hoping that would calm me. It didn't.

"Fine. Can you call an officer to give me a ride back to my car at least?"

"No, but you're free to call a friend for a ride and wait in our lobby."

I closed my eyes and drew in a slow breath.

"Fine. I'll call a cab."

Sutton nodded and pretended to look at something on her desk while I sat and pulled out my phone. Then she cleared her throat, getting my attention.

"What's with the notepad, by the way?"

I raised my eyebrows, confused.

"What notepad?"

"The one in your purse."

I opened my eyes wider and lowered my chin.

"Did you have a warrant to search my purse?" I asked.

"Didn't need one. We searched your purse for weapons and found the notepad inside."

"I see," I said, nodding. "It's none of your

business."

She crossed her arms.

"It was just a little weird," she said. "You must have written '*Take care of the dog*' forty times."

In fact, I had written *Take care of the dog* well over forty times. That notebook was my daily to-do list. Dr. Kessler suggested I keep it to remind myself to get out of bed in the morning. Sometimes I didn't need the reminder, but other times, I did. Some days had a lot of things written, but most didn't.

"If you were looking for weapons, why'd you open my notebook?"

"Because you had a razor blade shaped as a credit card in your wallet," she said. "There's no telling what you've got hidden in your notepad. You could have a razor blade shaped like a bookmark."

"Did you find one?"

"No."

"My notepad's none of your business."

She nodded.

"What happens if you don't take care of the dog?"

"He pees in his crate, and I become a lousy friend," I said, crossing my arms. "Good enough?"

"Yeah. Just curious."

I grunted and looked at my phone. The nearest Uber was forty-five minutes away, and the nearest taxi company was in Springfield. It'd cost him fifty bucks just to get here. It looked like I'd be walking until I could get my car back. I started to stand, but then an older couple walked into the station. The man was Hispanic. Sawdust clung to his faded yellow T-shirt, jeans, and graying black hair. His spouse looked a few years younger and had lighter skin and brunette hair. Her white cotton shirt draped off her athletic torso well. Sutton drew in a sharp breath. Her face turned red.

"Mr. and Mrs. Romero," she said, hurrying around her desk. "We didn't know you were coming in."

I sat back. Officer Sutton squirmed.

"Is Phil really dead?" asked Mr. Romero. Sutton licked her lips.

"Yeah, but I can't share any details. Troy will talk to you when he can, but we're slammed right now."

"Phil called us three days ago and said he knew who killed Oscar," said Mrs. Romero. "We need to find out what happened to our son."

Sutton held up her hands.

"I understand you're upset, and I'm so sorry for your son," she said, speaking slowly. "You have every right to be upset about Oscar, but I don't know why Phil called you. We haven't learned anything new in a long time."

The woman's glare turned icy.

"You don't get to tell me how I should feel."

Sutton, again, brought up her hands.

"I'm sorry," she said. "Poor choice of words. We've done our best to investigate Oscar's death, but we don't have anything new. I'm sorry. I wish we did."

"Phil said he knew Oscar's killer, and now Phil is dead. It's those people at the camp. They're covering it up again."

Things were making more sense now. Pollard rarely made the news in St. Louis, but Oscar Romero's death was sensational enough that reporters covered it for weeks. He was stabbed in the neck and allowed to bleed out on a sofa in a cabin at Camp Meadowview. The case had sex and violence, and it pitted the working-class town against the camp and its very wealthy campers. Despite the media attention, the local police never solved the case. It was a tragedy all around.

"If there's anything new to find, we'll find it," she said. "Don't worry."

"That's what you told us when Oscar died," said Mr. Romero, leaning forward to stand over Officer Sutton. Had I done that, I suspected she would have pulled a baton from her utility belt to beat me back. "I want to talk to Troy Lyons. Now."

Officer Sutton drew in a breath and then pointed to the chairs near me.

"Have a seat. I'll see what we can do."

The couple nodded and sat down. As fun as it had been watching Officer Sutton squirm, I wanted to get up and leave. Before I could, Mrs. Romero caught my eye.

"If you're here to report a crime, don't bother," she said. "They won't do anything."

Normally I would have said the police would do their best and that they'd spare no expense or resources in the investigation, but I had already seen the Bryant County Sheriff's Office at work. Their kid's case was unsolved for a reason. I couldn't do anything to help them, but if they needed to vent, I could—at the very least—be a sounding board.

"Tell me about your boy," I said, my voice soft.

Mrs. Romero did most of the talking, but her husband chimed in at times. Oscar had been young and handsome. He had run track in high school and dated a new girl every week. According to his parents, he had worked hard to go to college and earned extra money in the summer by cleaning pools, including the pool at Camp Meadowview. He had been twenty-one years old when he was murdered. The police investigated, but they never found his killer.

Mrs. Romero spoke for almost five minutes straight, barely taking a breath. With every word, her shoulders lowered, and the heat of her anger seemed to dissipate. When she finished, I lowered my voice.

"I'm very sorry," I said. "Oscar sounds like a remarkable person."

"No one here cared what happened to him," said Mrs. Romero, her voice trembling. "I don't know what to do."

"I'm sorry for your loss," I said again. They nodded but paid me little attention. Mrs. Romero put her head on her husband's shoulder. I started toward the door.

"You want to finish the firearms application before you go, Ms. Blackwood?" asked Officer Sutton. Had the Romeros not been in the lobby, I suspected she would have smirked at me. I looked her up and down.

"You're not worth the time," I said. Then I looked to the Romero family. "Good luck."

It took thirty minutes to walk to my car at the park. As Officer Sutton had said, a uniformed sheriff's deputy stood outside, smoking a cigarette as he leaned against his cruiser. He was probably thirty-five, and he had the uniformly tanned and leathery skin of a lifelong smoker who worked outside for a living. The nicotine had stained his teeth yellow, and the smoke had prematurely aged his skin so that he looked almost reptilian. When he saw me, he straightened, threw down his cigarette, and ground it beneath his heel. I didn't acknowledge him as I unlocked the driver's side door.

"Step away from the vehicle, miss," he said.

I touched the handle, but I didn't open my door yet.

"Do you have probable cause to search my vehicle?"

He opened his mouth.

"We arrested you this morning. You want me to take you back to jail?"

"I'm asking whether you have probable cause to search my car," I said. "If you had arrested me while I was inside my car, you could have searched it pursuant to the arrest. If you had impounded the car and driven it to your station for safekeeping, you could have conducted an inventory search. You didn't do those things, though. I'm legally parked in a public lot, and I'd like to go home. Can I do that or not?"

He looked me up and down. Then he stepped back.

"Stay where you are," he said. "Don't go inside."

I crossed my arms and waited while he walked toward his cruiser and spoke into the radio on his shoulder. He came back a few minutes later.

"My boss is trying to get a search warrant for the car, but he says we don't really need one. We only need probable cause to search. He's just trying to make sure the search'll hold up in court. He's already got the affidavit written up. Now he's just got to get a judge to sign it."

"So we're back to my first question. Do you have probable cause to search my vehicle?"

He considered me again and then stepped away and spoke into his radio. I waited for about five minutes before shouting at him again.

"Just search the car," I said. "You've got my

permission. You won't find anything illegal inside."

He looked at me and then said something into his radio. Then he nodded to himself and sauntered back toward me.

"Will you sign a release form?"

"Sure, fine," I said, shaking my head and holding out my keys. "Just get this over with."

He took the keys and walked to his cruiser, where he stayed for another five minutes filling out a form. Once he finished, he got out of his cruiser and handed the paper to me. The form looked similar to the ones we had in St. Louis. It granted the sheriff's department permission to search my vehicle and collect any evidence or contraband they might find. It also specified that I had been made aware of my constitutional rights and was granting my permission free of coercion, duress, or intimidation. I signed at the bottom, handed it back to him, and watched him work.

The entire process took about twenty minutes. He looked through the glove box, beneath the seats, inside my trunk, beneath my car, inside the wheel wells, and even in the depression in the back where my spare tire and jack sat. Aside from the .45-caliber pistol I kept in my glove box, he found nothing. He had no reason to confiscate the weapon, so he handed it back and wished me well.

The whole thing was a waste of time. Once he left, I sat in the driver's seat and used my phone to search for the local Humane Society's phone number. I found it and dialed but then discovered they were closed for the afternoon and would reopen tomorrow at eleven. Looked like I was stuck in Pollard.

I swore to myself and considered what the hell else I should do with the day. The nearest movie theater was in Springfield, and I didn't want to drive that far to sit in the dark and watch something crappy. Had the sheriff's department been just a little more efficient, I might have gone for a hike, but it was getting late, and I didn't want to get stuck in the woods once the sun went down. Then I opened my notebook and flipped to today's entry.

Take care of the dog.

Drive to Pollard and check out cabin.

Both of those were done. I drummed my fingers on the steering wheel. Dr. Kessler had said I should come here to reconnect with those things that once made me happy. I thought about calling her to tell her that I had checked out Mom and Dad's cabin, but she'd probably tell me to examine the cabin inside my heart next. I didn't know whether I had the patience to deal with her.

George was my friend, so I wouldn't leave town until I had him again. I thought about returning to Mom and Dad's cabin to see what it would take to repair it, but I found my thoughts straying to the Romero family instead.

Growing up, I'd had an almost mythic view of the police. In my childish mind, they had been heroes, modern-day knights out to protect their communities. Life had unburdened me of my naiveté since then. The police were far from perfect, and those officers in Bryant County were further from the mark than most. The Romero family deserved better than this town had given them.

I put my keys in the ignition and drew in a breath.

My life was in the toilet, but I had been a good detective for a long time. Maybe I could find something the locals missed. Maybe I could get lucky and break the whole case open. That probably wouldn't happen, but it was worth a shot. If nothing else, I was stuck here for now, and without George, my to-do list was short of activities. Hopefully the good deputies of Bryant County could refrain from arresting me for a while.

6

Every time her door opened, the stink of chlorine flooded the room. Elaine hated that smell. Lakeside Pools was a stepping stone on her journey, but the longer she stayed, the more it felt like a destination. She had worked too hard to settle. She had to finish this now.

She leaned back in her chair. Her office was twelve feet by twenty feet. The cinderblock walls were painted robin's egg blue. Navy blue Berber carpet covered the floor. The lack of windows made it feel like a basement. To brighten things up, she had hired a local artist to paint a mural of a family at the lake on two of the walls. The men and women who purchased pools and other services from Lakeside loved that painting, but Elaine didn't care for it. That painting represented their dreams, and as far as dreams went, they were fine and good. Hers were bigger, though. She wanted more.

Joseph Lipscombe walked into the room first. He was forty-five and handsome. The room's overhead lights caught on the wrinkles of his long, thin face, making him look distinguished instead of old. Years ago, the Army had forged him into a resourceful and intelligent soldier. Now, he used those same skills to solve her business problems. Elaine trusted him implicitly.

Daniel Nakamura came next. Elaine trusted him, too. His heavy jawline and thick neck gave him a menacing appearance, but when he smiled—a rare occurrence—he looked almost boyish. He had spent nine years as an active-duty Marine. His wife appreciated the money his new career gave him, but more than that, she—and their children— appreciated having him home. Elaine hoped Mrs. Nakamura wouldn't mind her husband working a few long days and nights in the weeks ahead.

"Gentlemen," she said, standing and nodding toward her door. "Close the door and sit."

Joseph sat in one of the two chairs in front of her desk, while his partner closed the door and then slumped into the open seat. Elaine sat and folded her hands in front of her.

"I already know Phil Mason is dead," she said. "That's unfortunate, but I'm sure he made his death a necessity. Will it pass as an accident?"

The two men looked at each other. Joseph leaned forward and rested his elbows on his knees and looked down at his hands. Daniel blinked and looked toward the wall. Elaine raised an eyebrow.

"Something I should know?" she asked.

"Lisa Mason was there," said Joseph. "As you suggested, we took a boat to avoid traffic cameras, but she saw us walking toward the house."

Elaine's skin felt warmer, and her heartbeat stepped up a notch.

"I see," she said, her back stiff. "Is she a threat?"

"She didn't see us kill her husband," said Daniel. "She left as soon as we arrived."

Elaine considered them and pushed back from her desk.

"Would she recognize your faces if she saw you again?"

The two men looked at each other. Joseph nodded.

"We talked," said Joseph. "She'd know us both."

Elaine sighed and swore under her breath.

"All right," she said. "We'll monitor the situation and kill her if necessary."

"She won't go to the police," said Daniel. "She wanted us to kill her husband."

Elaine considered him. Daniel had a good sense for people, so she trusted his judgment. This, though, she wanted to hear.

"Explain," she said.

"She knew we intended to kill him the moment we arrived," he said. "She saw us walking and knew we were covering our tracks, but she said nothing. You should have seen her eyes. She hated her husband. If Joseph hadn't been so focused on her breasts, he would have noticed her contempt."

She looked at Joseph. He shrugged.

"To be fair, her breasts are spectacular."

"I'll take your word for that," she said. "We'll monitor the situation. Next business, the buyers from Memphis are coming in this afternoon. The buyers from Kansas City are coming next week. My entire life has led to this. If we make this sale, we'll all end up very wealthy."

Joseph smiled a little.

"You're already very wealthy, boss," he said.

"I make a living, and I run a business, but I'm not wealthy," she said. "I will be, but we have to sell my company first. Once we're done, we'll share a three-thousand-dollar bottle of bourbon and toast our success. Until then, we work."

Both men nodded their agreement. Ten years ago, three thousand dollars would have been a life-changing sum. Now, it was nothing. Elaine hadn't grown up with money. Her mother had waited tables at a seafood restaurant in Hot Springs, Arkansas. She had never met her father and often wondered whether her mother knew his name. It didn't matter, though. They were fine without him.

Elaine's mother had followed every rule she was supposed to follow and worked as hard as she could as a waitress. At the end of every month, she made enough to cover the rent, food, insurance, and gas, but she had little left over. That was okay, though. They had enough.

Then her mom's employer sold his restaurant, and the new owner fired everyone so he could bring in a new staff. Elaine and her mom struggled for a while and moved into a car. Then Elaine's mom got another job cleaning houses, and they moved into a new apartment. Then the economy tanked, and demand for housekeeping services decreased. Her mom's employer went out of business, and she and Elaine moved back into their car.

That was Elaine's life. She watched her mom work until she collapsed from exhaustion, but she never saw her mom get ahead. It taught Elaine an important lesson. The rules, those social mores that extolled the virtue of hard, honest work, were bullshit. You didn't get ahead by working hard. You got ahead by finding opportunities and exploiting them. If that meant working an employee to death, you worked that employee to death.

The world wasn't fair, and it never would be. Elaine learned that lesson the hard way, but she learned it all the better because of that.

For the next hour, she practiced her presentation in front of Joseph and Daniel. If her meetings went well, two organizations would bid on her business, and every dream she'd ever had would come true. Nothing would stand in her way now. She had worked too hard and sacrificed too much. This was her world now, and she'd cut down anyone and anything that tried to stop her.

7

I drove for about five minutes and then parked in front of the local library. The building looked like more like a two-story warehouse than anything else. Narrow windows on the first and second floor spoke to the building's history and made me think it had been built sometime in the seventies. Hydrangeas along the front looked healthy, but the weeds that threatened to overtake them robbed them of whatever cheer they might have provided. Inside, the ceiling was low, the carpet was threadbare, and the overhead lights bathed the main room in an odd yellowish hue. The air held just a hint of mold and cigarette smoke.

A woman in her late twenties sat behind the reference desk. She looked up and smiled when she saw me walking toward her.

"Can I help you?"

"Maybe," I said. "I've got some research

questions."

She tilted her head to the side and smiled.

"What are you interested in?"

"A young man named Oscar Romero. Someone murdered him at Camp Meadowview a few years back."

She almost grimaced.

"We don't talk about Oscar here."

"I'm sorry to hear that," I said. "This is a public library, though, and I'm interested in background information on Oscar Romero and Camp Meadowview. If you have a moment, I'd appreciate you helping me find this information. If you're unavailable, I'll search the stacks myself."

"Are you writing a book? There are at least two authors right now writing books on Oscar. They're going to make him famous. You've got some competition."

"I'm not a writer," I said. She waited for me to say something else, but I had nothing else to say, so I kept my mouth shut. Finally, she pushed back from her desk.

"Because of the interest and the graphic nature of our files, Sheriff Mason suggested we restrict access to the materials to members of the press or academia. Sorry."

"Does the sheriff dictate a lot of library business?"

For just a second, her eyes narrowed. Then she caught herself and forced a smile to her lips.

"I've indulged you so far, but now you're bordering on being rude."

"Sorry you think that," I said. "Sheriff Mason died this morning. You'll hear about it on the news later."

She sucked in a breath and brought a hand to her mouth.

"Phil's dead?"

"You're on a first-name basis with him?"

She blinked but said nothing. Then she cleared her throat.

"Everybody knows Phil. Is Lisa okay?"

"She was out buying cookies or something when he died. I don't know."

She turned her head from me and straightened. I said nothing as she closed her eyes and inhaled.

"I'll show you the Romero files and get you set up in one of our study rooms."

I thanked her and followed her as we walked upstairs to a quiet corner of the library.

"Do many people research the murder here?"

"Not really," she said. Her voice sounded rough at first, but then it gained strength as she kept talking. "We show these files to two or three people a year. Interest rises on big anniversaries or when news stories come out."

"You ever meet him?" I asked.

"Oscar?" asked the librarian. I nodded, and she continued walking through the stacks of books to a row of small rooms at the far end of the second floor. "No. He was younger than me."

"What do you know about Camp Meadowview?" I asked.

She opened the study door with a key from her pocket.

"It's both more and less tawdry than the papers said," she said. "The younger campers sing songs and make wind chimes and tie-dye shirts. The teenagers drink, smoke, and screw. We close at eight. I'll get the files for you."

I thanked her and stepped inside. The room was ten or twelve feet by ten or twelve feet and had a table with four chairs and bright overhead lights. A window overlooked the stacks outside, but the door blocked the library's soft murmur. The librarian came back a few minutes later. Her hands were empty. I leaned back in my chair, not entirely surprised.

"I'm sorry, but our files are gone."

I grunted and shook my head.

"If you're going to blow me off, have the courage to blow me off. Don't pretend you lost the files."

The skin around her neck grew red, and she pushed her lips into a thin line. She was pissed. Good. That was what I wanted. I needed to provoke an honest reaction out of her.

"I'm not pretending. The files are gone. Someone must have borrowed them and not returned them. It happens. People steal things."

I nodded and crossed my arms.

"Where do you store them?"

She considered me and then crossed her own arms, matching my posture.

"Why do you care?"

"By your own admission, you restricted access to the files. The average person wouldn't be able to steal them because he or she wouldn't have access. You also said very few researchers come and look at them, so if a researcher had taken them, you'd know your thief. But you had no idea the files were even gone, let alone who took them. So where do you keep them and who has access?"

She looked down and seemed to be studying something on the carpet. I kept my eyes on her. Then, as if she had made a decision, she closed her eyes and spoke.

"They're kept in an empty office. The public doesn't have access. And nobody could have just walked out with them. The documents filled two bankers boxes. Any thief would have had to walk right by the reference desk, which is always manned."

I thought for a second and nodded.

"So a library employee took them."

She glanced at me but then looked down again without saying a word.

"Did anyone outside the library have access to the office?" I asked.

She said nothing again.

"Did Sheriff Mason have access?"

Her eyes shot up. This time, she didn't look down.

"He wouldn't have taken them. He wouldn't have needed to. His department investigated the murders. Half the information we had came from them."

I raised my eyebrows.

"Did he have access or not?"

She shifted her weight from one foot to the other.

"We had a fire in the building after hours a few years back, and the fire department had a hard time getting in. After that, we gave the sheriff's department and the fire department master keys to the building. That doesn't mean he took the files, though."

I brought a hand to my face and thought. She was partially right, at least. The library's publicly available documents wouldn't have aided a police investigation, but they sure would have helped civilian investigators and journalists. Their disappearance slowed things down.

I blinked a few times, thinking.

"How's the local real estate market?"

She furrowed her brow and tilted her head to the right.

"What do you mean?"

"If I wanted to buy a big cabin on the lake with ten or fifteen acres, how much would I have to spend?"

The librarian's lips moved, but she said nothing.

Then she cleared her throat.

"I don't know," she said. "Way more than my husband and I can afford."

"What's your husband do?"

She closed her eyes again and then drew in a breath.

"He's an accountant."

It was a good job, and it would have come with a decent salary. She may not have made a lot of money, but together the two of them should have made a very comfortable living. If the two of them couldn't afford a lake house with their salaries, I doubted the sheriff could afford one, either.

Maybe Sheriff Mason or his wife had family money, but, by all appearances, he lived well beyond his means. That was disconcerting considering he was now dead, that these files were missing, and that he had told the Romero family that he knew who had murdered their son.

"What do you know about the sheriff?" I asked.

"He's local. He's a good man," she said, shrugging. "Why is that relevant to Oscar Romero? And what does my husband have to do with anything?"

"Nothing," I said. "Just thinking. Tell me what you can about Oscar Romero's death."

Unfortunately, she knew little off the top of her head. His body was found early in the morning in the Pin Oak cabin at Camp Meadowview, a massive summer camp for very wealthy children, adolescents, and teenagers. Four young women lived in that cabin at the time of his death, but none cooperated with the police investigation. All the girls had recently turned eighteen and were enjoying one final summer before college. The police suspected a camper killed Oscar after an illicit tryst, but they never found enough evidence to prosecute anyone.

I took notes but not many. When she finished speaking, I glanced up.

"Who found the body?"

She blinked.

"Don't quote me on it, but I think it was the camp director. Dr. Turner."

That made me furrow my brow.

"Why would the camp director be poking around early in the morning inside a cabin?"

"You'd have to ask her," she said. She looked around and then to me. "I think I've said more than I should already."

"I will ask her. Thank you."

The librarian nodded, turned, and left. I read through my notes and followed a few moments later. When I reached my car, I looked up the camp on my GPS and headed out. As I left Pollard and pulled onto the only road that led to the camp, the asphalt narrowed and became rutted. Trees encroached on the roadway, forming an arch overhead. With a large number of campers and an equal number of staff members, the camp must have had a larger road somewhere for deliveries, but I hadn't seen it on Google Maps.

Eventually, the woods thinned, and I reached the camp's front gate. Two guards sat in a booth out front. A barrier arm blocked the driveway, and retractable spike strips stuck out of the ground, ensuring that no one could drive onto the grounds without permission. A wooden fence stretched east and west. I wondered whether the camp had featured similar security measures before Oscar's death or whether it had added them later.

I turned my car toward the gate and then stopped as a uniformed guard came toward me. He carried a clipboard but no firearm. His rounded shoulders and the arch in his lower back told me he likely sat at a computer or at a desk most of the day, while his pale skin and lined, weathered face told me he likely smoked. He wasn't a threat, but he had a radio to call the fitter members of the security staff. They'd chase me down if I tried to break in.

"Afternoon. What can I do for you?"

His gums had retreated from his teeth, and his breath smelled like spearmint. His eyes settled on my chest, so I cleared my throat to let him know I had noticed. Then I smiled as he straightened, his face red.

"I'm Hana Blackwood, and I'm here to see the director."

He furrowed his brow, surprised.

"Are you expected?"

I blinked and pretended to think.

"I'd say no."

He pointed toward the street.

"Do me a favor then and back up. This is private property. Next time, call ahead and make an appointment. We're not set up to accept unexpected visitors."

I wasn't above flirting with him if it'd get me what I wanted, but I doubted it'd work. The guard may have been fifty pounds overweight and ten years past chasing down an intruder on foot, but he wasn't stupid. He knew I had no business at that camp.

"I'll do that. In the meantime, I'll be investigating Oscar Romero's death. I was a detective with the St. Louis County Police Department, and I was pretty good at my job. My visit is a courtesy. This was Dr. Turner's opportunity to shape my investigation and the story I'll ultimately tell. If she doesn't want to do that, it's her loss. Thanks for your time."

I reached to my gear selector but didn't put the car in reverse. The guard considered and then stepped back.

"Hold on just a minute, Detective," he said. "I'll call Dr. Turner and see what she has to say about this...opportunity."

"Sure thing," I said.

He walked back to the guardhouse to call his boss. Nothing happened for a few minutes, but then the gate went up and the guard stepped out. He walked to my window and leaned down.

"Looks like this is your lucky day," he said. "Dr. Turner had some free time in her schedule. She can see you right away. Pull through the gate and park in the lot to your right. I'll drive you to the director's office."

He stepped back again, and I pulled through the gate and parked beside a golf cart in a small parking lot just inside the camp's grounds.

Then I sat and thought. This meeting was entirely too easy. If anything, Dr. Turner should have told me to call her lawyer. Instead, she agreed to see me immediately. I couldn't help but feel something was about to blow up in my face. I considered leaving, but then I found the security guard standing outside my door.

I rolled the window down.

"You ready to go, Detective? The camp's almost two thousand acres, so we've got a little ride ahead of us."

I considered grabbing my sole remaining pistol from the glove box, but somehow I didn't think the guard would appreciate that. Instead, I nodded, closed my window, and stepped out, hoping I wasn't walking into a trap.

8

The guard and I got on a golf cart, and he started driving. Camp Meadowview sat on a beautiful, rolling piece of property with pockets of dense trees interspersed with soccer fields, cabins, and larger buildings. I didn't see them, but somewhere, little girls sang songs about ants that go marching by. As we crested a hill and I got my first view of the lake, I almost held my breath.

"Pretty, huh?" asked the guard. I nodded.

"It's beautiful," I said. "I'm surprised you're not Camp Lakeview instead of Camp Meadowview."

"I agree, but the owners didn't ask for my opinion."

I cocked my head at him.

"You ever meet the owners?"

He cleared his throat.

"No."

"You ever meet Oscar Romero?"

He glanced at me and gave me a sour look.

"The camp's official policy is to defer comment on Mr. Romero to Dr. Turner and our general counsel."

"What's the unofficial policy?"

He focused on the road.

"To defer comment on Mr. Romero to Dr. Turner and the camp's general counsel."

"You think a camper killed him?"

He drew in a breath and seemed to consider the question before slowing the golf cart to a stop.

"You're not from around here, are you?" he asked.

"I own a piece of property just outside Pollard."

"But you don't live here," he said. I nodded. "Camp Meadowview is the largest employer in Bryant County. You lose your job at Meadowview, you'll have to drive an hour to Springfield to get another job, and it won't pay half as well. I like working here. You might be a nice lady, but I'm not risking my job to talk to you. I doubt anybody else will, either. Sorry."

At least he was polite about it. I nodded and kept my mouth shut for the duration of the drive. Within moments, we turned off the main road and onto a smaller road cut through a copse of fir trees. In the center was an oversized log cabin with big windows and six rocking chairs on the front porch. A woman with wavy, silver hair stood on the porch with her arms crossed and a tight smile on her face.

We nodded to one another, and she looked to the guard.

"Stick around, Jim. I don't think Ms. Blackwood will stay long."

He nodded and slumped at the steering wheel. Dr. Turner eyed me and then smiled.

"Why don't we have a seat on my porch?" she asked. "It's a comfortable evening."

"Sure," I said, joining her near the cabin. I sat in a chair kitty-corner to hers and looked at the surrounding woods. "It's beautiful here."

"Thank you," said Turner, drawing in a breath. "I don't know why Mr. Romero was in Pin Oak cabin the night he died, I don't know who killed him, and I don't suspect any of our campers or staff members. Beyond that, I can't say anything. My contract with Camp Meadowview contains a nondisclosure agreement that prevents me from speaking to members of the press or private investigators about anything that happens at the camp."

I nodded and lowered my voice.

"How about if I promised to keep anything you say between us?"

She shook her head.

"I wish it were that easy," she said. "Mr. Romero was a fine young man. Had he been born in other circumstances, he would have been Meadowview material."

"And that's a good thing?" I asked, lowering my

chin. She nodded.

"It is," she said. "If you'd like to learn more about his death, talk to Frannie Hopkins. She lives in Pollard and was on our housekeeping staff until her recent retirement. I suspect she'll have something to tell you."

I pulled my phone from my purse and typed in Frannie Hopkins's name.

"All right," I said. "Anything else you want to say?"

"No," she said. "Enjoy the rest of your day. I have to get back to work. Jim will drive you back to your car."

That was easy.

"Thanks for your time," I said.

She nodded, stood, and walked to her cabin while I left the porch. Jim, the security guard, nodded to me as I walked toward his golf cart.

"You get what you needed?" he asked.

"I got a name," I said. "Please take me to my car. I've got a busy evening."

Jim drove in silence. When we reached my car, he wished me luck, and I drove for about a mile until the road widened. Then I parked on the shoulder to give myself a moment to think. Dr. Turner knew far more than she let on, but—like Jim the security guard—I doubted she would have risked her job to help me. More than likely, Frannie Hopkins would be a dead end, but I had time to kill until I got George back. I figured I might as well see where this rabbit hole took me.

I used an app on my phone to look up Frannie Hopkins on a reference database provided by my local library in St. Louis County. The database didn't give me a phone number, but I learned that she lived in Bryant County and paid fourteen hundred dollars a year in property taxes. I put her address in my phone's GPS and headed out.

Hopkins's home had a single story, a small front porch, and clapboard siding. An air conditioner jutted out the front window to the right of the porch, and a late-model pickup was parked in the gravel driveway. The home was small, but someone kept the grass trimmed and watered the hydrangeas along the foundation. The light blue paint on the siding looked fresh and clean, giving the property a cheery feeling.

As I parked on the street out front, the home's front door opened. An older woman with an aged face and gray hair stepped onto the porch. She wore a colorful sundress and tennis shoes but no makeup. She nodded but didn't smile as I walked toward her.

"You the detective?" she asked. I nodded. She looked me up and down. "Dr. Turner called and said you'd be by. I guess we can talk outside."

She had no outdoor furniture, so I took a step back and smiled.

"Dr. Turner said you worked at Meadowview."

"That's right," she said. "I supervised the housekeeping staff."

I reached into my purse for a notepad.

"You mind if I take some notes?" I asked. She said she didn't, so I flipped to a clean page and smiled at her. "Did you like working at Camp Meadowview?"

She narrowed her eyes at me. For a moment, I didn't think she'd answer.

"What do you want to know?" she asked, finally.

"I'm asking whether you enjoyed working there," I said. "Was it fun? Was your boss nice? Did you like your co-workers? I'm just trying to make conversation."

She considered me and then shrugged.

"I had good and bad days. You don't care about my work, though. Speak your mind. If you want to know about Oscar Romero, ask me about Breanna Moore and Rachel Tibbals. They lived in Pin Oak cabin when he died. One of them killed him, but I don't know which."

I narrowed my eyes at her.

"That's a pretty big accusation," I said. "Why do you think they killed Mr. Romero?"

"*They* didn't do it," she said. "*One* of them did. There's a difference."

"There is," I said. "Who else lived in the cabin?"

"Angelina Lopez and Meredith Brown, but they didn't kill Oscar. They were good girls. Breanna and Rachel weren't."

"Okay. Why do you think Breanna of them

killed Oscar Romero?"

She broke eye contact with me to look out over her lawn. I let the silence drag on. Finally, she sighed and focused on me again.

"What do you know about Camp Meadowview?"

"Less than you," I said.

She gave me a tight nod.

"I earned forty-eight thousand dollars a year working at that camp. It was a good salary around here. It was enough to buy a decent house and car. I even help pay my daughter's college tuition. My son's working on an apprenticeship. He wants to be an electrician."

"That's a good job," I said. "And I'm sure your daughter's grateful for the help."

"Brat's never thanked me," she said. "That's not the point, though. I made forty-eight thousand dollars a year. Some kids at Meadowview spent more money than that each year on clothes."

I didn't know what she wanted me to say, so I told her I understood. She grunted and nodded.

"The young kids could be sweet and kind, or they could be monsters," she said. "Just depended on the kids. The bigger kids, though... We weren't people in their eyes. We were just furniture. We were robots without feelings. They didn't treat us like we were human."

I lowered my voice and tilted my face down.

"Did someone hurt you?"

She rolled her eyes and shook her head.

"I'm not talking about me," she said. "I'm talking about Oscar. He was sweet and handsome, but he was still a young man. He didn't know when to keep his fly zipped."

"A lot of young men make decisions with their penises. Few are murdered."

She lowered her chin.

"The ones who live didn't clean pools at Camp Meadowview."

It was a fair point, so I nodded.

"What made it different at Camp Meadowview?"

She blinked and then looked down.

"Like I said, the young kids could be nice. As they got older, though, the nice kids stopped coming. They went other places, or maybe they just didn't like summer camp. The teenage boys who come want to drink, play video games, and pick up girls. The girls did the same."

"What did Oscar do?"

She lowered her voice.

"He was a frequent overnight guest of a lot of the young ladies at camp. The two ladies I mentioned earlier—Breanna and Rachel—fought over him. I had to pull them apart. They would have killed each other."

"So they had a physical fight. They didn't just scream at one another?"

She nodded and crossed her arms.

"Knock 'em down, drag 'em out fight," she said. "I had to call in extra help to clean up the cabin afterward. Their daddies had to pay a pretty penny for all the stuff they broke, but I don't think they cared. They agreed to stay away from Oscar after that. A couple of days later, I found him dead on the sofa when I came to do my daily clean."

I drew in a breath as I considered the story.

"I thought Dr. Turner found the body."

"Nope," she said, shaking her head. "I found him and called Dr. Turner. She just called the police."

I jotted that down and glanced at her.

"What'd the police say about Breanna and Rachel's fight?"

"They never learned about the fight," she said. "Dr. Turner forbade me from talking to the police."

I straightened and drew in a short, surprised breath. Then I considered my next question.

"So you didn't talk to the police at all about that day?"

"I didn't want to lose my job."

"Understandable," I said, nodding. "You don't have a job to lose now, though. Tell me about that day. You found Oscar Romero's body in the Pin Oak cabin when you went to clean. You then called Dr. Turner. What happened next?"

She drew in a breath and leaned back just slightly.

"Dr. Turner drove a golf cart to the cabin and escorted the girls out of the house. Meanwhile, she ordered me to clean the cabin and remove the garbage. That meant liquor bottles, drugs, drug paraphernalia, condoms... Anything the girls would be afraid to show their grandmas, I threw away. When the police arrived, that place was pristine. I even made the beds and vacuumed the carpets."

And destroyed most of the forensic evidence.

"Were you there when the police arrived?"

She shook her head.

"No. Dr. Turner gave me the rest of the week off and a thousand-dollar check and told me to take a vacation. The kids and I went to Destin, Florida. We had a good time."

At least I now knew why the case went unsolved. The police never had a chance.

"You said Rachel or Breanna killed Oscar. Why?"

"It's obvious."

I said nothing, hoping she'd continue. Then she tossed up her hands.

"One of them, obviously, broke her promise and hooked up with Oscar again. The other girl killed him, probably out of jealousy."

Jealousy was a powerful motive, and I knew of dozens of murders committed for less, but I needed actual evidence.

"You cleaned the house," I said. "Someone stabbed Oscar. Did you find a knife?"

She shook her head but said nothing.

"What did you find?" I asked.

"Two used condoms in the first-floor bathroom. Each girl had a private bathroom, but guests used the first-floor bathroom. Dr. Turner told me to get rid of them."

Those condoms wouldn't have solved Oscar's murder, but the police could have used them in an interrogation room. Dr. Turner and her staff had cut the legs out from beneath this investigation before it even started.

"Are you sure the condoms were used the night of Oscar's death?"

She nodded.

"We emptied the trash cans every day."

"Would you be willing to tell the police what you've just told me?" I asked.

She hesitated and then shook her head.

"No, but I've got the condoms. I put them in a Ziploc bag and then stuck them in my deep freeze. After everything Dr. Turner did, I was afraid the investigation would turn on me. I wanted protection."

She hadn't intended to make the pun about protection, so I kept the smile off my face.

"You ever thought about giving them to the police?"

"I don't want to get involved," she said. She looked me up and down. "You seem like a nice lady. If you take my advice, you'll leave town tonight. Meadowview isn't what it seems. You go along with their plans, you'll be just fine, but if you go against them, they'll carve you up."

With George in the shelter, I couldn't leave. Still, I paused and considered her.

"Did Dr. Turner threaten you?"

"Turner's not the boss," she said. "I don't know the man in charge. Nobody does. He's dangerous, though."

I added what she had just said to my limited bank of facts about the case and nodded. Then I cleared my throat.

"If you give me the condoms, I'll make sure the police get them. Maybe they can do something. I'll need your phone number, too, in case I have questions."

She nodded and went into the house. About five minutes later, she came back with a sticky note on which she had written her phone number and a gallon-sized Ziploc freezer bag, inside of which I saw two used prophylactics. If a lab found Oscar's DNA inside and a camper's DNA on the outside, we'd have evidence tying a girl from that cabin to an intimate encounter with our murder victim the night he died. With that, they could get additional search warrants and break this case wide open.

That bothered me. Even aside from this mysterious boss, if Ms. Hopkins was correct, Dr. Turner had covered up a murder. If Turner felt guilty about that, she could have gone to the police years ago. They would have arrested her, but they would have worked the case. Instead, she sent me to Frannie Hopkins, who had the precise information I needed, and who was more than willing to share it.

This was way too easy, especially given the media attention and the failure of the sheriff's office to close the case when it first happened. Something was wrong here, and that made me nervous.

9

August 12, 1992.
Žepa, Bosnia and Herzegovina

Arman and I left our home in Višegrad and walked northwest with Mr. and Mrs. Stanković, our elderly neighbors, on trails cut through the mountains. We traveled at night and slept in the day to avoid snipers. They focused on riverboats and troop trucks, but they shot at us too, forcing us to hide behind trees. Sometimes, I wished they would just shoot us so we could stop walking.

Two days after we left Višegrad, we reached Žepa, a small village controlled by Bosniak forces. Serbian soldiers held the surrounding area, but there were enough fighters in Žepa to keep us safe. Mr. and Mrs. Stanković had to leave, but Mr. Stanković gave me a knife and prayed for me. They planned to walk to Serbia and be with their kids. I hoped they made it.

At first, Arman and I slept on mattresses in the

mosque. An old lady and her dog slept beside us. She had lived with her family on a farm, but then a Serb militia group came and killed everybody. Only she made it out. I didn't know her, so I stayed up at night with my knife and slept during the day in case she tried to kill us.

After a week, the imam introduced Arman and me to the Hadžić family. They took us in because they had empty bedrooms after two of their sons died fighting. Ibrahim, their remaining son, was fourteen, a little older than Sara. He treated Arman and me as his younger siblings, and his parents treated us as if we were their own. I think they needed people to love. They wept at night, but I pretended not to hear. Arman clung to them and never left their side. They weren't my parents, though. My parents were dead. Arman could believe what he wanted. He was a child.

Žepa was beautiful, but it wasn't home. Hills, valleys, and fields surrounded our house, but we couldn't play in them because of the soldiers in the woods. Men and boys from the village patrolled the streets and kept the soldiers away for now, but I had seen the army's weapons. Men with rifles and knives couldn't fight tanks.

Once the Serbs brought their artillery, they'd reduce Žepa to rubble, just as they had done to Višegrad. Then, when our defenders were too tired to fight, the soldiers would walk into the village and murder us—just as they had to Tata, Omar, Hamza,

Mama, and Sara.

I slept little. My eyes wouldn't close most days. When I did sleep, I had nightmares. Tetka—that's what I called Ibrahim's mama—held me at night some. She sang the same songs as Mama, but her hugs felt different. Sometimes, I'd close my eyes and pretend, though.

I missed Marko. Tetka had a cat, but I didn't like cats. They put their butts in your face, and they pooped inside of a box. That was gross, but Tetka cleaned it.

Everybody in Žepa had a job. Arman and I squished bugs in the garden. We had planted enough vegetables to last through the winter. We had potatoes and peas and lots of carrots. Dajdža—that's what I called Ibrahim's tata—had a big greenhouse with tomatoes and basil and eggplants, too. The chickens scratched at the soil and exposed little bugs, which they ate. Arman and I cleaned out the chicken coop, too, sometimes, and put the dirty straw behind the shed with the kitchen scraps. Ibrahim had to turn that with a big garden fork every few days. Tetka said it would become dirt one day, but I didn't know how that worked.

I had night work, too. Ibrahim, Dajdža, and I would go to the Drina River. Other men came, too. I'd climb a tree overlooking the water because I was the smallest, and I'd point to the bodies as they floated by. Then the men would use boats to bring them to shore for burial. Ten or fifteen bodies floated by some nights, but sometimes dozens and dozens came. Ibrahim said we worked at night because it was too horrible to do during the day, but really he was afraid of the snipers. They still shot at us at night, but they couldn't see us well. They killed one of Dajdža's friends, but I didn't know him. It was sad. He was a good rower.

The bodies came from Višegrad. Soldiers killed people and then dumped them in the river. The current brought them to Žepa. I hated the job, but I did it in case Mama or Sara floated by. I missed them, but I hoped they were dead.

That was how things went for months. I lived, but I felt dead. Then everything changed.

The Yugoslav army used big green trucks with tires as tall as me. They were flat at the front, and canvas covered the back. Their exhaust was choking. They didn't come near Žepa often because our fighters would shoot at them, so I didn't see them too much. I had never seen a white truck before until one showed up.

It was big, and it had a gun on top. The front reminded me of a frog. It had square windows like eyes. Angled panels beneath the windows rose up and formed a line like a mouth. The ground rumbled as it drew near, but people came out of their homes and waved instead of hiding. Someone had painted *UN* on the side in big black letters. Behind that truck came two minivans and then another big white truck.

Ibrahim was near me when I saw them, so I walked to him. We were in the garden outside the house by the plum tree. It was hot, but a breeze blew across the fields nearby, making it more comfortable. Arman was with Tetka inside. He was safe.

"What's going on?" I asked.

"Those are UN trucks," he said. "And they brought journalists. They're here to talk to us."

"I don't want to talk to anybody," I said. Ibrahim considered me but said nothing. He took care of me like Hamza and Omar had. He didn't wrestle like they did, but he kept me safe and carried me inside when the gunfire grew close.

"You have to talk to them," he said. "You're the most important person in Žepa right now."

I didn't know what that meant, but he ran down the road toward the trucks. I sat beneath the plum tree and pretended I was at home in Višegrad, beneath my willow tree with Marko instead of a cat that stuck its butt in my face and tickled my nose with its tail. Ibrahim returned a few minutes later with two women and a man carrying a camera on his shoulder.

"There she is," said Ibrahim. Tetka came out of the house, her brow furrowed. Her son waved her back. "Her name is Hana, and she's my sister. Be nice."

Ibrahim hadn't called me that before. It made my throat grow thick. The two women knelt near me. I pushed the cat away. The women spoke to each other. They were pretty, and they wore makeup despite the heat. Both wore jeans and clean shirts. They didn't look like they worked very much. They spoke together for a moment, but then they smiled at me.

"Hey, honey," said one. "I'm Vesna. The woman with me is Tracy. She works for a company called CNN in the United States. Can we ask you some questions?"

I looked to Tetka. She nodded, so I shrugged.

"Okay."

They asked me to tell them my story. It took time because Tracy, the lady from CNN, didn't speak our language. Everything had to go through Vesna. I told them about my house and Tata and my friend Petra and our dog. It was hard to talk about Mama and Sara, but I did. I also told her how Tata and Hamza had protected me and Arman, and I told them how Omar had died. Throughout the story, I didn't cry. They asked me about it, and I told them the truth.

"I have a hole inside me, and I can't squeeze tears out of it anymore. I don't know."

"Tell us about your life in Žepa."

I shrugged and told them about Tetka and Dajdža and Ibrahim. When I asked about Mr. and Mrs. Stanković, Vesna said she didn't know them. They asked about the snipers, but I had never met them, so I didn't know their names. They asked a lot of questions about the bodies in the river. When I finished, Vesna and Tracy talked for a long time in the yard. Then they talked to Tetka. Finally, Vesna gave me a hug. I didn't expect that, so I didn't hug her back.

"Tracy's getting a doctor," she whispered in my ear. "Tell him you have epilepsy and can't get medicine here."

I didn't know how to respond, so I nodded.

"Okay."

The cat sat on my lap, and Vesna spoke to Tetka. Then Tetka knelt beside me and whispered in my ear.

"Do as Vesna says," she said. "God will watch over you."

She kissed my forehead and hugged me. Then Ibrahim hugged me, which was strange. Finally, Tracy returned with a tall man. He wore camouflage and didn't look like a doctor, but he knelt beside me. Vesna translated.

"I hear you're sick," he said, smiling. "Can you tell me about it?"

I looked to Vesna. She gave me a tight smile, so I looked to the doctor.

"I have epilepsy."

"I see," he said, nodding. "When were you diagnosed?"

I shrugged.

"Today."

"Oh," he said, the corners of his lips curling

upward. "How are your seizures?"

"I don't have any."

"Does your head hurt?"

"No."

"Do you ever black out?" he asked.

"No."

He tilted his head to the side and smiled.

"Where are your parents?"

"Dead."

"Who takes care of you?"

I looked over my shoulder to Tetka but said nothing.

"Are you related to her?" asked the doctor.

"No, but she took us in. I don't think she's going to kill us."

"Do you have any family still alive?"

I thought and then shrugged.

"I don't know. The soldiers took Mama and Sara. Arman is alive, but he's little."

The doctor asked a lot of questions. I told him the same story I had told Tracy and Vesna. Finally, he stood and brought a hand to his face.

"If she stays, she'll die," said Vesna. "She's a child now, but children grow up. Young women get hurt here. She's lost everything already."

The doctor stared at Vesna and then me. Then he nodded and left. My stomach hurt, and my throat felt tight. I felt like I had done something wrong.

"I'm sorry," I said. "I didn't know what to say."

"You did everything right," said Vesna. "It's the

world that's wrong."

We stayed there in silence for a few minutes. Then the doctor came back. He spoke to Tetka, and she started crying and nodding. Then she hugged him. He knelt in front of me next and handed me a piece of paper on which he had written notes. I couldn't read it.

"If a doctor asks, tell him you have a history of seizures that's been ongoing since you were a baby. Tell them they've been getting worse. Tell them you have headaches that hurt so much you can't move and that food sometimes tastes funny. Tell them you fall asleep and wake up in strange places. Also say you see colors around people and that you're scared. Now repeat all that to me."

I didn't understand what was happening, but I spent a few minutes repeating what he had said. Then Tetka hugged me and told me she'd love Arman as her own son. I told her that was good. I went with Vesna and Tracy and a cameraman into a van. When they shut the door, I leaned over to Vesna, who was sitting beside me.

"The snipers will shoot us if we go in the day," I whispered. "They're in the hills."

"No, sweetheart," she said. "You're safe now. They won't shoot us."

"Where are we going?" I asked.

"There's a momentary cease-fire. We're getting you out of here while we can."

I didn't ask questions after that. We drove for

hours through the hillside of my country to Sarajevo. It had tall buildings, but most had big holes in them now. Some were burning. No one walked around outside. When we arrived, Vesna escorted me to a big crowd of women and children, who were boarding buses. Tracy spoke to a woman with a clipboard, while Vesna held my hand. Finally, the woman asked about my epilepsy. I repeated what the doctor had told me to say. Then the woman talked to Tracy. Vesna said I had done well and that they had a seat for me.

Before I left, Vesna hugged me one more time.

"Will you go with me?" I asked.

"I have work here," she said. "I have to stay."

"What do I do?"

She smiled and tucked a stray lock of hair back from my ear.

"You grow up," she said. "Now get on the bus, honey."

I swallowed hard and did as she said. When I got on the bus, I fell asleep and woke up in Croatia. Then I fell asleep again and woke up in Vienna, Austria. People flooded the streets. There were no tanks or artillery pieces. Snipers could have hidden in any of the surrounding buildings, but nobody ran and nobody hid behind the big planters or concrete benches.

I slept on a warm cot that night, surrounded by girls I had never even met but with whom I shared memories no one should have. We had left our homes and the war behind, but all of us had taken both with us as well. For the first time since my family died, I found fresh tears inside that hole inside me.

I didn't know what life held for me, but I would live because Tata and my brothers hadn't. I hoped I'd make them proud.

10

The potential buyers arrived in two cars. On TV, drug traffickers owned mansions in the hills and drove Bentleys, and they flashed money around like aspiring musicians in a rap video. In contrast, these men wore jeans and T-shirts and dusty boots, and they drove modestly priced family cars.

Conservatively, the organization they owned grossed thirty million dollars a year and sold several tons of marijuana each month to people young and old across the south. They owned legal distribution centers in which they sold products grown on their farms in California, and they moved unlicensed, illegal products through a network of street dealers across Memphis, Little Rock, Nashville, and Birmingham. One day, with the right leadership, they could jettison their illegal operations and focus on their legal dispensaries and farms, but for now, they were looking to expand their product lines.

They were perfect.

Elaine pushed open her building's glass door and stepped onto the gravel parking lot. Aside from Daniel and Joseph, she had sent Lakeside's employees home for the day and told them an industrial cleaning crew was coming in to remove hazardous waste that had spilled in the warehouse. She, Daniel, and Joseph had the building to themselves.

"Gentlemen, I'm glad to see you," she said. "Come on in. I've got coffee and pastries inside."

The five men—all related by blood or marriage —had come from Memphis. Though each man owned part of the organization, she only needed to convince one: William Forsyth. He was sixty-three and had partnered with his two sons, his son-in-law, and his brother. William's brother, Vince, was the family enforcer. Elaine knew little about Vince except to steer clear of him if possible.

William stepped forward and took her outstretched hand in a firm grip.

"It's nice to meet you, Ms. Alford," he said. "You are so much lovelier in person than you are on a video chat."

For a moment, she thought he'd kiss her hand, but, thankfully, he refrained. She flashed him an unreserved, almost coquettish southern-belle smile. A good woman, she had learned growing up, ruled her household, but she did it through subtlety and guile, whispers and smiles, sex but never violence. William Forsyth was a businessman, but he had a penis—as did everyone he brought with him. They ought to have sent their wives.

"I'm so glad you and your boys made it safely," she said. "Come on in. The building isn't much, but it keeps the rain off us. Joseph and Daniel, two of my loyal employees, are just inside. They're eager to meet you."

William stopped and cocked his head to the side. His entourage stopped as well.

"Can I ask you a personal question, Elaine?" he asked. "Assuming I can call you Elaine."

Elaine smiled and winked.

"Assuming I can call you William, I'm happy to answer your question."

His smile never left, and his eyes flicked down to her chest for a split second before meeting her gaze once more. She hoped he didn't expect to sleep with her as a price of the deal. She'd do it if required, but she'd prefer to pass him off to a prostitute instead.

"You may call me whatever you'd like as long as you tell me where you acquired that beguiling accent."

"Arkansas," she said. "Born and raised."

He nodded approvingly and looked her up and down. This time, he didn't hide his eyes as they settled on her breasts.

"If my boys weren't all married, I'd invite you to the family Labor Day party in a heartbeat."

She looked to the men he had brought with him. Vince was in his sixties. The other men were in their thirties or forties. All of them looked fit. They returned her smile without hesitation.

"Your boys are handsome, but my company keeps me busy," she said. "I don't get out in society often."

"I can help with that," said William, smiling again. He stepped into the lobby. She held the door for the others and walked in after them. The team from Kansas City would come in a week. They had partnered with a cartel in Mexico and carried a wider range of products. Her sales pitch to them focused on the value of her business and the ease with which they could integrate her products into their existing sales network. With them, the focus would be cold and businesslike. William and his boys required a gentler, more personal touch.

Inside, Joseph and Daniel introduced themselves and then led everyone to the conference room, where they sat around the long wooden table and ate locally made scones and donuts and drank coffee. Finally, William cleared his throat.

"All right," he said, nodding. "You've offered us your hospitality. Now it's time to work. I hear you're looking to jettison your business interests and retire."

"Sell, yes; but retire, no," she said, shaking her head. "I'm hoping to buy a stake in a technology startup that's training a neural network capable of analyzing the results of advanced genomic testing to create bespoke treatments tailored to the specific genetic makeup of individual cancer patients."

One of William's sons leaned forward and furrowed his brow.

"Can you put that in layman's terms?"

She smiled at him.

"I want to cure cancer. Your money's going to help."

The men all nodded as if they approved of her plans.

"That's a noble goal," said William. "Tell me what's on offer."

She walked to the head of the table.

"I own a turnkey business with profits of three and a half million dollars a year in a field adjacent to your own. The growth potential is substantial with the right hand guiding it. I would sell today for an offer of twenty-five million dollars cash. Otherwise, it will go to auction in two weeks with a reserve price of twenty million."

William closed his eyes and tilted his head to the side.

"That's a steep price."

"It's worth it," said Elaine. "Consider the assets. First, we have Lakeside Pools, the company in whose conference room we're now sitting. With gross sales of two million dollars a year and profits of almost three hundred thousand dollars, it's a valuable asset in its own right. Its warehouses also give us cover to import and store chemicals from overseas, its trucks give us license to transport those chemicals to our manufacturing facility, and its income and expenses provide opportunity to wash excess cash.

"On its own, Lakeside should be worth two to three million dollars. Its employees know me, but they do not know my business. We employ fifteen people here, including a very industrious manager who is growing the business at fifteen percent a year."

William took a few notes and nodded.

"It's good cover," he said.

"It's not our only asset," said Elaine. "I also own Camp Meadowview. It's a summer camp for wealthy children. Through Meadowview, I own two thousand acres of Missouri wilderness, including several miles of lakeshore. The camp is remote and isolated and has its own private security force. Because the camp has an Olympic-sized swimming pool, Lakeside Pools leases a building on site. That is our production facility. Lakeside's trucks allow us to carry chemicals onto and off of the property at our leisure without drawing the interest of law enforcement. Furthermore, the facility's isolated position within the camp allows us to work unimpeded."

William crossed his arms and leaned back.

"How much does that set you back?"

"The camp breaks even every year. With

expenses of approximately ten million dollars a year, though, it provides ample opportunity to obscure the source of its funding. It's run by an independent staff who know nothing of our business. We employ a full-time chemist who works on site. He's good at what he does and is loyal to us because we have pictures of him having a sexual liaison with a fifteen-year-old prostitute in Thailand."

The men from Tennessee snickered.

"Do you have similar relationships with all your employees?" asked William, flicking his eyes to Joseph and Daniel. They barely stirred.

"No," said Elaine. "I pay my employees well and treat them well. In exchange, they work hard. It's a mutually beneficial relationship."

William's son-in-law raised an eyebrow.

"How do you handle distribution?"

"Through a distributed network," said Elaine. "We don't touch anything on the streets. We're a supplier and sell to wholesalers. They're independent contractors who have developed networks of their own. We have assurances from all of them that they will continue working with you, assuming you treat them in the same professional manner that I do.

"While we're on this subject, let me also say why I contacted you. I know your products. My roommate introduced me to them at Vanderbilt. I liked what you sold me. More than that, I know the consumers who purchase your marijuana are the sort who purchase my product. My distribution team would love to sell your products, and I know your distribution team would have tremendous success with mine. If you buy me out, everybody wins."

William nodded but said nothing. Then he shifted and sighed.

"Your presentation's great so far, but already I'm worried about a couple of things. My boys and I are gardeners. We know gardening, and we know business. We're not chemists. Tell me about your product. We've never made it or bought it. We need to make sure it's a viable business for us."

Elaine walked to him and then put her hands on his shoulders and squeezed as if giving him a massage. Though his voice had an edge to it, his muscles were soft. He was relaxed and in his element.

"You don't need to do that, sugar," he said.

"I'd like to, though," she said, squeezing, her voice soft. "Before I speak to my product, know that Daniel and Joseph are capable operators. They've worked for me for years, and I trust them with my life. You will, too. They've agreed to stay with you for at least three years. They'll show you the business and introduce you to the right people. Twice a year, they fly to Cambodia to purchase safrole, and twice a year, they drive several barrels of it in a truck across the country from a harbor near

Seattle."

She let go of his shoulders and started pacing. He watched her, and she wondered whether he had an erection under the table.

"My product is methylenedioxymethamphetamine. MDMA. Ecstasy. You take it once, and you'll know why the kids love it. It's relatively safe, and the profit margins are through the roof. Moreover, we manufacture it domestically. We don't worry about Customs or Border Patrol or shortages of any kind. If demand rises, we make more. Our network doesn't go dry. To make our products stand out in a crowded market, my chemist has recently begun creating a secondary line of pills that contain powdered cocaine. Both drugs work in concert and produce similar highs, but they affect the body at different times. So far, our clients love them."

The men shifted.

"I don't know how I feel about cocaine," said William.

"If you'd like, you can discontinue that product line," said Elaine. "It's an experiment, but so far, it's working out very well. Our margins are very high, and collateral damage is low."

"How low?" asked one of the sons.

"There have been a few incidents," said Elaine, drawing in a breath. "Not enough to draw real heat. Like I said, if you're uncomfortable with that product line, you can discontinue it. Demand is extremely high, though."

They seemed to consider that. Then Vince cleared his throat, drawing Elaine's attention.

"Why do we need you?" he asked. "If this business is so easy, why should we buy you out? Why don't we just kill you and take over?"

She glanced to Daniel and Joseph.

"Well, first, if you hurt me, my employees will hunt you down and kill you in your sleep," she said.

"You're that loyal, huh?" asked Vince, looking to Joseph.

"Yes," said Joseph.

"Vince," said William, his voice a low growl. "This is inappropriate."

"It is inappropriate," said Elaine, cutting in. "But the gist of his question was fair. You need me and my organization because you don't know what you're doing. I'm guessing you've never negotiated with the Royal Cambodian Army, for instance. I have. Furthermore, I'm guessing you've never brought safrole through an American port. You probably don't know a good chemist, either. My team and I have done the legwork, we've set up the lab, and we have excellent employees. We have contacts and the know-how to produce MDMA at quantity within the United States. There are a lot of labs in Mexico that can do what we do, but transportation costs are extraordinarily high. I don't need to tell you how valuable a domestic source is."

William looked to his brother, his brow raised.

"That's worth something," he said.

"Is it worth her asking price, though?" asked Vince. "I don't know if I can answer that."

Elaine shrugged.

"It may not be worth it to you. It will be to my other buyers," she said. "You can't build what I have by making pills in a bathtub, nor can you purchase enough safrole domestically to produce what my lab can. Aside from that, remember I've also got three fifty-five-gallon barrels of safrole in my facility right now. That's enough to produce ten to fifteen million dollars' worth of product. I'm offering a bargain at twenty-five million. If you can't see that, then it's best that we end the meeting here."

Vince's lips curled into a sneer, but William said nothing. Finally, one of the boys cleared his throat.

"Can you scale up?" he asked. She nodded.

"Yes," she said. "Demand is huge and growing. My sales team is making strong inroads into Kansas City and St. Louis. I anticipate doubling my business this year. With your network, sales could quadruple. We might have to hire a new chemist, but my lab can produce ample product to meet that demand. In the right buyer's hands, you could turn a ten-million-dollar profit next year."

"And you'd give that up for a twenty-five-million-dollar payment?" asked William.

"I'd give that up for money I can use as seed

capital for something far bigger, but yes," she said. "I'm willing to gamble on myself because I know what I'm capable of. What are you capable of? I'm selling my life's work. It's important to me. Can you handle it?"

William closed his eyes and nodded.

"We can handle your business just fine," he said. "I'd like to see these facilities of yours, though."

Elaine tried to keep the smile off her face, but she had them. Now she just needed to close the sale. Everything would work out just fine.

"By all means," she said. "Camp's already expecting us. Let's go."

11

I took the bag of condoms, walked to my car, and sat. If I had trusted the sheriff's department, I would have driven right over and dropped those condoms off with the assistant sheriff, secure in the knowledge that he'd investigate. If he found Oscar's DNA on them along with the DNA of a camper, he'd be one huge step closer to closing his case.

And even if the DNA were too badly degraded to individuate anyone—as it likely was—he could still use the condoms in an interrogation booth. He could bring the former campers in, show them the condoms, and claim they were untested. Lying to a suspect about evidence during an interrogation may not be ethical, but it was legal, and sometimes the results justified the moral infraction. Teenage girls living in a communal environment knew more about each other's lives than most married couples. With physical evidence staring them in the face, somebody would break. They knew who slept with Oscar the night he died, and they'd say so. That person may not be the killer, but the sheriff's department would have a lead.

Since I didn't have enough information about who I could trust in Pollard, I drove to my hotel and stuck the condoms in the freezer of my in-room refrigerator. That wouldn't keep them as cold as Ms. Hopkins's deep freeze, but it should hold them long enough for me to think and investigate on my own.

By that point, it was getting late, and I hadn't eaten since breakfast, so I drove to the town's only restaurant, Frank's Downtown Diner. I sat at a table near the kitchen. Onions, meat, and something a little more earthy—probably mushrooms—sizzled on the grill.

After my day, I needed to hear a friendly voice, so I pulled out my phone and called Shane, my former partner from my time with the St. Louis County Police Department. I had liked most of the detectives with whom I worked, but I got lucky with Shane. He was a friend.

"Dude, hey," I said. "It's Hana. Just calling to say hi and see how you're doing. You at work?"

"Just left," he said. "You causing trouble down south?"

"Unintentionally. They accused me of murdering the sheriff this morning."

He laughed, thinking I was kidding. I'd tell him the truth eventually, but for now, I just wanted to talk to somebody I actually liked. We chatted for a few minutes.

Shane had spent the day working a case involving a young woman who had taken MDMA at a party at a local university and then overheated and died. The city and county had seen a few cases like that lately. We didn't know what was going on, but more and more, people seemed to be getting Ecstasy pills that contained cocaine as well. Both drugs produced euphoric highs, but they were tough on the body when mixed. This young woman was the third to have died in the past two to three months. Our narcotics division was trying to make inroads in the case but had yet to pinpoint the supplier. They would, eventually. They were good cops, and these drug pushers were killing young people. Dealers who did that didn't survive long in the wild.

I hung up about five minutes after the call began and then ordered a cup of potato soup and a turkey sandwich.

Before my dinner arrived, a middle-aged woman walked through the diner's front door, picked up a brown paper sack full of food, and talked to my server. Then she walked to my table. She was forty or forty-five. Wavy brown hair framed her oval-shaped face. She had a hooked nose and bushy eyebrows. No wedding ring or other jewelry adorned her fingers or wrists, and her hands looked soft. She wore blue jeans and a top, the fabric of which was decorated with big bushels of tight flowers.

I didn't know what she wanted, so I forced myself to smile.

"Hi."

"Hey," she said, darting her eyes around the room before sighing. "I heard you were a detective. That's what Jenny said, at least. She's your waitress."

"Rumors travel quick in Pollard," I said. "But I'm not a detective. Sorry."

"Oh," she said, her voice falling. "I heard you went to see Frannie Hopkins this afternoon. You asked a bunch of questions like a cop would."

I considered her for a moment and leaned back.

"I'm not a police officer, so if you need help, call 911."

"Are you sure you're not a cop?" she asked. "If you are, you've got to tell me. I saw that on TV."

She set her paper sack on the end of my table. Evidently, she planned to stay awhile. I sighed.

"Don't believe everything you see on TV. If you need the police, call 911. I'm here to grab dinner and then go to my motel."

Her back straightened, but she didn't leave. I forced myself to smile.

"Something else?" I asked.

"Somebody's been following me," she said. "My ex-husband just got out of prison. He was mean to me and my kids. Do you have kids?"

I had heard stories that started in similar fashion often when I worked the family crime beat. She didn't need to continue.

"If your ex-husband is following you or threatening you, call 911. I can't help you."

She looked down and shook her head.

"Before he went to prison, he hit me with a wine bottle. The cops asked what I did to provoke him," she said. "I moved my kids here to get away from him. He's not supposed to know where we are. I'm scared, okay? I just want to know if it's him following us. If it's him, we'll leave. If it's not…my kids are settling down. They've got lives here. I don't want them to lose that."

Her hands trembled. A hollow feeling began building in my gut, and I swore under my breath.

"How old are your kids?" I asked.

"Seven, nine, and eleven," she said. "They're good kids. I homeschool them because we bounce around so much. I was going to let Garrett play soccer this fall. He already picked out the cleats he wants me to buy. He wants friends, and I want to let him have them."

"Who's their father?"

She narrowed her eyes.

"Why does that matter?"

I leaned forward and raised my eyebrows.

"Things get very complicated if they're your ex-husband's children. Unless the court has said otherwise, he has the right to see them. Depending on custody arrangements, you might have even kidnapped them by taking them away from him."

She shook her head and lowered her voice.

"They're not his," she said. "They're from a previous relationship."

"You just want to find out if someone's following you?" I asked. She nodded, and I drew in a breath. "You'll need to buy a camera you can put outside your house and maybe a battery-powered one for your car."

"So you'll help me?"

I sighed. I had driven to Pollard to escape my life in St. Louis, not to pick up freelance investigative work. I didn't even know what I was doing, but I spoke before my mind could form a coherent refusal.

"I guess I will."

"Thank you," she said, reaching across the table to touch my hand.

I forced myself to smile at her, even though my stomach and throat felt tight. This was a mistake. I wasn't a private detective or a cop. I was just a woman waiting to pick up her dog.

"If I do this, I'll dig into your life," I said. "It's going to be invasive. I'll watch you go places, I'll see who you talk to, and I'll see what you do. If you're doing something illegal, or if you've lied to me about your ex-husband, I'll find out, and you won't like what happens."

"I'm not a criminal," she said.

"Good," I said, reaching beside me for my purse. I pulled out my notepad and wrote down my name and cell number and tore the sheet off. Then I pushed the paper and the notepad toward her. "Write down your name, address, and phone number on the notepad. Then write down your ex-husband's name, address, and phone number. I'll take things from there."

She did as I asked. Then she looked up to me.

"What are you going to do?"

"I'll talk to your neighbors and co-workers and see if they've seen anybody lurking around your home. I'll put up a camera by your house, too. If I need to, I can contact your ex-husband's neighbors and see if he's left his town."

She nodded.

"Just don't approach him," she said. "He's dangerous."

"Let me worry about him. You focus on your kids."

She nodded and took my information, leaving the notepad and pen on the table. I watched her walk away and then looked at the notepad. She had signed her name Crystal Valentine, but even as she had written it, I had known the name was bullshit. She had paused after writing the *y* in Crystal. The letters were uniform, thick, and neat. She had written it slowly and methodically to get it right. It was a new word for her. The lines on her phone number and address were irregular in contrast. She hadn't thought while writing. That was her actual number.

I thought about ripping the page out, wadding it up, and throwing it away, but I couldn't. She had lied to me about her identity, but her feelings were real. She was scared for herself and for her kids. I didn't know what I was walking into or who Crystal Valentine really was, but I suspected this would get ugly before I finished. Domestic violence cases almost always did.

I ate my dinner without saying a word to anyone else. Then I paid, put a tip on my table, and walked to my car. Somebody had slipped a folded piece of paper under my windshield wiper. None of the other cars alongside the road had papers under their wipers, so it wasn't a flier. I lifted my windshield wiper and opened a handwritten note.

I'm going to kill you and your fucking dog.

Beneath that, the scribbler had drawn a smiley face. My stomach tightened, and the fine hairs on the back of my neck stood. I looked around, but nobody seemed to be watching me.

People had threatened me before, but this one carried more weight than most. I clenched my jaw tight and exhaled through my nose. Very few people knew I had come to Pollard, and even fewer knew I had a dog. The sheriff's deputies had taken him almost the moment we stepped foot in town. Of those who knew about George, almost none would want me hurt. This hadn't come from a stranger I accidentally cut off in traffic or from the nice old lady I had met in the park. This had come from one of Bryant County's finest, a cop who thought I had murdered his boss.

I swore under my breath. I wished I had never driven to Pollard. In a single day, I had met an elderly woman who thought her son had been murdered, I had been arrested and accused of murdering the county sheriff, I had gotten involved in a cold murder case, I had been sucked into a domestic dispute between a woman and her violent ex-husband, and now a cop was threatening to kill me.

I opened my door, sat in the driver's seat, and then leaned over to unlock my glove box and the pistol I kept inside. The sheriff's department had confiscated two of my three pistols when they arrested me earlier, but they hadn't confiscated this one. It had belonged to my dad, and he had purchased it well before he and Mom adopted me. Twice a year, Dad took it to a firing range to practice. He said he kept it to keep us all safe, just in case. Now, it'd keep me safe. This never should have happened. I was starting to get pissed.

12

Joseph drove, while Elaine sat in the passenger seat. Daniel sat in the back. Even though it held no chemicals, a chlorine odor permeated the van's cloth seats. Equipment in the back rattled every time they drove over a pothole. No one spoke. Joseph didn't trust the Forsyth family yet, but he would in time. And if he didn't, he'd pull up stakes and leave.

Aside from his job, little tethered him to life in Missouri. He had an ex-wife and two kids in Springfield, but their entire household despised him. He doubted one of the kids was even his, but he gave Molly a couple thousand dollars a month as child support to keep her from bothering him.

Right after they learned Molly was pregnant with their first child, the Army shipped him to Iraq for a year. Then, when he got home again, the Army shipped him back for another year. Then, because of his combat experience in Iraq, the Army shipped him to Afghanistan. By the time his son started going to preschool, Joseph had hugged him six times. Joseph remembered every hug, but letters and phone calls from a war zone didn't make a relationship.

His relationship with his daughter was even worse. Molly claimed they had conceived her while he was on leave, but Joseph knew that was bullshit. They hadn't had sex on that trip. Still, he would have loved the little girl if given the chance. Molly poisoned that relationship, though.

Molly still called him some. Usually when she was drunk or needed money. She pleaded with him and begged him to "come home and spend time with his family." She said she still loved him and wanted him back. The first time she placed that call, he believed her and came home, hoping to rebuild what he had lost, but when he got to the house, he found a stranger playing with his kids. He then learned Molly, in a drunken stupor, had called not just him but also her ex-boyfriend. His own son told him to leave. That hurt.

Molly and their children survived on his child support payments, but they weren't family. Joseph didn't have one. He had colleagues at work and a job that paid very well. Once the Forsyths bought Elaine's company, he'd have more money than he'd ever need. Eventually, he'd retire and move overseas. He'd start over. He wouldn't have a family, but he could be happy. The universe owed him that.

"What do you think about the buyers?" asked Elaine. "You think you could work with them?"

Joseph glanced at her and nodded.

"They seem like professionals," he said. "I'd like to hear their plans for the future, but I don't see any issues with working with them."

She looked over her shoulder toward Daniel.

"What do you think?"

"They're family," said Daniel. "We're not. We'll always be outsiders."

Joseph glanced in the rearview mirror.

"You could always divorce your wife and marry into the family," he said. "I'm sure there's a single daughter or niece somewhere."

He didn't expect Daniel to laugh, but he had hoped Elaine would crack a smile. For some reason, he enjoyed making her smile. Her lips stayed thin and straight, and she crossed her arms.

"That is a concern," she said. "You both deserve to be taken care of."

"If I were in their position, I'd learn everything I could about the business and then kill everyone and bring in my own people," said Daniel. "It'd be the only way you could assure their loyalty."

Elaine went quiet as she thought. Joseph cleared his throat.

"You know, buddy," he said, "comments like that explain why you don't have more friends."

Elaine snickered and then touched him on the

forearm before looking at Daniel. He liked having her hand there and wished she had left it.

"You're right," she said. "You two will have to protect each other when I'm gone."

"No need," said Daniel. "I've got my own back. Take Joseph with you, though. You could use a bodyguard."

Joseph raised an eyebrow but said nothing. Elaine smiled but went quiet. The guards at Meadowview expected them, so the gate rose the moment they slowed. Joseph drove through, followed by the two vehicles from Tennessee. As he drove across the campgrounds, he glanced in his mirror to ensure the other vehicles followed.

The lab looked like a big storage shed with a rolling garage door for deliveries. At one time, its cedar siding had been brown, but Meadowview's maintenance team had painted it a deep blue color since then. An air conditioner thrummed on the side. Joseph parked outside. Elaine opened her door and stepped out. Joseph looked to Daniel.

"I'm not a bodyguard. Don't tell Elaine I am."

Daniel sighed and reached for the door handle but didn't open it yet.

"You're in love with the boss. She cares about you, too. I thought I'd move things along."

"I'm not in love with her," said Joseph, shaking his head. "And to her, I'm just an employee."

"Maybe I'm wrong on both counts," said Daniel, shrugging. "Come on. We've got work to do."

Daniel left the car. Joseph watched him through the window for a moment, but mostly he focused on Elaine. She was attractive, but anyone would have been attracted to her. That didn't mean he loved her. She was his boss, and he liked being with her. He cared about her, but only because they had worked together for years. That was natural.

He opened his door. Elaine glanced at him out of the corner of her eye and then smiled in his direction before focusing on the Forsyths. For a split second, Joseph caught himself smiling in return. Even if Daniel was right, it didn't matter. They had jobs to do.

He put his hands in his pockets and stayed near the van as Elaine answered questions about the camp and its staff and the building. Then, she walked to the keypad beside the door and entered her six-digit code. The lock buzzed, and the door unlocked. The interior had fluorescent lights and white walls. An epoxy coating covered the concrete floor. There were three workstations inside and a large chemical storage room.

Even at a glance, Joseph saw a problem. Three fifty-five-gallon barrels of safrole were missing. Without the contents of those barrels, this lab—in fact, their entire organization—was worthless. An empty feeling began growing in the pit of his stomach as he prepared a list of people they needed to visit. Elaine didn't let on that anything was amiss.

About ten minutes after arriving at the lab, the

Forsyths shuffled out to their trucks, and Joseph and Daniel climbed into the Lakeside Pools van. Elaine joined them a moment later. Her face was bright red, and she breathed through her nose.

"Where the fuck are those barrels?" she asked.

"I don't know," said Joseph, glancing in the rearview mirror. The Forsyths were already backing up, allowing him to reverse out of his spot beside the lab. "We'll visit Nick and see what he has to say."

"Do more than visit. The men we've met today are serious businessmen from an organization much larger than our own. If they think we're trying to cheat them, they will kill every one of us."

"We won't let them hurt you," said Joseph.

Elaine shook her head.

"I don't need chivalry," she said, her voice sharp. "I need answers. Drive me back to work and then find my safrole."

Joseph nodded and drove. He didn't like leaving Elaine alone with the Forsyths, but she could handle herself. He and Daniel had business. They drove her to work and then drove to the home of Nick Gilman, their chemist, and knocked hard on the front door of his Bryant County farmhouse. Like most of Elaine's employees, Nick worked odd hours and lived alone. He was a pervert, but he did his job without complaint.

The chemist cracked his door and furrowed his brow.

"Yeah?" he asked. He was in his mid-forties and had graying hair, bushy eyebrows and teeth stained a dull yellow. Joseph glanced at Daniel before kicking the door hard. Nick fell backward, and the door shot open. Daniel shouldered his way inside, a pistol drawn. Joseph knelt beside the chemist. Nick's eyes popped open wide, and he brought up his hands as if to protect his face.

"Don't kill me, guys," he said. "Whatever you think I did, I didn't do it."

"You sure about that?" asked Joseph.

"I didn't do anything. Whatever happened, I didn't do it."

"You go to the lab yesterday?" asked Daniel. Nick nodded.

"Yeah. Ms. Alford said she might bring people by, so I spent the day organizing and cleaning."

Joseph nodded.

"Did you move three fifty-five-gallon drums of safrole oil, by chance?"

Nick furrowed his brow.

"No. Of course not. They're too heavy to move. You'd need a pallet jack and a truck."

Joseph cocked his head to the side and glanced at Daniel.

"How much would they weigh?"

"Hundreds of pounds each," said Nick. "I can't lift that kind of weight. What happened?"

"They're gone," said Joseph. "And you're telling me you didn't move them?"

"Of course I didn't move them," he said. "What would I do with them?"

Daniel lowered his chin.

"Make drugs?"

"If I had a fume hood, protective gear, and a second lab, sure," said Nick, "but I don't. I'm not risking my health to make pills. I don't need the money, and I've never sold drugs in my life. I wouldn't even know what to do with a batch of pills."

Joseph sighed.

"If you didn't take the safrole, somebody else did. Who?"

The chemist shrugged.

"I'm a chemist, not a security officer," he said. Joseph raised his eyebrows, hoping for a better answer. Then he reached for his pistol. Nick held up his hands in a stop motion. "A cop came by this evening."

Joseph's eyes widened. Daniel leaned forward.

"Excuse me?" asked Joseph.

"A detective visited the camp this evening," said Nick. "Jim told me. He works security."

Joseph's gut began tightening. More questions raced around his head than he had answers for.

"What'd the detective want?" asked Daniel.

"You'd have to talk to the guard," said Nick. "I'm just a chemist. He told me like it was a joke because I was driving too fast. He said if I didn't slow down, the cop would get me."

This was a problem. Joseph looked at Daniel.

"You stay with him," he said, already reaching into his pocket for his cell phone. Daniel nodded, and Joseph left the house and walked toward the grass. There, he called Elaine. "Hey, it's Joseph."

"Hey," she said, her voice soft. "Everything okay?"

"No. We've got a problem at the camp. There might be a security breach."

13

Since Mom and Dad's cabin didn't have running water or electricity, I was staying at the only hotel in town. No one would ever call it nice, but my room was clean. It was probably popular with hikers and families on budgets. The sun had barely set, but already my eyelids were growing heavy. I hadn't dated anyone since my ex-husband, but George slept in a kennel beside my bed every night. Without him, I felt alone. I didn't like that. I hoped they were treating him well at the Humane Society.

A long, low dresser held my room's TV, while a round table and two chairs sat beside the window. The dresser wouldn't budge when I pushed it, so I pushed the light table and chairs in front of my door. The furniture wouldn't stop someone who wanted to hurt me, but it'd slow him down. Dad's pistol would do the rest.

That done, I showered and changed into pajamas

and opened my notepad to think about tomorrow's to-do list. I needed to pick up George, so that went right at the top. Beneath that, I wrote Crystal Valentine's name followed by a question mark. I still didn't know how I felt about her, but I'd look her up. Then I wrote *note on car*. No matter what else, I needed to deal with that. A cop with a vendetta could do a lot of damage to my personal life. Finally, I wrote *leave Pollard*. It seemed like a good list, so I let myself lie down after that.

For a few minutes, I stared at a water stain on the ceiling and hoped it didn't indicate structural damage to the roof. Then I rolled around before getting up and turning the air conditioner to a lower setting. Then I settled into bed again and forced myself to close my eyes.

I liked napping, but I hated going to sleep at night. Naps were great. I didn't have nightmares when I napped. Sleep at night was much harder. I had pills that would put me to sleep and keep me there, but they left me feeling groggy the next morning. Some days, that was worth it. Other days, they gave me eight hours of nightmares instead of the usual two or three.

I didn't want nightmares tonight, so I turned on the TV and watched an infomercial advertising an infrared oven that could, allegedly, cook a frozen turkey in an hour. Then I checked my email. Finally, I started reading a book on my phone. Gradually, I felt my limbs start to grow heavy, and my mind stopped racing. At a little after one in the morning, as my eyes started to close, two men started talking and laughing outside. It was annoying, but I was staying in a cheap motel. They were probably going to their rooms.

After ten minutes, the laughter and joking around continued, so I swung my legs off the side of my bed and walked to the window to peer outside. Two men sat on the hood of my Subaru. One smoked a cigarette. The other drank beer from a bottle. There were two six-packs on the ground. Apparently, they were having a good time.

I stepped back, rubbed my eyes, and then put on jeans, a belt, and a bra. Finally, I grabbed my pistol and attached its holster to my belt. I covered that with my shirt. Then I opened my door. The two men saw me immediately but stayed on my car. The one sipped his beer. The other tapped the end of his cigarette, knocking off a bit of ash.

"Hey, Hana," said the drinker. "Good to see you."

My pulse quickened, and I brought my left foot back to put me in a more athletic stance in case they did something stupid. The smoker had a wan complexion and thin face. He had shaved his head, but I could just barely see stubble on the sides in the moonlight. His partner, the drinker, had a paunch and a brown mustache and malevolent brown eyes. Both were likely in their mid to late thirties, and both wore civilian clothes now, but both had been part of the team that arrested me at the park.

"It's late, gentlemen, and it's time to move on," I said. "If you want to talk, we can talk tomorrow at your station. It's time to go home before anybody does something we regret."

"What makes you think we're going to regret being here?" asked the smoker.

I glanced at him, grateful that I had my back to a solid building. A covered walkway led to my left and right, giving me sight lines for at least a hundred yards in either direction. These two were the only threat I faced.

"Call it a hunch," I said. "You two drunk?"

"Getting there," said the drinker, before tipping his bottle back and tossing it to the concrete at my feet. The glass broke but didn't shatter. He expected me to jump. I didn't move except to raise my left hand in a stop motion.

"Don't throw anything else at me."

The smoker took his cigarette from his mouth and flicked it toward me. It, too, landed on the concrete in front of me. I lowered my right hand toward the pistol at the small of my back. Every muscle in my body was rigid. Two against one was bad enough, but these guys each had fifty or sixty pounds on me at least. Likely they were armed, too. If this went bad, it would go very bad very quickly.

"You guys have had your fun," I said. "It's time to leave."

"Why'd you kill Phil?" asked the smoker. "He

never hurt anybody in his life."

"I haven't killed anyone in a long time," I said. "I don't want to start now. Please leave."

"You're feisty," said the drinker, sliding off the side of my car. He walked toward the trunk. "I like that."

I kept an eye on the smoker but tried to watch the drinker, too. Then, as he reached his right hand to my hatchback's roof and kept his left hand at his waist, I realized what he was doing. The smoker laughed as the drinker moaned and urinated on my bumper. When he finished, he zipped up and walked toward me and his buddy.

"I think I've had all the fun I can handle for the night," said the drinker, looking toward his friend. Then he looked at me. "Unless you want to invite us inside."

I brought my hand behind me and wrapped it around the grip of my pistol.

"Leave and don't come back."

"Like I said, she's feisty," said the drinker. He snorted and then spit on the ground near my feet. His buddy laughed. "Stick around town, honey. I suspect we'll have some fun with you before this is over."

The drinker grabbed the remains of his six-pack, while the smoker slid off my car. Then they sauntered to a pickup and left. I watched until their car disappeared around a curve in the road before releasing a breath I hadn't realized I had been holding. My fingers unclenched the grip of my pistol. My legs trembled.

In a movie, the hero would have kicked one of them in the balls and then punched the other in the face. They would have run off, terrified. I wasn't the star of an action movie, though. If I had attacked them, they would have hit back. At the least, they would have beaten me up. I was alone in a small town, and they were cops. They could have dragged me into my motel room and done whatever they wanted to me. I didn't even have a dog to protect me.

I felt sick to my stomach as I went back into my room to pack. Pollard had one hotel, so I hadn't been hard to find. I threw everything I had into my overnight bag and then locked the room up and got in my car. My mom and dad's cabin had no running water or electricity, but it had a lock on the front door, and I had brought camping gear from St. Louis in case I couldn't find anywhere to stay.

I drove out to the cabin, unrolled my sleeping bag, and made a bed on the dusty old couch in my parents' living room. The room felt reasonably safe, but I'd feel a lot better once I had George back. I'd feel even better in my apartment in St. Louis. I fell asleep at about four in the morning and stayed asleep until almost nine when a songbird began singing outside. It was both pretty and annoying.

I sat up and swallowed hard. If I had planned to stay overnight, I would have gone by the grocery store to pick up supplies—bottles of water at the very least. My lips felt chapped, and my mouth felt dry. Even sitting in my parents' cabin—a place that had once made me feel safe and whole—I felt vulnerable. I didn't like that, so I put on my clothes hurriedly and strapped my pistol to the small of my back. My insides stopped quivering as much after that, allowing me to focus on the day ahead of me.

My parents' cabin was furnished just as it had been when they owned it. The sofas and coffee table came from Ethan Allen, the beds were made by a local woodworker, and the built-in bookshelves were made by a cabinet maker in Springfield. Mom and Dad had loved this place. I hated that I had let it go for so many years that a thick layer of dust now covered everything.

So I spent an hour cleaning. Realistically, I probably should have brought in a cleaning crew, but even an hour's worth of work made the place feel more like home. Afterward, I crashed down on the couch and looked at my phone. I thought about picking up George, but I also thought about Crystal Valentine, the woman from the diner. She had given me a fake name, but she might not have lied about everything. I needed to leave town, but she needed help, and I doubted the local police department would offer it.

I turned my phone into a Wi-Fi hotspot and opened my laptop. As best I could tell, Crystal wasn't on Twitter, Instagram, Facebook, LinkedIn, or Tumblr. Considering she was hiding from her ex-husband, that was good.

Next, I looked up her ex-husband. His name was Kevin Recinos, and he lived in Hopkinsville, Kentucky. Unfortunately, he had no property listed in any public tax records I could find; he had no social media accounts; and I couldn't find an address for him. The only reference I found to him was a newspaper article about a state-championship-winning high school basketball team from the late 1990s. He had played point guard for Hopkinsville High School.

Had I still worn a badge, I would have called the local police department in his area and asked about his criminal record and whether anyone had lodged complaints against him. That could verify Crystal's story that he had hurt her and the kids. Then I'd ask them to send officers by his house to see whether he was home. If Kevin had been to prison, he likely had a parole officer, too. I'd call him and tell him what was going on. If we could prove that Recinos had violated the conditions of his parole—by crossing state lines, for instance—I could send him back to prison. It would have been easy.

I closed my laptop, dressed, brushed my teeth as well as I could, and locked the cabin up before driving to Frank's Downtown Diner. The place had been relatively empty at dinner, but the residents of Pollard took Saturday morning breakfast seriously because someone occupied nearly every seat in the building. I ended up sitting at the bar beside two strangers and eavesdropping on conversations as I ate eggs and toast.

After half an hour, I returned to my car and drove to Crystal's address, an apartment in a small development a few blocks from the sheriff's office in Pollard. The L-shaped building wrapped around a parking lot and shielded a small swimming pool from the road. I knocked on a bunch of doors and talked to everybody I could. Universally, people described Crystal and her family as conscientious, respectful neighbors who kept to themselves. Nobody had seen anybody strange lurking around, either.

Then I went to the main office and found a man in his early forties. He had blue eyes and a wiry frame. His short black hair contrasted with his olive-colored skin and white button-down shirt. If he had smiled, he would have been handsome. Instead, he crossed his arms and blinked as I walked in.

"I heard a stranger was checking out the property," he said. "What do you need?"

"My family used to vacation in Pollard every summer, and I'm thinking of settling down here for a while. Tell me about your building."

He lowered his arms, and his face brightened now that he thought I was a potential tenant.

"Pollard's a great place to live," he said. "Congratulations on coming back. And I'm glad you're interested in leasing a place. I kind of thought you were here to sell something to my residents. We don't like solicitors around here."

I smiled, and so did he. My stomach got a little fluttery. It had been too long since I last got laid.

"Nope," I said. "I'm not here to sell anything. I'm just checking the place out."

"Unfortunately, every unit in this building is leased for the next year at least, but my boss has buildings across Bryant County. How many bedrooms are you looking for?"

"If this place is leased, don't worry about it," I said. "I liked the location by the police station. Security's a big deal to me. Does this building have surveillance cameras?"

He continued to smile.

"As I said, this building is fully leased. We've got some nice two-bedroom units a few miles away. I can put cameras or motion-activated lights on them if you're concerned about security."

I stepped back from the front desk.

"Thanks, but I was interested in this building," I said.

"We're booked. Sorry," he said. "If you change your mind about our other locations, I'm here every morning."

"Thanks," I said, taking another step back. "I'll keep that in mind."

I left and walked back to my car, where I took some notes. Crystal was doing everything right and keeping her head down. If her ex had pierced the veil she put up to protect her, he could be a real problem. Hopefully she was just being paranoid. I'd get a cheap web camera and put it in her window to make sure, and then I'd get out of town.

In the meantime, though, the Humane Society would open soon, so I could pick up George. I had better things to do.

14

October 19, 1992.
St. Louis, MO

It was raining, just as it had for the past two days. I stared out the window. Cars lined the streets. They didn't look like the cars we had in Višegrad or Žepa. Some had big hoods and trunks and looked like boats, but others looked like boxes with wheels. I saw pickup trucks, too. Contractors drove them. Lots of people fixed houses here. Everybody was always busy.

I had been in the United States for six weeks. It was nice, I guess, but nobody had asked where I wanted to live. If they had, I would have said Mallorca, Spain. Hamza had put up a picture of it in his room before he died. You could wear a bathing suit all the time, and it was always sunny. When I first got to St. Louis, it was warm. Then it snowed. Then it got warm again. And now it was rainy and cold. It was weird here.

Majda, my roommate, liked it here. She got here before I did. We—and a bunch of other kids—lived with Emil and Fatima Delić. They were nice. Fatima gave good hugs. They weren't as good as Mama's, but they felt good. Emil worked all the time. Before he moved to the United States, he had been the singing dentist of Visoko. Now, he was the singing carpenter of Bevo Mills. That was our neighborhood.

Emil couldn't work as a real dentist in America, but he still sang, and he still helped people. He said it made him feel like he was home. Every Saturday, people in the neighborhood lined up for Emil to check their teeth. They paid him in fruits and vegetables they grew. Sometimes people brought eggs, too. When he couldn't help somebody, he referred them to dentists with regular offices. Sometimes he even went with them if they couldn't speak English.

During the week, Emil was a carpenter. His tata had been a carpenter, so he knew what he was doing. He restored old houses and built doorframes and windows in new houses, too. Once, he drove us by an enormous house he had built in Chesterfield, a suburb west of St. Louis. Ten people could have lived inside, but he had built it for a mom and dad whose kids had left town years ago. I guess the kids had left their stuff. Otherwise, they wouldn't need that much space.

"Are you thinking about running away again?"

Fatima smiled and looked out the window beside me. She looked tired. She and Emil were older than Tata and Mama, but I liked them. Majda called Fatima mama, but Majda's real mama was dead.

"No," I said. "It's raining. Arman didn't like the rain, so he won't be outside today."

She put a hand on my shoulder and squeezed.

"Thank you for staying, sweetheart," she said. "I'm making lunch. Mr. and Mrs. Blackwood will be by after lunch to meet you."

I nodded and focused on the window again. I didn't run away. Fatima and Emil just thought I did. Arman needed me. That meant I had to find him. Nobody told me he had come to America, but he was probably here. Everybody who left Bosnia came to St. Louis. The city had entire neighborhoods of people from Bosnia. Somebody would know him. To find him, I knocked on doors and described him. I wished I had a picture, but I didn't. It would have made things easier. Nobody had seen him yet, but I hadn't asked everybody.

Fatima went back to the kitchen. Majda read a book on the end of the couch. She could read in English. I couldn't read English yet, but I was getting better. When Fatima left, Majda put her book down.

"Don't leave again," she said. "It's sad when you leave."

I shrugged.

"Everybody leaves," I said, "but when I find Arman, I'll bring him back. It'll be okay."

"He's probably dead. My brothers are."

I shrugged again.

"Maybe."

Majda went quiet. Then she started crying.

"I don't want you to leave again. Then they'll make me leave."

"They won't," I said. "They love you. And I always come back."

"Not last time."

I made it home most nights, but sometimes the police got me as I walked. Other times, people from the neighborhood spotted me and drove me home. Last time had been bad. I walked farther away than usual and got lost in a park and fell asleep on top of a picnic table by a pond. It was pretty, but I got in trouble for that. A lady jogger found me in the morning. She couldn't speak my language, and I couldn't speak hers well, so I ran away, and she called the police. They caught me in a tree and made me go home. Fatima had been crying, and Emil was mad.

"I won't go that far again," I said. "I think I know where he is now, besides."

"Where is he?"

It was a lie because I had no idea. I also knew that I'd never find him if I stopped looking.

"It's a secret."

"I hate you," said Majda, tears streaming down

her cheeks. "You make everybody sad."

I shrugged once more, unsure what else to say.
"Sorry."

She went quiet. I looked out the window again.
Majda's family was all dead, so she didn't have to
look. My brother was alive, though. Emil and
Fatima had given homes to six children, but other
families fostered even more. Arman could have
been anywhere. He'd come, though. All the kids like
us came here.

Majda picked up her book again and read, and I
kept looking out the window at the rain. It was
Saturday, so I didn't have school. That would give
me plenty of time to search for Arman if the rain
stopped.

A few minutes later, Fatima called us to the
dining room for lunch. We ate in shifts because the
dining room only had four chairs. Majda and I ate
with Fatima and a boy who had arrived a week ago.
I didn't know his name because he didn't talk. He
was younger than me but older than Majda. Fatima
said he would speak when he was ready, but it
might take him some time.

After lunch, somebody knocked on the door. I
opened it and found two old people outside. They
smiled at me. Then Fatima joined us and smiled,
too. Everybody was smiling, which meant I needed
to watch out. Fatima put a hand on my shoulder
and squeezed.

"Hana, this is Gloria and Henry Blackwood.

They're here to meet you."

I looked them up and down.

"What do they want?"

"To take a walk," said Gloria, holding out her hand. She had an accent, but she spoke my language. I narrowed my eyes at her, not trusting her. "The rain has stopped."

I crossed my arms.

"Where are we walking to?"

"Just around," said the woman. "We want to get to know you."

I looked at the man.

"Is he coming, too?"

They both nodded.

"I am," he said. "My name is Henry."

He spoke my language, too, but not very well.

"I'm Hana. My brother is Arman. He's still alive. My other brothers aren't."

"I've heard," said Henry. "I'm a lawyer, and I know a lot of people. Maybe I can help you find him."

I considered him anew then.

"Do you knock on doors?" I asked.

"I use the phone," he said, smiling. "Gloria and I have been learning your language."

"Keep learning," I said.

They both smiled but said nothing. Fatima stayed at the house, but Gloria, Henry, and I went for a walk. I pointed out my neighbors and the new deli up the street. Most people didn't listen to me when I talked, but they did. I told them about my school and about Majda. I was in the second grade, and she was in kindergarten. We walked to the same park in which I had fallen asleep on a picnic table. I pointed it out to them.

"I slept there one night," I said. "It was warmer, then. There were lots of flowers."

"We've heard," said Gloria. "Why did you sleep there?"

"I got lost looking for Arman," I said. "He's here somewhere, I think."

"If he is, we'll find him," said Henry. When I told other adults that I needed to find Arman, they just nodded and ignored me. Henry was the first person to say he'd help.

"There are a lot of doors I haven't knocked on," I said. "But it's too late today."

"You're probably right," said Gloria. "Thanks for walking with us. Can we do this again? Maybe Henry and I can show you our neighborhood."

"Maybe," I said. "I'm pretty busy."

"We'll try to work around your schedule," said Henry. "But only if you agree to stay in your house with Fatima and Emil. I'll keep looking for your brother on my own. I'm pretty good at searching for lost people."

Since he was the first person who had ever agreed to help, I nodded. We walked back to the house, and they dropped me off. As they had asked, I stayed home during the week. Then, on Saturday, they visited again. This time, they picked me up, and we drove to their neighborhood in Webster Groves. The houses there had bigger gardens, but I didn't know anybody. They had a dog named Lady. She was a girl, and she licked my hand. She wasn't as good as Marko, but I liked her.

They took me home afterward. Fatima called them a few days later and put me on the phone. I asked to speak to Lady. She didn't say anything, but I heard her breathe. That weekend, I stayed with Gloria and Henry. I had my own room in their house. We watched a movie. I couldn't understand it very well because it was in English, but it had a boy who learned karate. Lady stayed with me. I asked her to sleep on the bed, but she had arthritis and couldn't jump, so I put my pillows on the floor and slept beside her. Gloria and Henry saved a room for Arman, too, for when we found him.

When Gloria and Henry drove me home the next day, I gave them hugs. Fatima and Emil were nice, but they were always busy. They helped so many people. Emil checked people's teeth in the kitchen, and Fatima was always helping the other kids. I couldn't talk to them the way I talked to Gloria and Henry. They didn't have time.

During the week, I talked to the Blackwoods on the phone twice to tell them about school. Then I spent the next weekend with them at their house. It was nice. That was how it went for a few months. Then they asked whether I'd like to move in with them and Lady for good. I said yes. I missed Arman still, but I didn't think about him as much. Henry had kept looking for him, though, and they had kept his room open in their house. I packed up my clothes and moved in with them a few days later.

Henry, Gloria, and I shared their home in Webster Groves. I grew from a little girl to a young woman in their house, and I fell in love with them. I called them Mom and Dad. A horrible war had taken one family from me, but then the world gave me another. Gloria and Henry became my entire world. They taught a broken little girl to hope again.

But life was cruel and kind in equal measures. When I met them, Mom and Dad were in their sixties. Dad had spent a lifetime in the prosecutor's office, and mom had spent a life in the pediatric emergency room at St. Louis Children's Hospital. Neither of them had time to have kids when they were young, but then the opportunity presented itself, and they adopted me. They should have been traveling the world and seeing everything they missed.

Instead, they hauled a little girl to ballet and school and then to the mall, and, finally, to a bus outside an Army recruiter's office. I was in Iraq when Dad died. Mom followed about six months later. I wish I had been home. I wish I had been there to hold their hands in the hospital.

Mom and Dad sacrificed their dreams for me. They were the kindest, most generous people I had ever met. No one could replace Mama or Tata, but Henry and Gloria held the same place in my heart. I missed them every day. I hoped they knew all they had meant to me.

15

I picked up George at the Humane Society shortly after it opened. The instant I had his leash in hand, my chest loosened, and a weight seemed to leave me. He licked my hands and wagged his tail so hard it almost blurred. He was just a dog, but he was my friend. I was glad he was okay.

Afterward, we drove to a park, and I tossed him a ball for about twenty minutes. The last time I had visited that park, an older woman had told me someone was trying to kill her, just as they had killed her son Douglas. Very likely, she had dementia or Alzheimer's. I had seen it before. Her brain couldn't make sense of her perceptions, so it created theories that put things right. I hoped she was okay.

I hesitated and then put George's leash back on him. My older friend woman had walked to that park in slippers, so she couldn't have lived very far.

I looked up local businesses and found an assisted living center about a quarter of a mile west of the park. Then I looked toward my dog.

"Come on, buddy," I said. "We're going to make some friends."

George and I walked through the park and then alongside the road for about fifteen minutes before coming to the Pine View Assisted Living Center. The four-story white clapboard building sat in the middle of a big garden and had an expansive front porch holding a dozen rocking chairs, many of which were occupied. Ceiling fans provided airflow. A few of the residents watched George and me approach. One even waved.

As I walked, the front door opened, and a woman in scrubs emerged. She walked toward me with a smile on her face. I wondered whether they had surveillance cameras or whether she had been watching the front garden for residents who might have wandered away.

"Hi," she said. "I'm Danielle. You must be here for Mrs. Claypool. She liked your dog and said he was the finest animal she had ever seen."

I covered George's ears. He looked back at me, confused.

"If he hears that, he'll just get a big head," I whispered, patting George's shoulder. "I'm glad Mrs. Claypool liked George. I never learned her name."

She chuckled, and I smiled.

"Her name's Marilyn. She's had a colorful life. Can I ask why you're here to see her?" she asked. "I hear there was some trouble at the park when you met."

"The trouble's all sorted. Mistaken identity," I said before pausing. "I used to be a detective with the St. Louis County Police Department, and I worked a lot of cases involving the elderly. Mrs. Claypool told me some concerning things."

She nodded.

"Then I'm sure you realize that you can't always take people's statements at face value," she said. "Mrs. Claypool is well cared for here."

"This looks like a beautiful place, so I don't doubt that one bit," I said. "I was thinking about her son, though. Douglas. She said someone murdered him and that they were trying to kill her, too."

She straightened.

"No one is trying to kill her," she said. "As for Douglas, he no longer lives on the premises."

I raised my eyebrow and lowered my chin.

"He was a resident?"

"Of our minimally-assisted group home," she said. "Our elderly residents live in this building, but we provide safe housing for individuals with developmental disabilities. Douglas is autistic. Realistically, he could have lived on his own easily. I think he lived here to be close to his mom."

"What happened?"

She considered her answer.

"He checked himself out several years ago," she said. "We miss him. He was funny. The place is less lively without him in it."

"Do you know where he went?"

She hesitated but then nodded.

"He got married. His mother didn't understand and felt threatened. They fought in the lobby, and she spoke ill of Alice, Douglas's wife. He said he was never coming back. They live in Florida now. Last I heard, they were talking about adopting."

It was sad but not tragic. Maybe Douglas should have kept in touch with his mom, but I understood why he left. Life only gives you so many chances at happiness. You squander one, you may not get another.

"Good for Douglas," I said, my voice low. "Mrs. Claypool seemed like a nice lady. I'm glad she and her son are both safe."

"They are," said the nurse. "I'll tell her you and your dog stopped by once she wakes up from her nap."

I thanked her, and then George and I walked back to my car. The dog weighed well over a hundred pounds, so I secured him in a harness and connected that to a seat belt to keep him safe. He settled pretty quickly on the hammock that covered the rear seats. Before driving away, I turned and scratched his neck. He panted and seemed to smile.

"You'd never leave me, would you, dude?" I asked. He panted and licked his nose, and I petted him again. "You're all the family I've got left."

George and I stayed still, but then I took out my phone and searched for the nearest department store. Douglas and Marilyn Claypool were safe, but Crystal Valentine still needed help. If her ex-husband was in town, we needed to know it. A few moments after George and I got in the car, we headed north toward a Walmart in a town called Ozark.

Since I couldn't take George inside a store, I ordered a cheap camera online and did a curbside pickup. Then I grabbed lunch at a drive-through and ate at a picnic table in a public park. It was a nice break. Afterward, I went through an automatic car wash to wash away the urine from my bumper.

Finally, George and I drove back to Pollard and went to Crystal's apartment. She let us in right away. The interior was clean and had a dining room beside the front door. The living room and television were straight ahead. Three kids sat around the dining table with schoolbooks open in front of them. All of them wore clean, neat clothes. None had bruises or other signs of visible abuse or harm. It looked like a happy, healthy home.

I smiled and nodded to them. They seemed content to stare at George. One of them waved. The dog shifted on his feet and whined just a little, clearly wanting to say hello. I gave his leash a gentle tug so he'd settle down.

"Can we talk in private?" I asked Crystal.

"Sure," she said, nodding. "On the patio."

George and I followed her across the apartment to a glass door. She had made the most of her small patio by turning it into an extra living room complete with four comfortable chairs and a coffee table. Ivy-covered wooden dividers gave her privacy from the apartments next to her, and flowers and tomato plants in big, wheeled containers softened the look of the concrete pad. A rotating pedestal fan gave us a breeze.

"I purchased a video camera. It was thirty bucks, but hopefully it'll work. We can put that in your front window and monitor the parking lot for your ex-husband."

She nodded and went inside for her purse. After returning, she handed me cash and locked her eyes on mine.

"You haven't heard anything, have you?"

"No, but I've been working," I said. "You're keeping a low profile, which is great. In all honesty, I think you're probably okay here. Keep the video camera up for a few weeks, and keep your eyes open. If you see your ex-husband or feel threatened, call the police."

She nodded.

"I will," she said. She paused. "So you think this is enough? A camera?"

"Based on what I've seen, yes," I said. "Besides, I'm on my way out of town. Somebody left a death threat on my car yesterday, and two men showed up to my motel last night."

She drew in a breath and took a step back then sat down.

"Sorry."

"Not your fault," I said. "They think I killed the sheriff. I didn't, but it's hard to change somebody's mind when it's already closed."

"I guess so," she said. She paused. "My problems with Kevin don't seem that serious in comparison."

"Tell me about him."

She smiled wistfully and shook her head.

"You don't want to hear about it," she said. "Besides, you'll think I'm stupid or naïve for marrying him."

I shook my head.

"We don't get to choose who we fall in love with, and sometimes the people we fall in love with don't show us who they are until we've said our vows."

She stared at a spot on her coffee table, seemingly lost in thought. Then she cleared her throat and leaned back. Her wicker chair creaked.

"I went to high school with him. We fell in love and got married two years after we graduated. It was good for a while. We had kids and bought a house and settled down. I thought we were happy, but Kevin started drinking. He lost his temper a lot. Then our fights turned physical, and I decided to leave him before he killed me."

I looked down and grimaced.

"You told me they weren't his kids."

She said nothing.

"If they're his kids, your situation gets very complicated very fast," I said. "You told me earlier that he went to prison. Is that true?"

She nodded but said nothing.

"Did the courts sever his parental rights?"

She said nothing.

"Did you divorce him?" I asked. "Or are you still married to him?"

She folded her hands in front of her and then shook her head.

"I don't want to talk about this anymore."

I leaned forward.

"Your ex-husband may be a bastard, but he has legal rights. If these are his kids, he can file for an emergency custody order. You could lose them. You need a lawyer. I'm saying this as a former police officer who specialized in domestic abuse cases. You need help."

She blinked. Her eyes looked wet.

"When we first met, you told me he hit you with a wine bottle and that the police asked what you did to provoke him," I said. "Was that true?"

She licked her lips. Tears sprang in her eyes.

"Yeah."

"Why did the police think you provoked him?"

"Because he was a cop. He was their friend," she said. "They were covering for him. What could I do?"

That changed and complicated things. I considered her.

"Why'd he go to prison?"

"Because he took money from people he shouldn't have taken money from and got caught."

I fit that into what I knew. Finally, I sighed.

"Okay, Crystal—and I know that's not your actual name—find a lawyer who specializes in family law. You won't find one in Pollard, so go to Springfield. You can't do this on your own. At the very least, you'll need to formally file for divorce."

She nodded and looked down.

"I'm sorry for lying," she said. "And I'm sorry for getting you involved in this. It was stupid."

"No, it wasn't," I said. I paused. "Just to settle my curiosity, what name is your apartment under?"

She straightened.

"Crystal Valentine. That's my name."

"It's new, though," I said. "If I went to Hopkinsville and showed your picture around, nobody would know you as Crystal, would they?"

She hesitated.

"Are you going to do that?"

"No," I said, shaking my head. "What do you do for money?"

She looked down.

"I clean people's apartments, and I walk dogs. On the weekends, I drive an Uber in Springfield. The kids are old enough to watch themselves for a few hours."

I crossed my arms.

"What about the rent?" I asked. "This is a nice apartment. It's clean and big, and it's even got an outdoor area. Even in Pollard, a place like this with a pool and on-site management's got to run you, what, a thousand bucks a month?"

"About that," she said, her voice low.

"You make enough money to feed three kids, pay your rent and car payment, clean your clothes, and buy everything else you need by cleaning apartments and walking dogs?"

"And driving on the weekends," she said, her voice soft. "My landlord gives me a break on the rent sometimes. He's a good man."

"I met him," I said. "He seemed like a good man. Handsome, too."

She narrowed her eyes at me.

"What are you implying?"

"I'm not trying to imply anything," I said. "I'm trying to cover my ass and make sure you're not dealing drugs or doing anything else that could come back on me. Now tell me about your landlord. Are you sleeping with him to pay the rent?"

She closed her eyes and shook her head.

"That's none of your business."

"Normally, it's not, but if he's the kind of person who'd let you pay the rent with sex, he's the kind of person who'd call your ex-husband for money."

"No, he is not," she said. "He's a good man, the best I've ever met. You don't get to talk about him like that. You don't even know him."

I lowered my chin.

"So there's something between you," I said. Crystal looked away. Her sex life was her business, but if she endangered her kids, it would become a problem. "Set up the video camera in your front window. If your ex-husband contacts you or tries to hurt you, file for an emergency restraining order and call his parole officer. If he violated the conditions of his parole, you can send him back to prison. Your lawyer will advise you to file for divorce, too. He or she will do more for you than I ever could."

She looked at me and blinked and then drew in a breath.

"Thank you for your help. And good luck. I hope things work out for you wherever you go next."

"Me, too," I said. She escorted George and me out of the apartment. As long as she contacted a lawyer and stayed out of sight, she'd be okay. Marilyn Claypool was okay, too. I hadn't solved Oscar Romero's murder, but I had given it a good shot. Given time, I would have made some headway, but if I stayed in Pollard, eventually the deputies who came to my hotel room last night would make good on their threat. I needed to leave while I could.

I got in my car and headed north out of town. For a few minutes, it almost looked like I was home free. Then, I saw red and blue lights in my rearview mirror and heard a siren. A big sheriff's department SUV pulled off the side of the road from behind a tree and flashed its headlights at me. I groaned and pulled over. The SUV stopped right behind me. I reached back to George to make sure he was okay and watched though my rear window as a female officer—the same sergeant who had arrested me yesterday—walked toward my car.

She knocked on the glass, so I rolled down my window and forced myself to smile at her.

"Nice to see you again," I said. "Something I can do for you?"

"Yeah. I'm glad I caught you. You can turn around and follow me back to my station. My boss has a few questions for you."

I looked straight ahead and ground my teeth before speaking.

"And if I refuse?"

"Then I'll call my colleagues, and they'll call the Highway Patrol, and they'll pick you up at your place in St. Louis. Your choice, but cooperation would be easier for everybody."

There was less chance of anyone getting shot, too. I nodded.

"All right. I'll go back. There's no need for anybody to get hurt."

16

At ten feet by ten feet, the break room at Lakeside Pools was barely bigger than a closet. Joseph tried to avoid it, mostly because he didn't like interacting with Lakeside's employees. They were fine people, but he didn't know the first thing about pools or chemistry, so he couldn't answer their questions. They thought he got his job by sleeping with the boss. If they understood his actual duties, they'd know to keep their mouths shut around him.

He sighed and opened the cabinet doors. His coffee cup was gone. He kept a black, glazed stoneware mug in there so he wouldn't have to use the Styrofoam cups Lakeside supplied for its employees, and somebody had taken it. Joseph could replace a mug, but it pissed him off all the same. He didn't ask for much from his co-workers, just a little courtesy.

As he slammed a cabinet door shut, he caught a

whiff of Elaine's perfume and heard her clear her throat from the doorway. His shoulders fell a little.

"Did the cabinet wrong you in some way?" she asked, her voice light. He turned to her. This morning, she wore tight jeans, a white button-down shirt, and beige sandals. She looked casual and comfortable, and she gave him an almost mischievous smile.

"Somebody took my coffee mug," he said. "And I didn't sleep last night."

Elaine's back stiffened just a little.

"Some pretty young thing keep you up?"

"No," he said. "Work. We alone?" he asked. She nodded. "Daniel and I were at Meadowview until daybreak. Your safrole's gone. We couldn't find it."

Her body remained stiff, but she nodded.

"Thank you for looking."

"I'm sorry," he said. "I know what this means to you."

She gave him a tight smile and nodded.

"Stay here," she said. Then she turned and left. He leaned against the cabinet and crossed his arms. The boss came back a moment later with his coffee mug. "I took it home to wash it. You came in earlier this morning than you usually do."

He turned the mug in his hands and felt its rough sides.

"Do you wash my coffee mug often?"

"You clearly don't, so someone has to," she said, her smile wistful. He nodded and felt one knot in his stomach tighten and another loosen.

"Thank you. That's...thoughtful," he said. They were quiet for a moment, but then he cleared his throat. "Did you talk to Dr. Turner?"

"Yeah," she said, raising her eyebrows and walking toward the coffee station. She poured a drink and sipped from a Styrofoam cup. Then she stared at it and grimaced. "This is terrible coffee. You drink it every morning?"

"Regretfully," he said.

"From now on, come to my office when you want coffee. I've got my own pot."

Joseph allowed the corners of his lips to curl upward.

"I'll do that."

She smiled, but then she drew in a breath.

"Dr. Turner confirmed that a detective came to the camp yesterday to ask about Oscar Romero," she said. "Turner directed her to Frannie Hopkins, and Frannie gave her the bag of condoms and a story about two girls in the Pin Oak cabin."

Joseph sighed and nodded.

"They did their jobs," he said. "We need to pay them?"

"I took care of Dr. Turner," she said. "Frannie set up an appointment. I think she's going to ask for more money. Given everything else going on, I'd rather just pay her and be done with it than risk her going to the police."

"I'll call Daniel," he said. "We'll deal with

Hopkins. Anything else you need me to do?"

She hesitated but then nodded.

"I've been thinking. Daniel was right yesterday. I need someone I can trust by my side. Will you stay with me?"

He didn't have to think. He just nodded. She smiled.

"Good," she said. "We'll work out the details later. I'm glad I get to keep you in my life. Call Daniel. I'll get you money for Frannie from the safe."

She turned to go, but Joseph cleared his throat, stopping her.

"Thank you for trusting me," he said.

She blinked and then looked down.

"You might be the only person I do trust. I can't imagine taking anyone else with me. Now I'm going to get Frannie's money."

She left, and he called Daniel. Even as he spoke with his partner, though, he thought about Elaine. Going with her was the right decision. She needed him. What was more, he needed her.

Two hours later, Joseph smoothed the front of his shirt. Daniel wore dark jeans, a red short-sleeved shirt, and a brown belt. Frannie Hopkins had asked to meet them deep inside an enormous tract of land owned by a Canadian timber company. Heat and humidity made the air thick. Sweat beaded on Joseph's back, chest, and face. Birds and insects zipped around them, but he and Daniel were the only humans within miles.

"You think she'll show up?" asked Daniel.

Joseph glanced at him.

"Oh, yeah," he said. "She'll show. She's too greedy not to."

Daniel reached into his pocket for a pack of cigarettes. He lit up and sat on the car's front passenger seat with his legs outside. The smoke wafted on the gentle morning breeze and then dissipated.

"What's the plan here?" asked Daniel. "I'd hate to shoot her and learn you wanted to invite her to tea."

"Elaine wants to pay her," he said. "She just wants it over with. And while we're talking, I'm going to go with Elaine when she sells. She asked me this morning. She wanted someone around she could trust."

Daniel nodded.

"Good."

They settled into silence for a few minutes. Daniel smoked. Joseph listened to the birds and watched the trees sway. It was pleasant.

"I know what Elaine said, but we should kill Hopkins the moment she gets here," said Daniel eventually. "Then we should kill the detective who's been talking to her. Oscar Romero is a distraction we don't need right now."

Joseph considered him. Daniel didn't usually question orders. Maybe it was a good thing that he did. It showed confidence in his abilities. He'd need that in the months ahead with new employers.

"Killing a detective carries a lot of risk, and I don't think the reward is worth it," said Joseph. "She's a wild card. We don't know her or what she's capable of. Given the situation, I agree with Elaine— we should just pay Hopkins off and send the detective in the wrong direction."

Daniel took a drag on his cigarette.

"Hard to believe this detective just showed up and started investigating Oscar Romero the same day we took out Mason."

Joseph nodded.

"We'll deal with her next," he said. "For now, though, we've got to focus on Hopkins. One problem at a time."

They went quiet for a few minutes. Then Daniel furrowed his brow.

"I hear a car," he said.

"Then get scarce," said Joseph. "Hopkins thinks I'm working alone."

Daniel stood, headed toward the tree line, and disappeared behind a big pine tree. Joseph heard an engine a second later and then saw a pickup bounding toward them down the same lane he and Daniel had traveled. The timber company maintained these woods and trees, but it didn't come often enough to make an actual road. Instead, it had left an empty row just wide enough for two cars to pass between the trees.

Hopkins parked but stayed in her pickup. The air still held the scent of Daniel's cigarette. Joseph had five thousand dollars for her in an envelope and another fifteen hundred in the glove compartment of his car. If that wasn't enough, he could get more, but he hoped he didn't have to.

"Good morning, ma'am," he said, smiling as Frannie Hopkins stepped out of her truck. She closed her door, exposing the deer rifle at her side. He sighed and felt his shoulders sag. "The rifle's unnecessary. Put it away."

She raised the weapon toward him.

"Shut up."

Joseph brought his hand to his face and rubbed his eyes. Hopkins had brought an old bolt-action rifle. If she shot him with that at fifteen feet, the round would pass right through him. It'd hurt, but he'd survive unless she hit a major organ. After she fired once, she'd have to clear the bolt to fire again. That'd take time. She had chosen her weapon poorly.

"Calm down," he said. "Nobody needs to get shot here. We can talk our way through this. Bringing a gun out here was a mistake, Mrs. Hopkins. I'm here to help you, not hurt you."

"You're not here to help anybody," she said. "You're a murderer."

He held up his hands and took a step toward her. She jabbed the weapon at him as if it were a knife. Then she shook her head.

"You just stay where you are," she said. "I gave that detective a bag of condoms. Who did I set up, and who the hell are you?"

Joseph shrugged.

"I'm nobody, and I found the condoms in a hotel room in Kansas City last year," he said. "Any DNA inside is unusable. That's why we gave them to you. We have a plan for dealing with situations like this, and it's working. Everybody wins if we follow the plan."

She narrowed her eyes.

"I don't get it."

"I don't care," said Joseph.

She raised the weapon to her shoulder as if she were going to shoot him. Joseph sighed.

"You're not setting anybody up," he said. "You're gumming up the works. That's your job. You look as if you want to help, but you can't. This detective can work as hard as she wants, but she won't solve her case. More than that, she won't have anybody to blame for her inability to solve her case. That's the key. She won't come back to rework the case if she doesn't have evidence."

She seemed to mull that over.

"Who do you work for?"

"You don't need to know more than you already do."

Mrs. Hopkins lowered her rifle a little.

"Who killed Oscar?" she asked.

"That's none of your business," he said. "You want the money or not?"

She raised her rifle again.

"I never should have gotten involved with you people, but now that I am, I want to get paid. Give me the money."

He reached into his pocket for an envelope.

"You want me to toss it to you?"

"I want all your money, not just the envelope. I know you paid off Dr. Turner, too. How much'd you give her?"

"She dealt with somebody else. I don't know."

"How many people work for you?" she asked, scrunching up her face.

Joseph shrugged.

"What do you want me to say here?" he asked. "I work for a living, and so do you. You've got a boss, and so do I. You want the money or not?"

"Give me all your money," she said. "Put it in my truck and drive away. I hope you have more than five grand. If you don't, I'll blow a hole right through you."

"I don't doubt that," said Joseph, sighing. He raised his voice. "Daniel, this isn't working. Please shoot her now."

She barely had time to furrow her brow before three shots rang out. Each shot hit her within a three-inch cluster over her heart. She was dead before she even hit the ground. Joseph thanked his partner and then walked beside Mrs. Hopkins's body.

"Sorry, dear."

Daniel walked beside him and looked down at the body.

"How do you want to handle this?"

Joseph looked at the surrounding forest. Mrs. Hopkins had done almost everything wrong for her ambush, but she had picked a brilliant spot to dump a body. Joseph dug the tip of his boot into the soil. It was loamy and sandy, easy to dig.

"I keep a shovel in my car," he said. "We'll dig a grave here. Then we'll get rid of her truck."

Daniel nodded.

"This change anything?"

Joseph considered and then tilted his head to the side.

"Not with Oscar Romero," he said. "Phil Mason is dead, his wife is scared to death of joining her husband, Dr. Turner's in line, Frannie Hopkins is dead, half the girls in Pin Oak cabin are going to college overseas, and the other half are God knows where and have lawyers who could keep the Justice Department at bay for the rest of their lives. As long as this sale goes through, we're good."

"What about the detective?"

Joseph knelt beside the woman and patted her until he found the cell phone in her rear pocket. He then used her thumb to unlock it.

"She's only a threat if she comes looking for Frannie," he said, disabling the phone's security functions. "If that happens, we'll kill her. Elaine has plans for emergencies. We'll monitor the sheriff's phone lines. If the detective calls about Frannie, or if any of Frannie's relatives report her missing, we'll intervene. We'll clean house after we're done."

Daniel considered that and then nodded.

"All right," he said. "Let's bury the old lady."

17

George and I drove back to Pollard and parked in front of the sheriff's office's headquarters. The last time I had been inside that station, they had confiscated firearms from me. This time, I unholstered my .45 and locked it in my glove box before getting out of the car. The sergeant in the SUV behind me hurried out the moment she saw me. She tried to escort me inside, but I shook my head.

"I'm not leaving my dog in the car," I said. "It's too hot."

She considered and then nodded. George jumped out and stretched as soon as I opened the door. Once I had a leash on him, the sergeant seemed a little more sure of herself. We went inside, where, once more, Officer Sutton manned the front desk. She wore the same khaki uniform she had worn before, but her curly brown and gray hair hung loosely about her shoulders instead of being secured behind her. She smirked at me.

"Nice to see you back."

I wasn't in the mood for her brand of playful banter.

"Tell your boss I'm here."

"Oh, he knows. He's waiting for you in the interrogation room."

"Cool," I said, tossing George's leash and my purse and phone to the sergeant who had escorted me in. "I know where to go. I'll let myself back. If George isn't here when I come back, I'll call a lawyer."

I started walking before the other officers could stop me. Sutton stayed at the desk with George, but the sergeant hurried to my side. The interrogation room was empty but familiar. I sat and glanced at the sergeant.

"The sheriff will be in shortly," she said. "Can I get you something before I go? A drink, snack? If you need to use the restroom, I'll escort you over."

I considered the questions and then nodded.

"Coffee. Black. Last time I was here, it tasted like vanilla. If you've got some, I'd like some of that."

"I'll see what I can do. Before I leave you here alone, I need to pat you down. It's policy. We don't want anyone to get hurt."

It was a good policy, and the sergeant seemed like a good officer. I agreed, and she thoroughly— but professionally—patted her way up and down my body for weapons. After finding I was unarmed, she left and shut the door behind her. I would have tried to open it, but I didn't plan to go anywhere. If I didn't clear this up here, it'd follow me home. So I sat and waited for the assistant sheriff to knock on the door and come in.

Lyons ducked his head as he walked through the door as if he expected to hit it. He was taller than the average man—maybe a hair over six feet—but not tall enough to duck his head every time he walked through a doorway. Made me wonder what his home life was like if he had to lower his head every time he entered a room.

"Sheriff," I said, nodding toward him and noticing that he had gained a fourth star on his collar. "Congratulations on the promotion."

"It's probably temporary," he said, crossing the room. "By statute, the county needed a sheriff. I'm the highest-ranking law enforcement official left with Phil gone."

He sat down across from me and set a familiar Ziploc bag on the table between us.

"We'll get to this in a minute," he said. "You doing okay? Need anything? Coffee? Bathroom break?"

"I requested some coffee," I said. "And bully for you taking the advice I gave your officers the last time I was here. So why am I here? I was on my way out of town."

He grunted.

"I'm surprised you're so quick to leave," he said. "Yesterday, you seemed so interested in what went on in this town."

"I was under arrest yesterday," I said. "I wanted to understand the situation better."

"Have you done that?"

I considered and then shrugged.

"I've learned the world is more complicated here than I expected."

He nodded and then reached to a notepad on his utility belt.

"So yesterday we released you, and then you went to pick up your car. Thanks for letting us search it, by the way," he said, reading his notes. "Afterward, you went to the library, Camp Meadowview, and then the home of a woman named Frannie Hopkins. Is that right?"

"You're batting a thousand," I said. "I also went to Frank's Downtown Diner for dinner."

"And you met a woman there."

I smiled, but I didn't feel like smiling.

"Is that what this is about? You don't want me talking to the locals?"

"No," he said. "Who you choose to converse with is your business."

"Great," I said. "You obviously had someone following me. That's good. One of your officers left a death threat on my window at the diner. Who was it?"

The sheriff blinked and lowered his chin.

"Excuse me?"

"A deputy left a death threat on my car's window while I had dinner. The note said that the writer intended to kill me and my dog. No one in town knows I had a dog except you and your officers, so that note had to come from one of your officers," I said. "Two of them then showed up outside my motel room last night. They were drunk. They sat on my car. One of them urinated on the rear bumper."

He pursed his lips.

"Did they sign the note?"

"No."

He drew in a slow breath, his eyes distant.

"That doesn't sound like something my boys would do."

"You don't know your boys, then. It happened. Did the officer following me report seeing anyone slip a note under my windshield wiper?" I asked. He paused and shook his head. "Then he likely did it."

"I'm sorry you think that."

I leaned forward.

"I'm sorry your officers threatened to kill me, followed me to my hotel, got drunk in the parking lot, and peed on my car."

He looked at the table.

"I suspect you're misinterpreting last night's events," he said. "And if you aren't, I think you need to bear in mind that those men just lost a friend and colleague. They were blowing off steam."

"And if a civilian had done the same thing to them, he would have gotten shot."

He narrowed his eyes and crossed his arms.

"My men are professionals."

"Maybe during the day. The men outside my room last night were thugs, though," I said. "Now what do you want?"

"We searched your hotel room this morning and found these condoms in the freezer. My officer said you left Ms. Hopkins's house with a bag. Is this it?"

"No," I said. "She gave me some homemade cookies. They were delicious. As for the condoms... well, I'm a single lady. I don't think my sex life is any of your business."

His eyes flicked to the bag.

"They're used."

I shrugged.

"I don't get laid often. Sometimes it's nice to commemorate the occasion."

He shifted his weight on the chair and locked his eyes on mine.

"So you're not going to help us at all."

"I don't trust you."

He pushed back from the table, laced his fingers behind his head, and breathed through his nose.

"Believe it or not, we want the same things," he said. "You want to solve Oscar Romero's murder. I do, too. I also want to find out what happened to my boss."

"And I wish you all the luck in the world with both tasks. I didn't kill Sheriff Mason, though, and I have no idea who did. If I had any insight, I'd share it."

"What about Oscar Romero?"

I forced myself to smile.

"I don't know who killed him, either. You're going to have to figure that one out on your own."

"You want to find out, though, don't you?"

I shrugged.

"Of course I do," I said. "But to investigate Oscar Romero, I'd have to stay in Pollard. The longer I stay in town, the more likely your officers are to follow through on their death threat. I'm not interested in dying."

"Then help me. Tell me about these condoms."

He seemed sincere, but seeming sincere was easy. Still, he had the condoms now. I couldn't change that.

"They were collected by Frannie Hopkins from the Pin Oak cabin the day Oscar Romero died. She believes one of the girls in the cabin used them with Oscar and then threw them away. She also believes Oscar was murdered by either Rachel Tibbals or Breanna Moore because they fought over Oscar."

The sheriff's eyes went distant as he thought.

"I tried to interview Ms. Moore and Ms. Tibbals, but their lawyers refused to let me even see them," he said. "I've never heard the name Frannie Hopkins."

"She worked at Meadowview, but now she's retired. She found Oscar's body and then cleaned the cabin. Afterward, her boss gave her money and told her to take a vacation. That's all I know."

He nodded and went quiet. Then he cleared his throat.

"We'll find her," he said. "In the meantime, I need you to stick around town."

I shook my head.

"That's a negative, Ghost Rider. Oscar Romero is dead. As much as I feel for his family, he won't mind if his case goes unsolved. I'm going home before I get shot. Thanks, though."

The sheriff lowered his hands from his head but said nothing. I nodded toward the exit.

"Open the door. I'm leaving."

Again, he said nothing. Then I stood, and he got the hint and escorted me out. George was waiting for me in the lobby with Officer Sutton. She had tied his leash to a chair, but he stood when he saw me. His tail wagged. He looked happy, which was nice to see. Officer Sutton handed me my purse without saying a word. Then I got the dog and left.

I had planned to leave right away, but I walked George around the block first. Then, my cell phone started vibrating. I didn't recognize the number, but I answered anyway. It was a pleasant day with just enough of a breeze to make it comfortable in the sun.

"Hey," I said. "This is Hana Blackwood."

"Hi. Are you the detective?"

I wound my hand around George's leash so he couldn't get too far ahead of me.

"I guess I am. Who's this?"

"Lucia Medina," she said. "I saw you at Meadowview and heard you visited Dr. Turner. The motel gave me your phone number. I know the clerk."

I didn't appreciate the motel giving out my number to strangers, but I nodded.

"What can I do for you, Ms. Medina?"

She hesitated before speaking. I waited and forced a smile to my lips. Sometimes that helped brighten my voice on the phone. It made it easier to talk to me.

"Take your time," I said.

"Oscar was my friend," she said. "I work at Meadowview. I do the laundry."

"Oscar seemed to have a lot of friends," I said. "What kind were you?"

"Just the friend kind," she said. "I don't date men. He was nice, though. Most people at Meadowview aren't."

I waited for her to continue, but she didn't. I started to ask why she contacted me, but then she cleared her throat.

"Jim told me you visited Dr. Turner," she said. "I don't know what she told you, but you shouldn't trust her. We call her *la serpiente*. She's mean, and she lies."

I recognized the name Jim. He was the security guard who drove me to Dr. Turner's cabin.

"I see," I said, nodding. My car wasn't far away, but it seemed that Ms. Medina wanted to talk, so George and I kept walking. "What does she lie about?"

"Everything. When she hired me, she said she'd sponsor my brother's visa and hire him to work maintenance. He's a carpenter, and he can build anything. She won't even talk about it anymore."

I drew in a breath and nodded and considered my response.

"That's unfair, but I don't know the first thing about immigration law. Sorry."

"That's not why I called you. She's a liar. You can't trust anything she told you about Oscar."

"Can I trust Frannie Hopkins?"

She paused.

"Maybe," she said. "She wasn't nice, but if she promised something, she followed through."

"She told me either Breanna Moore or Rachel Tibbals murdered Oscar. She said they were both sleeping with him. Did you ever meet them?"

"No," she said, "but I knew Oscar. He liked girls like me. He said white girls were too skinny."

I smiled.

"Would he have turned down a pretty Caucasian girl who wanted to sleep with him?"

"Oscar only slept alone when he wanted to sleep alone," she said. "And he liked Latinas. He might have hooked up with white girls, but he wouldn't have sought them out."

My smile slipped. At the time of his death, four girls had been living inside Pin Oak cabin. Only one sounded Hispanic.

"Is the name Angelina Lopez familiar?" I asked.

"No. Why?"

"She lived in Pin Oak cabin at the time of his death," I said before pausing. "Why would Mrs. Hopkins tell me Oscar had a relationship with Breanna Moore and Rachel Tibbals if he didn't?"

"Probably for the same reason she cleaned the cabin after finding his body: money. Somebody paid her."

That was possible, so I nodded.

"Anything else you think I should know?"

"No, but be careful," she said. "Oscar was a good boy. I wish he hadn't died."

"Me, too," I said. I thanked her for her call and then hung up. I didn't know Ms. Medina, but her story corroborated some of my earlier suspicions of Dr. Turner and Mrs. Hopkins. Getting information from them had been too easy. They were setting me up.

I walked back to my car, put George on the hammock over the back seats, and sat in the driver's seat. My cell signal wasn't great, but I searched for Angelina Lopez on my phone and found results for thousands of women in the US. Luckily, Camp Meadowview had its own staff photographer who took a lot of pictures, some of which a reporter at the *St. Louis Post-Dispatch* had acquired and run in the newspaper. I knew what my Angelina Lopez looked like, I knew she was in her early twenties, and I knew she came from money.

Angelina probably had a Facebook profile, but I doubted she used it except to communicate with her parents and grandparents. Instead, I went to Instagram and browsed profiles of women named Angelina Lopez until I found the young woman I wanted. She had dyed her hair blond since high school, but she had the same basic bone structure as the woman in the newspaper pictures.

I browsed her pictures, hoping I could find something that would tell me where she was, and then stopped when I recognized the wrought iron front gate of Waterford College, a private liberal arts college in St. Augustine, Missouri. Nothing I did could bring Oscar Romero back, but I suspected this young lady knew something of his death.

Oscar Romero's death broke his parents' hearts. I saw that when I met them in the police station. The sheriff had given them a sense of hope when he called and said he knew who killed their son, but then they lost that hope when Mason died. It was unfair. More than that, it was wrong. Nobody deserved to have their hope stolen from them over and over. I sighed and looked over my shoulder to the dog.

"Settle in, buddy. We're going for a drive."

18

St. Augustine was a tourist town overlooking the Mississippi River on the edge of St. Augustine County. Once a year, the town had a massive spring fair that culminated in a hot air balloon race and brought in tens of thousands of visitors. Mom, Dad, and I visited when I was young, but Dad always felt there was something off about the place. I never got that feeling, but then I was a kid. It was beautiful now.

My clock said it was four-thirty as George and I pulled into the city limits. My stomach rumbled, but it was too early for dinner, so I parked downtown, and George and I walked to a little coffee shop called Rise and Grind. Since I couldn't bring the dog inside, I tied his leash to a shaded wrought iron table on the sidewalk and told him to sit down. He dutifully complied while I went inside to order a cup of coffee and a snack. As big as he was, George could probably drag that table down the street if he wanted, but he wouldn't go anywhere.

The line had two people in it, so I looked outside periodically while I waited. Shortly after I ordered, I turned and saw a blonde woman with a big brown dog kneeling beside George and petting his cheek. I nodded hello to her. She smiled and lightly tugged her dog's leash to get his attention before turning and walking away. George watched them go.

The woman looked familiar, but I didn't think I knew her. A couple of years back, I had met a detective from the St. Augustine County Sheriff's Department at a continuing law enforcement education seminar in St. Louis, and this woman looked a lot like her. I knew she wasn't Detective Court, though, because Detective Court never smiled or looked happy. That woman did.

Once I got my snack, I went outside and sat beside George. He begged for a piece of my pecan roll, but after one bite I knew I'd eat the whole thing. It wasn't healthy for him anyway. I petted his side and then told him to lie down.

I got George two years ago when I left my husband, Blake. George was a little furball, then, and I had needed him more than I knew. When Blake and I married, I had expected to spend the rest of my life with him. It wasn't even hope; it was expectation. I had loved him—or at least I thought I did—and I had thought he had loved me. In his own way, maybe he had. We had dated for about a year, and then lived together for six months. Then we got married. It had seemed like the natural progression.

We didn't fight much the first year, but then I got a promotion and became a detective—a job he had always wanted—while he stayed in uniform. He became resentful after that and blamed me—and every other woman with a badge—for the state of his career. The first time he pushed me, we laughed about it afterward, like it was an accident we had both survived and made it through unscathed. It was just so random and so out of my experience that my brain couldn't process it. I pretended it didn't happen—just like many of the domestic violence victims whose cases I investigated.

Then it happened again. Blake wanted me to put his name on the house's title. We were married, and he thought we should share everything. I tried to tell him that it wasn't even my house, that it belonged to my deceased parents. I wasn't ready to think of their things as mine yet. He pushed me against the cabinets in the kitchen and stormed off. Every neuron in my brain screamed at me to run, but I didn't. I kept thinking I had said something wrong and that if I avoided saying those kinds of things again, it wouldn't happen again.

Finally, a couple of weeks later, he slapped me, and I couldn't hide things anymore. In a book or a movie, I never would have let that happen. I'd be so tough that I could fight him off, or I'd be so clever that I'd handcuff him to the fridge and leave him. That didn't happen, though. I wasn't tough or clever or even brave. He was mad, and he took it out on me. Afterward, he left and went to the gym, and I cried in the shower until I didn't have any tears left.

Eventually, I called the only person I could think of who would help. Shane and Ivy came to the house immediately. Ivy and I packed a bag, while Shane kept watch in case Blake came home. He didn't, thankfully. Shane might have killed him if he had.

In the end, my marriage didn't explode; it fizzled. Blake didn't contest the divorce, and we divided our stuff with little difficulty. I owned the house, so Blake moved out, and I got a dog.

In a Hallmark movie, I would have left Blake and fallen in love with my soul mate. That didn't happen, though. Some dreams just didn't work out, and some failures didn't lead to future success. I did the best I could with what I had and tried to be happy. Some days were harder than others.

George and I stayed outside the coffee shop for about twenty minutes as I thought about the task ahead of me. If I'd had a badge, I would have visited the campus police department and told them I needed to interview Angelina Lopez about a homicide, and they would have brought her to me. It would have been easy. As a private citizen, I had work ahead of me. But I had a plan, too.

I searched for the local library on my phone. St.

Augustine had a compact downtown area, so I didn't need to get back in my car. George and I walked a couple of blocks and then headed inside. People looked askance at me for bringing a dog into the building, but I didn't plan to stay long, and I didn't want to leave him outside tied to a bench. He'd be fine.

We checked out the reference counter, where I found dictionaries, thesauri, almanacs, and a whole lot of other stuff, most of which was probably better accessed online. I also found a section containing phone books and Waterford College directories. According to the college's most recent directory, Angelina Lopez lived in a dorm in the middle of campus. I snapped pictures of her listing and a page containing a campus map with my cell phone and left.

It was half after five at that point, so my timing worked. George and I drove toward the school and then parked in a visitor spot near Ms. Lopez's dorm. Waterford College had a beautiful campus with lush landscaping, pristine lawns, and gorgeous Georgian-style buildings. It must have had an army of full-time gardeners to maintain the grounds. It was worth it. I would have loved to go to a college like that.

I spent two or three minutes doing some research on my phone before calling Angelina's room. She answered on the third ring with a hesitant hello.

"Hey, Ms. Lopez," I said. "My name is Hana Blackwood. I'm looking into the death of Oscar Romero, and I was hoping I could talk to you for a few minutes."

She didn't hesitate to respond.

"I'm not interested. If you call again, I'll consider it harassment and call the police."

"I just want to run some names by you. Breanna Moore and Rachel Tibbals. You remember them?"

I waited, expecting her to hang up.

"What about them?"

"Somebody is trying to make it look like they killed Oscar," I said. "I don't think they did, though. I doubt they even had a relationship with him. Did you?"

She paused. Again, I half expected her to hang up.

"He was my friend, not that it's any of your business."

"You're right," I said, softening my voice. "It isn't my business. But he's dead now, and he shouldn't be. I'm trying to find out what happened. His family deserves to know the truth. If you come down and talk to me, I'll buy you dinner. I'm not looking to jam you up, and I'm not a cop. You don't have to talk to me, but it'd be nice if you could."

She paused.

"Who are you?"

"Just another person. I'll leave you alone if you ask, but I'd like your help."

She paused again.

"Where are you?"

"Outside your dorm. I'm in a blue Subaru."

"Okay."

She hung up. She was either calling the campus police or coming down to visit. I gave it fifty-fifty either way. About five minutes later, the front door opened. Angelina stepped out and looked around. A tie held her dyed-blond hair back from a heart-shaped face. She wore jeans and a baggy T-shirt. As she came toward my car, I opened my door and waved. Her green eyes looked tired.

"So I'm here," she said. "What do you want?"

"Just to talk," I said. "Like I said, I'm investigating Oscar Romero's death. He seemed like a nice guy. People liked him a lot. Did you?"

She paused and then nodded.

"Why's he dead?" I asked.

She swallowed and blinked. It almost looked like she was going to cry. If campus security happened to drive by and see us, they'd probably arrest me for trespassing. I needed to hurry this up.

"I don't know," she said.

"But you liked him?" I asked. She nodded again. "You hungry? I saw a place called the Pizza Palace nearby. I'll buy you a slice."

She looked down.

"Their food sucks. Buy me a sandwich at Able's Diner. It's just up the road. Then we'll talk."

I looked back to my car and then to her.

"You like dogs?" I asked. She shrugged and then nodded.

"I guess."

"Good. I'll give you a ride."

19

January 12, 2020.
St. Louis County, Missouri

It was two in the morning, and I sat on the rear seat of a narcotics detective's Honda Accord. We were the third car in a four-car convoy, and we planned to arrest Lavan Michael Johnson, a twenty-six-year-old independent pharmaceutical salesman with a criminal history stretching back to his early teenage years. He and his girlfriend—Kenna Washington—had recently murdered a witness who planned to testify against Lavan at an upcoming assault trial. Unfortunately for Lavan and Kenna, they had committed this murder in front of a homeowner's surveillance camera. We had the whole thing on video from beginning to end.

The car in which I rode shuddered as it slammed into a pothole. I bounced on my seat but stayed upright. Detective Hogan looked in the rearview mirror.

"Sorry, guys," he said. "I'll try to avoid those from now on."

"Good luck," said the detective beside me, snickering. "Welcome to north county, where city pothole repair crews dare not tread."

Nobody laughed. Every street in St. Louis County had potholes, and Jennings wasn't worse than any other suburb in that regard. Detective Hogan had hit the pothole on purpose and watched me in the rearview mirror the whole time because he liked watching my boobs bounce. He was classy like that.

My lieutenant had asked me to come along on this assignment because Lavan and Kenna had two kids and I had experience working with traumatized children. We already had a foster home lined up for them and a social worker on standby to take over when we secured the home and adults. I lost my family at a young age, so I knew some of what those kids had ahead of them. If they found a new family who loved them, they'd be okay. If not, they'd face hardships for a long time. At least they'd have a chance, though.

The dashboard clock read 3:15, and the sky was black and cloudy. It was forty degrees outside, and not a single person loitered on the sidewalks. The homes around us were small and single story. Most had brick exteriors and likely held two or three bedrooms. As often as not, a chain-link fence surrounded the backyard, and wrought iron bars covered the windows. Small, neighborhood parks appeared every few blocks. The trees and flowers had gone dormant for the season.

The lead car in our convoy parked half a block from Lavan's rental home. The rest of us parked in a row behind it. Lieutenant Jorgenson, the major case squad's commanding officer, got out of the first car and then waved to the rest of us to gather around him. Because we knew Lavan had firearms and little compunction about using them, we had brought ten officers and a no-knock warrant for his arrest.

I met the lieutenant near the hood of his black SUV. The rest of the team huddled around us. The air wasn't quite cold enough to turn my breath to frost, but I was grateful for my jacket and the heavy bulletproof vest it concealed.

"Okay, folks," said Jorgenson. "You know the drill. We're here for Lavan Johnson and Kenna Washington. Expect both to be armed and willing to shoot. We will go in hot. Lavan and Kanna, in addition to being a loving couple, are alleged to be St. Louis's sole supplier of Yankee Speedball. It's ecstasy combined with very high-quality cocaine in easy-to-conceal pills. So far, their drugs have killed three people. We also have them on video murdering a rival who tried to move into their Speedball market.

"Upon arrival, Detective Blackwood, Officer Short, and I will proceed north through the house to the master bedroom. Detectives Hogan and Puglisi and Officer Harding will go through the kitchen and living areas. There are two children in the home, and their safety is our first priority. Lindsay Morgan from CPS is here to deal with the kids once we get them. Officer Davenport will be with her at all times."

Lindsay was a social worker with the Children's Division of the Missouri Department of Social Services. I had worked with her before and liked her. She smiled often and easily, which was rare for someone in her job. I nodded hello to her and then focused on my boss.

"If I haven't said your name, your job will be to wait in front of or behind the house in case Johnson or Washington bolt. If they do, please arrest them. Questions before we go?"

He had already given us a thorough briefing earlier, so we all knew what to do. I chambered a round in my service pistol and checked to see that I had extra magazines. The other officers around me did likewise.

Jorgenson drew in a breath.

"You know your jobs. Let's go."

The bulk of our team hurried toward the house. Only Lindsay and Officer Davenport stayed behind. Upon arrival, two uniformed officers ran toward the backyard, while two others hustled to the front of our group with a portable battering ram between them. Behind them came Officer Harding with a breaching shotgun.

The boss held up five fingers and looked at each of us. Then he counted down. With each change in count, my heart beat faster. Jorgenson patted the uniformed officers on the shoulder. They pulled their battering ram back, and for a split second, the entire world went quiet. I could hear the blood whooshing past my ears, I could smell ash from the cigarette Detective Puglisi had smoked before we left, and I could feel the cold on my cheeks and seeping into my lungs.

Then the battering ram slammed into the door.

The house shuddered, but the door didn't open. I held my breath as they hit it again. As before, it didn't budge.

"Shotgun," said Jorgenson. "They've reinforced the door."

I hustled back while Officer Harding aimed the breaching shotgun toward the hinges. His first shot blew a hole six inches wide clean through the door. My ears rang. I grimaced and tried not to flinch as he lowered his weapon and aimed where the lower hinge would be. When he fired again, the door shifted in its frame. He kicked it down and then jumped to the side.

"Police officers," shouted Detective Hogan. "We've got a warrant."

Hogan, Puglisi, and Harding sprinted into the house. Lieutenant Jorgenson, Officer Jermaine Short, and I ran after them. Hogan and his team took a short hallway to the left, while we went straight ahead to the master bedroom. As soon as we reached it, Jorgenson kicked the door at the knob, splintering the frame and forcing it open. Jorgenson and Short rushed inside.

The first shot rang out. It hit the doorframe to my right. My instincts told me to dive to the ground, but I stayed on my feet. My heart pounded, and my skin tingled. Jorgenson and Short returned fire, and I sprinted forward and swept the room with my pistol. Lavan lay on the bed with a pistol in his hand. His eyes were open, but his chest wasn't moving. We'd get him an ambulance as soon as we could, but he had drawn his last breath.

"Suspect down," said Jorgenson. "No sign of Kenna Washington or the kids. Blackwood and Short, check the closet."

Officer Short ran toward me. I heard a muffled cry from the closet door to my left. The crying transformed into a soft wail. I waved the boss over. Officer Short positioned himself to the right of the door. Jorgenson went to the left. I stood in front of it, my heart thudding against my breastbone.

The lieutenant counted down from three on his fingertips. Adrenaline poured through me. Every muscle in my body felt ready to run, so I drew in a deep breath to calm myself down. After hitting one, he pointed at me, and I kicked the door as hard as I could. It exploded inward, exposing a walk-in closet that had been transformed into a nursery. There was a crib and a changing table. An infant kicked and screamed in the crib, terrified. There were no adults or anywhere to hide.

"Room's clear," I said, holstering my weapon. "I've got the infant, and I'm getting out of here."

I picked up the baby and then grabbed a pacifier from the crib. She quieted instantly when I put the pacifier in her mouth.

"You're okay, sweetheart," I said. "I've got you."

I hurried out of the room and through the front hallway. Outside, Detective Hogan and his team were waiting on the sidewalk.

"Baby okay?" he asked.

"Yeah. She's fine. Lavan pulled a gun on us. Jorgenson and Short shot him. He's down. You find the toddler?"

"His room was empty," said Hogan. "Maybe he and his mom were staying elsewhere for the night."

"Maybe," I said. "Call an ambulance for Lavan."

Hogan considered and then shook his head.

"I'll wait for the lieutenant's order. Don't want to waste resources we don't need to waste."

"Lavan's been shot multiple times. Do your job and call an ambulance, jackass. I'm going to find Lindsay and Davenport."

He muttered that I was a bitch as he took out his phone. One of the uniformed officers lit up a cigarette, apparently thinking his job was done. I rubbed the baby's back and walked up the sidewalk to get away from the smoke. Lindsay and Officer Davenport were half a block away. I filled them both in on what had happened and handed the baby to Lindsay. She had a pair of car seats in her vehicle for the kids, and hopefully we'd put them both to good use soon. She checked out the baby, and Davenport looked to me.

"You mind switching places?" he asked. "I'd rather search the neighborhood than stand around."

"Call the lieutenant to see what he says, but sure," I said, nodding.

Davenport took a couple steps away and got on his radio, and I looked to Lindsay. She was probably twenty-five and had blond hair. I didn't know whether she had kids of her own, but she knew how to care for them.

"Baby looks healthy," she said, bouncing the little girl on her hip. "Did you see any infant formula in the house?"

"I didn't look," I said. "Sorry."

"No problem," she said. "Once you've got the house secure, I'll go in and see what we can find. If they don't have anything, we'll have to see what works for this little girl's system on our own. We'll sort it out."

I nodded and looked around us. A siren blared in the distance, but I didn't hear any shouts or further gunfire. As Lindsay and I stood there and smiled at the little girl in her arms, I found the muscles of my shoulders relaxing. At least this part of the job was done.

"I always wanted a little girl," I said. "Maybe if I

get married again."

Lindsay smiled.

"Forget the marriage part," she said. "You don't need a husband to become a mom. If you want a kid, you should do it."

I started to say it'd be nice to have a bigger support network than I'd have, but then I caught movement between two nearby houses. It was a figure.

"Get behind me," I said, my voice a little more strident than I meant. Lindsay drew in a breath and straightened. She grasped the baby tighter and stepped behind me. I unholstered my weapon but kept it low at my side.

"I'm a police officer," I said, my voice taut with adrenaline. A muscle in my shoulder twitched. "And I can see you between the houses. Please come forward and into the light."

The figure walked forward. It was Kenna Washington. A small figure—a child—hung back in the shadows.

"You killed him," she said, tears evident in her voice. "Lavan."

"He shot at us first," I said. "Please come forward, Ms. Washington. Nobody else needs to get hurt. And call your little boy forward, too. Ms. Morgan can take care of him. I'll take you into custody safely. No one will get hurt. There's no need to resist. We've got officers all over the neighborhood looking for you."

She took another few steps forward. She had a pistol. I raised mine. The night felt warmer all of a sudden, and my heartbeat sped up.

"Drop your gun," I said. "Nobody needs to get hurt."

"Give me my baby," she said. "Put her on the ground and walk away. I didn't do anything."

"We can't do that," I said. "If you ever want to hold your daughter again, put the gun down. We'll talk, and we'll get you a lawyer. I promise that we'll take care of her and you. There are police officers all around here. If they see you with a gun, they may not react well."

She looked around and seemed to consider it.

"If I put this gun down, I'll go to prison."

"You don't put that gun down, you're going to die. Your kids could get hurt, too. I don't want that, and neither do you."

She looked around again. Then her shoulders lowered.

"I don't see any other cops," she said. "I think I'll take my chances."

She raised her pistol. Maybe she thought I wouldn't shoot her, or maybe she thought I'd miss. Or maybe she was bluffing and wanted to see what I'd do. She didn't know I had spent eight years in the Army and that I had qualified multiple times as an expert on the Combat Pistol Qualification Course. She didn't know I put fifty rounds through my pistol every month at a firing range.

In the end, her thoughts—whatever they were—
didn't matter. A social worker and an infant stood
not ten feet behind me. I wore a bulletproof vest, but
they didn't. I could risk my own life, but not theirs.

As Kenna aimed at me, I squeezed the trigger.
The first round hit her in the chest. The next four hit
within a three-inch cluster over her heart. She fell
backwards, and her toddler ran from the dark
toward his mother. I reached Kenna before the kid
and picked him up. He kicked and fought and bit
my arms, but I didn't let him go. My colleagues
weren't far, so they heard the gunshots and came
running.

"We're okay," I shouted. "Kenna's down. Get a
medic."

Officer Davenport arrived first. He saw me
struggling with the toddler and took him from me. I
knelt and checked Kenna's pulse, but she had likely
died with the first shot. My legs felt shaky, and my
stomach roiled. I fell to the grass a couple of feet
from her body and breathed deeply.

I watched Officer Davenport and then Lindsay
struggle with a terrified little boy who only wanted
to hug his mother and who never would again. My
back hurt. I felt sick. My hands trembled as I
brought them to my face. Lieutenant Jorgenson
walked toward me and knelt beside me.

"Stand up, Detective," he said. "We need your
pistol."

I looked down at my hands. I still had my

weapon out, so I handed it to him, and he put a hand on my upper arm.

"Stand up," he said again. "I need to get you in a car before the news people get here."

"Oh, okay," I said, nodding. I put my hands on my knees and forced myself to stand. It felt like I was floating. I looked at Kenna and then drew in a breath. "I did that. I shot her."

"She pulled a weapon on you," he said. "You didn't do anything wrong."

"I murdered a woman in front of her children."

I didn't even realize what I had said until the words left my mouth. Then I felt a tear in the corner of my eye. Jorgenson squeezed my arm tight.

"Do not say another word until you talk to an attorney, Detective," he said. "Come on."

To my shame, I did as he said. I let him lead me to an SUV, and I let him call my union rep so I could have a lawyer meet me at our station. After a three-week investigation, a team of detectives from our Professional Standards Division concluded that my shooting was justified and that I had saved lives, my own included.

My department gave me a medal of valor. No award could make right what I had done, though. My colleagues said my shooting was justified, but the facts didn't change. I did to a little boy in St. Louis what a Serbian militia group did to me in Bosnia—I killed his family in front of him. He'd hate me for the rest of his life. And I would deserve it.

The day my department exonerated me, I turned in my badge. Police work gave my life meaning, but I couldn't do it anymore. When doing the right thing turned me into someone I hated, it wasn't worth it.

20

Angelina, George, and I drove to Able's Diner just off the edge of campus. I had a turkey melt sandwich and a chocolate and peanut butter milkshake. Angelina had a meatball sandwich and fries. Thankfully, she was up for eating at a picnic table outside, so I fed George two cups of dog food right there. It was a pleasant night, so the dog and I could even walk dinner off afterward.

As we ate, I introduced myself again and told her how I had stumbled onto the case and what I had done so far. She didn't seem too interested, which was fine. I didn't need enthusiasm, just honesty. When I finished speaking, Angelina raised her eyebrows but said nothing.

"So, the sheriff's office in Bryant County has a Ziploc bag full of condoms. Presumably, they'll find Oscar's DNA in them. Are they going to find yours, too?"

She shook her head.

"Nope," she said. "I was on the pill, and I trusted him. He said he didn't have any diseases."

Her judgment left something to be desired, but I appreciated her honesty.

"So you had a romantic relationship with him," I said. She shrugged and tilted her head to the side.

"I don't know if I'd call it a relationship," she said. "Oscar and I hooked up. It was Meadowview. If you weren't there to hook up, why'd you go?"

"It's like spring break in Cancun," I said. "If you're not guzzling tequila, you might as well have gone to Disney World."

"Yeah, exactly," she said. I didn't know whether my reasoning held, but I nodded as if it did.

"So you hooked up with Oscar," I said. "Did other girls from your cabin hook up with him, too?"

She shook her head.

"They might have tried, but they weren't his type. He was a nice guy, and he was gorgeous. I cried when I heard he died."

"You didn't cooperate with the police, though," I said. "You liked this guy and slept with him, but you didn't talk to the detectives investigating his death. Why?"

She held my gaze but then blinked and looked away. I gave her a minute.

"I know that's not a fair question," I said, "but Oscar's loved ones deserve an answer."

For a moment, she said nothing. Then she drew

in a breath.

"They do," she said. "But I wasn't at Meadowview that morning. I told the police the truth. I didn't know anything."

"Where were you?"

"Jail."

I smiled and then chuckled.

"Let's talk about that," I said. "Why were you in jail?"

"Meredith and I snuck out of camp and hitchhiked to town. We had fake IDs, so we went to a bar and got drunk. Afterward, some lady saw me puke on her azaleas and called the cops."

"Okay," I said, drawing the syllables out. "So the police arrested you for public intoxication?"

She looked down.

"Yeah. When they showed up, Meredith and I ran. She got away, but I tripped on a stick. I guess they booked me after that. Since I didn't have my real ID on me, I gave them my fake ID. They knew it was fake and said they wanted to charge me with identity theft. I had to call my dad in the middle of the night. His lawyer got me out the next morning."

When people lied, they usually tried to make themselves look good. Ms. Lopez's story was stupid enough that I believed it. Plus, unless her lawyer had it expunged, she'd have an arrest record somewhere that could corroborate everything. It was a good alibi.

"So you returned to the cabin to find Oscar

dead."

She nodded.

"The other girls were on the porch. Dr. Turner was telling them that she had pictures of us drinking and smoking weed and said that if we cooperated with the police, she'd put those pictures on Facebook for college admissions people to see. If we talked to the police, she'd ruin our lives. She told us to call our lawyers and keep our mouths shut. We did what she wanted."

I considered and then crossed my arms. If she were lying to me, there'd be multiple witnesses who could contradict her.

"How'd the cabin look?"

She shrugged.

"I didn't go inside. After I talked to the police, my mom and dad took me home. I haven't been back to Meadowview or Pollard since."

"Is it possible that Oscar had spent the night with Breanna, Rachel, or Meredith?"

She shrugged.

"It's possible, but I doubt it," she said. "Meredith was with me, and Rachel and Breanna only hooked up with rich guys. Oscar was hot, but they joked about how poor and dirty the staff were. I don't think they'd go slumming and hook up with the pool boy."

I added her story to everything else I knew.

"So you didn't sleep with him because you were in jail, Meredith didn't sleep with him because she was hiding from the police, and Rachel and Breanna didn't sleep with him because he was poor."

She narrowed her eyes.

"Why do you think somebody slept with him before he died?"

"Because the lady who cleaned your cabin found condoms in the downstairs bathroom."

She shook her head.

"Nobody used the downstairs bathroom," she said. "The door latch didn't work. Maintenance was supposed to fix it, but they never did. And if you tried to use it, the door would swing open on you while you were mid-pee. If the housekeeper said she found condoms in that bathroom, she's lying to you."

I nodded and rubbed my eyes. It looked like I wasn't done with Pollard, after all.

"I think a lot of people are lying to me," I said. "Unless you want to hang around here, I'll drive you home."

She said sure, so we piled into my car, and I drove her back to her dorm. Afterward, I drove to a park that bordered the college and walked with George for about half an hour. Aside from his morning and evening meals, walks were his favorite time of the day. They were probably mine, too. The world slowed and quieted when George and I walked, giving me time to reflect and even daydream. Today, though, I focused on Oscar Romero.

Everywhere I turned, people were handing me evidence, and none of it made sense. That bothered me.

The sun was still up when George and I reached the car, but already it was kissing the horizon. I hated driving in the dark, but I took out my phone anyway and called Frannie Hopkins. Her phone rang several times before she answered.

"Hey," I said. "This is Hana Blackwood. We talked on your porch about Oscar Romero."

She said nothing, but I could hear her breathe.

"How sure are you that Breanna Moore and Rachel Tibbals had sexual relationships with him? You said they fought over him, but I've found no evidence of that."

Again, I paused. She said nothing.

"If you're covering for somebody, now's the time to come clean."

I counted to ten before speaking again.

"I don't think you were honest with me," I said. "We should talk. Where'd the condoms come from?"

I waited.

"If you don't want to talk on the phone, we'll talk in person. I'm in St. Augustine now. I'll see you in a few hours."

I hung up and looked to George. He seemed to grin back at me. I didn't want to go back to Pollard, but I was getting somewhere.

"Want to drive back to the cabin?"

He furrowed his brow and tilted his head to the side, signaling his confusion. Then he started panting happily. I wished I could smile that easily.

"Okay, bud," I said. "Let's go."

21

Elaine slid Frannie Hopkins's phone back in her pocket and looked to Joseph. He had already been working for over ten hours and had hours more work to do. The pair stood in front of Frannie Hopkins's home. Joseph wore a stiff Bryant County sheriff's deputy uniform that Elaine had stolen years ago.

When he woke up that morning, he hadn't expected to stand on the porch of a murdered woman in a stolen sheriff's deputy uniform, but circumstances had compelled Elaine to enable long-planned emergency measures. Joseph appreciated her foresight. It made his job much easier.

"That was Ms. Blackwood," she said. "She knows Frannie lied to her about the condoms, and now she's coming for a chat."

Like many rural police departments, the Bryant County Sheriff's Office had a limited budget and relied on the State Highway Patrol at night for its emergency calls. Elaine paid the local department's sole IT professional to keep her apprised of the comings and goings of the department. He was expensive but helpful. Today, he had earned his paycheck by rerouting those calls to her instead of to the Highway Patrol's dispatcher.

"Blackwood's quick," said Joseph. "You have a plan for her?"

Elaine shook her head.

"No, but she's coming here to the house. We have a few hours."

"I'll set up, then," said Joseph. "Daniel's better with a pistol than me, but I'm far better with a rifle. I'll shoot her as soon as I have a clean shot."

Elaine considered the suggestion but shook her head.

"We need information from her first. Take her alive."

Joseph drew in a breath and let it out slowly as he thought.

"We'll take her to the cabin, then. She'll talk if we hurt her enough."

"No," said Elaine, shaking her head again. "I don't trust information gleaned through torture. Blackwood's a cop—or at least she was. She thinks like a cop. If she thinks we're cops, too, she'll believe we're following the same rules she does. We'll use that."

Joseph furrowed his brow.

"How?"

"We'll call Leeland and see if he can get us into the station. It's empty now and will be all night. We'll use interior rooms and the back door. No one will see us. If we get her to trust us, she'll tell us everything she knows. Then we'll drive her to the middle of nowhere and shoot her."

Joseph considered her.

"Using the station is audacious."

"It's also our best shot to get what we need. Call Leeland and set it up." She paused. "You look good in a uniform, by the way. You should keep it."

"I will," he said. "If Leeland can get us into the station without getting caught, he deserves a bonus."

She tilted her head to the side.

"Probably. I'll consider it. In the meantime, I'm going to interview Zane Hopkins and see what he knows and who he's talked to. We'll kill him, too, but I've got an idea for that. We need to stop this before it spirals."

Joseph looked down.

"Any word on the safrole yet?"

The skin around Elaine's face looked tight, and her lips curled downward. For a moment, she clenched her jaw. Then she shook her head.

"I contacted Colonel Sok in Cambodia. He has twenty-eight barrels available, but they'll cost us. I'm pissed, but we have to play the hand life dealt us."

"Daniel and I can pick it up," he said. "It'll be one last job."

"I'm glad I can count on you," she said. "Now talk to Leeland. And remind him to disable the security system. I don't want that going off while we work."

Joseph nodded. He had soft blue eyes. She had noticed them before, but she hadn't focused on them. She liked the way they looked. He wished her luck and then stepped outside. She walked into a tidy kitchen with cabinets on two walls and a wooden breakfast table. Daniel sat on one side of the table. Zane sat on the other. Zane was in his early twenties. His unkempt black hair tumbled down his forehead, partially covering his eyes and forcing him to rake it back every few moments. Stubble covered the pale skin of his chin and cheeks.

Elaine smiled at them both.

"Your partner needs you out front, Officer Nakamura," she said. "I'm going to talk to Mr. Hopkins."

Daniel stood.

"Good luck, Detective."

She thanked him, and he left the room. Elaine sat in Daniel's still-warm chair. She smiled apologetically at Zane.

"Sorry about having to step out," she said. "We run with a minimal staff at night, and I got a call. Let's start over. I'm Detective Elaine Johnson with the Missouri State Highway Patrol. Your mom is

Frannie Hopkins, and you think she's dead. Tell me about that."

"I know she's dead. I saw it happen," he said, his voice soft. "Two guys killed her this morning and then buried her in the woods. I was hiding in the back of her truck. Then, when they shot her, I ran. They didn't see me."

She nodded.

"Could you identify these men?"

He shook his head.

"Not really. I didn't see it well. One had light brown skin. He may have been Hispanic. He had black hair. The other guy was white and really old. Like forty or fifty. The white guy was in charge. He talked to my mom while the Hispanic guy shot her."

Zane's observational skills lacked precision, but he still posed a threat.

"Did you film this murder or take pictures?"

He looked at the table.

"I should have," he said. "Sorry. I wasn't thinking, I guess."

"It's okay, honey," said Elaine, reaching across the table to touch his arm. "You were scared, and you saw your mom die. Nothing here is your fault. You're the victim, but you're safe now. Did you tell anybody else about what you saw?"

"I didn't have the chance. Mom set this up in the woods, so it took me a while to reach the road. I didn't have a cell signal out there. As soon as I had one, I called 911. You picked me up."

The story had more holes in it than a colander. A real detective would have pushed him and tried to figure out why Frannie Hopkins had met two trained murderers in the middle of nowhere, but she already knew—Frannie Hopkins had gotten greedy. She deserved a bullet to the chest. Elaine pretended to consider Zane.

"Here's the problem: the Hispanic guy and the white guy are known to us, and they're very dangerous. They're suspected in the deaths of half a dozen people. We don't have the resources to keep you safe here, so we'll drive to Springfield as soon as my men come back. Is that okay with you?"

He nodded.

"The men who killed your mom are expert marksmen, and your house has an awful lot of windows," she said. "These guys could shoot you at a thousand yards, and there'd be nothing we could do to stop them."

He lowered himself in his chair.

"What are we going to do?" he asked.

She pretended to think.

"We'll take you to the county sheriff's office. It has holding cells in the basement. They're not comfortable, but at least you'll be safe there for a while. And I need you to make me a promise."

He swallowed and nodded.

"Okay."

"Don't trust anybody but me. This situation is more dangerous than you realize. The men who killed your mom are the most dangerous people I've ever investigated. I don't know how deeply embedded they are in Pollard. This isn't my station, and I don't know the officers here. You can't talk to anybody but me, and you can't let anybody know you're here. In fact, give me your cell phone. You're alive because nobody knows where you are. The men who killed your mother are tracking you, though. I can almost guarantee it."

"They can find me with my phone?"

"Oh, yeah," she said. "These men are professionals."

He handed her the phone as if it were molten metal. She made a show of removing the battery before slipping it in her pocket. Then she told him to stay in the kitchen and away from the windows. He practically dove to the floor. Elaine almost felt sorry for him. Then again, he had gone with his mother when she had tried to steal from her. Joseph or Daniel could have gotten hurt. That Frannie died instead was a matter of luck. He deserved what he was getting.

She left the house and joined Joseph and Daniel on the front porch. Joseph was still on the phone.

"Is that Leeland?" she asked. Joseph nodded. "May I talk to him?"

"Sure," he said, holding out the phone. She took it and held it to her ear.

"Leeland, it's Elaine," she said. "Are you able to get us in?"

He grunted.

"It's complicated," he said. "The building's empty, but I'd have to alter the logs for the security system, and I'd have to alter video from the surveillance system, too. It's doable, but if I get caught, I'd go to prison."

"That's true," she said. "And that's the bargain you struck when you agreed to work with me. I've paid you good money for years, and you've done good work for me when I've asked. Now I need you to continue doing your job. If you refuse, I'll bury you six feet in the ground, and you won't have to worry about prison. Is that clear?"

"Yeah," he said, his voice soft.

"When can we get in?"

"The station's empty now. Text me when you get there., and I'll unlock the back door remotely."

"Thank you, Leeland," she said. "You're a valuable employee, and I appreciate your service."

She hung up and handed Joseph his phone.

"Drive Zane to the station in Daniel's pickup. I'm going to go to the office and pick up the Volvo."

"The Volvo's a junker," said Joseph. "What are you planning?"

"Something that'll get both Zane and Blackwood off our backs for good. Do your jobs. We'll all be safe. Put Zane in a cell in the basement and get a pair of cruisers. Ask Leeland where the keys are stored. We're going to end this Oscar Romero nonsense tonight."

22

George and I got in the car and headed south once more. The longer I drove, the more uneasy I felt. Everybody who knew Oscar said nice things about him and then lied their asses off about his death. That made no sense. You don't tell me you cared for a guy in one breath and then lie about his murder in the next. Someone was playing us all.

Once we reached Pollard, I drove to my cabin and set up the dog's portable kennel in the living room. I loved George, and I loved having him around, but dogs his size needed a lot of sleep. If he stayed up too much longer, he'd get cranky and start making my job harder. So I put him in the kennel and zipped him up. He curled into a ball and started snoring before I left again.

Then I drove to Frannie Hopkins's house. The moment I parked, though, I swore aloud. A pair of uniformed police officers exited the home. One officer was Asian and probably thirty. The other was forty or forty-five and Caucasian. They waved. I assumed they were expecting me. I kept my hands on the steering wheel as they came toward my car.

The Asian officer pulled my door open with his right hand while keeping his hand over the grip of his pistol.

"Show me your hands and get out of the car, ma'am."

I drew in a slow breath and tried to keep the stress out of my voice.

"Before I move, know that there's a .45-caliber pistol in the glove box. I don't plan to reach for it. It's loaded, but there's not a round in the chamber. You can get it out yourself."

The Asian officer nodded.

"I will."

The Caucasian walked to the front of my Subaru and pointed his weapon at my chest through the front window.

"Keep your left hand on the steering wheel. Then bring your right hand down to the seat belt," he said. "If you make a sudden move, I will shoot you."

"I don't doubt it," I said, doing as he asked. Once my seat belt was unhooked, I brought my hand back to the steering wheel, at which point he ordered me to extend my arms outside the car and then step out. The Asian officer, meanwhile, pulled a cruiser to a stop behind my Subaru.

After searching me for weapons, the Caucasian officer had me sit in the cruiser while he and his partner searched my vehicle. About an hour later, an unmarked Volvo sedan parked on the road, and a woman got out. She was in her early thirties and pretty. Her makeup was impeccable, not something I saw in police officers often. A navy jacket hugged her trim torso and pantsuit.

She conferred with the officers and then opened my door.

"Evening, Ms. Blackwood," she said. "I'm Elaine Johnson, and I'm a detective with the Missouri State Highway Patrol. You were seen near Phil Mason's house at the time of his death. It's on video. You said you own the cabin next door?"

I furrowed my brow.

"That's what this is about?" I asked. "I thought we cleared this up."

She crossed her arms and said nothing, so I swore under my breath.

"You're wasting your time," I said. "I own the property next door, but I didn't kill Sheriff Mason."

She considered me and then tilted her head to the side.

"Someone bashed Sheriff Mason's head in with a rock," she said. "We found the rock. Care to guess where we found it?"

"No, but thank you."

She lowered her chin and narrowed her eyes.

"Not even a guess?"

"Only a moron would guess. If I guessed and got it right, I'd look guilty. If I guessed and got it wrong, you'd call me a liar. I'm not interested in games."

She straightened and blinked as she considered me. Then she nodded.

"Okay, fine. No games. I found the rock in your cabin. It had a significant quantity of dried blood on it. It also contained hair that appears to be a match for Sheriff Mason's. It had your fingerprints on it. We got them from St. Louis County."

I looked away.

"I have nothing to say."

"Why'd you kill him?" she asked. "We'll start with that."

I snickered.

"You're not very good at this, are you?"

She straightened.

"What do you mean?"

"The rocks around here are limestone. It's nearly impossible to pull latent fingerprints from limestone. It's too porous. If you're going to lie to me, give me a reasonable lie."

For just a split second, she stared at me, her eyes hard. Then she cleared her throat and looked down.

"If you didn't kill Phil Mason, who did? Yours was the only car anywhere near his house at the time of his death."

"No idea," I said. "Can I go now?"

Instead of answering, she shut the cruiser's door and walked to my Subaru. I shook my head and closed my eyes, hoping my growing headache would dissipate. After ten minutes of searching, the detective called the uniforms toward her. A moment later, the Asian officer retrieved a plastic evidence bag from the cruiser's trunk, and the detective walked toward me, holding a bagged firearm.

When she pulled open my door, she said nothing. I opened my eyes wide.

"Congratulations! You found a firearm," I said. "It's a Colt 1911. It's older than me, but it's a good gun."

She looked at the bag and shook her head.

"Guess again, Ms. Blackwood," she said. "This is a SIG Sauer P229R. Looks like it's chambered for a .40-caliber Smith & Wesson round. That's the same caliber that was used to kill Frannie Hopkins."

I drew in a surprised breath.

"Frannie's dead?"

The detective nodded. The muscles at the small of my back tightened, my skin tingled, and a knot grew in my gut.

"Where'd you find that gun?" I asked.

"Beneath your front seat," she said.

For just a split second, I wondered whether I had put a gun there. Then I realized how absurd that was.

"It's not my gun. My hands are small, so I can't comfortably shoot the 229. And I hate the .40-caliber round. It's all compromise with little upside."

"It was in your car, though."

Again, I shook my head and started to tell her it wasn't my gun. Then I paused as I realized something.

"When did Mrs. Hopkins die?"

"We haven't established the time of death yet."

"Was it today?" I asked, lowering my chin. The detective blinked.

"We haven't established the time of death yet."

"I haven't been here today," I said. "I spent the morning with a friend in Pollard, and then I drove north to St. Augustine. If Hopkins died today, I couldn't have done it."

The detective rolled her eyes.

"As I've already stated, we don't know when Mrs. Hopkins died yet. I think I just found her murder weapon, though."

I looked at the gun.

"I knew the sheriff's department had dirty cops, but I didn't know the Highway Patrol did, too."

She raised her eyebrows and leaned forward.

"What are you accusing me of?"

It didn't matter what she did or what I said. She and the officers with her had firearms, and I didn't. Nothing I said would improve the situation.

"I'm invoking my right to remain silent."

"Fine."

She slammed the cruiser's door shut, and I leaned my head back against the seat and sighed.

"Damn."

23

The cops talked in front of my Subaru for several minutes, giving me a moment to think. My best option was to sit quietly and let Detective Johnson and the uniformed officers work. Once they pressed charges, I'd get a lawyer, who'd poke so many holes in their case even a blind person would be able to see through it. Then I'd sue everyone for harassment and wrongful prosecution. The trick would be surviving long enough to make it to court. That wasn't a sure bet.

Eventually, the Asian officer got in the cruiser in which I sat.

"I'd like to call a lawyer."

The officer looked over his shoulder to back out of the driveway but didn't acknowledge me or my request. Detective Johnson's unmarked Volvo followed us. I gritted my teeth and waited.

We drove for a few minutes and then parked

outside the Bryant County Sheriff's Office's headquarters. My driver opened my door and reached for my elbow to escort me out of the car. The department already had my personal information, and Detective Johnson declined to take my fingerprints or confiscate my civilian clothes. Once we were inside, she patted me down again but declined to give me a full body search for drugs or other weapons. More than likely, that meant they didn't plan to hold me here. Or that they were terrible at their jobs. Either was possible.

The station had three holding cells in the basement. The Caucasian officer escorted me to the one nearest the stairs. A young man sat in the far cell. Like me, he wore civilian clothes. An empty cell separated us. Tears streaked down his cheeks, and his eyes were red. Hopefully he wasn't talkative. The uniformed officer removed my handcuffs and was about to shut my cell door when I cleared my throat.

"Hey," I said. "I'd like to make a phone call, please. My dog is alone in my cabin. I need somebody to take care of him, and I'd like to call an attorney."

He smiled at me.

"I'll see what I can do."

"Thank you."

He left. Then I sat down on the bed and lowered my head. The kid looked at me and opened his mouth to say something, but I cut him off.

"I'm not in a talking mood, buddy," I said. "I've had a bad day."

"My mom was murdered today."

I shifted on the cold, metal slab. If they had planned to keep me overnight, they would have given me a mattress. Hopefully I wouldn't be here too much longer.

"Sorry for your loss," I said. "Are you Frannie Hopkins's kid?"

He nodded but said nothing.

"Why'd they arrest you?" I asked.

"I'm not under arrest. This is protective custody."

I looked at him. His cell door was closed.

"Can you leave if you wanted?"

He shook his head.

"If you can't leave, you're under arrest," I said. "Why are you in protective custody?"

"They thought I was in danger," he said.

"From whom?"

"I can't talk about that."

Nothing about this situation was right. My stomach hurt, and muscles all over my body ached. A heavy weight seemed to press down on me as I stood and paced.

"Who'd you talk to at the police department?" I asked.

"I'm not supposed to say anything."

"I used to be a detective in St. Louis. This isn't right," I said. "Anybody know you're here?"

"Just the police."

I nodded and felt the knot in my gut tighten.

"Did they take your cell phone?"

"Only so the people after me wouldn't use it to track me down."

I walked to my cell door and half-heartedly tried to open it. It didn't budge. He watched me and then walked to his own door. It, too, didn't move. Then he kicked it and nearly fell backwards.

"You could kick that thing until your leg falls off, and it won't move," I said. "They should return soon to let us go to the bathroom. I'll talk to them then and see what's going on."

He nodded. I sat down to think. We needed to get out of here. Even if Detective Johnson thought I had killed somebody, she had no reason to lock this kid up. So I sat and waited and felt my stomach tighten and my heartbeat quicken with every minute.

Eventually Detective Johnson came into the basement. She looked as if she were in decent shape. If she opened my cell door, I could probably kill her if I had to, but it might be tough. Unfortunately, as she walked to my cell, she kept her back to the far wall, well out of my reach. Her eyes passed from me to the kid.

"Okay, guys," she said, her voice low. "You're both in a cell because I don't trust this department or its officers." She looked to the kid. "I'm sorry about your mom, Zane, and I'm sorry you're in a cell now. This isn't how we usually do things, but I'm trying to keep you safe."

She looked at me.

"Ms. Blackwood, I don't know what you're doing here, but you stepped into a hornet's nest. You and Zane would be dead now if you weren't in this cell."

I crossed my arms, unsure how much I bought this. Zane leaned forward.

"I don't want to die."

"I know," said Johnson. "Tweedle Dee and Tweedle Dum are on an errand, so the station's empty. We're getting out of here while we can. A US attorney is waiting to talk to you in a federal courthouse in Springfield. You can call your own lawyer if you want one, too. Sound okay to you two?"

Zane nodded and looked to me.

"I knew we could trust her."

"Why does the US attorney want to talk to us?" I asked.

Johnson hesitated but then lowered her chin.

"Because he thinks you witnessed a crime."

"Okay," I said, nodding slowly. "He's the US attorney and won't involve himself in a local murder or some other local crime. What federal crime did we witness?"

Her eyes flicked up and down me.

"I'm the messenger, okay? The situation sucks, I get that, but I can't change it," she said. "From what

I've gathered, you're in Pollard to investigate Oscar Romero. Are you working with anybody?"

"No," I said, surprised she'd asked. "And I came here because my parents own a cabin in town. Why?"

She furrowed her brow.

"So you're not investigating Oscar?"

"I am, but that's not why I came. What's going on, and why do you care?"

"If you had a partner, we'd pick him or her up, too, to keep him safe," she said. "Beyond that, I don't have time to explain anything. The police in this station are corrupt. Come with me, and we'll talk."

"Why'd you take Zane's phone?"

"Because that's what you do when you put someone in protective custody," she said, her voice growing sharper. "I had to make it look real. Do you want to leave or not?"

I crossed my arms.

"Give him his phone and let him call an attorney."

She smiled.

"I would, but his phone is in an evidence bag in a safe. Yours is, too, by the way."

"Then let him use your phone."

She closed her eyes and held up a hand.

"Fine. He can use my phone, but we need to get going."

"Thank you," I said, not moving. "Give it to

him."

She gritted her teeth and smiled again, but it looked pained.

"I'll give it to him in the car," she said, walking toward Zane's cell. She unlocked it with a button on the far wall. "Let's go."

Zane walked out of his cell, and then Johnson walked in front of mine and paused. Then she sighed and hit the button, unlocking my cell. I slid the door to the side but didn't step out.

"Well?" asked Johnson. "You coming or not?"

None of my choices were good. I didn't trust anyone from the sheriff's office, and Johnson's explanation of the situation made no sense. Zane, though, was just a kid. If I left him on his own, I suspected a tourist would find his body bobbing in the lake tomorrow morning.

I stepped forward.

"Give Zane your phone now, and I'll go with you. He can use it in the car."

She glared at me before reaching into her pocket and handing him a slim black phone. Then she gave me a cold, black smile.

"Happy?"

"No, but let's go anyway."

24

Detective Johnson led us through the station, out the back door, and to the parking lot. The night air smelled sweet and held just a hint of impending rain. I had seen the detective's Volvo before, but I hadn't looked at it up close. The red paint obscured rust that had eaten into the wheel wells, while duct tape covered a tear in the rear seat's black leather. Even from a distance, it smelled like burning engine oil.

"The Highway Patrol doesn't give you a car?" I asked.

"Budget cuts," she said. "This one runs, and I can afford it after my divorce. You have a problem with that?"

"No," I said. "Sorry about your divorce."

"Me, too," she said. "I wish I had a better lawyer."

"Or at least that your husband had a worse one,"

I said. She smiled and nodded. Then she unlocked the car, and we got in. The interior smelled like stale coffee, but the leather seats felt comfortable, and the seat belts worked. The fan belt squealed as she turned the key. The noise stopped, though, as she shifted into gear and left the parking lot.

I looked to Zane.

"You've got her phone. Make a call."

"To whom?" he asked, his brow furrowed.

I almost said he should call his lawyer, but he was a kid, and his mom spent her career on the housekeeping staff at a summer camp. He wouldn't know an attorney. The engine noise rose as Johnson rocketed through town. The acceleration pushed me back into the seat.

"You got an aunt or uncle who cares about you?"

"My aunt Jean lives in Iowa, but I don't know her phone number," he said. "It's in my phone."

I thought back to my conversation with his mom. We were practically flying down the road and had already reached the edge of Pollard. I closed my eyes.

"Your sister goes to college, right? Call her."

"She's a bitch."

I squeezed my jaw tight.

"Just call her," I said. "Your mom's dead, and you're in police custody. Tell her you're on your way to the courthouse in Springfield. Ask her to meet you there. Tell her that if you don't show up, she should call Alexa Swaine in St. Louis. She's a defense attorney, and she'll be able to help if there's an emergency."

He narrowed his eyes.

"Why do I need a lawyer?"

"Just give me the phone," I said, my voice sharp. "I'll take care of it."

He handed me the phone, and I hit the home button to power it up. Then I glanced up front.

"Hey, Johnson, I need your fingerprint."

"You'll need both my fingerprint and my passcode," she said. "Give me a minute. Once we're out of Bryant County, I'll find somewhere to pull off."

It seemed reasonable. The streetlights ended, and the road narrowed. My stomach churned as we drove around hills, over them, and sometimes in valleys cut straight through them. At the speed Detective Johnson was driving and with the loose shocks on her Volvo, it was like riding in a boat on choppy water.

I glanced at Zane. He sat straight up with his hands at his sides as he swayed.

"You okay, Zane?"

He closed his eyes.

"I feel sick."

He didn't seem up to moving, so I leaned over and hit the button to open his window, but nothing happened.

"Can we get some air back here? Zane looks like he's going to puke."

Johnson reached to the center console and flicked a switch for the air conditioning. Nothing happened.

"Sorry," she said. "Doesn't look like it works. Windows don't work, either. It's an old car."

She should have known the air conditioner didn't work. She shouldn't have needed to touch the switch.

"Park somewhere and unlock your phone," I said, trying to force the tension from my voice. "We've got to be a couple of miles outside of town already."

"I'll park when I feel safe. We might be away from town, but I don't want to get hit by a drunk high school kid taking his dad's pickup for a joyride. Highway Patrol picks up a lot of those accidents on roads like this."

I covered the phone with my hand and hit the home button to wake it up. Johnson glanced in the rearview mirror.

"Can you turn that off?" she asked. "It's creating a glare."

"In a minute," I said, hitting the emergency button in the lower left of the screen and bypassing the phone's security feature so I could make an emergency call. I dialed 911 and put the phone to my ear. Nothing happened.

"Put the phone down, Hana."

Our car slowed and then stopped. We were in the low point of a valley between two big hills. I pulled the phone from my ear and swore. The terrain must have been blocking my signal.

"Who are you calling?" asked Zane. "We're fine. She's taking us somewhere safe."

Johnson turned off the car and opened her door. Moist but warm air rushed inside. Something smelled almost fishy, making me wonder whether we were by the lake. The hills around us blotted the starlight and cast a shadow over our vehicle. Johnson grunted as she jammed the door latch up. Then she did it again, and the plastic broke. Afterward, she slammed the door and walked straight ahead, up the hill, ignoring us completely.

"Shit," I said, watching her leave. I tried to open my door, but it didn't budge. "Open your door, Zane."

Zane's door didn't budge, either.

"She must have child locks or something," he said. "Where's she going?"

I ignored him and unhooked my seat belt so I could lean forward. Somebody had already broken the front door latch on the passenger side. I hadn't thought to look earlier.

"I'm going to break my window. Cover your face."

I slid down so I could kick the window. My heel didn't do a damn thing. I kicked again, but the glass continued to hold.

"What are you doing?" asked Zane. "She's probably just trying to get a cell signal or something."

"I've got her phone. She's not trying to get a signal, and she's not trying to take us somewhere safe. She locked us in her car in the middle of nowhere, and she's leaving. We need to get out of here before we find out why."

Joseph breathed easier as he saw the Volvo crest the hill and then descend into their kill box. He breathed even easier when Elaine opened her door, stepped out, and broke the interior door handle, locking Blackwood and Zane inside. Joseph slid the receiver back on the Colt 1911 they had confiscated from Blackwood earlier. It seemed almost cruel to kill Blackwood with her own pistol, but Elaine's plan required it.

Once Blackwood and Zane died, Daniel and Joseph would take her body out of the Volvo, torch the car, and dump her corpse in the deepest part of the lake. The fire would burn away her blood and other forensic evidence she left behind, leaving the police to find Zane's body inside the cab, riddled with bullets from Hana's pistol.

Joseph didn't like complicated plans, but this solved multiple problems at once. The police would think Blackwood killed Zane and ran. They'd look for her, but they'd never find her. Meanwhile, her upstart investigation into Oscar Romero would flounder, a witness to Frannie Hopkins's murder would die, and Elaine's business would sell. Everything would work out.

"Can I have some keys, please?" asked Elaine, once she drew close.

Daniel tossed her a set of keys from his pocket. She barely broke stride toward the pickup he had driven.

"Blackwood's smarter than we realized," she said. "You need to move before she and the kid break out of the car. I'm going to the office in Springfield. We'll swap cars there, Daniel. And Joseph, I want to see you tonight, too. We need to talk at my place."

Joseph nodded.

"I'll text you before I head over."

"Good," she said. "I'll see you later."

He watched her climb into Daniel's pickup. Then Joseph turned to his partner.

"What do you think she needs?"

Daniel raised his eyebrows.

"I believe the term is booty call."

Joseph shook his head and positioned himself on the hill overlooking the Volvo.

"We don't have that kind of relationship."

"Drink some wine with her and see what happens."

Joseph reflected on his last few engagements with Elaine and nodded. She was attractive—beautiful, even—but his feelings went well beyond that. He cared about her and wanted good things for her. He wanted to share the world with her and see her smile. She was important to him.

"I think I will."

"They're moving," said Daniel, nodding toward the car. "Car's rocking. They're trying to break out."

Joseph cleared his mind and slipped his finger from the trigger guard to the trigger.

"Goodnight, Ms. Blackwood," said Joseph. "Nothing personal. This is just business."

He took the slack out of the trigger and fired.

25

The window flexed and absorbed every kick I threw at it—just as it was designed to do. I needed a hammer or center punch...or something.

"People are moving outside," said Zane. "They're climbing the hill."

"Forget them. Just break the window," I said. "Try to get the headrest off. It should have a metal pole on it to connect it to the seat."

Zane tried pulling on the headrest, but it didn't budge. Then he started hitting it. I ignored him and looked around. The carpet had vacuum lines as if someone had just cleaned it. Not even a single soda can or stray receipt littered the floor. There was nothing here. I swore under my breath.

Then the first shot rang out.

My heart skipped. I dove to the floor as a round pinged against the vehicle. A second shot followed the first. Then a third hit the driver's seat.

"Are they shooting at us?" asked Zane, his hands over his ears.

"Get down, dumbass," I shouted, reaching for the seat belt. I pulled it down as fast as I could and slunk as low as I could in the footrest. The terrain elevated the shooters above the car, and most of their rounds hit the driver's side. My hands trembled, and sweat beaded on my forehead and dripped into my eyes.

I bunched up the seat belt and flung the metal clip at the window like a sling. On the first strike, nothing happened. On my second swing, though, the hardened steel clip struck the tempered glass, cracking it. I hit it a third time, and the window shattered. My hands trembled, and my heart thudded against my breastbone.

I balled my hand into a fist and punched the glass. Fragments flew outward. I cleared the rest with my seat belt sling and shimmied out. The gunfire echoed against the hillsides. I dove to the ground and ducked behind the engine block for cover. Those same hills that blocked a cell signal cast shadows that hid me well.

"Get out, Zane," I said. "Climb through the window."

It took him a moment, but he started climbing through slowly. The rounds kept coming, hitting the side of the car. Then, the metallic clink of a heavy rifle replaced the sharp reports of a pistol. Round after round slammed into the car, shattering glass. I pulled Zane's hands and dragged him out. He hit the asphalt and rolled onto the grass beside the road, dazed. The kid didn't move, so I slapped him in the face to get his attention.

"Stay low and run to the woods."

He nodded, but I didn't know whether he understood. I couldn't help him if I was dead, so I crouched and sprinted toward the woods, hoping he'd follow. Once I reached the tree line, I ducked behind the thick trunk of a silver maple and looked back toward the car. I couldn't see Zane, but hopefully he had run away.

I ran deeper into the forest. Thorns and briars tore at my exposed skin and clothes, but I couldn't slow down until I put some distance between me and the car. Then I reached a small creek and ducked down in the cold water. Two men shouted behind me, but nobody fired another weapon.

My heart thudded. Whenever the trees thinned overhead, the moonlight shone down on me like a spotlight, making me easy to see. I smeared mud from the creek on my face, on my arms, and in my hair. It wasn't perfect, but I was dark enough.

Then I started running again.

For about half an hour, I followed an old deer trail through the woods, stepping as lightly and delicately as I could. Finally, I crouched low beneath a bushy pin oak, the lowest branches of which touched the ground and formed a dark cocoon. Squirrels skittered on the tree above me. I hid there long enough for the mud on my arms, face, and hair to dry and crack. Aside from the animals, I heard nothing.

Then I ran again. After half an hour of jogging, I found a road. The air smelled fishy, so I followed the odor until I reached the lakeshore, which I then followed to Pollard.

My gut ached dully, but otherwise, I felt almost numb. If I'd had any tools, I would have stolen a car and left town. Since I didn't, I walked until I found a familiar street and used that to orient myself until I found the Hopkins's home. My Subaru was no longer in the driveway. I brought my hand to my face. Dirt caked my skin and cracked when I moved. I smelled like shit.

"Damn," I said, my voice low as I looked around. The night was dead quiet. Nobody was out. My cabin was about five miles away, so I started walking. The sun was rising by the time I reached the driveway. The instant I saw it, I stopped midstep. My Subaru was parked outside.

The hairs on the back of my neck rose as I walked toward the car. This made no sense. If anything, Johnson and her thugs should have dumped the car in the lake. They had no reason to bring it to my cabin. The car's interior looked just as it should. I didn't know what to think, so I left it alone and walked to the cabin. The front door was unlocked. The instant I opened it, George started barking. At least he was okay.

"Hush, dude," I said. "I've had a long night."

The cabin looked undisturbed at first, but then I found my purse, wallet, and keys on the mail table beside the door. They shouldn't have been there. The Asian cop had confiscated them when he arrested me. George whined.

"Hush, buddy," I said, bringing a hand to my mouth. Three cops arrested me, took me to their station, and then tried to kill me. Then they moved my car back to my cabin and put my stuff back inside. Everything they did carried a risk. They would have known that, and yet they went out of their way to break into my cabin and return my car. Why?

I didn't have an answer. Then I looked to George. He had a thick rawhide bone in his kennel. I kept a bag of rawhides with me when I traveled because George loved them, but I never would have given him one in his kennel. Little pieces of rawhide could have come off and choked him. It would have kept him quiet, though.

I had been in the woods for several hours, so Johnson had time to do all this, but why?

I unzipped his kennel and let George out. He tried to take his rawhide with him, but I grabbed it from him. Then he whined before focusing on me. He smelled my hands and then my face before licking his lips and yawning. Apparently, he didn't know what to make of my appearance.

"I'll take you outside soon," I said. "First, I'll

change and think. Watch the door."

He didn't understand, but he lay down while I stripped off my soiled clothes. My cabin didn't have running water, so I used bottled water to clean off the mud. Then, I changed into fresh clothes and realized how much my old ones stunk. I threw them in a trash bag and took them to the porch. Finally, I took George out for a quick walk in the woods.

When I got back, I called Shane on my cell phone. Two hundred and fifty miles northeast of Pollard, his cell phone rang in Clayton, Missouri, and he answered in a confused, sleepy voice.

"Hana, hey," he said. "It's still dark. You okay?"

"Not really," I said. "Sorry it's early. I didn't know who else to call. Something weird just happened."

He cleared his throat.

"Okay. Tell me what's going on."

"I'm in Pollard. The police arrested me for murder a few hours ago, and then they tried to kill me. I was in a Volvo 850 with a kid named Zane Hopkins. He may be dead. The lead detective was named Elaine Johnson. She claims to be a detective with the Missouri State Highway Patrol, but she's not. She drove me and Zane Hopkins out to the middle of nowhere and tried to kill us. I escaped, but it took a couple hours. When I got back to my cabin, I found my car in the driveway. My wallet, keys, and cell phone were inside the cabin. They brought everything back."

He paused.

"I don't know how to respond."

I ran my right hand through my hair and sighed heavily.

"My car shouldn't have been outside the cabin. It should have been at Frannie Hopkins's house. And my keys and wallet should have been in the police evidence locker. Instead, they were in my cabin." I paused for a moment. "I'm not crazy."

Shane paused and then drew in a breath.

"Are you hurt?"

"No," I said. "I've got some cuts on my hand when I broke a window to escape a car, but they're superficial."

He drew in another slow breath.

"Okay. You should get those cuts checked out at the hospital. Tell them everything you told me. They'll keep you safe there."

I rubbed my eyes. If I told them the truth, they'd pump me full of tranquilizers and label me psychotic. Which Shane knew.

"I'm not having a mental breakdown, but thanks," I said. "I'll talk to you later."

I hung up before he could say anything else. Then I looked to the dog.

"I'm not crazy," I said. George panted but said nothing. Talking to a dog didn't help my case, but I didn't care. "Come on, buddy. We've got to disappear before they come looking for us."

George stood as soon as I grabbed his leash. I

wanted to leave town, but I needed to figure this out first. I needed to find Zane Hopkins, too. He could back up my story. Detective Johnson had already tried to kill us once. We had both seen her face and the faces of her men, which made us both threats. They'd come after us again. Next time, at least, I'd be ready.

George and I left the cabin and hid in the shade beneath a pine tree across the street. The landscape sloped downward, blocking any driver's view. George had no idea what we were doing, but he liked me, and he enjoyed being outside. He would have lain in pine needles beside me all day.

As I lay there, my adrenaline faded, leaving weary exhaustion in its place. I had been awake for over twenty-four hours. At eighteen, that wouldn't have slowed me down. At thirty-two, my legs felt heavy, my back ached, and I hated everyone in the world.

I watched the cabin until noon, but nobody came. Maybe I was wrong about this. Or maybe they thought I was dead. Either way, I needed rest. George could watch the door for me.

We walked back inside, and I gave him a cup of food before I crashed on the sofa. I fell asleep almost the moment I closed my eyes. I slept hard for a few hours, but then the dog licked my face, and my eyes shot open. George wagged his tail and seemed to grin. I gently pushed him away.

"Go away, butthead."

He sat down, but then somebody knocked on the door.

"It's me. Open the door."

I recognized the voice, so I groaned and swung my legs off the sofa. The moment I opened up, George vaulted up and ran to greet our guest. Shane knelt and petted his cheeks. My old partner glanced at me.

"At least George is happy to see me."

"You shouldn't have come," I said. "How'd you even know I was here?"

He lowered his chin.

"If you didn't want me coming down, you shouldn't have called me at five AM with a crazy story. And I knew you were here because I asked Candace Miller to track your phone."

Candace was a cyber crimes analyst in my old department. My cases rarely required her expertise, but she was good at her job, and she had a great sense of humor. I liked her a lot. Had I made more effort, we could have been friends. Shane must have called in a favor to convince her to track me at five in the morning, which meant he really had been concerned about me. I lowered my voice.

"Does Ivy know you're here?"

He shook his head.

"No, but I left her a message. She had a ten-hour shift yesterday and didn't get in until six this morning. By then, I was already gone. What's going on?"

I stepped back.

"Come in," I said. "I don't want to stay outside if I don't have to. The locals will probably arrest me if they see me."

Shane didn't move. Then he looked down and sighed.

"I already went by the sheriff's office before coming here," he said. "Nobody arrested you last night. I even called around to neighboring states. There are no open warrants against you in Missouri, Illinois, Tennessee, Arkansas, or Kansas."

I shook my head.

"That's not right," I said, stepping back. "They arrested me last night at Frannie Hopkins's house. Detective Johnson accused me of murdering Phil Mason with a rock. Then they tried to kill me. They may have killed Zane Hopkins. I don't know."

Shane smiled, but the look he gave me was more concerned than happy.

"Are you sure you're okay?"

"I'm fine," I said, my voice growing heated. "They're the problem. I don't know why they're lying to you, but they are. They arrested me last night."

"Okay," he said. "Let's take you by the motel. I'll get a room, and you can shower."

"You don't believe me," I said. "Do you?"

He tilted his head to the side.

"When was the last time you had something to eat?"

It was the kind of thing he might have asked a schizophrenic person raving on the street.

"I'm not crazy."

"I know," he said, softly. "Are you hungry?"

I sighed and raked my fingers through my hair. Dried grit scratched my scalp. "I'm telling you the truth."

"And I'm asking whether you're hungry," he said. "I haven't had lunch yet, and I'm going to get something to eat. Would you like to come?"

I closed my eyes and counted to five.

"If I go, will you listen to me before assuming I'm having a breakdown?"

He nodded and answered softly.

"I will."

"Good. Let me get George's leash."

26

Joseph's legs ached, and his hands and forearms itched from the poison ivy that had grown in the woods surrounding their ambush point. He sat in the front seat of a full-sized panel van. Even his fingers hurt from wrapping around the steering wheel. They had tried to track Hana Blackwood through the woods last night, but she had disappeared. Because of her, they had lost Zane Hopkins, too. At least they knew Zane. With his mother dead, he had nowhere to go but his sister's house. She was a college student at the University of Missouri. Now they just had to wait for him to show up.

Joseph wanted to close his eyes, but it was his turn to watch. Daniel lay in the back of their van, snug in a sleeping bag. His eyes were closed, and his chest rose and fell with regularity. He deserved the sleep after their night.

They had parked in the lot beside a big apartment building a block from campus. Across the street was an American Foursquare home with clapboard siding and a big front porch. The unkempt lawn had more weeds than grass, and window air conditioners protruded from three windows out front. Joseph wouldn't want to touch the metal handrail that led to the porch for fear of getting tetanus. With a massive renovation, the home could be beautiful. Its present owner, though, seemed content to let it fall apart.

Kate Hopkins had a two-bedroom unit on the third floor. It would have been the attic at one time, so her rooms were probably freezing in the winter and blazing hot in the summer, spring, and fall. Living off campus, though, gave her independence that students on campus didn't have. That'd be worth a few cold nights.

Zane should arrive any moment.

Joseph stretched and rubbed his eyes. After chasing Blackwood and Zane through the woods, he and Daniel had returned to the scene to rake the grass for shell casings and sweep the asphalt for broken glass. By the time they finished, it was cleaner than it had been upon their arrival. The old Volvo had been a junker they purchased on Craigslist for eight hundred dollars cash. It barely drove to begin with and wouldn't turn over after they shot it up, so they had to tow it behind Daniel's pickup. They dragged it to a scrap metal yard and left it just outside the fence, the last in a long line of ruined vehicles. Weeds would overgrow it soon enough.

After disposing of the Volvo, they stashed Daniel's pistol—the one that had killed Frannie Hopkins—beneath the front seat of Hana Blackwood's Subaru and then returned the Subaru and her personal items to her cabin. Leeland at the sheriff's office altered his station's security alarm's logs and rerouted emergency calls to the Highway Patrol's dispatcher. They hadn't killed Blackwood, but they had covered up their trail.

After an hour of waiting, a Honda CR-V the color of split pea soup pulled into the driveway and parked in front of the garage. A young woman stepped out and scanned the area. Then she opened the rear. Zane Hopkins jumped out. He wore clean clothes and looked as if he had taken a shower after running through the woods. Elaine had confiscated his cell phone, but Zane had friends in Pollard. They had probably sheltered and clothed him while his sister drove south.

"Zane and Kate are here," said Joseph, glancing in his rearview mirror at his partner, who was rubbing his eyes and already sitting up. "Once you're awake, we'll drive over there and block them in."

Daniel drew in a breath and nodded before climbing into the front seat. They had driven an unmarked white panel van, one of six owned by

Lakeside Pools. Anyone who looked at them would think they were plumbers or electricians on a break between jobs.

Zane and Kate entered the house through a side door. Daniel drew in a breath, rubbed his eyes, and then cleared his throat.

"I'm ready. Let's go."

Joseph reversed their van from its parking spot and then drove across the street. The home's gutters barely clung to the roof, the paint had chipped, and the exterior wall bowed outward. A rock propped the side door open. Joseph never would have let his kids anywhere near that house.

Joseph and Daniel both donned latex gloves, slipcovers over their shoes, and red baseball caps before stepping inside. Each wore navy coveralls with the insignia of a fake air conditioning company on the breast.

An empty hallway led straight ahead with apartments to the left and right. A dingy, red carpet covered the floor, and peeling floral wallpaper covered the walls. Stairs led up. It looked like a shitty retirement home.

The second floor matched the first. The third floor, though, held only one apartment. Kate had locked the door, but it only took Daniel ten or fifteen seconds to pick the deadbolt. Joseph pulled Blackwood's .45-caliber pistol from his pocket and screwed on a suppressor.

"Ready?" he whispered. Daniel nodded, and

then Joseph opened the door, his pistol extended in front of him. Music thumped from the apartment downstairs. Marijuana smoke wafted toward them as they stepped into the living room. Kate had arranged three couches in a U shape facing a television. The coffee table in the middle held a water bong. Zane and his sister sat in front of the TV. Zane's eyes were red with tears. His sister's looked little better.

Neither of them had more than a second to react before Joseph fired. The first round hit Zane in the forehead and exited straight out the back, taking parts of his brain with it. Kate died next from a similar wound. Blood spattered the walls, but no one screamed, and no one ran.

"We're good," said Joseph. He unscrewed the suppressor. It was warm but not too hot. After slipping the pistol and suppressor into his pockets, he and Daniel shut the door and left. There could have been cameras around, so they kept their heads low.

When they reached the van, they drove away without saying a word. A mile later, they stopped by a storm drain. Joseph tossed in the suppressor. Several miles after that, they stopped at another storm drain, and Joseph disposed of the pistol. Columbia wasn't a large town, so it didn't take long for them to reach its outskirts. Once they were far enough away, they pulled into the parking lot of a Baptist church. They both got out and removed their coveralls. Those they put into the church's dumpster. Daniel unscrewed the license plate—which they had stolen from a minivan in the parking lot of an apartment complex in Jefferson City—and replaced it with their actual plate.

They then headed south and drove for several hours before fueling up in Osage Beach, a tourist town near the Lake of the Ozarks. As Daniel filled the tank, Joseph tossed the stolen license plate—along with the remnants of their fast-food breakfast—in a trash can. Finally, they headed home, and Joseph called Elaine.

"Hey," he said. "It's done. Daniel and I are driving back."

"Your tools?" asked Elaine.

"Gone," said Joseph. "We're clear. Everything went as planned."

"I'm glad," she said. "Drive safely. I need you here for another job."

27

Shane checked into the town's only motel, and I showered while he and George walked. Afterward, we went by Frank's Downtown Diner, where we ordered sandwiches to go. Finally, we drove by the park so we could eat in privacy. For twenty minutes, I told Shane about my time in Pollard. He nodded and asked questions, but mostly he listened. When I finished, he wiped his mouth with a napkin and nodded.

"Bad vacation. Next time, consider Disney World."

"People are dead, buddy. It's inappropriate to joke."

He put his elbows on the wooden picnic table. Around us, the grass waved in a slight breeze. A lawnmower droned somewhere nearby, but I couldn't see it.

"What's your plan?" he asked.

"Three police officers tried to kill me last night. You may not believe it, but it's true. I plan to go to their station and ask them why."

Shane considered me and then wadded up his sandwich wrapper.

"Gutsy."

"You're going to be with me," I said. "If we get in trouble, we'll shoot our way out."

"I hope you're kidding," he said.

"Sure. We'll say that."

He looked at me askance. I smiled.

"Okay," he said, shrugging. "Let's go."

He, George, and I left a moment later. Officer Sutton sat behind the counter at the sheriff's office. She nodded to me and then looked to Shane. Finally, she saw George and stood and pointed toward the door.

"You can't bring your dog in here."

"He's my emotional support animal," I said. "Without him, I fall apart. I need to see Troy Lyons and the county prosecutor."

Sutton arched her eyebrows while tilting her head down.

"Why do you need to see them?"

"I went to visit Frannie Hopkins last night, and I was taken into custody by two uniformed deputies and a detective with the Missouri State Highway Patrol. They then tried to kill me."

She narrowed her eyes.

"This supposedly happened last night?"

"Yeah," I said. She blinked.

"Let's get back to this arrest at Frannie Hopkins's house. You said two uniformed officers and a detective arrested you and tried to kill you?"

"That's right."

She considered me and then pointed to the waiting room.

"You sit right there. Sheriff Lyons will be out soon."

Once Shane and I sat down, Sutton hurried toward the rear of the station. About ten minutes later, she and Sheriff Lyons joined us in the waiting room. He seemed to recognize Shane, but he focused on George. I wound my hand around the dog's leash.

"You're not allowed to bring animals into the station."

"He's a service animal," said Sutton. The sheriff raised his eyebrows at me as if to confirm. I shrugged.

"Emotional support," I said. "I'd like to talk about my arrest last night."

"Detective Lewis came by this morning," said Lyons, glancing at Shane. "He asked about it, too. We have no arrest on record."

I told him what had happened, and he asked a lot of questions. The more I spoke, the colder his eyes became. Finally, he crossed his arms.

"We've got a couple of problems here, Ms. Blackwood," he said. "First, my office doesn't operate at night, so nobody was here. Second, we try to maintain a diverse workforce, but we don't have any Asian men or women on staff at the moment."

Muscles all over my body tensed as I looked to Shane.

"If you don't work at night, who takes your emergency calls?"

"The Highway Patrol," he said. "We don't have the call volume to justify a night shift. Anything else you want to accuse us of?"

I looked to Shane.

"Zane Hopkins will back up my story. This really happened."

Shane drew his eyebrows together and pursed his lips. Then he squeezed my shoulder.

"Let me take you home," he said. "You've had a rough time lately. Ivy and I have a guest house. You can stay with us."

I brushed his hand off and stepped back, shaking my head.

"I was arrested last night. I'm not lying, and I'm not making this up."

"We're not saying you are," said Lyons, his voice low. He held a hand toward me the way a hunter might have approached an ensnared animal. "Let's take a couple of breaths and calm down, Ms. Blackwood. Everything's going to be okay."

"Fuck off," I said. "Both of you. Elaine Johnson arrested me at Frannie Hopkins's house. She said she found the rock used to murder Sheriff Mason in my cabin. Then she locked me in the holding cell in the basement. Zane was in a cell, too. She told him he was in protective custody after witnessing his mother's murder. Later she told us she didn't trust the people in this station because they were corrupt."

Shane looked down. George whined, apparently hearing the anger in my voice. I patted his head, and he calmed.

"Frannie Hopkins is dead, too?" asked the sheriff.

"That's what Johnson said," I said. "I didn't ask for proof. Zane said he witnessed the murder."

Lyons looked down and sighed again.

"Ms. Blackwood, if my officers had arrested you, they would have taken you to the Tri-county Justice Center. We don't use the basement cells anymore. I understand that you're scared, but—"

"How would Hana know you had holding cells in the basement unless she had seen them?" asked Shane, interrupting him.

Lyons paused. Then he opened his mouth to speak, but I responded before he could.

"There are three of them," I said. "The bars are painted yellow. Each cell has a single metal slab for a bed. None of them have a toilet. A button on the wall unlocks each cell door. That's a mind-bogglingly stupid arrangement, by the way. Any inmate could throw his shoes at the button and unlock the door."

Shane's gaze hardened. I crossed my arms. The sheriff shifted his weight from one foot to the other.

"You probably saw them in pictures. Every Halloween, we host a party for kids in the community. They go all around the station and the parking lot trick-or-treating. Every year, Jackie Sutton sets up a graveyard scene in the holding cells. There are dozens of photos on our Facebook page."

Shane glanced at me.

"I've never seen the station's Facebook page," I said. "Why the hell would I look up the department on Facebook?"

"I don't know," said Lyons. "You weren't here last night. I don't know what else to tell you. No one from my department arrested you."

"They had a cruiser, and they wore your uniforms."

Lyons closed his eyes and drew in a breath.

"I've indulged you more than enough, Ms. Blackwood," he said, his voice growing sharper. "Detective Lewis came this morning, and I heard him out. I searched our station's logs to make sure nobody came into the building last night. Officer Ellison locked the building up at 8:11 PM last night, and I unlocked the doors at 7:47 AM. Our locks are electronic, and everyone has a unique passcode. No one was here."

"I was here. So was Zane Hopkins."

The sheriff drew in a slow breath and gave me a pained smile.

"It's time for you to leave, Ms. Blackwood," he said. "You've overstayed your welcome."

Shane put a hand on my shoulder and gently squeezed before I could object.

"We'll head out," he said. "Thank you for your time."

The sheriff grunted. I wanted to hit him, but Shane was right. We needed to get out of there before they arrested me again.

Outside, the sun beat down on the concrete walkway. Windows reflected the light like mirrors. A gray-haired woman drove by slowly and stared at us as if we were criminals. I wanted to give her the finger and ask what her problem was. Shane cleared his throat.

"You okay?"

"No, I'm not okay," I said. "Somebody tried to kill me last night, and the local sheriff thinks I'm crazy."

"You're not crazy," said Shane. "I'm going to call a friend. You care if I sit in your car?"

I shook my head. Then I thought better of it and glanced at him.

"If you call a psychiatric hospital and have me admitted against my will, I'll never forgive you."

Shane lowered his chin.

"I'm your friend," he said. "I won't do that."

"Sure," I said. "Fine. I'm going to take a walk."

Shane nodded, walked to my Subaru, and sat in the passenger seat. George and I walked around the block. The heat sapped the raw edge from my anger and allowed me to think again. Having George beside me helped, too. When I got back to my Subaru, Shane was standing outside the car, hanging up his phone.

"We need to find Elaine Johnson," I said. "She's going to be the key to breaking this."

"That was my thought, too," said Shane. "She's not a detective with the Missouri State Highway Patrol. The license bureau has over fifty Elaine Johnsons listed, but I suspect it's a fake name. If you really want, we'll look at pictures later. It'd be weird for her to lie to you about everything but then give you her real name."

"It would be," I said. "So you believe me?"

He considered his answer before speaking.

"It's not about believing you. You've been under a lot of stress lately. You're seeing a therapist, aren't you?"

"For depression," I said, narrowing my eyes at him. "Not psychosis."

He crossed his arms and stood.

"Are you on any drugs?"

"Illegal drugs?" I asked. He nodded. I snickered and turned away, shaking my head. "I can't believe you have the nerve to ask me that."

"You called me at five in the morning to tell me you had just escaped from the police. The sheriff has no idea what you're talking about."

I looked toward the building.

"The sheriff is incompetent," I said, turning to look at my partner again. "If you don't believe me, let's find Zane Hopkins. He'll back up my story. And if we can't find Zane, we'll find the spot where Johnson dumped us off. There'll be evidence. And no, I'm not taking drugs."

Shane drew in a breath but said nothing for a good minute. Finally, I raised my eyebrows.

"You have something to say?"

Shane shifted his weight from one foot to the other as he looked down.

"I think of you like a sister," he said. "You know that, right?"

I softened my voice.

"Yeah."

"What if you're wrong? What if Zane can't corroborate your story?"

I shook my head.

"It doesn't matter," I said. "I'm not wrong. If we can't find Zane, we'll find the spot where Johnson ambushed us. Pollard doesn't have that many roads. We'll find the right one."

"But what if we can't?" asked Shane. He paused and cleared his throat. "Will you talk to Ivy? She's a surgeon, but she's a doctor. Or maybe we can call your therapist together. Maybe she can help."

I sighed.

"I've talked to doctors, and my therapist is a

moron," I said. "She's convinced I'm going to kill myself unless I give myself a reason to get out of bed every morning. She even made me fill out a daily to-do list in a stupid notebook. Every day, I write '*take care of the dog,*' and that's it. Because that's all I can do, apparently. Nobody wants me to do anything else. Nobody wants me to be a cop, nobody wants to be married to me, nobody even wants to talk to me except my dog."

As I spoke, my anger began dissipating, and something else took its place. My throat felt tight, and my eyes grew wet. I shut up and turned away so I wouldn't say anything else. Thankfully, Shane knew me well enough to give me space. After a minute, I drew in some deep breaths. Shane began to speak, but I held up a hand cutting him off.

"I'm fine," I said. "Everything's fine."

I turned. He looked to the ground.

"Let's go for a drive. We'll find the spot they ambushed you and go from there. I can drive if you want."

"Thank you," I said. I paused. "And sorry if I yelled. I didn't mean to. I didn't get a lot of sleep last night."

"It's okay," said Shane. "You've got a lot on your mind."

I did, but I didn't want to share it—even with someone I cared about.

"Let's just drive."

28

Shane drove my Subaru, and I sat in the passenger seat. Pollard was not a pretty town. The landscape was gorgeous, but when its founders built the town a hundred years ago, they cut down and paved over great swathes of forest. The brick shops and offices that remained looked like a thousand other strip malls across the Midwest. Once you left town, though, and entered the forested hills of southern Missouri, it grew more appealing.

For half an hour, I didn't recognize a single road. Then, after turning around half a dozen times, the car rolled to the right as it came over a hill, and my stomach dropped as we descended.

"Go faster," I said. "Johnson drove faster."

Shane pressed on the accelerator. Johnson's old Volvo had such loose shocks that it felt as if we were floating. My Subaru wouldn't win too many drag races, but it had a much firmer, more athletic ride.

Despite that, the road felt familiar. This was it. I looked out the window. Trees whipped past us, and I could just see the lake shimmer through the forest. I closed my eyes and listened to the sound of the tires.

"Take the next right. It should be coming up soon."

Shane paused.

"I don't see anything."

"Johnson didn't, either, until she was right on top of it."

Shane kept driving. Then we crested a hill, and I felt the car nearly shudder as he braked and flicked the wheel to the right. The asphalt changed. The road here was older and cracked. It sounded different...and familiar. Then we topped a second hill, and I knew exactly where we were. The highway department had blasted through hillside and built the road through the valley cut between two limestone ledges.

"Pull over."

Shane pulled off the road. Birds chirped outside. A bumblebee flew from clover flower to clover flower, and the air smelled fishy. As my foot hit the ground, mud squished around my shoe—just as it had last night. George hopped out, yawned, and sniffed the air but then focused on me and panted.

"It's a good spot for an ambush," said Shane.

"It was," I said.

"If this is the right spot, there'll be evidence," he

said. "Let's find it."

I agreed, so George and I climbed the ridge to search for shell casings while Shane searched along the roadway for tire tracks, glass, shell casings or anything else that would corroborate my account of the night's events. At first, I found nothing. Then, after about ten minutes, I stepped on a shell casing.

"I've got .223 rifle brass," I said. "It's just the one casing so far, but I'll keep looking. There should be more."

"I've found a few glass fragments," said Shane. He paused. "I expected more based on your description of what happened."

I agreed and knelt in the grass. A few minutes later, I found a .45-caliber casing. Then I found another .223 casing followed by a second .45-caliber casing. Eventually, Shane joined me on the hill to see what I had. He put his hands on his hips and furrowed his brow and shook his head.

"I don't know," he said. "You sure this is the right spot?"

I looked around and nodded.

"Yeah," I said, pointing toward the woods and a big silver maple visible from where I stood. "I hid behind that tree."

"They shoot at it?"

I shrugged.

"I don't know."

"How many shots did they fire?"

I glanced at him and shrugged again.

"A lot, but adrenaline and stress can distort memories," I said. "More than four shots, though. They've cleaned up."

Shane put his hands on his hips and looked around. Then he looked at me. His smile was almost pained.

"I'm on your side," he said, finally. "You know that, right?"

I clenched my jaw and drew in a breath through my nose.

"You're on my side, but you think I'm delusional."

"I didn't say that," he said. "But you're under a lot of stress. It's understandable that you wouldn't be in your right mind right now. Stress can do funny things to perceptions. You found some shell casings, but I only found broken glass. There should be more here."

I pinched my lips tight.

"Just say it," I said. "You think I'm making this up."

"No. I don't think that," he said. "Something happened to you. I think your mind is misinterpreting it."

I crossed my arms.

"So we're back to me being crazy. Thanks."

George nuzzled my hand. His tail thumped against my thigh. I petted him so he'd know I was fine.

"Detective Johnson held you captive in a jail

cell," said Shane. "She could have killed you at any time. Why would she drive you to the middle of nowhere, lock you in a car, and shoot up that car? Why didn't she kill you in the police station? She took a risk driving you out here. It doesn't make sense. And think of the expenses involved. She trashed a car. Even a crappy car will run you a couple thousand bucks, right? Not only that, you got away. Zane Hopkins did, too."

He was right. Johnson's ambush didn't make sense. I blinked and considered.

"She got something out of ambushing us she couldn't have gotten by killing us in a jail cell," I said. I looked down the hill toward the road. Then I looked at the shell casings I had picked up. "When Johnson and her men picked me up, they confiscated my dad's Colt 1911. I found .45-caliber casings on the ground."

Shane went quiet for a moment. Then he furrowed his brow.

"You carry an AR-15 in your car?"

"No," I said, "but I'm willing to bet they tried to kill me with my own firearm, the .223 casings notwithstanding."

He considered that. Then he crossed his arms.

"That doesn't explain why she drove you out here."

"The ambush itself must have been necessary for whatever she was doing," I said. Then I paused as my mind made a connection. "When she and her men arrested me, they claimed to have found a .40-caliber pistol in my car. She then claimed Frannie Hopkins had been killed by a .40-caliber pistol. She also claimed to have found a rock in my cabin with Phil Mason's blood on it. I think she was trying to set me up for murders she and her thugs had committed. Maybe she wanted to kill Zane with my gun to make it look like I had killed him."

Shane shook his head.

"She could have done that in Pollard. Besides, if she had succeeded, the police would have found your bullet-riddled body right beside his."

I rubbed the back of my neck and sighed heavily.

"I don't know," I said. "We're missing something."

Shane looked out over the road.

"Why would she want to kill Zane?" he asked. "Frannie Hopkins and Phil Mason clearly knew things about Oscar Romero. Why'd she go after Zane, though?"

"I don't know. He claimed Johnson had put him in protective custody, but he wouldn't say why." I paused. "You believe me?"

He looked to the road.

"Something happened to you here," he said. "Maybe it's time to call the professionals."

"And who are the professionals?" I asked. "The Highway Patrol? Johnson had a Highway Patrol badge. The FBI? Even if I could get in to see them, they wouldn't believe me. They'd write a report and never think of Pollard again. You don't even really believe me, and we've worked together for years."

He drew in a breath.

"Then come home," he said. "Nothing you do will bring Oscar Romero back from the dead."

"If I leave, more people will die. Johnson is cleaning house. She already took out Phil Mason and Frannie Hopkins. If Zane Hopkins isn't dead yet, he could be next. And if not him, it'll be someone else."

Shane crossed his arms and adjusted his stance, almost looking like someone readying himself for a fight.

"Best-case scenario," he said, "what do you hope to accomplish by staying? You gave up your badge. Even if you do find evidence that Johnson killed the sheriff, you can't introduce it in court. You're not sending anybody to jail."

"You're right," I said. "I won't send anybody to jail."

He wrinkled his brow and lowered his chin.

"Then what are you doing?"

I wished I had an answer for him, but I didn't. So I shrugged.

"I don't know," I said. "When I got to Pollard, I found people who needed help, so I helped...or at least I tried to. Maybe I made things worse."

"You did your best."

I looked at him and tried to smile.

"That's the problem. I did my best, and I failed,"

I said. I couldn't keep the smile on my face, so I let it slip as I considered what I wanted to say. "You know that expression about pain so bad you wouldn't wish it on your worst enemy? You ever felt pain like that?"

"My appendix burst when I was fifteen. It hurt."

"But you knew you'd survive," I said. "The doctors pumped you full of antibiotics and painkillers and operated. Every surgery has risks, but you knew you'd wake up and probably be okay. You knew that pain would go away."

"Yeah," he said, his voice soft.

"I'm talking about pain so bad you never want to wake up," I said. "You can't escape pain like that. The Romeros felt it when they lost their son. I didn't come to Pollard for them, but I'm staying because nobody should ever feel like they do. If I can keep some other mom and dad's son or daughter from dying, I will."

Shane swallowed and looked down.

"You lost your family, too. Is that how you feel? Like you just want to sleep and never wake up?"

"Sometimes," I said. "Other times, I'm angry, sometimes I'm lonely, sometimes I just ache. And other times, I'm fine. That's how grief is. It doesn't always make sense."

"You're not a superhero. If you stay, you're going to get hurt. I don't want that."

"If they kill me, investigate my death and finish the job I started."

He shook his head.

"I don't know what to say to that."

"Then don't say anything," I said. "Let's go back to town."

He nodded. I put George in the back and sat in the driver's seat. The drive took little time, and we didn't bother speaking until we reached Pollard. Then Shane drew in a breath.

"What's your next step?" he asked.

I glanced at him.

"I need to focus," I said. "This started with Oscar Romero's death. If we can find his killer, everything will make sense."

"Okay. Who killed him?"

"I have no idea," I said.

Shane considered.

"Why is he dead? He was a college kid who cleaned pools. Who profited from his death?"

"I don't know."

Shane opened his mouth to say something but then stopped himself.

"What do we know about him?"

"Not nearly as much as I'd like. We've got to figure out a way to change that."

29

Camp Meadowview had two thousand acres and two entrances. One led to a private cabin in the woods and had a wrought iron gate secured by thick chains and a hardened-steel padlock. Few people had a key. The other entrance had a guardhouse manned twenty-four hours a day. Elaine's safrole hadn't left through either entrance. An enterprising thief could have removed it via boat, but it would have been hard to wheel three fifty-five-gallon drums of oil through the camp and to the dock unseen.

It was here somewhere. They had spent hours looking for it already and found nothing. It had to be here, though. More importantly, their thief had to be here.

Joseph, Daniel, and Elaine sat on one side of a long conference table in the camp's administrative building. Dr. Turner sat at the head of the table.

Daniel and Joseph had driven straight to the camp after killing Zane and Kate in Columbia, but they should have gone home. They had interviewed nine people so far, and none had seen a thing.

Before calling in the next employee, Joseph held up a hand.

"We're wasting our time interviewing everybody. Those barrels weighed hundreds of pounds each. Our thief didn't just carry them away. He didn't roll them away, either. They would have broken open, or somebody would have noticed. What vehicles does Meadowview own?"

Dr. Turner seemed startled that someone had asked her a question. She closed her eyes and thought.

"Our housekeeping staff has golf carts, but our landscapers have trucks and trailers. We've also got four Chevy Tahoes for traveling off-site."

"What about the security team?" asked Daniel.

"They've got golf carts," she said. She thought for a second. "They've also got a Gator. It's like a souped-up golf cart for carrying things. I don't know if it could carry your missing barrels, though. They sound heavy."

Daniel looked at Joseph. Then Elaine cleared her throat.

"Call in Bill Arians," she said. "He's still the lead groundskeeper, right?"

Dr. Turner nodded.

"He is, and he'd have access to a truck," she

said. She reached for a walkie-talkie and excused herself from the room. Elaine looked to Joseph.

"Bill played football at Mizzou," she said. "He's the only Meadowview employee I know who could lift a fifty-five-gallon barrel full of safrole."

They waited almost twenty minutes for Bill to arrive. He could have passed for twenty-five, but Joseph suspected he was a bit older. He smiled to everybody in the room and then waved. The sun had tanned the skin of his arms, neck, and face an even light brown. Grass stains and dirt covered his jeans, but his white shirt looked clean. His shoulders brushed both sides of the doorway.

"Afternoon," he said. "I changed my shirt, but these are the only pair of pants I had with me. Sorry if I smell like gas or grass."

"You're fine," said Elaine. "Have a seat. I'm Elaine, and I represent Lakeside Pools. We maintain the swimming pool. You might have seen my guys around. We also rent a storage shed on-site. With me is Lakeside's vice president, Joseph, and our branch manager, Daniel."

"Hi, folks," said Bill, waving an enormous, calloused hand. "What can I do for you?"

"They're here to ask about a theft at Lakeside's storage shed," said Dr. Turner. "Someone stole some dangerous pool chemicals. We need to find them before someone gets hurt."

Bill straightened.

"Oh," he said. He blinked a few times and then

shook his head. "That's awful."

"Have you heard anything about the theft?" asked Elaine.

"No, sorry," he said. "One of my guys trims the grass around your shed, but I rarely make it out there myself. Dr. Turner keeps me pretty busy."

He smiled. Joseph tried to smile back, but he wasn't in good humor.

"We're looking for three fifty-five-gallon barrels," he said. "They would have been full and would have weighed about three hundred pounds each."

Bill leaned forward and narrowed his eyes.

"Were they blue?"

Elaine leaned forward. Joseph and Daniel both straightened.

"They were," she said. "Have you seen them?"

"Maybe," he said. "I saw some barrels on the burn pile yesterday. I wondered what they were doing there, but I figured you wouldn't drag them all the way to the burn pile unless you really needed to."

Elaine looked to Joseph.

"You didn't see them on your search before?"

He shook his head and looked to Bill.

"Can you drive us there?"

"Sure. I can fit two of you in the truck, but it's a tight squeeze. The rest of you can ride in the back if you want."

Joseph looked to Elaine. Her face had grown red,

but she said nothing. Then he looked to Dr. Turner.

"Call security and ask them to get a golf cart," he said. "Ms. Alford would appreciate a ride, I'm sure. Daniel and I don't mind squeezing in with Bill."

Elaine agreed, so Daniel, Joseph, and Bill climbed into his Chevy F-150 truck and headed toward the burn pile. Bill waved and smiled to every kid they passed. Joseph couldn't prove anything, but he doubted Bill had done anything wrong. He fit into the summer camp too well. Maybe one day he'd run it. Assuming he wasn't a thief. If he was, he'd have to die.

Joseph smelled smoke before they reached the burn pile. About two hundred yards from the groundskeeper's six-car garage was a smoldering pile of wood, weeds, and other refuse. Right on top were three fifty-five-gallon barrels. Flames had scorched the exteriors, and someone had pierced their bases to create holes. The air had an almost sweet smell amidst the acrid smoke.

"Here they are," said Bill, parking at the edge of the gravel lot beside his building. "I don't know who put them there, but they burned pretty well."

"Thank you," said Joseph, opening his door. He and Daniel stepped out. "You should leave before my boss gets here. She's going to be angry."

"Sure," said Bill. "Let me know if I can help."

"Just leave," said Daniel.

Bill nodded. Joseph slammed his door shut and stepped back. Bill turned the pickup around and left. Daniel sighed.

"He doesn't know anything," he said. "It's going to be a shame if Elaine tells us to kill him."

"If she does, I'll talk her out of it," said Joseph. "It'd be dirty business to kill a loyal employee just because she's pissed."

Daniel grunted but said nothing. Elaine and Dr. Turner arrived about ten minutes later in a golf cart. Elaine focused on the burn pile. Then she looked to Dr. Turner.

"If you'll excuse us," she said. "I need to talk to my employees."

The doctor straightened.

"How are you going to get back?"

"We'll walk," she said. "It's a nice afternoon."

Turner didn't look convinced, but she nodded and left. The golf cart's electric motor whirred, and then it disappeared. Elaine turned to the burn pile and covered her mouth. Then she looked down.

"There's nothing left," she said. "It's gone, isn't it?"

"Looks like it," said Joseph, his voice soft.

Elaine circled the smoldering pile, staring hard at the debris.

"This was supposed to be it. It was my ticket out of here," she said.

"We'll rebuild," said Joseph. "We've already got more barrels on the way."

Elaine went silent. Then she sighed.

"We will," she said. "First, though, find out who

did this. Then crucify him."

"I understand revenge, but we've got a lot of work already," said Joseph.

"No, Joseph," she said, shaking her head. She was nearly trembling. "This isn't about revenge. The man who did this tried to ruin me. And if he did it once, he'll do it again. Find him and tear his lungs out."

He looked to the ground and then sighed.

"Okay," he said. "We'll talk to the security team and review their logs to see who was on the grounds. Then we'll talk to Bill again to find out exactly when he found the barrels."

Daniel agreed. Joseph looked to his boss and nearly asked whether she wanted him to stay with her, but she waved him away. She needed some space, but she'd be okay. And he'd hunt down the man who had hurt her. It would all work out. He and Daniel started walking.

"Hey, Joseph," called Elaine. Joseph turned. "If Bill did this, kill him. Never hesitate to act. They'll see it as weakness."

He nodded.

"Of course," he said. Then he paused. "Zane Hopkins is dead, but Blackwood's not. She can identify us. How do you want to handle her?"

Elaine brought a hand to her face and sighed.

"Leeland already called me to say she went by the police station today," she said. "They think she's crazy. We'll kill her, but she's not our priority right now. Just do your job. Find the son of a bitch who's sabotaging my business."

"I will," he said.

This would be a very long day.

30

Shane and I drove back to Pollard, where we parked in the lot of the motel near his room. My thoughts felt scattered, and I felt restless. Walking usually cleared my thoughts, and I highly doubted George would mind a stroll around town.

"How's your dad's cabin?"

I hadn't expected the question, so my mind took a moment to process it.

"Something broke a vent, and an animal got inside. Staying there's a bit like camping. It'll take some work to make it habitable again."

"But it's got running water and electricity, doesn't it?"

"Theoretically, but they're turned off," I said. "Why?"

He shrugged.

"Just thinking it'd be nice to have a friend with a beachside cabin," he said. "For long weekends with

Ivy."

I let myself smile.

"If Ivy's okay sharing her love nest with a raccoon, you're welcome to visit all you want. I'll give you a key."

"You should fix it up. Might be worth something if you sell it."

I shook my head.

"It's not mine to sell. It was my mom and dad's place."

He seemed to accept that because he asked nothing further. As he opened his door, his phone beeped half a dozen times in quick succession. I glanced at him as he pulled it from his pocket and thumbed through his messages.

"Everything okay?" I asked.

He smiled.

"Yeah. It's Ivy. She wants to make sure you're okay and wanted to know whether she should come down."

Ivy was a trauma surgeon in a major emergency room, so she kept busy. I liked her a lot, and I loved seeing her, but I couldn't ask her to take a day off just because I was having a bad one.

"Tell her thanks, but no. Maybe you should go home, too."

"So you can investigate without me looking over your shoulder?"

"So you can spend time with your beautiful, young wife before she comes to her senses and finds a more suitable husband."

He smiled.

"Will you stick around if I make a call?"

"I'll warn you before I go."

He nodded and got out. I opened my door and started to get out, too, when my phone started buzzing. It was Crystal Valentine. I answered before it buzzed again.

"Hey," I said. "It's Hana Blackwood. You okay?"

"Kevin's in town," she said. "I saw him drive by my apartment. I don't know what to do."

It took me a moment to reorient myself to Crystal's situation. Kevin was her violent ex-husband. He never should have found her.

"Are you safe now?"

"I think so," she said. "The doors and windows are locked, and the kids are inside."

"Good. For now, stay inside. If you see him again, call 911 and tell them you're afraid for your life," I said. "We'll talk in a minute. I'm in my car, and I'll be at your apartment in a few minutes."

Once she thanked me and hung up, I texted Shane to let him know I had somewhere to be. He hurried toward the car and put his thumb over the microphone on his phone.

"You okay?"

"I am, yes," I said. "Another lady I know isn't. I've got to go, but I'll be back."

"All right," he said. "Good luck. I'll be here when you get back."

I thanked him, and then George and I drove to Crystal's complex. Unlike my previous trip, no teenagers sunbathed by the pool, and nobody walked around. The dog and I hurried to her apartment. She opened the door, but she didn't beckon us inside. Instead, she bit her bottom lip, looked at me up and down, and used the door to shield part of her body.

"You look rough," she said. "You okay?"

I had taken a shower after my trek through the mud this morning, but I hadn't looked at myself for longer than it had taken me to put toothpaste on my brush.

"Long story, but I'm good," I said. "You said Kevin is in town. Can I come in?"

She nodded and stepped back so we could come inside. The blinds were drawn, but her kids sat at a table in the front room, schoolbooks open in front of them. The kids fidgeted and wouldn't look at me. None had written on the papers in front of them. Kevin hadn't hurt the kids before, but they looked nervous.

I wished I could tell them it'd be over soon, but I had worked enough domestic violence cases to know otherwise. If Kevin had spent the time and money to track them to Pollard, he'd never stop harassing Crystal. This would end badly.

"Can we talk out back?" I asked. Crystal nodded and led George and me through the living room to her back patio. She nearly jumped with every sound. She had lied to me about her name—I knew that—but she couldn't fake this kind of nervousness. "Tell me what happened."

She drew in a breath. I waited for her to say something, but she didn't. Then she brought a hand to her face as tears began falling down her cheeks.

"It's okay," I said. "We'll sort this out, but you've got to talk to me. What happened?"

She kept her eyes closed. Then she bit her lip and looked at me again.

"I think I'm just going to take the kids and run."

"Think hard about that. Your family has a life here. You came to me—a stranger—for help because you wanted to fight for your kids. Your ex-husband hurt you, but that's the past. Focus on your future. We can make it better, but you can't run. If you run today, you'll run every day of your life."

She nodded and seemed to consider what I'd said.

"I'm so scared."

"It's okay to be scared," I said. "Just don't panic. Pollard is small. If Kevin's in town, I'll find him and see what he's up to. In the meantime, make some coffee."

"To throw on him in case he comes in the house?" she asked, furrowing her brow.

"I guess that could work, but I was hoping for a drink," I said. "I had a late night."

She straightened a little.

"Oh, okay."

I thanked her and left George in the apartment with her kids as I walked to my car for a travel mug. Unfortunately, my mug wasn't in the front cup holder where I thought I had left it, so I looked under the seats and discovered that I ought to clean my car out more often. I didn't find my coffee mug, but I found a pistol under the front passenger seat. It was a SIG Sauer P229R, and if I had to guess, it was the same one Detective Johnson had shown me at Frannie Hopkins's house. She said someone had used it to kill Frannie.

So that was bad.

Leaving it there and hoping for the best wasn't an option. If a teenager broke into my car hoping to steal my purse or cell phone, he could find a gun and hurt himself or someone else. Calling Sheriff Lyons seemed little better. Two people wearing uniforms and driving a cruiser from his station had tried to kill me last night. Giving them another gun seemed like a bad idea.

I hesitated and then picked the weapon up. It had a nearly full magazine and looked clean. A hero in an action-adventure movie would pick it up, use it against his enemies, and then toss it afterward so the police couldn't trace it back to him. Since I wasn't a sociopath intent on killing everyone opposed to me, I removed the magazine and the round in the chamber and put those in my glove box. Then I removed the slide assembly, recoil spring, and barrel. Those, I stashed with my jack and spare tire. Finally, I put the receiver beneath the front seat. If a kid broke into the car now, at least he wouldn't find a working weapon.

I went back to the apartment. Crystal opened the door for me before I could knock. Then she looked down at my hands.

"I made coffee. If you don't have a travel mug, I can give you one of mine."

I told her I'd appreciate that. The kids were still working on schoolwork at their dining room table, so Crystal and I walked to the kitchen, where she poured coffee into a silver travel mug with a gas station's logo printed on the side.

"Do you mind if I leave George here for a few hours?" I asked. "He's a good dog. He shouldn't bother you. I have to run some errands. Plus, if someone comes near the door, he'll bark. He likes you guys, and he's protective."

She looked to him and nodded. Already, her youngest had left the table to sit beside George on the ground.

"The kids would like that. I would, too."

I thanked her and wished her luck. Then I reminded them all to stay inside and to call the police if Kevin showed up.

As I walked back to my car, I let my mind wander. If Crystal's ex-husband was in town, he had to be staying and eating somewhere. Considering Pollard had one hotel and one restaurant, I should be able to find him.

Frank's Downtown Diner was close, so I drove by there first, but I couldn't find any cars with a Kentucky license plate. Next, I tried the hotel. Few cars waited for me in the lot, but one—a red Ford Fusion—had a license plate from Christian County, Kentucky. According to the map on my phone, Hopkinsville was the county seat. I had found Kevin.

I snapped pictures of the car, the parking lot, and the hotel with my cell phone and then called Shane to tell him what I was up to. He wished me luck finding Recinos and said he planned to take a nap.

Afterward, and as I waited for Kevin to emerge from the hotel, I searched for local gun shops on my phone. Bryant County had about ten thousand year-round residents, and apparently, those residents loved their firearms because I found eight shops and two custom gunsmiths within a twenty-mile radius. I made note of the nearest store and then yawned and stretched and sipped the coffee Crystal had given me.

About half an hour after I arrived, a middle-aged man emerged from a room and walked toward the Ford. I snapped pictures of him and then hunkered down in my seat and pretended to be texting someone as he opened his door. He drove off within thirty seconds. I waited until he was almost out of sight and then followed, expecting him to drive by Crystal's apartment. Instead, he drove to the headquarters of the Bryant County Sheriff's Office.

I parked half a block away and took pictures of him walking through the front door. That trip complicated things. I called Crystal. She answered right away.

"Hey. It's Hana. Did you or your ex have friends in Pollard before you got here?"

"No," she said. "Why?"

"I found Kevin's car, and then I followed him to the sheriff's office."

"Did they arrest him?" she asked, her voice almost hopeful.

"No, and I don't trust the locals. Pack your bags and get out of town. I'll pick up the dog."

She paused.

"I don't have family. It'll take time to set up a new place."

"You don't have a secret security system at the apartment, do you?"

"No."

I grimaced and thought.

"Then keep George for the next day or two. He's a sweetheart, but his bark will scare people off. Your apartment complex has a couple of teenage girls in it, and I bet you could pay one of them to walk him around the block. He likes kids a lot."

She hesitated.

"We'll take care of George. I'm sorry that I got you involved in this."

"Don't be," I said, shaking my head. "I'll get George's stuff. Keep your door locked and your head down until I get to your place. I also need you to get on your computer and look for the Kentucky Probation and Parole Office. It's probably part of the Department of Corrections. Call them and tell them your name—and be honest—and tell them you've spotted your ex-husband in Pollard, Missouri.

"Tell them you think this violates his parole. They'll forward your complaint to his parole officer, who will go by his house and try to track him down. When he can't find him, the parole officer will either contact the police in Pollard to arrest Kevin, or he'll come down here himself to find him. Either way, he'll go back to prison. You've just got to keep your head down and survive until that happens."

She thanked me before hanging up. I loved George, but they needed him more than I did at the moment. Plus, he'd love playing with her kids. After everything they had been through, they deserved a new friend—even a four-legged one.

I turned on my car and put it in gear, knowing I had better things to do than to worry.

31

I got George's stuff and drove back to Crystal's apartment. By the time I arrived, the dog had already fallen asleep on their couch. The kids were back at their homework, but they kept eyeing him. They even smiled a little. If he could make them happy for a few days, this was the right thing to do.

I put his bed, his food and water bowls, a leash, and a bag of food in the living room. Then Crystal hugged me and thanked me. I told her it was no problem and that I was glad to help. It wasn't a lie, either. She and her kids deserved a safe home. If I could help give them that, I would.

Afterward, I drove by a small gun shop that provided custom smithing services. There, I purchased a holster, a used Glock 19, and fifty nine-millimeter rounds. I would have bought a second pistol, but I didn't have the money. Until I got another job and a steady paycheck, my income consisted of rent payments on the three-bedroom house my mom and dad had left me in Webster Groves, Missouri.

When Blake and I were married, we had lived together in that house and had talked about starting a family. I imagined myself braiding my daughter's hair or digging in the garden with a little boy. I even had names picked out. Sara for a daughter and Henry for a boy. Dreams were fickle, though. You had to work for them. Sometimes you had to fight for them. I had fought for my dreams, and I still fell short.

That house held the naïve hopes of my childhood, and now it held the hopes of the family who rented it. They seemed like nice people, so they deserved a happy family home. Maybe their dreams would come true. As for me, I quit chasing fantasies a long time ago. Now, I had a dog and a car and a vague hope that the future would look different than the past. It wasn't much.

I forced my maudlin thoughts down, left the gun shop, and drove to the sheriff's office's headquarters in Pollard. Officer Sutton sat at the front desk. When she saw me, she wrinkled her nose. Her lips curled into a humorless smile.

"You've got guts coming in here after what you told Troy this morning."

"Sure. Thanks."

The skin at the corners of her eyes wrinkled as her predatory grin widened.

"You accused me and my colleagues of murders," she said.

"If I had accused you of murder, I would have used your name," I said. "Tell me about Kevin Recinos."

Her smile faded.

"I'm not familiar with Mr. Recinos."

"He was in here earlier," I said. "Middle-aged, brown hair, maybe six feet tall, and he has a slight paunch. He beat his wife with a wine bottle. Now, she and their kids are scared to death of him. She lives in town."

She looked down.

"You have a remarkable gift for stepping into situations that are none of your business, Ms. Blackwood."

"It's one of my many character flaws," I said. "Where is he?"

"I'm not going to have that conversation with you."

"So you do know him," I said, nodding. "If Crystal calls, please send her help. He's a dangerous man."

She raised her eyebrows.

"We'll do our jobs," she said. "Speaking of which, sit down. A detective from Columbia would like to talk to you."

"About?"

Sutton pointed to the seating area.

"Something important. Sit down."

I had driven through Columbia several times, but I had spent little time there. The Columbia PD shouldn't have even known my name. They might have known the name of Zane Hopkins's sister, though. She was a college student at the University of Missouri—which was in Columbia—and I had told him to call her last night.

"Is this about Zane Hopkins or his sister?"

"You tell me," said Sutton.

If Zane or his sister were dead, I gained nothing by talking to the police now. On television and in books, clever criminals talk their way out of trouble all the time, but in reality, that doesn't happen. If you're in an interrogation booth, the police aren't looking for information, and they're certainly not looking to clarify anything; they're trying to shore up their case against you by getting you to say something stupid.

"Am I free to go?"

She nodded to the chairs.

"Sit down," she said. "I'll tell Troy you're here. He'll call the detective from Columbia."

I considered her.

"Do you have probable cause to charge me with anything?"

She said nothing.

"If you do, arrest me," I said. "If not, I'm going to go. Sound good with you?"

She, again, said nothing.

"You need to answer so I know how to respond,"

I said. "Am I under arrest?"

"Not at this time," she said, "but it's in your best interest to clear this up now."

"You haven't even told me what happened," I said. "How can I clear anything up if you don't tell me what's going on?"

Sutton crossed her arms and shifted. Something had happened in Columbia, but it wasn't her case. Sutton had no business discussing it with me, but I hoped I could cajole her into it, anyway.

"Since you're not even going to bother telling me what happened," I said, "I'm going to leave."

Her eyes narrowed.

"Zane Hopkins is dead. So is his sister. It's a professional job, too. Sheriff Lyons called the Columbia PD to ask about Zane, and lo and behold, he and his sister were dead. Care to explain that?"

My stomach tightened. It felt like somebody had punched me.

"Poor kids."

"Yeah," said Sutton. "Poor kids. That's all you've got to say? Since you arrived in Pollard, people have been dropping left and right. I think we deserve an explanation."

"One day, I hope you get one," I said. "Who's your station quartermaster? I need to know who maintains your stockpile of uniforms. It's for the lawsuit my lawyer plans to file against you."

Her eyes popped open.

"You are one cold bitch," she said. "Two kids are

dead, and you're talking about a lawsuit. If you're not going to cooperate, get out."

"Sure. Thanks for your time."

She said nothing, so I turned and walked to my car. Once I sat, I rubbed the back of my head. I had only met Zane the one time, but he was barely in his twenties. He should have had sixty years ahead of him. Now he didn't.

I sank into my seat. My entire body felt heavy. I needed to think and focus on the work in front of me, but I kept picturing Zane in the holding cell. He had been scared and heartbroken over his mother's death, but he had been hopeful, too. He really thought Detective Johnson wanted to help him.

I had lost friends in the Army, and I had seen dozens of bodies as a detective. Death never became easy, though. It left me feeling hollow. My therapist would probably tell me to take the day off and think about that feeling and allow my mind to process what I had experienced. I didn't have time to grieve or process, though.

The police already wanted to talk to me about Zane's death. They had no reason to charge me with his murder yet, but they'd find cause if they tried hard enough. A witness would claim she had seen a woman matching my description near the murder scene, a forensic technician would find a stray hair that looked suspiciously like mine near the bodies, a detective would find smeared fingerprints that could have been mine on a handrail. You could charge anybody with anything.

And that's all it would take. Once the police had me in custody, I'd die in a cell. Jail was the easiest place in the world to commit murder. You knew where your victim would be at all times, and you could find people willing to kill for a hundred bucks in a commissary account.

I rubbed my face. It was too late to run away now. The monster was already out. I had to face it now. First, though, I needed information. Someone gave Detective Johnson the uniforms her thugs had worn and the cruisers they had driven. If I could find that someone, I could use him to find her.

I pulled out my phone. The last time I visited the station, Sheriff Lyons had mentioned his station's Facebook page. Apparently, they kept it updated. I browsed through almost two hundred pictures until I found a photograph of a man in civilian clothes standing in front of a big storage room inside the station. The picture's uploader captioned it *Christopher Key, hard at work.*

I had my quartermaster.

I searched through Bryant County's publicly available property tax information until I found listings for Christopher Key. The first was for a two-acre vacant lot near the lake. The second listing was for a two-story brick home just outside of Pollard. I looked up the address on Google Maps and headed out.

When I arrived, I found a man standing in the

driveway beside a minivan. A duffel bag rested on the ground beside him. He straightened and furrowed his brow. His thinning brown hair topped an oval-shaped face with evenly tanned skin and a thin, brown beard. As I opened my door, he placed his bag in the van and then nodded.

"You lost, miss?" he asked, smiling.

"That's always a possibility," I said. "Are you Christopher Key?"

The smile slipped off his face, and he nodded and crossed his arms.

"I am. What can I do for you?"

"Officer Sutton at the sheriff's office told me I could find you here," I said, hoping he wouldn't sniff through the lie. "My name is Hana Blackwood. I hear you're in charge of the inventory at your station. Can I ask you a few questions?"

He narrowed his eyes and lifted his chin.

"Are you an auditor?"

I smiled.

"Just think of me as a friendly woman asking questions," I said. "Are you missing any uniforms?"

"No," he said. "Why?"

"How do you keep them?" I asked. "Are they under lock and key twenty-four hours a day, or are they available for sworn officers to take as needed?"

"We keep them in a closet, but you have to sign the uniforms out. Why? Who would steal a uniform?" he asked. "And who are you again?"

"I'm Hana Blackwood," I said. "Tell me about

your fleet. Who has access to your vehicles?"

He took a step back and blinked several times.

"Our sworn officers," he said. "We don't have the budget for take-home vehicles."

"Who had vehicles last night?"

He narrowed his eyes at me.

"Nobody. We don't have an overnight shift," he said. "Emergency calls are routed through the Highway Patrol. If necessary, our own officers can respond in civilian vehicles."

I nodded and smiled.

"Are the keys locked up?"

"No need. The station's locked up. No one can get in. We keep the keys on a bulletin board. What's this about?"

So everybody in the station had access to everything. That didn't help. I forced myself to smile.

"Looks like you're going on vacation," I said.

"Yeah. Why?"

"Just making conversation," I said. "Did you work yesterday?"

"Is that relevant to your audit?"

I smiled.

"I'm lousy at small talk," I said. "Sorry."

He nodded his agreement and then turned to go into his house. I got back in my car and left. When I reached town again, I parked in the lot in front of a strip mall and pulled my notepad from my purse to jot down a few quick thoughts.

People had threatened me before during investigations, but nobody carried out those threats. Outside of movies and books, bad guys don't come after cops. I wasn't a cop anymore, obviously, but that basic rule should have still held. The bad guys probably wanted to stop my investigation, but their own rational self-interest should have stopped them from trying to kill me. Obviously, it didn't.

The bad guys were willing to take a lot of risk to stop me. This wasn't about a cold murder. Something else had to be going on. If I didn't find out what, people would die. Maybe even me.

32

I sent Shane a text message to see what he was doing. He called back right away.

"Hana, hey," he said. "I'm at the motel still. Some cops came by looking for you. They wouldn't tell me what they wanted."

"Zane Hopkins and his sister are dead. Somebody murdered them. A detective from Columbia wants to question me. I declined."

Shane went quiet.

"You have any details?"

"Not really," I said. "I also found out that anyone with physical access to the station could have taken uniforms or a cruiser."

"That's a liability," said Shane.

"Risk management isn't their strong suit," I said. "I'm going to go visit the Romero family and see what insight they can provide me. You want to go with me?"

"Just give me an address."

"Once I get it, I'll text it to you."

I used my phone to research the Romero family. According to the Bryant County tax assessor's website, they owned a home on two acres. I texted the address to Shane and headed out. Shane must have been closer because I found his BMW parked on the street half a block away when I arrived. The Romeros lived in a white Craftsman bungalow with a big front porch and dormers that protruded from the roofline. A thick row of hedges screened the home's foundation and gave the family some privacy.

Shane and I walked to the front porch, just as we had done hundreds of times before. Mrs. Romero answered my knock. She wore jeans and a pink T-shirt.

"We're not interested in…" she began. Then her voice trailed off. "I know you."

"We met at the sheriff's office in Pollard," I said. "I'm Hana Blackwood. With me is Shane Lewis. Do you have a few minutes to talk to us?"

She looked at us both. Then she crossed her arms.

"What do you two want?"

When I had been a detective, I had hated this part of the job. The dead were easy to deal with. The living were hard.

"I own a cabin near Pollard, but I was a detective in St. Louis County for many years. This is abrupt, I know, but I had hoped to talk to you about Oscar."

Mrs. Romero's breathing grew shallow and quick.

"Please leave," she said. "We don't talk to reporters...or whatever you two are."

She almost stepped back and shut her door, but I spoke up before she could.

"I'm not a reporter," I said. "I'm just trying to figure out who killed your son, and I could use your help. That's it."

Her nostrils flared as she exhaled, but she stopped shutting the door.

"Why should I help you?"

I hesitated and then tilted my head to the side.

"Because I'll find out who killed Oscar and why."

Her eyes widened. Then she looked to Shane.

"Do you have anything to say? Or does she talk for you?"

"She does talk a lot," said Shane, "but she's also honest. She's a good detective. If anyone can solve your son's case, it's her."

Her nostrils flared.

"And who are you?"

He considered his answer.

"I'm here as a civilian, but I'm a detective with the St. Louis County Police Department. Hana was my partner."

Mrs. Romero looked at us both. Then she shifted her weight from one foot to the other.

"Why do you care when nobody else does?"

I considered lying to her and saying I wanted justice. That wasn't the truth, though.

"I just do. Oscar died, and he shouldn't have. That matters to me. I don't know what else to say," I said. "You either trust that I've got good intentions, or you don't. I won't stop working the case either way."

She blinked and seemed to consider that. Then she blew out a long breath. Her expression was softer when she spoke again.

"I miss my son."

"I know."

She looked down and sighed. Then she stepped back.

"Come in. Both of you."

We followed her into the wood-paneled entryway, down a short hallway, and to a kitchen at the rear of the home. The paint on her white cabinets had chipped, and her Formica countertop had scratches, but the bright yellow walls and big windows overlooking her backyard gave the room a cheery feeling. She gestured to a round breakfast table beneath the back window, pulled a pair of coffee mugs from a cabinet beside her stove, and poured us coffee. I sat and took a mug from her. Shane sat beside me and did the same.

"Thank you," I said.

Mrs. Romero sat across from us.

"What do you want?"

I sipped my coffee. It was lukewarm and tasted bright and acidic. I would have liked it over an hour ago when it was fresh, but I rarely turned down coffee, mediocre or otherwise.

"As I said, I've been investigating. When the sheriff's office investigated your son's death, they —"

"He was murdered," she said, interrupting me. "Someone stabbed him in the neck and left him to die. If you can't say that, you belittle his death and me."

I nodded and looked at my coffee mug and considered how to continue. On those few occasions in which I had interviewed the families of murder victims, I always did it shortly after their loved one's death. The timing hadn't given them the opportunity to become angry or to think about all they had lost.

"You're right. Oscar was murdered. I don't have kids, and I can't imagine what you're feeling. I won't pretend that I do. Everything about this is unfair, and our investigation will hurt. You okay with that?"

She sipped her coffee.

"I don't have a choice."

I stayed quiet until she looked at me again. Then I shook my head.

"You do have a choice. I want to find out what happened to him, but I won't put you or your family through something you can't handle."

For a moment, her eyes went dark, and her jaw moved as she clenched her teeth tight.

"My husband and I can handle it fine."

"Good," I said, reaching into my purse for a notepad. "The original investigators believed a camper at Meadowview murdered your son. Nothing I've found supports that theory, though. Unfortunately, the camp cleaned up the cabin to save the campers the embarrassment of the police finding their drugs and alcohol. They destroyed the forensic evidence."

She considered that and nodded.

"If the girls didn't kill him, who did?" she asked, looking first to me and then to Shane.

"We don't know, but we'll do what we can to find out. Can we see his room?" I asked. "I assume it looks the same as it did when he was alive."

She blinked and looked to Shane.

"Why? Sheriff Mason didn't need to see it."

"He should have searched it," said Shane. "It could have provided background information on your son that he couldn't get anywhere else."

She looked down at the table as if considering my request. Then she stood without saying a word. We followed her upstairs to Oscar's second-floor room. He had no siblings. The house was quiet.

Mrs. Romero pulled open the door. Sunlight filtered through the built-in shutters that covered the windows on the north and east walls. It was a pretty room. The air smelled stale, but no dust covered the end table beside the bed, the dresser, or the chest of drawers beside the door. A colorful abstract painting on canvas leaned against the foot of the bed. I looked at it and then to Mrs. Romero.

"Your son was an artist?"

She sighed and shook her head.

"No, but a girl he dated was," she said. She paused. "He dated a lot of girls. You should know that."

"So I've heard," I said. "I talked to several people about him, and everybody liked him. He seemed like a special person."

She nodded but said nothing.

"I come in here sometimes," she said, finally. "I sit on the bed and close my eyes and pretend he's in college."

I used to do the same with my family. Reality had a way of intruding on my fantasies, though. Finally, Mrs. Romero cleared her throat.

"So this is it," she said. "I don't know what you two expect to find."

"We don't either," I said. "Since we're here, can you do us a favor? Write down a list of Oscar's closest friends."

She straightened and drew in a breath.

"You could have asked me that downstairs," she said, narrowing her eyes. "You don't want me here while you look around."

"You're astute and right. I don't want you here," I said. "I promise that we won't damage anything, and we won't take anything without your permission."

Her nostrils flared as she drew in a breath.

"I've already searched for drugs, if that's what you expect to find," she said. "He had marijuana in his end table. He was a college student, and he smoked weed. Does that bother you?"

I shook my head.

"Will you get me the names?"

She hesitated but then relented and turned. I waited until I heard her footsteps down the stairs before surveying the room. Then I turned to Shane.

"You take the closet and dresser. I'll take the bed, end tables, and chest of drawers."

Shane agreed, so we started to search. Inside the chest, I found socks and boxer shorts in the top drawer. The drawer beneath that held T-shirts and pajamas. The bottom drawer held sweaters, the top of which felt like cashmere. Oscar had had good taste.

I felt around and between the clothes and beneath the drawers, but I didn't find any weapons, drugs, or hidden envelopes full of cash. Then I checked out the end table beside his bed. It was a simple Shaker-style piece with spindly legs, nice lines, and a single drawer. In that drawer, I found three red Omega watch boxes. I knew little about men's watches, but I recognized the brand from an elder abuse case involving theft. Those three watches had probably cost Oscar ten to twelve thousand dollars.

"Kid had money," I said. "He's got some expensive watches here in the end table, and he's got very nice sweaters in the chest of drawers."

Shane came out of the closet and nodded and opened drawers on the chest. Then he pulled out an off-white, cable-knit sweater.

"This is Purple Label from Ralph Lauren," he said. "Ivy gave me a sweater like this for Christmas last year."

"Your wife has good taste."

"She's got expensive taste," he said, raising his eyebrows. "This is a thousand-dollar sweater."

"Oh," I said, standing straighter.

"In the closet, he's got jeans from Alexander McQueen. Those are probably five or six hundred each. He's also got polo shirts from Hugo Boss, Versace, and Emporio Armani. Assuming they're genuine, he's got twenty grand worth of designer clothes in this closet. It's hard to believe a kid who cleaned pools could afford this wardrobe."

"The watches in his end table are probably worth ten to fifteen grand," I said. "We haven't even seen his shoes."

We went quiet. No amount of thought could explain this, though. As we left the room, my gut felt unsettled. Mrs. Romero met us at the bottom of the stairs.

"Did you find what you needed?" she asked, holding out a piece of paper for me. I pretended to look at the names and phone numbers.

"I don't think so," I said, lying. "Your son seems like a pretty straight shooter."

"He was," she said. "He was a good boy."

"Before I go, can I ask you one more question?" I asked. She nodded. "Did he have any other jobs? I heard he was handsome. Did he do modeling jobs or anything that would have given him free clothes?"

Her eyes took on a distant gaze, and she smiled.

"He had the looks, but no," she said. "During the school year, he worked as a DJ. He did parties on campus and at bars."

I didn't know how much a DJ on a college campus made, but I doubted it would have covered his clothes budget.

"Did he work for somebody, or did he freelance?" asked Shane.

"He had a manager," she said. "His name's on the list. Chase Andrews. They were friends."

We'd track Chase down as soon as we could.

"Thank you for your help," I said.

Mrs. Romero nodded and opened the front door but said nothing. Shane and I left the house. I didn't know what—if anything—we had learned, but one thing was certain: this case wasn't what it had first appeared to be. This wasn't about a romance that went awry. This was about money and a college kid who had way too much of it. Something was rotten in Pollard, Missouri. Shane and I needed to find out what before anyone else died.

33

Outside, the sun had already slunk low, and the sky was turning orange. It'd be dark in another half hour. My stomach rumbled, but I doubted Detective Johnson had stopped work for the evening, so Shane and I couldn't, either. We walked to our cars and then stopped near the hood of his BMW.

"What do you think?" I asked.

"Oscar didn't pay for his clothes or watches cleaning pools, I can tell you that," said Shane. "You heard the name Chase Andrews before?"

"No," I said, already reaching for my phone. I opened a browser and searched for him. He wasn't hard to find. "According to his profile on LinkedIn, he's the founder and CEO of Chase Andrews Talent Management."

"What kind of talent?" asked Shane, crossing his arms.

"Let's find out," I said, searching for the

company. The corporate website had a lot of pictures of scantily clad women. "He's a pimp who hides behind a party-planning service. His company specializes in sending women to corporate events, work retreats, birthday parties, or any event the host desires his guests to remember forever."

"Does he pimp out men, too, or does he specialize in women?"

"The website only mentions women, but if Oscar was a high-end gigolo, he probably needed expensive clothes to fit in with the clientele. I'm going to call and set up an appointment. See what we can get from him."

Shane sat on the hood of his car. I dialed Andrews's number, which went to voicemail.

"Hey," I said. "My name is Hana Blackwood, and I'm kind of in a dilemma. My boss has a bunch of clients in from out of town, but our entertainment has fallen through. We were given your name and think your entertainment offerings are perfect for our needs. Call me when you can. I know this is last minute, but we're willing to pay extra for expedited service."

I hung up.

"Voicemail?" asked Shane.

"Yeah," I said. "Hopefully he'll call back soon. In the meantime, I'm hungry. You want to get dinner?"

"Yeah. Let's do that. We can drop your car off at the motel. No need for us to keep driving two cars around."

I agreed and started toward my car when my cell rang. I pulled it from my purse. Shane stopped and watched. The caller ID said *Chase Andrews Enterprises*.

"It's him," I said before answering. "Mr. Andrews, thanks for calling me back so soon."

"Of course," said Andrews. "I'm always available to talk business. If your boss is looking to throw a party, I've got the perfect entertainment. What time are you thinking and what do you have in mind?"

"We've got three clients in from Atlanta. They're property developers, and they're accustomed to high-end entertainment. Unfortunately, we don't have a lot to offer in southern Missouri. Geoff plans to take them to dinner and then to a bar, though. We were hoping we could hire some models for an after-hours party. I figured we'd start at eleven, and we'd keep the party going all night. Can you accommodate that?"

"With ease," said Andrews. "How many models are you looking for?"

"Three," I said, glancing to Shane. "But they need to be fun, and they need to be willing to earn their paycheck. We're not looking for dancers in skimpy clothing. We want a little more than that. Since we've never worked together, I'd like to meet you in person to discuss the arrangements and ensure that we're on the same page."

"I wouldn't have it any other way," said

Andrews. "I'm in Springfield, and I'm available to talk right now."

"I can meet you in an hour."

He gave me directions to his office and thanked me for my business before hanging up. I put my phone in my purse.

"We've got an appointment," I said. "You mind driving to Springfield? Andrews expects somebody with money. You look like you have it."

"Sure. Let's go."

We dropped my car off at the motel and headed north. The sun set as Shane drove, and the night sky blossomed into a beautiful star-strewn panorama. Shane followed Andrews's directions to a vacant portion of a parking lot outside a Home Depot. Cars filled the parking lot of an Applebee's across the street. The air smelled like exhaust. It wasn't the office I had expected.

We hesitated before getting out of Shane's car and looking around. Chase—I had seen his picture when I looked him up earlier—leaned against the side of a late-model white limousine wearing a navy suit, white shirt, and red tie. Just a hint of scruff covered a lean, handsome face. He stood as we walked toward him.

"Ms. Blackwood?" he asked. He extended his hand as I nodded. "I'm Chase Andrews, and I'm glad to meet you. Who's your partner?"

"Shane Lewis," said Shane, holding out his hand. They shook. "Nice to meet you. I work with

Hana."

"This isn't what I expected," I said. "You asked to meet in your office."

Andrews looked to his limo. Rust ate into the wheel wells.

"I like to move around. You know how it is, I'm sure."

"No, but we're in different businesses," I said.

He nodded and flicked his eyes down my body.

"You're not what I expected, either," he said. "It's hard to believe a beautiful woman like you needs the services of a firm like my own."

He smiled, apparently believing he was charming.

"I'm not a prostitute. I hope your employees are, though, because my clients want to get their rocks off." He started to respond, but I cut him off. "Tell me about your talent. How do you recruit them?"

He shook his head.

"Tell me about yourself and your firm first," he said. A semi passed on the road behind me. Its engine noise drowned out everything around us. When the noise dissipated, I crossed my arms.

"I'm the assistant in a firm that requires services," I said. "Assuming you can provide suitable talent for my employers, we're willing to pay market rates."

The smile stayed on his face.

"What services do you two want?"

"The discreet kind," I said. "My firm's brought

in three clients. They're middle-aged men, and they're away from their spouses and partners. We plan to show them the town and everything the region can offer. Some of them might become repeat customers if your talent is enthusiastic enough."

He nodded.

"Let's talk numbers. You said you want three models earlier. Is that right?" He glanced at Shane. "We could add a fourth if you'd like."

"No, thanks," said Shane. "I'm good."

"The women you provide need to be special," I said. "Our clients are educated men. We're not interested in girls so young they can't walk into a bar or women who can't hold a conversation."

He waved that concern off.

"All of my employees are legal adults," he said. "Several of the young ladies I work with are college graduates. One even has a master's degree in economics. She's brilliant, and she's great at parties."

"That could work," I said, glancing at Shane. He nodded as if he picked out prostitutes often.

"Good," said Andrews. "Tell me about yourself, Ms. Blackwood. Will your clients be cops, too?"

"Excuse me?" I asked, raising my eyebrows.

"I looked you up. My business is tough. I've got to protect myself and my employees. You're a detective in St. Louis. Are you allowed to work in Springfield? Or are you part of some kind of intra-state task force? And is Mr. Lewis a cop, too?"

The smile left my face.

"You looked me up. Good for you. I used to be a detective in St. Louis, and I specialized in family crime. I was also a member of the major case squad."

He gave me a big smile and nodded.

"I'm leaving now," he said. "You two have a nice day."

"I'm no longer a cop," I said. "I quit."

He started toward his car, so I cleared my throat.

"How was Oscar Romero at parties?" I asked. His footsteps faltered. Then he turned around. "You said your employee with a master's degree was great at parties. I bet Oscar was even better. I know he didn't have a master's degree, but everybody loved him."

He considered me and then shook his head. His eyes narrowed, and he opened his mouth to speak but then seemed to reconsider.

"I'm not interested in talking about Oscar. Have a nice day."

He turned and started toward the limo. Shane and I followed him.

"You employed him, though," I said. "You gave him designer clothes and watches as a bonus?"

We reached the back of the vehicle. He stopped and turned.

"Please stop following me."

"Oscar's dead," said Shane. "We don't care about your business or your employees. We're interested in him."

Andrews stepped forward. He wasn't a hulking brute or anything, but he had forty or fifty pounds on me. Shane probably could have dropped him in a heartbeat, but I brought my hand to my firearm at the small of my back.

"Please don't try to intimidate us," I said. "That will end badly for you."

His eyes traveled down my torso again.

"You want a job?" he asked. "I could use a more mature woman."

"No, but thanks," I said. "Tell me about Oscar."

Andrews sighed and put a hand on his vehicle and leaned forward. His shirt billowed out, making him look bigger than he was. It reminded me of a puffer fish, trying to blow itself up and scare off a shark.

"Oscar is dead. What do you want to know?"

"Someone murdered him," I said. "I hear he was a good guy, too. Why would somebody murder him?"

He looked down and shook his head before removing his hand from the vehicle.

"He wasn't a good guy. Please leave me alone."

He tapped on the roof of his car. A man stepped out of the driver's seat. He wore a black suit, and he crossed his arms. I shook my head at him.

"I'd stay where you are, buddy," I said. "This is between us and Mr. Andrews."

The muscle looked to his boss. Andrews nodded,

and the guy stayed put. I looked to Andrews.

"Tell us about Oscar," said Shane. "Did you send him to Meadowview to engage in amorous congress with a camper?"

He furrowed his brow.

"I don't even know what the hell amorous congress means."

"Did you send him to fuck a client there?" I asked.

He straightened.

"No. Just please leave me alone."

He reached for the door handle.

"You leave, I can't guarantee you won't show up in a police report," said Shane.

He lowered his hand and turned to us.

"You said you weren't cops."

"To be fair, Hana said she wasn't a cop," said Shane.

"He's right," I said. "We're not looking to jam you up. Oscar's murder is our only interest here. If you give us what we need, you'll probably never see us again. If you stand in our way, we'll make life hard for you. How do you want to approach this? Given the nature of your business, I'd be cautious if I were you."

The muscles of his jaw twitched as he clenched his teeth. Then he crossed his arms.

"Fine. Oscar worked for me, but I fired him. Now he's dead. He deserved it."

I shifted my weight to my back foot and

considered.

"I've spoken to dozens of people, and they all liked him. Why did he deserve to die?"

"Oscar ruined my business," said Andrews, leaning forward. "I was a party planner. He was a DJ. That's it. No matter what you think, I didn't pimp him out to anybody."

I crossed my arms and nodded.

"I checked out his house. He had Alexander McQueen jeans, Omega watches, and more cashmere sweaters and scarves than I've ever seen. How'd he afford all that?"

Andrews lowered his chin and raised his eyebrows.

"He was a drug dealer."

I shook my head.

"He wasn't a drug dealer," I said. "Try again. I searched his room. His mom found some weed there, but there weren't any drugs there, and nobody else mentioned them."

"You've been talking to the wrong people. He worked as a DJ so he could sell drugs to kids. Because of him, the police raided my office, took my computers, tore my home apart, and interrogated my staff. They didn't find shit, but they still put me out of business. I had six full-time employees, and I had to let them go. I lost everything because of him. We specialized in sweet sixteen parties and bar mitzvahs. No parent wants to book a guy suspected of dealing drugs at parties."

I narrowed my eyes.

"Start over and tell us what happened. What'd he do to you?"

"Four years ago, a lawyer booked us for his daughter's birthday at the family's lake house in Pollard. They wanted everything. Music, food, lights, decorations, flowers...the whole shebang. It was a forty-thousand-dollar job, the biggest we ever had. My staff was pumped. Oscar would DJ for us, a restaurant in Springfield would provide the food, and my florist would provide the flowers. It was the birthday girl's coming-out party, and we planned to show the world what we could do."

He paused as if waiting for one of us to say something.

"Sounds like you worked hard," said Shane.

"We busted our asses," he said, his voice growing louder. "And it was going great. The weather cooperated, the food tasted amazing, and the house looked fantastic. Everybody was having a good time. Then at sunset, Oscar went on stage. The kids danced and sang, but he kept disappearing. The sound system and lighting kept working, so that was okay. Whenever Oscar left, though, a different girl would go with him. A parent noticed and thought Oscar was hooking up with the partygoers."

I nodded.

"Go on."

"The parent called the police, and a pair of

officers came out. They caught Oscar with Ecstasy in individual baggies and shut down the entire party. Then the Bryant County sheriff came out and started interviewing everybody. They dragged Oscar to jail, but the sheriff mislabeled the pills and lost them in his evidence vault. Without evidence, the prosecutor dropped the charges but not before Oscar said I was his supplier.

"I lost my business after that. After word got out, we couldn't book another party. We had plans. We were going to do weddings. I was even researching commercial real estate. We were going to buy a kitchen and cater our own events. We were good at what we did. Then Oscar told that sheriff I forced him to sell drugs. I don't even know why. He didn't have to."

Andrews may have been a pimp, but he evidently didn't understand the narcotics trade. I tilted my head to the side and considered him.

"Oscar pointed the finger at you because he was terrified of his real supplier. He needed to blame somebody, and he knew you wouldn't kill him. His actual supplier would—and probably did."

"Whatever. I'm still broke," said Andrews. "This isn't what I wanted to do. I've got a degree in tourism management. Until Oscar came along, I was going places. Now, I hook up rich old men with college girls who can't pay their tuition. I don't even like what I do."

"That's unfortunate. You had no idea Oscar was

dealing when you hired him?"

"No," he said, shaking his head. "I hired him because women loved him and because he knew how to set up a sound system."

The story made sense, but it didn't explain everything. I had no idea where Oscar got his drugs, where he stored those drugs, or why he cleaned pools in the summer. If he made enough money to buy his clothes and watches by selling drugs, a summer job seemed like a complete waste of time.

"Did Oscar's arrest make the newspapers?"

Andrews scoffed and rolled his eyes.

"This is Springfield. You don't need to make the news for everybody to know your business. It was all over Facebook."

Then his boss at the pool company should have known about it, too. No sane employer would keep an employee suspected of dealing drugs on staff. He'd come with too much liability. I needed to find out what I could about that pool company.

"Thanks for your time, Mr. Andrews," I said. "I won't bother you anymore."

"Good."

He got into the limousine. My muscles felt tight, and my skin tingled as Shane and I walked back to the car. We were getting somewhere with this case. Oscar Romero wasn't the man the world thought he was. Who he truly was and who he worked for, I had no idea.

But we'd find out—and soon.

34

Shane and I drove back to Pollard and stopped by the grocery store for food, bottles of water, and a few other things. Sheriff Lyons had already looked for me once at the motel, which meant Elaine Johnson likely knew to look for me there, too. So Shane and I abandoned his motel room and drove to my cabin. The place looked secure, and it was certainly quiet. Even without running water or electricity, we could stay there for a few nights.

We ate on the back porch. The wooded landscape sloped downward toward the lake. During the winter, you could see the water clearly through the leafless limbs, but the leaves obscured the view during the spring, summer, and fall. It was peaceful. On nights like that, I missed my mom and dad most of all.

"So what do you think?" asked Shane. "About Andrews."

"He's a shit bag who chose to pimp out women," I said. "Hard to feel sorry for him, even if Oscar ruined his business."

"You think he killed Oscar?"

"He had motive," I said, picking at the remnants of my salad. "The killer had access to the camp, though."

Shane nodded his agreement, and we settled into an easygoing silence. After dinner, we went inside. He took one of the bedrooms, while I slept on the couch in the living room. That night, I dreamt of throwing rocks in the lake with my dad, of baking muffins with my mom, and of watching the sunset on the porch with Lady, our elderly dog. I couldn't remember the last time I slept without nightmares, but this cabin held too many wonderful memories for the bad ones to find hold. I felt at peace here.

Unfortunately, memories—no matter how wonderful—didn't make the toilets flush or lights work. I had to pee in the woods the next morning, which wasn't entirely fun. Afterward, I washed my hands with bottled water. Shane did likewise. Then we ate granola bars, and I dug my hiking boots out of the car while he spoke with his wife.

Nature had overtaken the trails Dad made, but that didn't matter. I hiked to the lake and then sat and watched the water ripple. Then I hiked back to the cabin. Finally, I sat on the back porch and watched the morning pass.

As a child, I knew pain and sacrifice. I survived a civil war because people loved me. Now that I was an adult, I needed something more. I wanted a reason to live, something that made my life meaningful. For a while, I thought I had that. Blake and I were in love, and we were going to raise children in my parents' house. It'd become our home. We'd be happy.

Then he hurt me. He was a bastard, but he didn't break me. I poured myself into being a detective and worked seventy hours or more a week. The hours didn't matter, though; I helped people. I made the world better. Then, I lost that, too. I didn't know what I had left to give now. Sometimes, you just get knocked down so often and so hard that getting up stops being worthwhile. I didn't know what to do anymore.

Shane came out of the cabin a few minutes after I sat down.

"If it's okay with you, I'm going to go to the motel and enjoy the running water for a while. You can shower after me if you want, but I can't guarantee there'll be any hot water."

"You're a true gentleman," I said, smelling my armpit. "I feel compelled to take you up on your offer."

We left the cabin. As he pulled into the motel's parking lot, any thoughts I had about showering and getting ready for the day disappeared. Kevin Recinos stood outside my Subaru. It looked like he was trying to break in. Shane slammed on the brakes and pulled up behind the car. Both of us got out. Recinos straightened. I snapped pictures of him with my phone.

"Put your hands on top of your head and come toward my car," said Shane, lifting his shirt over the badge clipped onto his belt. "I'm going to pat you down for weapons, and then I'm going to call the sheriff's department."

Recinos furrowed his brow.

"Who are you?"

"Nobody," said Shane. "Now do as I ask."

"No need to pat me down," said Recinos. "I've got a Glock 17 on my hip, and my badge is in my back pocket. It's gold and has an eagle on top. Who do you work for?"

Before Shane could respond, I called out.

"You're not a cop anymore, Kevin. You lost that when you went to prison."

He focused on me and shook his head.

"Never been to prison, honey. I work at the FBI's resident agency in Hopkinsville, Kentucky."

My gut tightened, and I drew in a breath.

"I caught you trying to break into my car," I said. "I don't believe you."

He shrugged.

"Your beliefs don't matter, Detective Blackwood."

I narrowed my eyes.

"How do you know I was a detective?"

"The same way I know you're divorced, that you live alone in a little apartment in northern St. Louis County, and that you resigned from the St. Louis County Police Department after shooting a suspected murderer. Is this guy Shane Lewis?"

I lowered my weapon and felt the fine hairs on the back of my neck stand. Shane looked at me, confused.

"We'll talk in a moment," I said to him. Then I looked to Recinos. "Why did Crystal Valentine tell me you were her ex-husband and that you had beaten her?"

"Is Crystal Valentine an attractive woman in her early forties with olive-colored skin and brown hair?"

"That's more or less her," I said.

"Her actual name is Julie Fisk, and her husband is Tony Fisk. They lived together in rural Kentucky near Hopkinsville. Tony is a convicted drug trafficker and murderer. He imported fentanyl from labs in Mexico and repackaged it for sale in Louisville, Indianapolis, Cincinnati, Chicago, and St. Louis. He and a network of associates murdered almost two dozen of their rivals over the past decade. His wife, Julie, was his partner. When we arrested them, Julie turned on her husband and his suppliers. Because of information she supplied, we've arrested three dozen people in four countries. She a friend of yours?"

I brought a hand to my face and let that sink in.

"Why are you here now?" I asked. "If Crystal—or Julie—is free, she must have made a deal. Why are you looking for her?"

"I'm not looking for her," he said. "I'm looking for two button men who work for Tony Fisk's former partners. At the time of his arrest, Tony Fisk owed them thirty-five million dollars. They want their money and probably think Julie has it."

"And you tracked those bad guys here?" I asked, lowering my chin.

"Yep."

"Why were you trying to break into my car?"

He considered and then shrugged.

"I was hoping to find out who you worked for. Now I know—Julie," he said. "Word of advice? Don't trust her. She's a liar who uses and discards everyone around her. Now, if you'll excuse me, I have work to do."

I watched him walk to his car. Then I snapped pictures of him with my phone. He was both right and wrong: Crystal had lied to me, but she hadn't used and discarded me. She came to me because she and her family needed help. She wasn't a monster. Real monsters didn't hide in apartments in the middle of nowhere with their children.

As he left, Shane walked to me.

"That was unexpected," he said.

"It's a long story, but I'll fill you in," I said. "In the meantime, take a shower. I'm going to do some research."

Shane agreed and went to his room. I, meanwhile, sat in the front seat of my car with my phone. A Google search turned up a dozen articles on Tony Fisk. A reporter in Louisville had followed his arrest and trial, but the story didn't really take off. Fisk may have dealt drugs, but the government's case against him focused on tax evasion and securities fraud, two of the least sexy crimes on the books. He'd spend the rest of his life in prison, but not for the most serious crimes he allegedly committed. No article I found mentioned Julie Fisk, so I couldn't confirm Recinos's story.

Kevin Recinos and Crystal Valentine had given me competing stories but few verifiable facts. If Crystal was really Julie Fisk, a woman who testified against her drug-trafficking, murderous husband, she should have been in witness protection with the Marshals Service. Even if she had turned witness protection down, she should have had a contact with the marshals who would have helped her in cases like this. If Recinos was telling the truth, she had no reason to contact me.

FBI agent or not, Recinos terrified Crystal. He— or someone—scared her kids, too. Whoever Crystal really was, that wasn't right. I wanted to tell her he was in town, but I couldn't interfere with a federal investigation. Instead, I sent her a text message.

Stay safe, stay inside, and keep George with you. Everything's going to work out.

I hoped I hadn't just lied to her.

35

Once Shane was dressed, it was my turn in the shower. Since neither of us had eaten a real breakfast, we went by Frank's Downtown Diner afterward and had eggs and toast. Our conversation focused on Oscar Romero. He had sold drugs, but he still cleaned pools for Lakeside Pools.

I knew of a high-end cocaine dealer who worked a menial nine-to-five job at an investment brokerage, but only because that job gave him access to very wealthy potential clients. When he tapped one office out, he moved to another. The kids at Meadowview might have bought Oscar's drugs, but there wouldn't have been enough of them to support his lifestyle.

Lakeside Pools brought Oscar to Camp Meadowview, but something else must have drawn Oscar to Lakeside Pools. We needed to find out what, so we drove my car to the company's address in Springfield after breakfast. There, we found row after row of warehouses and light industrial buildings. A semitrailer was parked in the lot out behind Lakeside Pools, but nobody walked to or from the building. A dozen white commercial vans were parked in a row in the lot to the side. Most had a greenish-blue wave painted on the outside and *Lakeside Pools* stenciled on the doors.

I parked across the street in the nearly full parking lot of a trucking company, and we watched. For four hours, nothing happened. My eyelids started growing heavy, and I yawned. On television, stakeouts were glamorous and exciting. In reality, they were boring, resource-intensive, and rarely successful.

"We're wasting our time here," I said. "It's just a pool company."

"A busy one," said Shane. "They've got a lot of trucks moving in and out."

"I'm sure their owners appreciate that," I said, reaching for my keys. Before I could turn on my car, the building's front door opened. An attractive blonde woman stepped out. I grabbed my phone and used its camera to zoom in on her. She wore a navy pencil skirt and sleeveless top, and she carried a dark coffee mug. By the way she swung it, it held no coffee. "That's Elaine Johnson."

"The detective?" asked Shane, sitting straighter. I nodded and snapped pictures of her as she opened the front door of a red four-door Mercedes.

"The one who tried to kill me."

She sat, closed her door, and then reversed out of her parking spot. I put on my seat belt and twisted my keys in the ignition.

"You're not going to ram her, are you?" asked Shane, reaching for his own seat belt.

"The thought crossed my mind, but no," I said. "We need information. She's going to give it to us."

Johnson pulled out of the parking lot and hung a left. I followed a few minutes later. We drove for about half an hour. Eventually, we reached a middle-class neighborhood full of winding streets, big brick homes, and mature landscapes.

Johnson pulled into the driveway of a brick home with a two-car garage. The yard sloped downward behind her house, making me suspect she had a walk-out basement. A pair of dormers protruded above the garage. It was a big house for a single woman. I drove past and then parked a block away.

"You're sure that's the woman who tried to kill you?" asked Shane.

"I wouldn't forget her," I said, taking pictures of the nearest cross street with my phone so I'd remember where I was. Then I looked up Johnson's address online to see what I could find in publicly available databases. "The home is owned by Lakeside Trust, and it was purchased two years ago for four hundred thousand dollars. Elaine Johnson doesn't appear anywhere on the tax record."

I looked up from my phone. Shane had a distant look on his face.

"You with me, buddy?" I asked.

"Look up the street about half a block."

I followed his gaze to a white Chevy pickup. A man sat in the front seat. He didn't move. He just sat there, as if he was waiting for something. It wasn't the first time I had seen him, either. I thumbed through other pictures on my phone until I found those I had taken outside Lakeside Pools. The same pickup had parked on the road there, too.

I showed a picture to Shane.

"We're not the only people watching her," he said.

I held my phone toward the pickup and zoomed in as tightly as I could. The driver looked at me, so I waved and smiled. Then he put his car in gear and left. My phone had a decent zoom, but it didn't have a telephoto lens. The details of his face were fuzzy, but the driver looked as if he was in his fifties or sixties, and he didn't look happy. A detective would have hidden in a surveillance van. This guy was a freelancer. Interesting.

I doubted Johnson ran a drug ring out of her home, but clearly she drew attention. She wouldn't expose her business accidentally, but if I pushed her hard enough, she might make a mistake.

"You're armed, aren't you?" I asked, glancing toward Shane. He nodded. "Come on, then. This is going to be fun."

* * *

Elaine sighed as she entered her home. She had bought it with cash and had dreamt of filling it with furniture and flowers and memories. A landscape designer she hired had designed a terraced garden on the hillside out back. It'd have tomatoes and cucumbers on one end and rose and lilac bushes on the other. In the front yard, she planned to place tulips and daffodils.

Unfortunately, that garden never materialized. In the past two years, she had spent more nights in hotels than home. No furniture decorated her living room, the kitchen held few plates, and only one bedroom contained a bed. Soon, she'd put the home on the market. A family would love it, but she had no attachment to it.

She plucked two bottles of wine from the rack in her kitchen and considered their labels. Both were good but not great bottles. She didn't even know whether Joseph liked wine. Maybe he was a beer man. He drank—she knew that because she had seen him come in hung over once, after the Kansas City Chiefs won the Super Bowl. He had looked so sheepish that morning. It was almost cute.

She put the white wine in her fridge and poured the red into a decanter so it'd breathe. The day had been unpleasant, but their plans were progressing. Zane Hopkins and his sister were dead, and Elaine had already wired two million dollars to Colonel Sok in Cambodia for four fifty-five-gallon drums of safrole oil. It was a lot of money, but it'd be worthwhile if it secured the sale of her business. Her safrole would reach Thailand within the day. Then, a dockworker would hide the barrels amidst barrels of palm oil. They'd reach Seattle in two weeks and her warehouse in three.

Everything would work out. She needed to stay strong. She poured herself a glass of red wine, stripped off her clothes, and put on a pink silk robe before drawing a bath in her ensuite. Then the doorbell rang.

She expected Joseph to come by but not for another couple hours. Maybe he was eager to see her. The thought made her heart flutter and her lips curl into a smile. She tightened her robe but stayed naked beneath it. If Joseph played his cards right, maybe they could take a bath together.

Unfortunately, her smile left as she opened the door. For a moment, she could only stare. She had a gun in her bedroom but no weapons here. Her lungs felt tight, and her throat felt dry. She licked her lips and looked around. Hana Blackwood and a man she didn't recognize stood outside.

"Ms. Blackwood," she said, her voice lower than she expected. "I didn't..."

"Expect me?" asked the detective, flicking her eyes downward. Elaine tried to cover herself. "Nice robe."

"Every other house on this street has a surveillance camera," Elaine said. "If you kill me, you'll go to prison."

"I don't doubt that," she said, holding up a bundle of magazines and letters. "I'm not here to kill you. In fact, I got your mail. Your real name is Elaine Alford. I looked Elaine Johnson up earlier and couldn't find anything."

Elaine stepped to her left, hiding herself behind the thick, wooden door. If she slammed it, Blackwood and the man beside her would kick it down. Or maybe she'd just shoot through it.

"What do you want?"

Blackwood held out the mail. Elaine's back stiffened. Then she reached forward and snatched it. Blackwood's mouth curled into a tight smile.

"You think I'm just going to shoulder my way inside and kill you?"

"I don't know what you want," said Elaine, "but I want you to leave."

"Just a second," said Blackwood, reaching into her pocket for her phone. She flicked her finger across her phone's screen and then held it up for Elaine to see. "You see that white pickup?"

Elaine looked at the screen and nodded, wary.

"I found it in front of your house. It was also parked in front of Lakeside Pools, where you work. The man driving it was probably sixty. He was kind of ugly. Sound familiar?"

Unfortunately, it sounded like Vince Forsyth. It could have been William Forsyth, but Elaine wouldn't have called him ugly. Either way, the potential buyers of her business shouldn't have been following her. Her skin started getting warm.

"What do you want?" she asked.

"Nothing," said Blackwood. "I just thought I'd show you the pictures and let you know that I know where you live." She paused. "Who's the guy in the truck?"

"Nobody."

Blackwood lowered her chin. Elaine straightened.

"If he was nobody, your face wouldn't have turned that white. Consider calling the police. They'll protect you."

"Goodbye, Ms. Blackwood," she said, stepping back. "Don't come here again."

"I won't. It's probably going to be a crime scene soon, anyway, after the guy in the truck murders you in your sleep."

Elaine narrowed her eyes but said nothing. Blackwood and the man with her wished her luck and walked to her cheap little Subaru and drove off. Elaine squeezed the door hard and then slammed it shut. She went straight to the kitchen and grabbed her phone. Joseph answered right away.

"Hey," he said. "Everything okay? I wasn't planning to come over until later."

"Hana Blackwood just came to my house."

"Are you alone now?"

"Yeah. She left after showing me a picture of Vince Forsyth. He's been following me."

Joseph said nothing for a moment.

"Have you called William?"

"This requires more than a phone call," she said. "I want him to understand how unacceptable his behavior is."

Joseph paused. Elaine clenched her teeth. Her chest rose and fell with every breath.

"All right," he said. "We know where they're staying. Daniel and I can kill him. We've still got the police uniforms from Pollard. If we get a pair of cruisers, it'll be easy. We'll send a message."

It felt like a bubble had burst inside her, and she exhaled a slow breath.

"Thank you," she said. "You're the best friend I've ever had, Joseph. I want you to know that."

She'd spoken without thinking, but she had meant it. Joseph cleared his throat.

"You're my friend, too, and I say this as your friend—if we go after the Forsyths, we'll start a war. I'm willing, but I'm not sure that we can win. People will die, and I don't know if the rewards will be worth it."

She blinked and looked down. Then she sighed and rubbed her eyes.

"Fine. Then don't kill anybody. Go to Springfield and show William we can get to him. Put the fear of God into him."

"We will," said Joseph.

"Be safe. I don't know what I'd do without you."

"You, too," he said. "I'll call you soon."

He hung up, and she walked back to her bathroom to turn off the water. The tub had nearly overflowed. A big part of her wanted to call Joseph back and tell him to forget everything. She had some money saved up. They could just run. They could fly to Mexico and buy a place on the beach. She'd learn how to cook, and he'd learn how to sail. He had always wanted to do that, he once told her.

Elaine didn't pick up the phone, though. She deserved more than a retirement in Mexico, as wonderful as it sounded. She deserved to win. Joseph did, too. They had worked too hard to lose. No, they'd finish the game and make sure the losers —Hana Blackwood in particular—paid the price.

36

As I drove from Alford's house, Shane crossed his arms.

"What'd you hope to accomplish with that conversation?" he asked.

"She knows we're watching her now," I said. "She also knows the guy in the pickup was watching her. He scared her, so we know she's got enemies. We didn't know that before."

"What does that get us?"

"I don't know yet, but the harder we push her buttons, the more likely she is to lash out. She'll make a mistake, and we'll have our opening."

Shane looked ahead. The sun would set in another hour.

"It was reckless," he said. "If she goes under, she could disappear before we can prove anything. We know she came after you, but we still don't know why or who works for her, or whether she killed

Oscar Romero. If your goal is to piss her off, congratulations. If your goal is to solve your case, though, knocking on her door was a mistake."

I shut my mouth and scowled but said nothing. Maybe he was right, but playing offense for once felt good. Once we reached the outskirts of Springfield, I drew in a breath through my nose.

"Alford's dirty, her company is dirty, and so is the police department in Pollard," I said. "Now, she knows I'm a threat to her personally. She and her thugs will come after me, but before they do that, they'll clean house. I'm going to use that."

"What does that mean?"

"It means, maybe you should go back to St. Louis."

Shane crossed his arms.

"What are you going to do?"

I glanced at him and then to the road ahead of me.

"I'm going to stake out her business tonight. If she's got drugs in the building, she'll clean them out. I'll watch. Then, once I see her cleaning crew, I'll call the Springfield PD and tell them I see suspicious activity. They'll come out."

"Easy as that, huh?" asked Shane. "The local PD will show up, the bad guys will roll over, and happy days will be here again."

"Do you have a better plan?" I asked.

He said nothing. Then, a few minutes later, he cleared his throat.

"Where are we going?"

"I'm dropping you off near your car. Then I'm going to go by the grocery store for some food and water."

He uncrossed his arms and shook his head.

"Just turn around. I'll go with you."

"So you like my plan now?"

"I think it beats sitting around in a cheap motel."

I turned around as soon as I found a safe place and then drove to a grocery store in Springfield, where I purchased bottles of water, premade sandwiches, pretzels, and other snacks for our stakeout. Then, I drove back to Lakeside Pools and parked in the lot of a business nearby. Shane settled into his seat, while I dug out a pair of binoculars from the back of my car. My mom had loved birds, and she had left me three sets of binoculars. I had brought a pair to Pollard in case I saw a bald eagle near the cabin. They were usually farther north this time of year, but I thought I might get lucky.

After that, Shane and I sat and watched the building. Lakeside Pools connected both Oscar Romero and Elaine Alford. There had to be something here. The hours ticked by. At one in the morning, I walked to a convenience store about half a mile away to use the restroom while Shane continued his watch. I might as well have caught a movie while I was gone, though, because nothing happened. By five in the morning, I realized we had wasted the entire night.

As the sun started to rise, Shane stretched and yawned.

"You ready to go home?"

"To Pollard," I said. "I'm not done with the case. You can go if you want, though. I won't hold it against you."

"If you're here, so am I," he said. "Ivy's orders."

I smiled, more to myself than to him.

"I have always liked her."

I drove back to Pollard and dropped Shane off near his car at the motel. He'd stay there for a few hours to rest, and then we'd regroup. Once I reached my cabin, I locked the door and crashed on my sleeping bag in the living room. I was asleep almost the moment I shut my eyes. Unfortunately, I woke up about three hours later when somebody pounded on the door. At first, I wondered why George wasn't barking, but then I remembered he was with Crystal Valentine and her family.

"Open the door, Blackwood. Now."

The voice belonged to Kevin Recinos. I rubbed my eyes and rolled over. Wrinkles covered my shirt, but I was dressed.

"Give me a minute," I said before clearing my throat.

"No. Open the door, or I'll kick it down."

I rubbed sleep out of my eyes before wriggling out of my sleeping bag.

"One...two..."

Recinos hadn't told me what he was counting to,

but I hurried toward the door anyway and threw it open. He wore a gray suit, white shirt, and blue tie. His hair was combed, but he had bags under his eyes and several days' worth of hair on his chin.

"What do you want?" I asked, squinting in the morning light. He looked me up and down.

"Are you drunk?"

"No, I'm exhausted, and you woke me up," I said. "What do you want?"

He looked over my shoulder and then pushed past me and into the entryway.

"Where are they?"

"Where are who?" I asked. "Why are you here? How'd you even know where my cabin was?"

He walked past me and into the living room. Along the way, he picked up my pistol from a table. I sucked in a breath.

"What the hell are you doing here?" I asked.

He ignored me and stuck his head in each of the cabin's three bedrooms. Satisfied we were alone in the cabin, he came back to the living room and glared at me.

"I want to see your phone," he said.

"No," I said, shaking my head. "I've been more than accommodating. Give me my firearm and get out of my house. If you want to talk to me again, I'll give you the name of my attorney."

"Crystal Valentine and her family are gone," he said. "They left their shit in their apartment and disappeared."

My mouth opened.

"Did they leave a dog?"

He furrowed his brow and shook his head.

"No, there was no dog," he said. "They disappeared. Why would they leave a dog?"

I stepped back and sat on the couch. Crystal and the kids had liked George, so they wouldn't hurt him. That didn't mean they could take care of him, though. He'd slow them down. They couldn't keep him if they were running. Maybe they took him by the Humane Society before leaving.

I reached for the phone on the end table nearest me.

"Are you calling them?" asked Kevin, his voice sharp.

"No, I'm looking for my dog," I said. "They had George. I'm going to call the Humane Society."

He crossed the room and grabbed my phone from my hand. I jumped.

"Stop it," he said, throwing my phone to the couch. "Focus. You're helping me find them."

My back stiffened, and muscles all over my body grew rigid. If I had a pistol, I would have drawn it. Kevin had probably fifty pounds on me. In a fight, he'd win. I needed a weapon. Unfortunately, I didn't have much. My mom kept a reproduction Tiffany lamp on an end table. It was heavy glass, so if I could reach that, I could use it as a club. It'd crack his head clean open.

I edged toward it.

"Never touch me again," I said.

He looked me up and down. Then he stepped back.

"Sorry. I'm worried about Crystal and her family. My job is to keep them safe, and now they're gone."

At our last meeting, he told me he had followed a pair of bad guys from Hopkinsville. Button men, he had called them. He hadn't seemed to care about Crystal.

"Where would they go?" I asked. Kevin stood between me and the front door. My fingers trembled as adrenaline began building.

"If I could answer that, I wouldn't be here."

"Think. You're an FBI agent, and she's a witness to multiple federal crimes," I said. "She moved from Hopkinsville to Pollard. Would she go back to Hopkinsville?"

"No."

"After Hopkinsville, where'd she go?" I asked. "You told me last time we met that she testified against her husband at trial. Where'd she live?"

He sighed.

"A safe house in Bowling Green, Kentucky, but she wouldn't have gone back there. It was too close to home. She could run into people she knew. We only kept her there because it gave us an easy commute to Hopkinsville."

I had worked with FBI agents before. They were tight-lipped—even to police officers working parallel investigations. Kevin spoke about things he never should have told anyone. The hairs on the back of my neck stood up.

"Does she have any family?" I asked. "Someone who would take her in?"

Kevin started pacing. He chewed on a fingernail.

"I don't know," he said. Then he stopped. "She trusts you. Call and ask where she is."

"She's smart, so she won't answer," I said. "She knows I was a detective. If she doesn't trust you, she won't trust me." I paused. "When I worked in St. Louis, I took a continuing law enforcement education course with the FBI. We flew to their orientation center in Arlington, Virginia. It's where they took witnesses before major federal trials. You think she'd go back there? Maybe she felt comfortable there. If she's scared, she'll retreat to somewhere familiar."

He considered me and then nodded.

"I'll look into it and call our contact there. In the meantime, I need you to call her."

The FBI had no orientation center in Arlington. I had made it up. And Kevin had jumped on it. He had lied to me. Crystal had lied to me, too. I didn't even know her real name. The lies flowed from both of their mouths as easily as the truth.

Now, though, Crystal's lies made sense.

"We should go to the sheriff's office," I said. "They'll help us look for her."

"No. This is a federal matter," he said, pulling the firearm from the holster at his belt. I thought quickly and then drew in a breath.

"I know somebody who can help," I said. "Crystal had a friend in town. They were close. I'll take you to him. Just don't hurt me. I'm not a threat."

He grabbed me by the arm and squeezed and then pointed the pistol at my waist.

"Good. You're driving. Let's go."

37

Outside, Kevin had parked his red Ford Fusion behind my Subaru, blocking me in. He pointed to his car with his pistol.

"Get in the driver's seat. I'll be in the back. If you try anything stupid, I'll kill you and jump out."

I held up my hands and wished my parents had purchased a cabin on a busier road.

"Okay."

We got in the car, and I drove to Crystal's apartment building and parked beside the office. Kevin raised an eyebrow and cocked his head at me.

"I already told you they left."

"And I heard you," I said. "We're here to see the manager. He and Crystal were sleeping together."

Kevin raised his chin.

"I hope you're telling me the truth."

Kevin was a danger, but I knew enough dangerous men and women to control myself around them. I forced a tremble into my voice.

"You're not an FBI agent, are you?"

"If you behave, you'll live," he said. "If you run, you'll die. And so will this manager and everyone I see afterward. What do you want to do?"

Though I tried to keep my anger from my face, I seethed inside. Kevin had come here to hurt a woman and her children. Crystal may have broken the law, but her kids were innocent. Kevin would have hurt them. That pissed me off.

"The manager will know where she is. He's probably hiding her," I said, forcing my voice to sound high and tight. "Please don't hurt me."

He grunted.

"Get out of the car and walk toward the office. You'll go in first. I'll have a gun at your back, and I will shoot if you decide to play hero."

"I'm no hero," I said, reaching for the door handle.

"Good."

We stepped out of the car. Once more, the pool deck was empty, and no children played nearby. I walked toward the office, wishing again that I had a pistol. Kevin followed so closely I could hear him breathe and smell his musky, woodsy cologne. My heart raced, and I almost felt light-headed.

As I pulled the door open, a bell rang. The office was about ten feet by fifteen feet. Chairs, a desk, and a row of mailboxes on the wall cluttered the interior. Brown cardboard packages with UPS labels rested against the desk. They probably belonged to residents. Rough-sawn cedar covered the walls. Little sunlight filtered through the dirty windows in front.

"Hold on."

The voice came from an open doorway at the far end of the room. Kevin stepped up beside me. The man who stepped out of the interior office was in his late fifties or early sixties. He wore a maintenance man's coveralls, but his cool, blue eyes scanned the room at a glance and then focused on Kevin. Then he brought his right leg back and turned his left hip toward us, the smile never leaving his face as he put his body between us and the firearm hidden on his right hip.

"Morning, folks," he said. "Can I help you?"

"Is the manager here?" I asked. "The young guy. The handsome one. It's about Crystal Valentine."

He flicked his eyes up and down me before giving me a sympathetic look.

"I heard you were friends," he said. "Ms. Valentine and her family no longer live here. Sorry."

"They take the dog with them?"

He considered me again and nodded.

"They did," he said. "Crystal's a good mom. She'll be a good momma to that dog, too."

"We're not here to talk about dogs," said Kevin, reaching behind him for his wallet. The maintenance man stiffened but stayed where he was even as Kevin exposed his badge. "Where'd they go?"

"That real?" asked the maintenance man, raising an eyebrow. Kevin nodded.

"Sure is."

The maintenance man stepped closer to peer at the badge. Then he straightened and lowered his hands below the desktop. If I had read the situation correctly, he had just hit an emergency switch similar to the ones a bank teller might toggle in case of a robbery.

"I don't think I can help you, partner," said the maintenance man. "Come back in an hour. I'll have my boss in by then."

Kevin raised his weapon.

"Try again," he said, pointing it at the maintenance man's chest. "Where is Crystal?"

I brought my hands up as if I were under arrest. The maintenance man kept his hands at his waist, near his weapon.

"He said he doesn't know," I said. "We should go."

"Shut up, Hana," said Kevin.

"Walk out and leave this complex. Nobody has to get hurt," said the maintenance man, his voice bereft of friendliness. "Lower the gun and go."

Kevin leaned forward. I shifted my weight and edged toward him half a step.

"You're not in a position to threaten anybody," said Kevin. "Now tell me about Crystal. Where is she? Pretend your life is on the line."

The instant he finished speaking, the office's exterior door opened. Warm air came in. No one spoke. Kevin cocked his head to the side but didn't turn.

"You should leave, friend," he said. "This is a law enforcement matter. It doesn't concern you."

I drew in a breath. The world slowed, and my senses seemed to heighten. I could smell Kevin's cologne and the stale coffee in a mug on the maintenance man's desk, and I felt the heat from outside wafting through the door.

Then, everything moved at once.

The maintenance man lunged forward and reached for Kevin's weapon. Kevin's finger traveled from the trigger guard to the trigger.

As the maintenance man grabbed the firearm, I stamped down hard on Kevin's foot and lowered my elbow. Kevin grunted and stepped backward, and I swung my arm and arched my back, getting as much of my body into it as I could. As my elbow struck his face, he reared back.

Somebody fired a gun. Insulation and bits of the acoustic-tile ceiling rained down on us. The guy at the door hit Kevin in the back. He fell forward against the desk as the maintenance man ripped the pistol from his hands. Before I could move, a pair of arms wrapped around my chest and yanked me backwards. Two men with pistols stood in the parking lot. One wore a bathrobe. The other wore slacks and a white Oxford shirt. Somebody threw me to the ground. My elbows and knees hit hard.

"US marshals. Face down on the ground."

My ears rang, and I felt dizzy. I swallowed hard as the world seemed to spin around me. Then I put my hands in the air and lowered myself to the ground.

"I'm unarmed. My name is Hana Blackwood. I'm not a threat."

One marshal patted me down. Then another secured my hands behind me with zip ties. At least I was right about one thing—Crystal hadn't paid her rent by driving an Uber.

For the next half hour, I hung out on a lounge chair beside the pool under the watchful eye of a female marshal. Neither of us spoke. Eventually, the handsome building manager, the one Crystal had vehemently defended at our earlier meeting, escorted me to a black SUV and cut the zip ties over my wrists.

"Have a seat, Ms. Blackwood. I'm Deputy US Marshal Kyle Dyer," he said, opening a rear door. I sat on a leather bench seat. He stayed outside and squinted at me. "So...why is a former St. Louis detective here with what appears to be a spectacularly corrupt FBI agent?"

"That's a long story."

His lips curled upward, but his eyes stayed flinty.

"We've got time."

I sighed and closed my eyes.

"It started with Crystal Valentine. She came up to me while I was having dinner."

Dyer let me talk for a few minutes and interrupted only to ask clarifying questions. I told him that Crystal had approached me and claimed that she needed help with her violent ex-husband, whom she suspected was in town. Her story made little sense, but I had worked domestic violence cases before and knew victims rarely told the complete story during an initial interview. I agreed to help and installed a video camera in her apartment and told her to contact an attorney.

Dyer reached into his pocket for a notepad. He scribbled notes and then drew in a breath.

"Tell me about Kevin Recinos. How'd you meet him?"

"He came to me a couple of days ago. Nearly everything Crystal told me was a lie, but she was so scared of Kevin that I loaned her my dog. He's a sweetheart, but he has a big bark."

Dyer blinked and considered me.

"Let's focus on Recinos. How well did you know him?"

"Not well at all. I caught him trying to break into my car, and he flashed his badge at me and told me that Crystal's real name was Julie Fisk and that she had been married to a major drug dealer from Hopkinsville, Kentucky. Crystal's story had changed so often I didn't believe anything she said. I didn't believe Kevin, either, but he had a badge. I backed off."

He considered me for a few moments.

"If you backed off, how'd you show up here?"

"He came back to my cabin with a gun this morning. I suggested we come here because I knew there'd be marshals waiting for us."

He narrowed his eyes.

"Did Crystal tell you there'd be marshals here?"

"No, but she didn't have to. Every time Crystal and I met, her story changed. She was lying, but I didn't know why. Clearly, though, she was scared and living under a false identity so believable she could use it to rent an apartment. Not only that, I knew she could afford the rent and her monthly expenses without working. Most women on the run stay with family or friends. They don't concoct new identities and run to the middle of nowhere."

Dyer considered that, but he wrote nothing down.

"Continue."

"The first time I met Kevin, he said Crystal was on the run after working out a deal with the US attorney's office to avoid prosecution. This time, he said the FBI had hidden her. Neither made sense, but then I started putting the lies together. I didn't know the truth, but I saw its outline."

Dyer shook his head.

"I don't understand."

"Consider the key to it all," I said. "You. Crystal loved you. She said you were the best man she ever met. Her eyes lit up when she talked about you. I'm guessing you cared about her, too. Otherwise, you wouldn't have risked your job by sleeping with her."

His head shot up.

"That's quite an accusation to lob at me."

"It is," I said. "Crystal witnessed a crime and then testified about it. To keep her safe, the government moved her here, paid her rent, and gave her money for food. You swore an oath to protect her. Instead, you slept with a vulnerable woman, and she fell head over heels for you.

"She risked everything to stay with you. She knew someone was after her, but if she told you the truth, the Marshals Service would whisk her and her family to Idaho or Florida. If she went to the police, she'd have to tell them the truth. They'd refer her to the marshals, and the marshals would send her away. Either way, she'd never see you again.

"So, she came to me with a crazy story she thought I'd believe. When I called her on the details, she changed that story until I bought it. She wanted me to solve her problem. It was the only way she and her kids could stay here and be with you. Crystal made lousy choices, but you crossed the line, Marshal. Everything that happened today was your fault. You're lucky no one died."

He drew in a breath and eyed me.

"That's a whole lot of speculation."

"That doesn't make me wrong, though."

He stepped back and swung his arm toward the street in front of the apartment.

"You're free to go, Ms. Blackwood. I don't think we'll be contacting you again."

At the very least, Dyer deserved to lose his badge, but that wasn't my call. I wasn't a detective anymore. I was a civilian who'd tried to help a woman in distress. Maybe I shouldn't have even done that.

I slid out of the car. Dyer slammed the door shut and walked toward a crowd of officers near the front office. My cabin was miles away, but Shane's motel was nearby, so I started walking. Before I reached the edge of the parking lot, though, the complex's maintenance man hurried over to me.

"Hold up, Ms. Blackwood," he said, smiling. "I'm Chief Deputy Marshal Gus Tannehill. Can I buy you a cup of coffee? I'd like to talk to you about Kyle Dyer and his relationship with Crystal Valentine."

I considered him.

"Are you two friends?" I asked.

"Nope."

"Make it breakfast," I said. "And you're driving. My car's still at my cabin."

"Sounds good."

38

The Forsyths had five rooms in a midmarket hotel near the Springfield airport. To ensure they were comfortable, Joseph had contacted the hotel staff a week before their arrival to make sure the Forsyths would be treated well. He had brought coffee and donuts and met Ms. Sharon, a supervisory member of the housekeeping staff. She was in her mid-fifties and had three children and a new grandchild. He had given her three hundred dollars so she could buy a new crib, and she had agreed to keep him updated on the Forsyths. Everybody profited.

Those early contacts were about to pay off royally.

When they reached the hotel, Joseph texted his contact. Ms. Sharon responded and said four of the men were in the hotel's dining room, eating breakfast. The family patriarch, William, was still in his room. Unknown to Ms. Sharon, William was nursing a hangover after spending an amorous, liquor-filled evening with a twenty-year-old woman from Missouri State University. Elaine had hired her to help cement a sale, but now the girl would be helpful in ways she didn't envision.

Daniel parked at the rear of the building. Ms. Sharon opened the rear door and smiled as soon as she saw Joseph step out of the pickup.

"Good morning," she said. "How are y'all doing this fine morning?"

"We're great," said Joseph, reaching for his wallet. He counted five one-hundred-dollar bills and held them toward her. Daniel got their supplies together. "There's a room I'd like you to let us into. Afterward, tell your boss you feel ill, or that you've got to go home to take care of that grandbaby. Do you have a locker to store your stuff while you're at work?"

She looked at the money.

"This is too much money to open the back door."

"It's also to stay quiet when the police come," he said. "Do you have a locker here for your stuff?"

She hesitated but then nodded.

"Leave it open as you leave," he said. "When the police come, tell them somebody broke in and that you left your master key in your locker. The man we're going to visit this morning is a drug trafficker, and he's done some bad things. We're going to visit."

She shook her head.

"I thought you were businessmen."

"We are," said Joseph. "And you're a co-conspirator. Do you know what accomplice liability is?"

She shook her head.

"It means you'll be charged with every crime you've helped us commit," said Joseph. "You can either go to prison, or you can take the money I've given you and do as I say. Buy your grandbaby diapers, live your life happily, and never speak of this again."

She stepped back. Joseph reached for his wallet again and gave her three more hundred-dollar bills. It was all the money he had on him.

"Take care of yourself, Sharon. And please give me your key card. Remember what I said—make it look like somebody opened your locker."

She nodded and held the rear door open and then handed Joseph her master key card. He thanked her and then walked inside. She disappeared down the long hallway that led to the lobby. The hotel's interior was clean, functional, and bland. Rather than wait for the elevator, Joseph and Daniel took the stairs to the third floor. William Forsyth had the room nearest the stairwell.

Once they reached William's door, Joseph pulled his firearm from its holster while Daniel unspooled a length of silver duct tape from the roll he carried. Both men knew their jobs, so neither spoke. Sharon's key card opened the door without issue.

The interior smelled like bourbon and musk. William Forsyth lay asleep in the bed. Joseph shut the door, while Daniel crossed the room.

Once they were in position, Joseph counted down from three on his fingers. As his last finger disappeared, Daniel secured the duct tape over William's mouth and then pinned his arms to the bed. Joseph held the gun to the older man's head as his eyes popped open. He kicked his feet and thrashed, but Daniel had been a high school wrestler and knew how to hold somebody down. After a few minutes, William's strength ran out. His eyes shot from one captor to the other.

"Morning," said Joseph. "Have a nice night?"

He thrashed again. The blankets slid off the end of the bed. Daniel held him easily.

"You keep fighting, I'll shoot you."

William narrowed his eyes but stopped kicking. Daniel let off some of his weight.

"Can my partner remove the duct tape, or will you scream? Remember that if you scream, you'll die, and your spouse will find out you spent your last night alive with a hooker."

William exhaled through his nose, but he didn't kick or fight. Daniel ripped off the tape. No one spoke for a few seconds. Then William cleared his throat.

"What the fuck are you two doing? And where are my boys?"

"They're eating breakfast," said Daniel. "They're

fine. Everybody's fine for now."

William snorted.

"What do you want? Elaine put you up to this?"

"She did," said Joseph, "but only because your brother's been following her. He already threatened to kill Elaine and take over the business instead of buying it. Now, we've got a picture of him outside her house. That makes us nervous."

"That's not how we do business," said William. "I explained that to you. And I appreciate the assets your company possesses. I'll talk to him. If you need him to, he'll apologize. If he had done his job right, Ms. Alford never would have seen him. He wasn't the problem, though. He was studying a business we intend to acquire and found a pretty young woman studying the same business. My brother wasn't following Ms. Alford. He followed that woman. It just so happened she was following your boss."

"Good for your brother," said Joseph, stepping back. He holstered his pistol. "I'd suggest you leave town now. We'll consider this a misunderstanding and move on with our lives."

William sat up and held his hands in front of him.

"Hold up a minute," he said. "If your company can't stand up to scrutiny, I don't want to buy it. You've got problems, but the assets might be worth it. I'm here to make a deal."

Joseph crossed his arms.

"Our problems are none of your concern."

"But they are. Tell me about the pretty brunette who followed your boss home and knocked on her door. What are you doing to her?"

Daniel said nothing. Joseph blinked.

"She's none of your concern," said Joseph.

"Is Oscar Romero my concern?" asked William. Joseph tried not to grimace. William's eyes glinted. "You didn't think we'd research the area? Romero's death is the biggest crime Bryant County's ever seen. It made the news in Memphis. As soon as Elaine mentioned Meadowview, I knew we had a problem. Do you have it under control?"

Daniel stepped forward.

"It's none of your concern."

"But it is," said William, panning his gaze to Daniel. "My boys and I drove out to that camp with you. You gave us a private tour. For all I know, the police have surveillance footage of us all together discussing the sale."

"We've got the police under control," said Joseph.

"Do you?" asked William. "I hear the sheriff's dead."

Neither Joseph nor Daniel spoke. William looked at both men.

"I admire Ms. Alford's business acumen, her facility is top notch, and her distribution network works," he said. "Security is lacking, though."

"Given the circumstances we're both in, our

security seems fine," said Daniel. "We've got guns. You don't. We're going to walk away from this encounter. Will you?"

"You're right," said William. "You got me with my pants down. Congratulations. I'm not the threat, though. You gentlemen have a dead kid problem. Romero is your business. I don't really care what you did to him. That woman—the private detective, or whatever she is—bothers me. I want your company, and I want that woman dead. Make it happen, and I'll wire Ms. Alford her twenty-five million. If you do your jobs, everybody wins."

"We'll talk to the boss," said Joseph.

William shook his head and scoffed.

"If she's not interested in selling to me because my brother knows where she lives, she's got bigger problems than Oscar Romero."

"She'll call you," said Daniel.

"I look forward to it," said William, smiling.

Joseph turned and left. Daniel followed. When they reached Daniel's pickup, Joseph pulled his phone out and called Elaine.

"Are they gone?" she asked.

"It's complicated," said Joseph. "He still wants to buy you out. He said Vince was following you as part of his due diligence."

"That's bullshit," said Elaine. "You don't follow your business partners."

"They weren't following you. They were following Hana Blackwood. He wants us to kill her.

If we do, he'll wire you twenty-five million for everything."

Elaine remained silent.

"What should we do?" he asked.

"The only thing we can," she said. "We'll kill Hana Blackwood. She's staying in Pollard. Find her. This is your area of expertise. Take care of her before something else goes wrong. I'm ready to leave Missouri."

"We're on it," said Joseph. Elaine wished him luck and hung up. He glanced at Daniel. "Head to the motel in Pollard. We've got one more job, and then we're done."

39

I spent an hour with Chief Deputy Marshal Tannehill. He seemed jovial, but his questions held an undercurrent of anger. Marshal Dyer's relationship with Crystal had compromised a long-standing emergency safe house and endangered a number of people. No one had died, but he had disrupted a lot of lives. It was a mess, but it wasn't a tragedy. Hopefully they'd change their procedures and ensure it wouldn't happen again.

Afterward, he drove me to my cabin. I crashed on the couch again and fell into a dream-filled but pleasant sleep. At noon, Shane knocked on the front door and called out for me. I rubbed my eyes and let him in.

"Morning," he said, his voice chipper. "It's a little late for breakfast, but you up for lunch?"

"Not hungry," I said. "I had a big breakfast at the diner about an hour ago. It's been a long morning."

Shane smiled, probably thinking I was kidding.

"The locals arrest you for murder again?" he asked.

"Nope. This time, I foiled an attempt to murder a witness in federal protective custody."

His smile faded.

"For such a little town, Pollard has a lot going on."

"It's a lively place. You got plans for the day?"

He shook his head. I walked to the kitchen.

"Granola bar?"

He declined.

"I've been thinking," I said. "Sheriff Mason is dead. Alford claimed I bashed his head in with a rock and then hid that rock in my parents' cabin. She also said the rock had my fingerprints on it."

Shane considered that.

"Can you lift fingerprints from a rock?"

"Depends on the porosity of the surface," I said. "That's beside the point. The sheriff's death was public knowledge, but his manner of death wasn't. She killed him, but before she did, he called Oscar Romero's parents and said he knew who killed their son. He had evidence against Alford, and she—or her employees—killed him to keep him quiet."

"And you want to find that evidence."

I nodded.

"How do you plan on doing that?" he asked.

"I was thinking of breaking into Phil Mason's house. I haven't seen his wife around lately. She's probably staying with family. We should be able to do it without getting caught."

"That sounds like a terrible idea," he said.

"It is," I said. "You in?"

"Ivy told me to stay until we figured this out. I guess that means I am."

"Good. We'll keep her number on speed dial in case we need her to bail us out of jail."

Since no one else lived near the Masons' home, Shane and I walked along the road rather than through the woods. Once we reached the house, we both paused.

"How should we approach this?" asked Shane.

"Same as if we had a search warrant, and we were looking for drugs or documents that indicate he's involved with an illegal organization," I said. "We'll knock on the front door to make sure the house is empty. I'll pick the lock on the basement door. If you have misgivings, I'll go in alone. You can stay outside."

He considered me for a long moment.

"How sure are you about this guy?"

"Pretty sure he's dirty," I said.

He drew in a slow breath.

"I'll trust your judgment. Let's go."

We crossed the lawn toward the house. The desiccated, dormant grass crunched whenever I walked, and a comfortable breeze blew up the hill from the lake. The air held just a whiff of lake water.

Before knocking on the front door, I pulled a pair of latex gloves from my pocket and slipped them on my hands. Shane did likewise. Then I rang the doorbell twice. Nobody came, so I rang the bell twice more. Then I looked to Shane.

"Nobody's home. Check the perimeter and keep your eyes open for signs of an alarm."

He went left, and I went right. I looked at every window for sensors but found none. The backyard had a flagstone patio and an elevated deck overlooking the lake. The log walls gave way to huge sheets of glass that would have maximized the view from inside. Further down the hill, the water sparkled. When we met back up, Shane whistled.

"It's beautiful," he said. "How much money you think a small-town sheriff makes?"

"Not enough to afford this," I said. I followed the patio beneath the deck to a set of glass French doors. The basement's interior looked dark but modern and clean. I knelt and pulled my pick set from my purse and worked on the lock. The tumblers fell into place, and the deadbolt slid back.

I waited for an alarm to blare. None did, so I opened the door. The interior smelled stale. A television hung on the far wall. A wooden bar dominated the room's eastern side. With the lake sparkling in the background, it looked like something from a celebrity's Instagram feed. I wondered how many felonies Mason had perpetrated to afford it.

Shane stayed in the basement while I went upstairs. If we'd had time, Shane and I would have opened every cabinet, checked every toilet tank, lifted acoustic tiles in the ceiling, and checked beneath and inside of every piece of furniture in the house. Considering we had broken in, though, we needed to move and focus on those places most likely to hide something important.

I checked out the home office first. Mason kept a couple of police files in his desk, but none mentioned Oscar Romero, Elaine Alford, or Lakeside Pools. The bedrooms and bathrooms held nothing of interest, either. I went downstairs again and called out for Shane.

"I'm in the kitchen."

I hesitated because the kitchen was upstairs. Then I followed his voice to a room just off the main entertaining space. When we first entered the basement, and I saw doors off the main room, I assumed they led to a laundry or storage area. One, though, led to a commercial kitchen with stainless steel tables, a stainless steel commercial oven, and a subzero freezer. It was spotless.

"The Masons must take Christmas dinner seriously," I said.

Shane nodded toward a stainless steel oven.

"That's a proofing oven. This is a bakery."

I nodded and furrowed my brow.

"How do you know that?"

"Ivy's been talking about renovating the kitchen," he said. "She watches some baking show on Netflix and wants to get serious about baking."

"You checked out the fridge?"

"Yep. Milk, cream, beer, wine…it looks like the baker only buys what she needs as she goes along."

"What about flour and sugar and that kind of stuff?"

Shane turned and pointed to a stainless steel door.

"The pantry's over there. It's full."

I crossed the room and pulled the door open. Inside, I found five-gallon buckets stacked on top of each other. Shane joined me in the doorframe.

"They've got enough food to survive for years," he said. "It looks like they're prepping for a disaster."

I walked toward the buckets and turned one so I could see its label. They had purchased the bucket from a commercial company. The label said pinto beans. The bucket beneath it said brown rice, and the bucket beneath that said it contained black beans. I stepped back and considered the scene.

"Somebody broke the seals on these buckets," I said. "Brown rice is oily. It'll go rancid in about a year stored like that. If they had kept the seal intact, it would have lasted a lot longer. And they should keep their beans in an oxygen-free environment. They'd last a lifetime that way. With the seal broken, they'll spoil in a year. A disaster prepper would know that."

Shane furrowed his brow, crossed the room, lifted a bucket from the top of the stack and put it on the ground beside me. Then he pried off the lid.

"Looks like black beans to me," he said, glancing up.

I nodded and reached inside. At first, I felt only black beans. Then my hand touched something flat. It felt like a narrow book wrapped in cling film. I pulled it out and found a bundle of hundred-dollar bills secured by a currency strap. Ten thousand dollars. Then I reached in again and found more straps of hundreds in that bucket. I found five additional straps in a bucket of rice.

"Let's check some more buckets and see what else they're hiding."

Shane agreed and got to work. I checked four buckets and found money in each. Shane did as well. Then he called out to me.

"Hey, Hana, I've got something new."

"Not cash?"

He nodded and pulled out a Ziploc baggie containing small round pills. They looked like little blue candies, but each had been imprinted with the logo of the New York Yankees. Shane said nothing as he reached into the bucket again. This time, he pulled out a Ziploc baggie with little red pills. These held the logo of the St. Louis Cardinals.

"You didn't bring an MDMA testing kit, did

you?" I asked.

Shane shook his head.

"Nope, but this is the stuff we're finding in St. Louis," he said. "The Cardinals pills have been around for years. The blue pills are new. They've killed three kids so far. It's MDMA and cocaine. Apparently, it's pretty high-quality stuff."

I knew those pills. Yankee speedballs. Obviously, the pills had nothing to do with the actual baseball teams, but the pill maker didn't care about trademarks when he branded them.

"I thought Lavan Johnson and Kenna Washington were the sole distributors of Yankee speedball."

"We thought so, too, until we found them again on a kid from St. Louis University," said Shane. "Someone's evidently taken Lavan and Kenna's place. Why would the sheriff have these? And why would he have all this money?"

"Because he's dirtier than I thought," I said, reaching for my phone. I snapped pictures of the cash, the buckets, and the drugs. Then I looked to Shane. "Let's lock up the house and get out of here. You haven't checked out of the motel yet, have you?"

"I have not."

"You mind if I take advantage of your running water and shower?"

He looked me up and down.

"I insist on it, in fact. While you're doing that, I'll

get lunch. Then we can figure out our next move."

"It's a plan," I said. "Let's go."

40

Joseph sat in the passenger seat of the white paneled van and focused on his phone. Daniel sat behind the steering wheel. Joseph and Elaine hadn't decided where they'd end up, but she had several million dollars to spend on a house. Ostensibly, he'd live in a guest house as her guard, while Elaine would have the big house to herself. He suspected—and hoped—he'd spend most of his nights with her.

"That one's nice. I like the stone," said Daniel. "Where is it?"

They had parked in a hairdresser's lot a block from Blackwood's motel.

"Devon," said Joseph. "It's in the United Kingdom. Elaine thinks she could get an investor's visa to move there. It's a beautiful area. There are lots of walking trails along the coast."

"And at your age, walking's good exercise," said Daniel, smirking. "Make sure you find restaurants that serve an early-bird special for senior diners, too. You might need that."

Joseph glanced at him.

"I'm forty-five, buddy," he said, wrinkling his forehead. "How old are you?"

"Forty-one," said Daniel. "To be fair, I thought you were much older. Time has not been kind to you."

Joseph gave him the finger and focused on his phone again as Daniel laughed. Though he tried to keep it from his lips, Joseph smiled, too. And why wouldn't he smile? Life was good. Elaine's safrole had shipped from Cambodia, the Forsyths would buy the company, and then he and Elaine would disappear.

Daniel would keep working, but the Forsyths would pay him half a million a year or more to manage their operations in Pollard. Combined with everything Elaine had paid him over the years, Daniel could retire at forty-five and spend the rest of his life doting on his wife and playing with his kids.

For the next hour, Daniel watched the street while Joseph searched for homes on his phone. Then it was Daniel's turn to relax while Joseph watched. About half an hour into his shift, a blue Subaru Outback pulled into the motel's parking lot. A black BMW followed, and a man in his early to mid-thirties stepped out. The two of them went into a motel room.

"We've got her," said Joseph. "But she's not

alone. Looks like a booty call."

Daniel glanced up. He had been reading a novel on his phone, but he focused quickly and grabbed binoculars.

"Who's the dude?" he asked. Joseph couldn't say. The two walked into a motel room, and Joseph scribbled down the black BMW's license plate number.

"Leeland can look up the license plate if necessary," he said. He paused. "We can take her and her boyfriend out right now."

Daniel lowered the binoculars.

"In a hurry?"

"Yeah," said Joseph. "I've been working full time since I was fifteen. I'm ready for a break."

Daniel considered and then nodded.

"All right," he said. "We go in just like in Columbia. We've got coveralls and protective gear in the back. You can shoot her with her own pistol. Then we'll disappear."

"It's a plan," said Joseph, glancing to his left. "Get changed, and we'll get going."

Daniel grunted, unbuckled his seat belt, and climbed into the rear of the van. Joseph kept watching the motel in case Blackwood left. Then he swore under his breath as two SUVs pulled into the lot. One was a black Chevy Suburban without markings. The other was a white Ford with the Bryant County Sheriff's Office badge painted on the door. The deputy sheriff stepped out.

"She's got company."

"Other than the BMW driver?" asked Daniel.

"Yeah," said Joseph. "It's the sheriff's office."

Daniel—now wearing plain gray coveralls—climbed back into the driver's seat. The sheriff wore a uniform. The other guy wore a suit. They knocked on the door of the room Blackwood and her partner entered. It opened, and they went inside. Neither Daniel nor Joseph spoke for a moment. Then Joseph swore again.

"Let's go," he said. "Before the police notice us."

Daniel turned the keys in the ignition. The heavy van's engine roared and then quieted as he pulled away.

"We can't kill her if she's under police surveillance," said Daniel.

"She'll shake 'em," said Joseph. "Let's find out who her boyfriend with the BMW is. If she cares about him, she's vulnerable. We'll use that. Blackwood's going to die soon. There's too much riding on this for her to live."

41

A few minutes after Shane and I got to the motel, somebody knocked hard on his door.

"Bryant County Sheriff's Office. We know you're in there, Ms. Blackwood. We need to talk to you."

I looked to Shane.

"You didn't see anybody outside the Mason place, did you?" I whispered. He shook his head. I considered the door, but we didn't have a choice but to open it. So I did. Sheriff Lyons stood outside beside a balding man in a gray suit so voluminous and ill-fitting that it could have been a poncho

I nodded to them both.

"What do you guys need?"

"Just some conversation," said the bald man. "Can we come in? I'm Detective Raymond Leach. I'm investigating the deaths of Zane and Kate Hopkins."

I looked to Shane. He nodded, so I swung my

arm.

"You came all the way down here, so come on in," I said. The two officers stepped inside, and I shut the door. They stood awkwardly and smiled at me, so I pointed to the table and chairs. "Sit down. The room is rented by Detective Shane Lewis. Whatever you have to say to me, you can say to him, too."

They sat. The detective looked to Shane but smiled at me.

"Sheriff Lyons said you were a direct woman," he said, reaching into his coat. He pulled out a cell phone. "You mind if I record our conversation?"

"Record away."

He flicked his finger across the screen and opened an app. Shane crossed his arms.

"Should I call my union rep and get a lawyer?" he asked.

"No need," said the detective. "We're here for Ms. Blackwood. You can have a seat and watch if you'd like."

Shane nodded and continued standing a few feet from the table, his arms crossed. The sheriff and detective focused on me once more.

"As you know, Zane and Kate Hopkins are dead now," said the detective. "Sheriff Lyons says you knew Mr. Hopkins."

I held up a hand.

"Let's stop here. I heard they died in Columbia. Why are you here interviewing me?"

The detective looked to Lyons. Then they both looked at me.

"Mr. Hopkins died in my jurisdiction, but he came from Pollard," said Leach. "I had hoped to gain insight into his death by interviewing those who knew him."

"So this is an interview," I said, nodding. "You're not charging me with a crime."

"Should I?" he asked.

"I've already told Sheriff Lyons how I knew Mr. Hopkins. That's all I have to say on the matter. You can leave now."

Neither man moved.

"The sheriff did tell me a story, but it was a little hard to believe," said Leach, raising his eyebrows. "You claimed a blonde woman pretending to be a Highway Patrol detective arrested you and then tried to kill you and Mr. Hopkins."

He paused. I nodded.

"You were a good detective once, Ms. Blackwood," he said. "Major case squad. Commendations out the wazoo. If you hadn't quit, you'd have made captain in another decade. I've seen your jacket. How would you react if someone off the street told you that crazy story?"

I considered the question and what it meant.

"Let's pause for a second. If you know that much about my career, the police in St. Louis must have given up my personnel file," I said. "Which means you got a court order, which means you convinced a judge that you had probable cause to believe I was involved in a crime. In that case, this isn't an interview, but a prelude to an interrogation." I paused and looked at Lyons. "You should read me my rights if I'm under arrest. If not, get out."

Detective Leach knocked on the table and smiled.

"You are certainly direct, Ms. Blackwood," he said, standing. "It was good to hear from you."

"Since you came all the way out here, Detective, your murderer is named Elaine Alford. She told me she was Elaine Johnson, but that was bullshit. She lives in Springfield and works at a company called Lakeside Pools. It's the same company Oscar Romero worked at. Ask Sheriff Lyons about Oscar."

Leach smiled again.

"Thanks for the tip," he said. "I'll see you around."

Then they left. I shut the door after them and sat on the bed. Shane went to the window and peered out. After a minute, he stepped away.

"They're gone," he said. "You need a lawyer. That detective wouldn't have driven all the way down here for information. He expected to make an arrest."

"I know," I said. "He's probably got a witness who saw somebody who looks like me near the scene of the murder."

"That's possible," said Shane.

"I didn't kill them," I said. "Just in case you're

wondering."

"Innocence won't stop a police investigation. Leach thinks you did it, and the sheriff's probably egging him on. That's a problem."

My shoulders felt heavy.

"I know. I'm going to get dressed in the bathroom. Then we should get out of here before they come back."

Shane agreed, so I showered and changed. Then we drove to my cabin.

As a kid, I enjoyed my family trips to the cabin, but I didn't consider what they had meant to my dad. He loved it there. It was his escape from the world. Dad had been a good man, but as a prosecutor in St. Louis, death and despair had surrounded him his entire adult life. He had tried to protect people and use the power vested in him fairly, but it had worn on him. He had often smiled at me, but it had rarely lingered at home. At the cabin, his smile rarely left. I loved that. Mom did, too. I wished I had taken better care of his dream.

I dug my keys from my purse as we stood on the front porch. Shane looked around.

"We should fix this place up," he said. "It wouldn't take much to make it nice again."

I looked at him and then to the driveway overrun with vegetation, to the overhanging roof that sagged, to the slowly deteriorating boards of the deck.

"Repairs cost money, and I don't have a job."

"We can fix a few things now to prevent future damage," he said. "If we close up the gable vent, we'll keep other animals from coming in. Then we can clean up the interior."

"We need to focus on Oscar Romero. He's the priority right now."

Shane looked down at the ground.

"I am focusing on Oscar," he said. "I just think best when I keep my hands busy. And you're the priority. Oscar's dead. He's not coming back. I came down here to keep you alive, not solve his murder."

I found my keys and unlocked the deadbolt but didn't open the door or look at my old partner.

"Why'd you break into the Masons' house with me, then?"

"Because solving Oscar's murder might be the best way to keep you alive," he said. "You're a friend. I don't want you dead."

"That's nice of you to say."

He chuckled.

"Preferring your continued existence is the barest minimum of friendship. Just so you know."

I looked around me. A knot had grown in my stomach. My throat felt tight.

"But you're here. I didn't have to ask. And you didn't leave or kick me out when the police showed up at your motel room."

"That's true," he said. "And I'm willing to patch up your gable vent if you drive me to a hardware store for materials."

I nodded.

"Thank you. I think I'd like that," I said. "Let's buy nails or screws or something. I don't know. I'm not a carpenter."

So we spent the afternoon and then the evening working on my cabin and talking about Oscar. We drove to three different hardware stores for supplies, but neither of us had a revelation on Oscar. Finally, we went to Frank's Downtown Diner for a quiet dinner and then back to the cabin. I slept on the couch in my sleeping bag, while Shane slept on a bare mattress in one of the bedrooms.

I dreamt about Afghanistan that night. I had been a twenty-five-year-old staff sergeant in the Army then, and I had already spent a tour in Iraq. In my dreams, I rode in a truck and laughed with two friends I had met in basic training. In reality, I had never been deployed with either woman.

Kate became a motor transport operator, a truck driver, after basic. Now, she was buried in the Abraham Lincoln National Cemetery in Ellwood, Illinois, after an IED hit a vehicle in which she rode. Jamie became a technical engineer. Now she had a family and lived outside Washington, DC, with her husband. I hadn't spoken to her in years, but I hoped she was well.

When I woke up at seven the next morning, a sour feeling had invaded the pit of my stomach. Despite having Shane in the same house, the cabin felt cold and empty. I dressed quietly in a bedroom and went for a run. When I got back, Shane was on the front porch.

"Hey," he said. "Have you talked to Ivy lately?"

I shook my head and walked inside for a bottle of water. Shane followed.

"She's not answering my calls, and she's not at work."

I would have joked that she was at a boyfriend's house, but Shane had a serious expression on his face. He looked worried.

"Let me call her," I said. "Maybe your phone's having a problem."

He nodded and shifted his weight from one foot to another as he waited. I dialed Ivy's number on my phone, but it went to voicemail. I put the phone to my chest and told him. Then I put it beside my ear again.

"Hey, Ivy," I said. "It's Hana. Shane and I are in Pollard. He's been trying to get in touch with you, but he can't. If you get this, call him."

I hung up and looked to him. He started pacing the room by the window.

"This isn't like her," he said. "Even if she were mad at me, she'd take my calls."

"Call the dispatcher and ask for a resident safety check," I said.

Shane nodded and drew in a breath.

"I already did, but she wasn't at the house. I also called her sister, but she's not there."

I considered and tilted my head toward the door.

"I'm sure she's okay. Think about where else she could be. I'm going to go outside for a minute," I said. "Get some fresh air."

He didn't respond, so I grabbed my phone and left the room. Once I got outside, I walked away from the porch and then started calling hospitals in St. Louis. Shane would have called Ivy's boss, but her colleagues may not know if she had been in a car accident. I talked to nurses at Barnes-Jewish, Mercy Hospital, St. Luke's, and the Missouri-Baptist Medical Center, but she wasn't a patient at any of them. Shane was right to worry. This wasn't like her.

As I walked back to the cabin, my phone rang. My breath left in a rush, and my shoulders sagged as I saw the caller ID.

"Ivy, hey," I said. "You scared us. Let me get Shane."

"Stop first. I want to talk girl to girl about that cool drink of water you're traipsing around with."

My footsteps stopped. Cold spiked throughout my body. That wasn't Ivy's voice.

"Ms. Alford," I said, trying to force the emotion out of my voice even as my heart raced, "I'm disappointed to hear from you."

"I'm sure you are," she said. "Tell me. Did you sleep with your partner last night?"

"No," I said. "Of course not. He's like a brother."

"And that would make Dr. Lewis your sister-in-law," she said. "What would you do to keep your sister-in-law alive?"

Shane popped his head out the door. He gave me a curious look.

"Everything okay?" he asked. I waved him away.

"Tell me what you want," I said.

"I want to talk to Shane. Is he around?"

I glanced at him and then held a finger to my mouth to keep him quiet.

"Let me call you back. Can I call you on this number?"

"No," she said. "I'll call him."

The call ended. Shane's phone rang. He pulled it from his pocket and looked at the screen. Then he looked to me.

"What's going on, Hana?"

"That's not Ivy," I said. "It's Elaine Alford."

He blinked and then answered the phone.

"Hello?"

"Put her on speaker," I whispered. Shane nodded and did as I asked.

"Detective Lewis," said Alford. "I'm glad to hear from you. My name is Elaine Alford, and I'm an associate of your friend Hana."

Shane stared at the phone. His throat bobbed as he swallowed.

"Why do you have Ivy's phone, and where is my wife?"

"Ivy is well, I assure you," said Alford. "Whether she stays that way is up to you and Ms. Blackwood. If she's not around, I'd suggest you get her."

Shane looked at me.

"I'm here," I said. "What do you want, and how did you get Ivy's phone?"

"The same way we got Ivy," said Elaine. "I walked into her bedroom and took it. Shane, your paisley bedspread is fabulous, by the way. I love it with the gray walls."

Shane's breath became ragged.

"What do you want?" he asked.

"You and Hana went into Phil Mason's home yesterday. I want the documents you found. Phil found his conscience at the wrong time. He was going to tell Oscar Romero's parents what happened to their son. I couldn't have that."

"We didn't find—" said Shane.

"You can't have the papers. They're the only leverage we have," I said, interrupting Shane. He furrowed his brow. "Enjoy prison."

I looked to Shane and mouthed for him to hang up. He furrowed his brow again but then looked down at the phone.

"Bye."

He hung up. Alford called back immediately.

"I hope you have a good reason for that," Shane said.

"I do," I said. "We've got to let her think we have whatever she wants. If we don't, she has no reason to keep Ivy alive. The longer we keep Alford talking, the better chance we have of tracking her down before she hurts anybody."

Shane's phone rang once more.

"Let it go to voicemail," I said.

He considered me and then sent the call to voicemail.

"I hope you're right."

"Me, too," I said.

We walked into the cabin to think and regroup when his phone beeped. Alford had left a message. Shane played it aloud. His face went white. It took me a moment to hear Ivy crying.

"Please do as she asks," said Ivy. "They're going to hurt me."

Then Ivy went quiet.

"Call me back when you're ready to talk about the exchange," said Alford. "You've got five minutes."

Shane brought a hand to his forehead. He put the phone on the table in the cabin's entryway.

"What do we do?" he asked. "We don't have any documents."

"I know," I said. "We'll get some. Call her and tell her we need time. Tell her we rented a car and drove to Little Rock, Arkansas, because we were afraid to stay in Pollard."

"What if she doesn't believe that?"

"One step at a time," I said. "Until we figure this out, she's in charge. We'll get Ivy back. We just have to think."

"I hope you're right," said Shane, picking up the phone again.

"I am."
My words held far more certainty than I felt.

42

Shane sat on the sofa and called Alford back for a tense but short conversation. He scribbled notes and hung up and balled his hands into fists without looking at me. His body shook. I said nothing until he drew in a breath.

"She wants to meet tonight for an exchange," he said. "She gave me coordinates in the Mark Twain National Forest. You're supposed to come, too. If we go to the police, she'll kill Ivy."

"It's an ambush," I said. "If we go out there, she'll kill us."

"If we don't, she'll kill Ivy. She said that, and I believe her."

I shook my head and started pacing behind my sofa.

"We won't let that happen," I said. "You're a detective. Call in every favor you've got and track her phone. I'll look into the meeting site and see what's there."

Shane picked up his phone.

"I know a Verizon tech. He owes me."

He got to work, and I opened up my laptop. I used my phone as a mobile hotspot and searched for the coordinates. As Alford had said, they pointed to a spot in the Mark Twain National Forest. From the satellite view on Google Maps, a lone, narrow road ran to a cabin nearby, while a thick canopy of trees stretched for miles. A shooter would have hundreds of potential hiding spots to choose from. If we go there, we die.

Ten minutes after I closed my laptop, Shane hung up.

"Both calls came from cell phones moving southwest at thirty-five miles an hour," he said. "They're in a car near Fort Leonard Wood. The phones are off now, though. We can't track them further."

"Did you call the Highway Patrol?"

"The search area expands every second, and we don't know what they're driving. There are too many roads and escape routes. For all we know, they're on I-44 now heading northeast."

"We'll find them."

He nodded but said nothing.

"I checked out the coordinates she gave you," I said. "The spot is about two hundred yards from a cabin in the Mark Twain National Forest. It's a wooded area. The nearest town is several miles away. If we go there, they'll kill us."

"They won't," said Shane. "They want police files from the Masons' house. We need to find them. We must have missed them the first time."

I blinked and drew in a slow breath as I thought through my response.

"They're not after police files," I said. "If we found files, we could make copies and send them to every newspaper in Missouri. Alford couldn't stop that. This isn't about documents. This is about us. They want us to drive to the middle of nowhere to kill us. They're hoping we're desperate enough to do that."

He covered his face with his hands.

"I'm not thinking straight."

"You've got a lot on your mind," I said. "We're going to find them, and we're going to get Ivy back."

"How?"

I paced in front of the room by the television.

"I don't trust the sheriff's office in Pollard," I said. "At best, they're incompetent."

"What about the Highway Patrol?"

"If we call them, they'll call Sheriff Lyons," I said. "How about your people in St. Louis?"

He leaned back and crossed his arms.

"Things got political after you left. People protested over your shooting. Deputy chief retired, and every captain in the department fought for his job," he said. "It got ugly. People blamed you for things you didn't do. I stuck up for you and made enemies."

I lowered my voice.

"Sorry."

"Don't be. It was my choice," he said. "Ivy and I are trying to have a kid. I was going to put in my papers when she got pregnant."

"You'll make a good dad," I said, my voice soft. He grunted but said nothing. Then I drew in a breath and focused on our situation. "If we can't expect help from St. Louis, we might be on our own. The FBI can't come in without an official request from the local police department, but even with that, they're a big, slow agency. I doubt they could put a team together fast enough to help Ivy."

Shane sighed and leaned back.

"I'm worried," he said. "I won't lie."

"You've got reason to worry," I said, "but Alford doesn't have that many places she could be. I doubt they're at Lakeside Pools's warehouse. It's too public. They wouldn't take Ivy to Alford's house, either. It's in a residential neighborhood, and it'd be too easy for them to get caught. I think they're at the summer camp."

"Wouldn't the summer camp have hundreds of kids at it?"

"Yeah, but it's enormous," I said. "Everything in this case comes back to that camp. Oscar Romero was a drug dealer. He didn't need money, but he went to that summer camp every day. Why? What did Lakeside Pools gain by sending him there? How much maintenance does a swimming pool even require?"

Shane seemed to think.

"I don't know."

"And the camp has armed guards, fences, and perimeter checkpoints. It's a fortress. Ostensibly, they protect the campers, but what kind of threat are these kids under?"

Shane settled into his seat.

"Even if Alford is there, we can't just storm the place, guns blazing," he said. "Kids could get hurt."

"One problem at a time," I said, going to my laptop. I called up Google Maps again and then hovered over the camp. The satellite view had limited resolution, but I could see the buildings. Most of them, I recognized from the map I had seen at the library. I pointed out three buildings I didn't recognize. Two looked like small sheds. The third looked like a big cabin. It was distant from the rest of the camp, and it looked as if it had its own entrance.

"I'm willing to bet Ivy's here," I said, pointing to the big cabin. "We can rent a boat and see it from the water. If the place looks abandoned, we'll move on and figure things out. We'll put some fake documents together and scope out the drop-off location in the forest."

"We'll be taking a lot of risks," said Shane.

"We'll be taking risks no matter what," I said. I

paused. "Alford wants me dead. If Ivy's not in the cabin, I'll call Alford and offer her a trade. Me for Ivy. If the bad guys drop Ivy off at one location, I'll offer to turn myself over to them at another. If they don't drop her off, we'll go after them. We'll hunt Alford down and kill her."

"That's dark," said Shane.

"Life's dark."

Shane considered and then gave me a tight nod.

"Let's check out this cabin, then."

I searched for boat rental companies and then reserved a pontoon boat from a marina with a dock about a mile from the camp. Shane and I then headed out in my Subaru. My gut twisted. Shane and Ivy didn't ask for or deserve this. He came to help me, and she got hurt. We had to find her. I felt sick.

When we reached the marina, I paid the deposit, signed the contract, and agreed to pay seventy-five dollars per hour for the entry-level "party barge." I also agreed not to drive the boat while intoxicated.

Fifteen minutes after parking, Shane and I were on the boat, casting off. It was a warm day, but the boat's canvas canopy kept the sun off us. Combined with the breeze, it was comfortable.

Neither of us had driven a boat before, but it wasn't hard. Water-skiers and swimmers dotted the lake. Shane pointed out a roped-off area with flags bobbing on the water. There must have been scuba divers. Even with our boat's weak engine, we made good time to the camp. It had its own covered dock with eight boat slips. Kids paddled in canoes near the shore. On the hill nearby, a massive tower suspended a zip line that terminated on a much shorter platform near the lake. Boys and a couple of counselors played with a Frisbee on the grass. It looked like fun.

I throttled down and looked around.

"This isn't what I expected," said Shane. "Based on your description, I thought there'd be wet T-shirt contests on the beach and beer bottles on the ground. This is a summer camp."

"The older kids get rowdy. The young kids just play."

"Where's the cabin?" asked Shane.

"About a mile further," I said, pushing the throttle forward once more. Gradually, we left the children behind us. Though the camp owned several miles of lakeshore, its fields and recreational facilities ended at a line of deep woods. I piloted our pontoon boat for another ten minutes before Shane tapped me on the shoulder and pointed.

An A-frame log cabin jutted from the hillside. Its windows reflected the sunlight like a mirror, while fir and other coniferous trees provided it privacy from prying eyes on the lake. It was a pretty house and much larger than my cabin. I throttled down and felt our boat drift before Shane dropped the anchor over the side. Then he grabbed a pair of fishing poles the marina had supplied us.

Neither of us had come to fish, but the poles let us blend in.

"This is it," he said. "You see anything?"

I took Mom's binoculars from my purse and trained them on the shoreline. The trees around the home cast it in dark shadows. At first, I saw little. Then, as my eyes adjusted, I nodded.

"I see a red Mercedes," I said. "It's Alford's car."

Shane squeezed his mouth shut and stood near the side of the boat.

"If you're thinking of swimming to shore to rescue Ivy, think again. We don't know what we're up against yet. We need a plan."

"I know."

I studied the terrain. A limestone ridge rose behind the home, and the ground sharply sloped downward to the lakeshore. A narrow road led east to the rest of the camp. Rocks lay strewn about the sandy beach. If we moored our boat on the beach, a shooter could pick us off from the front porch as we climbed the slope out front, but if we docked the boat half a mile to the east, they wouldn't see us. We could then hike through the woods.

"If she's there, we'll get her," I said. "We'll use the terrain and have surprise on our side, too. They won't see us coming."

He swallowed.

"You ever done this before?"

"Sort of," I said. "But I was a combat medic, and my team had air support and artillery."

"Then it's time we get some bigger firearms," said Shane, already pulling up the anchor. "Let's get my wife."

43

We returned our boat to the marina and then went to the office. The guy behind the counter smiled.

"Did you guys have a good time?"

"We had a great time," I said. "We found a little quiet nook and dropped anchor. It was peaceful."

The clerk focused on his computer.

"If you give me just a minute, I'll print you out a receipt, and you guys can be on your way."

"That's something I want to talk about," I said, leaning against the desk. It came to my chest, allowing me to rest my hands under my face. "Is it possible to rent a boat overnight? We'd love to camp out on the water."

The clerk and I negotiated for a few minutes. He didn't seem enthusiastic about the idea until I offered him five hundred bucks for the night. That got his attention. I hoped I had enough headroom on my credit card to pay it. Fifteen minutes after I got there, I signed a new contract to use the boat overnight. We'd have the means to get to the camp, at least.

After that, we drove to the cabin. We had eight hours to kill before we hit Camp Meadowview. I intended to sleep and plan. Shane had other ideas.

"I'm going to pick up supplies in St. Louis," said Shane. "You have a vest?"

"I had to turn mine in when I left the department."

"I'll see if I can get one that'll fit you," he said. "You're, what, five-foot-seven and a hundred-thirty-five pounds?"

"You flatter me, but you're in the neighborhood."

"I'll get you a medium."

I considered him and then blinked.

"You're not planning to rescue Ivy alone, are you?"

Shane said nothing. Then I noticed the quiver in his lower lip.

"No. I'm not getting her alone," he said. Then he paused before speaking again. "This may be something you've done a dozen times, but I haven't. I didn't join the Army when I turned eighteen. I went to college and acted like a moron for four years. You fought insurgents in Iraq and Afghanistan while I did keg stands with my friends. I don't know what I'm doing, but I'm angrier than I've ever been, and I don't want to be near you right now. Okay?"

I wanted to apologize, but it sounded hollow even in my head. Instead, I nodded.

"Okay. I understand. Drive safely."

He left my car and got into his BMW. Then he drove off, and I went into the cabin. I felt like someone had just scooped out my guts with a spoon. My throat was tight, and every part of my body felt heavier than it should. I fell onto the couch and lay there for a while. Exhaustion overtook my sense of dread, and I fell asleep. I woke a little after six. My stomach rumbled, but I didn't have any food.

I rolled over and checked my phone. No one had called or texted me. I thought about texting Shane to make sure he was okay, but he needed space. At least I could give him that. I got up and then drove to Frank's Downtown Diner for dinner. Every waitress in the building knew me by sight.

Dinner was fine, but I couldn't focus on the food and tasted little. Afterward, I walked to the park and watched the sunset and thought. The plan I came up with was a simple smash-and-grab job, but a lot could go wrong. I tried to visualize the night we had ahead of us, and every time I ran through the scenario, I found new flaws. I hated this.

Shane may have thought I was some kind of hero, but I wasn't. I had been an Army medic. I went on patrol with my team, and I carried a rifle, but I rarely shot it. My job had been to protect my team, patch up wounds, help exfiltrate the injured, and try not to get shot myself. I was terrified the whole time.

Today brought a new fear. I loved my teammates in the Army like family, and I had fought for them as if they were family, but they knew what they were getting into when they signed their enlistment contracts. They had training and protective gear. Shane was a cop. Ivy was a doctor. They didn't deserve this.

I got back in my car and drove to the hotel to wait. Shane returned at about ten. Instead of his BMW, he had brought Ivy's gray Infiniti SUV. I walked outside as his headlights flashed in my window.

"Hey," I said, as he got out of the car. "You okay?"

He looked at me and then motioned me toward him. I hugged him tight.

"We're going to get her back," I whispered. "Okay?"

"I know."

We stayed there for a moment. Then he let go and nodded to the rear of his SUV. As the door beeped and swung up, the interior lights came on. Shane had, apparently, raided the armory at his station.

"I brought you an M4 carbine and a vest," he said. "You're comfortable shooting the M4, aren't you?"

"I am," I said. "It's what I carried in the Army."

"Good," he said. "I've got two flash bangs for you, too. You know how to use them. Pull the O-ring and toss it. It should scare the shit out of anybody in the house."

"I see you got a shotgun," I said, nodding toward a weapon still inside the car. He picked it up.

"It's a Benelli M4 tactical shotgun," he said. "Your rifle will be good at a distance. I figured this would be good up close. It's loaded with rifled slugs, so it'll go right through body armor."

I considered him.

"Will the slugs go through a wall?"

"Depends on the wall. Drywall and wooden siding, of course. Brick or cinder block, probably not. It'd cause damage, though."

"Okay," I said, considering. "So, here's what I've come up with. It's simple and should be easy to execute. There's an elevated ridge above the cabin and a slope below it. You'll go on the ridge, and I'll wait on the slope. Once we're in position, you're going to shoot the house with your shotgun. The guys will hear the shot and investigate. Fire on them and then run. They'll chase you.

"Once you draw the bad guys away, I'll kick down the front door, toss in a flash bang, and search the house. I'll get Ivy out. We'll get back to the boat and travel east along the lake to Camp Meadowview's beach. You can then circle back and meet us. If the bad guys are still following you, I'll have the rifle and give some covering fire. I'm accurate to about five hundred yards with an M4. Much beyond that, things get iffy."

Shane shut the SUV's door.

"It's a plan," he said. "Let's get to the boat. I want to get this over with."

"You and me both," I said. "Let's get her back."

44

Water lapped against the sides of our pontoon boat. The air smelled earthy but clean and pleasant. Starlight shimmered across the greenish-black water. Our boat had lights, but we kept them off to reduce visibility. I held the throttle as low as I could while still making decent time toward Meadowview.

Shane and I both wore dark outfits beneath bulletproof vests. The night hid us well, but the moon spotlighted the aluminum pontoon floats on our boat. Hopefully, we'd look like a couple out for a late-night rendezvous under the stars.

"You ready?" I asked as we approached Camp Meadowview's dock.

Shane nodded, pulled his pistol from his holster, and checked the magazine. He had done that three times already. It seemed like a ritual now.

The fields and zip line of Camp Meadowview

slid by. The camp had guards, but they seemed to stay by the cabins where the kids slept. Within minutes, the fields passed, and we reached the wooded terrain that held our target. I pointed our pontoon boat toward a beach and then killed the engine. Our momentum carried us to the sand. The front pontoons slid onto the embankment, while the rear bobbed on the water. Shane lowered the anchor and then drew in a breath.

"This is it," he said. "Any last advice?"

"Keep your head up, your eyes open, and do your job. Come back alive."

It was the same advice my CO had given me on my first combat patrol in Iraq over a decade ago. Hopefully Shane took it to heart. If we both did our jobs, everything would work out fine. Shane checked his pistol once more before grabbing his shotgun. Then he stepped off the boat and disappeared into the woods. I could hear his footsteps, but I couldn't see him at all.

I picked up my rifle. It'd take Shane five to ten minutes to reach the ridgeline, giving me more than enough time to position myself as well. Little starlight penetrated the canopy of trees. Alford's cabin was about five hundred yards away and two hundred yards elevated above the beach.

A curious sense of calm descended on me as I ascended the hill. As dark as it was, I had to step lightly to avoid tripping on tree roots, loose rocks, or other hazards. Sweat beaded on my forehead and slid down my back. We had operated at night often in the Army, so it felt both normal and surreal to carry my rifle up that hill.

Eventually, I found a well-beaten trail that looked as if it headed straight to the cabin's front door. I followed it for about a hundred yards before ducking behind the thick trunk of a sweetgum tree. The front door of Alford's cabin was about a hundred yards ahead of me. With my rifle, I could sprint there in twelve to fifteen seconds. I'd be exposed that whole time, but I couldn't change the topography.

As I stayed there and felt my sweat cool, my mind, once more, began picturing ways this could go wrong. Shane's shotgun might not be loud enough, they may not be home, or they might have more people in the house than we could handle. They might even shoot Ivy as soon as they heard us. Panicking wouldn't help anything, though. I took a couple of breaths and squeezed my rifle hard, concentrating on those things that were in my control.

Then the world seemed to stop moving as Shane's shotgun fired. The report echoed off the cabin, the limestone hills, and the trees. Then a second shot rang out to the west. It wasn't Shane. The weapon boomed, but it was higher pitched than his shotgun. Alford may not have known we were coming, but she had set up her team to intercept us, anyway.

Adrenaline spiked through my system. I raised my rifle to my shoulder and crept forward, hoping to see the shooter. The cabin's front door opened. I dove to the ground. A man ran out with a long gun. I lined him up in my sights and eased my finger to the trigger. He had night-vision goggles strapped to his forehead. He panned his eyes around the cabin.

"Shooter's to the east," said a voice to my left. "I may have clipped him. He's running."

"Give me covering fire."

Instead of answering, the sniper fired. The sound echoed around the hillside. I could kill the man with night-vision goggles, but that'd give my position away. The sniper would kill me. If he had an infrared scope—which I suspected he did—he could pick Shane off from five or six hundred yards. Then they'd kill Ivy. The landscape and trees kept me alive for now, but the moment I moved, they'd have me.

So I stayed put while the man with night-vision goggles ran. The sniper fired again. I knew vaguely where he was, so I watched and waited. Then he fired again. I saw the muzzle flash and focused, but the position made little sense. He'd have to be hanging from a tree.

Then I realized that was exactly what he was doing. He must have been on a deer stand. His torso blocked the starlight, allowing me to just see his form.

I aimed at the darkest shadow and switched the

selector knob on my rifle from single-fire to a three-shot burst. He fired again, and I lit him up. The butt of my rifle rested against the pocket of my shoulder, while my cheek rested against the stock. I squeezed the trigger and felt the recoil hit my shoulder. Then I squeezed again and then again as I walked forward.

For a split second, I held my breath, unsure that I had hit him.

His rifle fell. A second later, he tumbled fifteen or twenty feet down. I didn't have time to celebrate before a pistol cracked to my right. It came from the house. I dove to the ground. The pistol fired again. The round hit the ground to my right, so I slithered backwards toward a bush, the closest cover.

"You killed him!"

It was Elaine Alford. Her voice was ragged. The bush concealed me, but a bullet would pass right through it. I switched the fire-selection knob to single-shot and squeezed the trigger twice in Alford's direction. Then I shot my eyes around the yard. There was a walnut tree with a thick trunk about ten feet away. If I could get to it, I'd have some cover.

Alford, unfortunately, had a better position than me. She had hidden behind a wooden whiskey barrel turned into a planter. Geraniums spilled over the side. If the whole thing was filled with dirt or sand, I could shoot an entire magazine at it without damaging it. Her hair peeked over the right edge. I fired twice at it. Then she disappeared behind it.

"You fucking killed him!"

She fired twice wildly. Neither round came close to me, but that didn't mean I could run. I scurried to the left. The planter still hid Alford well. A shadow moved near the cabin's front door. It was Ivy. She held her hands in front of her, and she crouched low in the doorway. Cuffs secured her wrists together, but she carried a heavy-looking brass lamp.

For a split second, my eyes met hers, and she pretended to raise the lamp as if she were going to hit someone. I shook my head. This wasn't a cartoon. She couldn't sneak up on Alford and club her. She was going to get shot. She ignored me and kept walking, so I did the only thing I could.

I rose and put the butt of my rifle against my shoulder and squeezed the trigger. The round hit the planter with a dull thud. Then I fired again and again as I crept forward, using my own gunfire as cover and hoping Alford would focus on me instead of Ivy. Wood particles flew, but the planter stayed upright, and Alford stayed behind it.

"Run, Ivy," I said, my voice soft. "Don't do this."

Ivy kept coming, though. I hurried to the left, continuing to fire at the barrel and knowing I'd run out of rounds well before that planter broke. Then I saw Alford. Her eyes locked on mine. Her face was red. Wood splinters and dirt covered her shoulders. She raised her pistol. I squeezed my rifle's trigger. It clicked, but nothing happened.

"Shit."

Alford rose. I threw my rifle at her, but she batted it away.

"I loved him," she said, her hands trembling, "and you killed him. I'm going to kill your—"

Ivy's lamp thudded against her skull. Alford dropped to the ground, limp and silent. For a moment, we both stared at her. Then Ivy knelt beside the prone woman and felt her neck.

"She's alive."

"Anyone else in the house?" I asked. Ivy shook her head. "Tie her up with the cord as well as you can and then get inside and hide. We'll get your handcuffs off as soon as we can."

I picked up my rifle and started running to the east but slowed when Ivy called out.

"Where are you going?"

"To find your husband."

I followed the road toward camp and dropped the empty magazine on my rifle and popped in a fresh one. As I ran, the trees began thinning until I reached a grassland. Soccer goals stood on either end. Without trees, the moon shone down brightly enough to cast shadows. My breath caught in my throat. Shane stood in the middle of the field. An Asian man knelt in front of him. His fingers were laced behind his head. Shane had his shotgun. His hands trembled.

"Lower the weapon, Shane," I said. "It's over."

"How's my wife?"

"She's fine," I said. "She clobbered Alford over

427

the head with a lamp and tied her up. I got the sniper. He's dead. Put the gun down. He's not worth it."

Shane looked at me.

"You're not just saying that?" he asked. "She's okay?"

"Yeah," I said. "I'm telling you the truth. I told her to hide. She's in the house now. If you go back, I'll take care of this guy."

Shane stayed still, his eyes locked on the man in front of him. Then he started to lower his rifle. At that same instant, the Asian man lunged forward. Moonlight glinted off the knife in his hand. I raised my rifle without thinking and squeezed the trigger twice. His body rocked with each shot, and then he fell forward.

I lowered my rifle and felt the strength leave my arms and back. The lights of a golf cart were coming toward us from across the field. Someone—a guard, presumably—was running toward us with a flashlight. I pointed them out to Shane. He reached to his waist and held up his badge and his pistol to show he wasn't a threat.

"I'm a police officer, and this is police business," he said. "Stay back and call 911. I need paramedics and the police."

The guards stayed away. Shane looked at me.

"Can you handle the locals?"

I nodded.

"Yeah. Go find your wife. She's in the cabin.

Good luck."

45

The sun shone as I walked toward the Bryant County Sheriff's Office's headquarters. It was eight in the morning, and I felt good. Three days had passed since Shane and I had rescued Ivy, and I had been staying in my cabin. No animals had gotten in since we patched up the exterior, and, after a recent visit from a plumber, I even had running water and working toilets. The shower was brisk without a water heater, but it beat paying sixty dollars a night to sleep in a terrible motel.

This was a damage-control meeting more than anything else. I'd sign some paperwork, listen to some lawyers bloviate, and then leave. I had better places to be than the sheriff's office.

From the exterior, the station looked exactly as it had on my last visit. Officer Sutton sat behind the front desk. She hadn't noticed me yet, but the instant I opened the door, I heard a soft whine and then a familiar bark. My breath caught in my throat.

"George?"

Sutton looked up. She didn't smile, but her eyes looked softer than on my last visit. George barked again as she led him around the desk. When he saw me, he ran. I knelt in front of him. He nearly knocked me over, but I didn't care. I petted his cheek and put my forehead against his neck. His tail wagged like a propeller.

"Hey, sweetheart," I whispered. "I missed you."

There was a lightness in my belly I hadn't felt in days. George barked and bowed in front of me.

"He's been doing that a lot," said Sutton. "The bowing, I mean. A lawyer from Springfield brought him by this morning. We knew you were coming by, so we kept him for you. There's a note here, too."

"I'll get it in a moment," I said. "George needs to go outside. That's what the bowing means."

"Oh, sorry," said Sutton. "I'm a cat person."

I nodded and took George outside. When we returned, Sutton handed me an envelope. I opened it and found a handwritten note and a picture of Crystal Valentine's children playing with a golden retriever puppy. Everybody was smiling. The note was quick.

Hana—My name is Julie. I'm sorry I lied to you. You and George are better friends than I deserve.

-JF

I looked up at Officer Sutton.

"Thank you for taking care of George and for the

note."

"Of course," she said. "Sheriff Lyons and the others are waiting for you in the conference room. You need an escort?"

I knew where it was, so I told her no. Then I wrapped my hand around George's leash and walked him back. The conference room had a long table ringed by office chairs. Framed photographs depicting the history of the police department covered the walls, including a few from the annual Halloween party Lyons had mentioned to me a few days ago. Half a dozen men and women sat around the table. Sheriff Lyons stood when he saw me.

"Take a seat, Ms. Blackwood," he said, gesturing to the chair beside him. "Hi, George."

The dog perked up upon hearing his name and panted. We sat where the sheriff directed us. Then he smiled, drew in a deep breath, and exhaled.

"What a week, folks," he said. The assembled group tittered and smiled. "I think everybody knows everybody else around here, but if not, I'll make introductions. I'm Troy Lyons, and I'm the sheriff here in Bryant County. To my left is Hana Blackwood. She's a civilian contractor with my department. To Ms. Blackwood's left is Jason Blystone, the Bryant County prosecutor."

Lyons continued introducing the attendees, but I paid little attention. I wasn't there to make friends.

"First things first," said Lyons, sliding a stack of papers toward me. "I need Ms. Blackwood to sign the paperwork making all this official. She's been the best consultant this department's ever hired. Your paycheck's in the envelope on top, by the way."

I signed. According to the paperwork, the department was hiring me on a temporary one-day consulting contract for five thousand dollars. How they planned to spin that and claim I had been on staff for the past two weeks, I had no idea, but they'd figure it out. My contract also included an agreement offering me transactional immunity for my actions of the past week. It was a good deal for all of us.

At the time of her arrest, Elaine Alford had millions in cash stashed around her various businesses. The federal government had begun proceedings to seize Camp Meadowview and Lakeside Pools for their roles in an illegal enterprise. Both would be worth millions. Bryant County wouldn't get all of that money, but it would get a good portion of it if the county could prove to the federal government that its people had run the investigation.

After signing, I slid the paperwork to Lyons. He scanned the document and smiled at me.

"Thanks, Hana," he said. He exhaled a long breath and looked to the assembled lawyers and law enforcement officials. "This has been a roller coaster couple of weeks. We have a press conference coming up, but I wanted to speak here first and share everything that's happened.

"Foremost, Elaine Alford is sitting in the women's section of the Tri-county Justice Center. The charges she faces include the murders of Sheriff Phil Mason, Zane Hopkins, Frannie Hopkins, and Kate Hopkins. She'll face further charges in multiple jurisdictions for various drug offenses, but neither Ms. Alford or the drugs she and her team produced at Camp Meadowview will ever hurt another citizen of Missouri.

"As best we can tell, the staff at Camp Meadowview was ignorant of Ms. Alford's endeavors. The exception, though, was Dr. Kristen Turner, Ms. Alford's mother. Dr. Turner used her position as camp director to hide her daughter's drug manufacturing operation. Dr. Turner faces significant state and federal charges."

He paused as if for applause. No one obliged him.

"Two days ago, the police in Springfield raided Lakeside Pools, Inc., and found a safe containing nine hundred thousand dollars cash. Again, most of the staff was ignorant of Ms. Alford's drug manufacturing. Deputies from my department have been scouring Camp Meadowview. So far, we've found approximately forty thousand individual doses of the drug MDMA. The street value of those drugs approaches one million dollars. We also found twelve thousand doses of MDMA combined with cocaine. These cocaine-laced pills have been implicated in the deaths of multiple people statewide."

Lyons cleared his throat and glanced up from his notes.

"After finding the drugs, my team entered a private cabin on the campgrounds. There, we found restraints used to hold Dr. Ivy Lewis hostage. Immediately outside, we found the body of Joseph Lipscombe, one of Ms. Alford's employees. To the east, we found the body of Daniel Nakamura, another of Ms. Alford's employees. Both died of multiple gunshot wounds. We've determined their deaths were justifiable homicides.

"Aside from the weapons and bodies, we also found a cell phone that once belonged to Frannie Hopkins inside the home. We used that phone's GPS to find a remote location at which Ms. Hopkins had set up a meeting with Nakamura and Lipscombe. At that location, we found a shallow grave that contained Ms. Hopkins's body. The weapon used to kill her was found disassembled in Ms. Blackwood's vehicle. The magazine inside that weapon contained the fingerprints of Mr. Nakamura. We believe he murdered Ms. Hopkins and tried to make it appear that Ms. Blackwood had done it.

"After searching Ms. Alford's phone, we were led to Leeland Walker in my department. Leeland was our IT manager. He's admitted giving Ms. Alford access to our station, to rerouting the 911 system so that Ms. Alford received emergency calls that should have gone to the Highway Patrol, and to providing her access to our station, vehicles, and equipment. We plan to charge him with several felonies."

He paused and shuffled his notes again. The men and women around the table nodded.

"Okay... What else do I have to say..." he said, his voice low. He looked up. "Oscar Romero. He died years ago. We think Ms. Alford killed him. She denies it, but she's denied everything so far. We knew he sold drugs for Ms. Alford, and we think she killed him to prevent him from going to the police."

He paused again and clicked his tongue.

"I think that's just about it," he said. Then he looked to me. "Is that it?"

"Tell us about Jim," I said.

Lyons straightened and nodded.

"Yeah. Jim Darrisaw. I should mention him," he said. "Jim was a security guard at Meadowview. He helped to search Camp Meadowview and ensure Dr. Turner didn't escape. Prior to that, though, he and his colleagues borrowed a utility vehicle and broke into Lakeside's storage shed, where they found three suspicious barrels containing an unknown substance.

"They should have called us. Instead, they loaded the barrels onto their utility vehicle, pierced them with a garden pick, and burned them. They thought the pool company planned to dump dangerous chemicals in the pool and hurt the kids."

Lyons looked at me again and raised his eyebrows.

"That sounds like everything," I said. "You guys did good work."

"It's not done yet, either," said Lyons, focusing on the lawyers. "We're working with forensic accountants from the FBI to identify Ms. Alford's bank accounts and track down her remaining assets. This may be the biggest drug bust southern Missouri has ever seen."

No one had mentioned that Alford could only create such a massive organization because the former sheriff—Lyons's friend—took bribes to help hide her business, but we couldn't all be perfect. Lyons and the lawyers talked for another half hour, but I didn't pay attention. I had my dog and a paycheck. I needed nothing else from them.

As I got up to leave after the meeting, Lyons walked toward me, a smile on his face.

"Can we talk before you leave?" I nodded, and he lowered his voice. "The station has some extra funding coming now that we've arrested Ms. Alford. I know Pollard is a far cry from St. Louis, but you've already got a cabin here. I could use an experienced detective."

I furrowed my brow and considered him.

"Are you serious?" I asked.

A tight smile cracked his lips.

"I am."

I blinked again.

"You arrested me for murder with evidence so thin a first-year rookie at the academy would have known better, and multiple officers from your station harassed me. At least one even threatened to kill me. Meanwhile, you missed your boss's corruption and the growth of a major drug syndicate at a summer camp in your jurisdiction. All the while, your station's IT manager gave regular updates to a murderous drug kingpin in Springfield. So, respectfully, no. Thank you."

Lyons crossed his arms.

"You could have just said no."

"I could have," I said. "Good luck, Mr. Lyons."

He grunted, and I left the building. George panted beside me, so I reached down and patted his side. Once I reached the car, I got him settled in the backseat and then sat in the driver's seat to call Shane. He answered right away.

"Meeting's over," I said. "You ready to ruin somebody's day?"

"I am," he said. "Everybody'll be in place here shortly."

"Good. See you soon."

46

I drove out to the cabin and found a pickup beside Ivy's SUV in the driveway. Technically, I still owned the cabin, but I wouldn't for long. The property was beautiful, and the cabin held so many wonderful memories that I couldn't count them all, but I couldn't afford to keep it up. This was my dad's place, and I had let it fall apart. I loved my memories of the cabin, but it was just a building. To Ivy and Shane, it would become more. It'd be a place they shared with their kids once they had them. They'd make new memories and fill it with laughter and love again. That's what Dad would have wanted.

Ivy, Shane, and their contractor emerged from the house a moment later. The contractor held a clipboard and a camera. Ivy wanted to expand the porch in back and possibly add another bathroom. She had good taste, so whatever she did, it'd be beautiful. I looked forward to seeing it.

I walked toward the three of them.

"You mind if I borrow Shane for a little while?"

Ivy looked at him and smiled.

"Sure. Walt and I are just about done."

Shane squeezed his wife's hand and then came toward me. We walked back to the road.

"Meeting go well?" I asked.

"For the contractor," he said. "Ivy's taste has gotten more expensive over time."

I tilted my head to the side and started walking toward the Masons' cabin.

"Think of it as an investment in the local economy."

He kept walking but said nothing. I smiled just a little. The lawn outside the Masons' home was trimmed and neat, their azaleas and hostas were lush, and the walkway looked freshly swept. According to my calendar, fall would arrive in two weeks, but I suspected it would feel like summer for far longer.

We crossed the grass and knocked on the front door. When no one answered, I knocked again and then rang the doorbell twice. Finally, Lisa Mason opened the door. She was a beautiful woman with blond hair and green eyes. A flour-speckled apron covered her chest and hips.

"Yes?" she asked.

"Mrs. Mason," I said, smiling. "I'm Hana Blackwood. I own the cabin next door. This is Shane

Lewis. He and his wife are buying the cabin from me, so they'll be your neighbors soon."

She narrowed her eyes.

"We own that cabin," she said. She closed her eyes and reconsidered. "I own the cabin, I mean."

"Your late husband sure thought that," said Shane.

She stepped back.

"I'm working, so I don't have time to chat," she said. "You'll hear from my lawyers about the cabin."

I stuck my foot in the doorframe before she could close it. She pulled back.

"Please remove your foot, or I'll call the police."

"I wouldn't do that," I said. "They might search your basement and find all the money and drugs your husband hid in the buckets."

She drew in a sharp breath and straightened. Then she shot her eyes up and down me.

"What do you want?"

"I saw your Facebook page," I said. "Your cookies look great. Are you catering a wedding?"

"A birthday party," she said.

"I also heard you teach baking and decorating classes."

She blinked and shook her head.

"Not anymore."

"But you did," I said. "At Camp Meadowview. You quit after Oscar Romero died. It's a shame. The kids there could use some wholesome entertainment."

She looked down but said nothing.

"So how'd it happen?" I asked. "Did he wink at you while he cleaned the pool? Did you introduce yourself in the dining hall?"

She said nothing.

"I guess that doesn't really matter. You were thirty-three and married to an older man you barely saw. Oscar was in his early twenties and handsome. Phil gave you a beautiful home, but he was busy. I bet it was flattering when Oscar started flirting with you. He usually went for Latinas. You were special, though."

She swallowed and blinked.

"I don't know what you're talking about," she said, "but if you don't leave right now, I'll call my lawyer."

"That's actually not a bad idea," I said. "He should be on standby."

I reached into my purse for a manila file folder and pulled out a surveillance photo of Lisa standing next to Oscar. She was giggling and looking directly into his eyes. He had his hand on her elbow.

"You and Oscar had a fling. You loved him."

She closed her eyes and shook her head.

"This is ridiculous," she said. "You have a picture of me with Oscar. So what? I barely even knew him. He made me laugh, but that doesn't mean anything."

I opened my file folder again and skipped past the pictures to the printouts of text message exchanges between the two of them.

"'I love the way you touch me,'" I read, glancing at Mrs. Mason. "'You're a master musician, and I'm your instrument. Your fingers know just what to do.'"

Mrs. Mason said nothing. Shane cleared his throat.

"If you don't mind, I'm going to use that one on Ivy."

I smiled, but Mrs. Mason didn't move.

"The other texts are more lurid," I said, flipping through the printouts. "'*I love your cock…you make me so wet…you're bigger than my husband.*' You also sent pictures." I closed the folder. "You loved Oscar, didn't you?"

She blinked and shrugged.

"Well, you found out my secret," she said. "I had an affair. My husband found out, and we went to counseling. Happy? Thanks for making me relive my worst memories."

"That wasn't your only secret," I said. "You loved Oscar, but he didn't love you. When he broke it off, how did you feel?"

"*I* broke it off," she said, stepping back again. She started to close the door, but my foot still blocked it. "Get away from my house, or I'll call the police."

Shane reached to his belt for his badge.

"They're already here," he said.

"I don't blame you for the affair. You were lonely

and in a miserable marriage," I said. "Oscar was charming and handsome, and you cared for him. I can see it in your text messages. When he broke it off, you couldn't take it. He broke your heart, so you stabbed him in the neck with a scalpel. The police searched for the murder weapon, but they didn't consider the scalpel you use to cut and shape fondant. You use a similar one in your demonstration videos on Facebook and YouTube."

Her lips curved downward.

"He didn't even fight back. He trusted you," I said. "That's why he didn't have defensive wounds on his hands."

She held up a trembling hand.

"Please leave me alone."

"I can't," I said. "Once you killed Oscar, you called your husband and told him what you had done. He already knew you were sleeping together because he had been monitoring your text messages. He even had Camp Meadowview's photographer take pictures of you and Oscar flirting. I think he planned for it to become evidence in your divorce trial. Your husband took bribes, but he had never before covered up a murder. You pushed him over the edge. Part of him, I think, even loved you. He wanted to protect you."

Lisa crossed her arms but said nothing.

"After you told him what you did, he contacted Elaine Alford, Meadowview's owner. He told her about the body, but he left out your role. She gave him half a million dollars to make the problem go away. That was on top of his monthly stipend for ignoring her drug business. She was afraid that any investigation into Oscar or Meadowview would turn up things she wanted kept secret."

When I finished speaking, the three of us went quiet. Mrs. Mason drew in a breath and nodded.

"You're a detective?" she asked, looking to Shane. He nodded. Then she looked to me. "My affair wasn't a crime. You're harassing a widow and have no evidence of anything. My lawyers will take you for everything you own."

"They might if you and your husband could read a property survey," I said. "Elaine Alford kidnapped Detective Lewis's spouse and demanded documents that we supposedly found in your house. It was crazy because we didn't find any there. Her demand got me thinking, though.

"Your husband was a decent detective when he wanted to be. He loved you, but he didn't trust you. He wouldn't store anything that could incriminate you where you could get it. Instead, he broke my cabin's gable vent and shoved everything in my attic. Shane's contractor found it yesterday. Your husband kept the scalpel you used to kill Oscar, your bloody clothes, printouts of text messages you and Oscar sent one another, pictures of you two together at Meadowview, and copies of security logs that put you at Meadowview at the time of Oscar's death.

"For years, he stored the evidence. Then he decided Oscar's parents deserved the truth. Elaine Alford found out and ordered his murder. She sent Joseph Lipscombe and Daniel Nakamura. You were here that day gardening. I saw you in front of your house. You didn't kill your husband, but you knew what would happen and why. You let them murder your husband so you wouldn't go to prison."

She swallowed.

"I have close to a million dollars cash in the house," she said. "It's yours if you let me go."

"No, thanks," said Shane, reaching behind him for a pair of handcuffs secured on his belt. "You're under arrest for the murder of Oscar Romero. Deputies from the Highway Patrol are on their way to take you into custody. It's a nice day, so why don't you wait for them outside?"

Thankfully, she didn't fight. Shane secured her hands and sat her down on the front step. She cried, but I had little sympathy for her.

"You okay sitting with her?" I asked. Shane nodded, so I walked back to the cabin. The contractor had left, and Ivy stood in the front yard, marking off areas where she planned to put flower beds. I told her what had happened and where Shane was.

"I'm glad it's over," she said. "Shane and I plan to stay through the weekend. You and George want to stay with us? Soon we'll have electricity and hot water."

I shook my head.

"This is your place now. I hope it makes you happy."

She straightened.

"Shane and I haven't signed the paperwork," she said. "I know what this cabin means to you. I don't want to take it from you unless you're sure."

"No, it's yours," I said. "Every time I walk through those doors, I can almost smell my dad's cologne, and I can almost hear my mom calling us in for lunch. I love this cabin, but it's my past. If I stay here, I'll never move on. And I want a future. I don't want to be sad anymore. I deserve better."

Ivy put a hand on my elbow.

"You do," she said. "What's next, then?"

I blew a raspberry and shrugged.

"I don't know. When I first got to Pollard, I met a woman named Marilyn Claypool in the park. She's got memory issues, and she thinks her son is dead. I'm going to find him. He should see her before she dies. After that, I plan to explore. The last time I visited another country, an asshole blew up my Humvee. It'd be nice to see places where the locals aren't so militant. And who knows? Maybe I'll find something that makes me happy."

"I hope you do."

I looked to the cabin and put my hands on my hips. I was leaving it in good hands. Mom and Dad would have been happy.

"Show me this garden of yours."

Ivy was only too happy to comply. I stayed with her in the cabin the rest of the morning. Then the Highway Patrol came and picked Lisa Mason up. Shane went with them. He'd have reams of paperwork and reports to write, but then he and Ivy would spend time together in their cabin.

Until then, Ivy and I talked and laughed. Then I showed her a spot beside the cabin where my mom had planted day lilies, and then I showed her the place at which I used to stand and throw rocks with my dad.

At noon, George and I left. When I went to Pollard, I had brought a notebook with me with my daily to-do list. Most days, my list had centered on George. He had kept me alive by giving me a reason to get out of bed every morning. I hadn't touched that notebook in days. I hadn't needed it.

Everyone faced hardship and tragedy—some of us more than our fair share. Life had knocked me down more times than I could count. It was cruel. But too many people had loved me too much and sacrificed too much for me to quit. Maybe I'd never be happy, but I'd try. And maybe, one day, if I searched hard and far enough, I'd find peace. Until then, I'd keep looking and hoping to find a world in which my dreams could come true.

Enjoy this book? You can make a big difference in my career

Reviews are the lifeblood of an author's career. I'm not exaggerating when I say they're the single best way I can get attention for my books. I'm not famous, I don't have the money for extravagant advertising campaigns, and I no longer have a major publisher behind me.

I do have something major publishers don't have, something they would kill to get:

Committed, loyal readers.

With millions of books in the world, your honest reviews and recommendations help other readers find me.

If you enjoyed the book you just read, I would be

extraordinarily grateful if you could spend five minutes to leave a review on Amazon, Barnes and Noble, Goodreads, or anywhere else you review books. A review can be as long or as short as you'd like it to be, so please don't feel that you have to write something long.

Thank you so much!

Did you like Night Work? Then check out The Lost Ones!

Two girls walk to school one morning but never arrive. The same day, their grandparents die in a bank robbery. It isn't a coincidence.

Former detective Hana Blackwood came to Florida to look for someone. But when she goes to the bank to deposit a check to fund her Florida excursion, she finds herself in the middle of an armed robbery.

In the wrong place at the wrong time, Hana shoots a stranger who tried to shoot her. It's a pointless death.

Or was it?

Nothing about the robbery makes sense. There's a bigger game being played, one with deadly consequences for two innocent children who have gone missing.

Hana hunts the wicked. It's what she's done her

entire adult life. Now, though, hunting isn't enough. She has to save two innocent girls, and she has to do it quickly before they're lost for good.

The Lost Ones is the second novel in New York Times' bestselling author Chris Culver's thrilling Hana Blackwood series. If you like mysteries and thrillers, give the series a chance. You'll be hooked in no time.

Stay in touch with Chris

As much as I enjoy writing, I like hearing from readers even more. If you want to keep up with my world, there are a couple of ways you can do that.

First and easiest, I've got a mailing list. If you join, you'll receive an email whenever I have a new novel out or when I run sales. You can join that by going to this address:

http://www.indiecrime.com/mailinglist.html

If my mailing list doesn't appeal to you, you can also connect with me on Facebook here:

http://www.facebook.com/ChrisCulverbooks

And you can always email me at chris@indiecrime.com. I love receiving email!

About the Author

Chris Culver is the *New York Times* bestselling author of the Ash Rashid series and other novels. After graduate school, Chris taught courses in ethics and comparative religion at a small liberal arts university in southern Arkansas. While there and when he really should have been grading exams, he wrote *The Abbey*, which spent sixteen weeks on the *New York Times* bestsellers list and introduced the world to Detective Ash Rashid.

Chris has been a storyteller since he was a kid, but he decided to write crime fiction after picking up a dog eared, coffee stained paperback copy of Mickey Spillane's *I, the Jury* in a library book sale. Many years later, his wife, despite considerable effort, still can't stop him from bringing more orphan books home. He lives with his family near St. Louis.

Made in the USA
Monee, IL
29 November 2021

83427942R10263